Cara Colter lives on an acreage in British Columbia with her partner Rob and eleven horses. She has three grown children and a grandson. She is a recent recipient of the *RT Book Reviews* Career Achievement Award in the Love and Laughter category. Cara loves to hear from readers, and you can contact her or learn more about her through her website, www.cara-colter.com

To all the men and women who serve,
with deepest gratitude.

Wakefield Libraries
& Information Services

This book should be returned by the last date stamped
above. You may renew the loan personally, by post or
telephone for a further period if the book is not required by
another reader.

the feeling of warmth away. His darkness could
put out her light in a millisecond. And he'd better
remember that—and remember this is—about how
beautif

Dear Reader,

I've just had another perfect summer. I had the opportunity to do plenty of swimming in two of the world's most wonderful lakes: Lake Pend O'reille in Idaho, and Kootenay Lake in BC, in Canada. I also had lots of company this summer, ate ice cream, drank iced cappuccinos and sat in the shade just contemplating life.

And while I was having this fantastic, carefree summer so many young men and women who have answered the call to protect their nations were so far from home.

I write about soldiers because I have always thought it takes a special kind of courage to leave all the comforts (that I generally take for granted) behind. I am aware that the peace and prosperity I enjoy are ultimately linked to a young stranger's willingness to serve and to sacrifice.

So this one is dedicated to them, with heartfelt gratitude.

Cara Colter

BATTLE FOR THE SOLDIER'S HEART

BY
CARA COLTER

First published in Great Britain 2012
by Mills & Boon, an imprint of Harlequin (UK) Limited,
Eton House, 18-24 Paradise Road, Richmond, Surrey TW9 1SR

© Cara Colter 2012

ISBN: 978 0 263 89446 2
ebook ISBN: 978 1 408 97120 8

23-0712

Harlequin (UK) policy is to use papers that are natural, renewable and recyclable products and made from wood grown in sustainable forests. The logging and manufacturing processes conform to the legal environmental regulations of the country of origin.

Printed and bound in Spain
by Blackprint CPI, Barcelona

CHAPTER ONE

THERE were Shetland ponies everywhere.

They were gobbling the long strands of grass that sprouted around the brightly painted legs of the children's playground equipment. They were chowing down on the weeping-willow fronds at the edge of the duck pond.

Three had found their way through the chain-link fence and were grazing with voracious appetite on the green temptations of the Mason Memorial Soccer Field.

One had its face buried in the remnants of a birthday cake, and another, wandering toward the wading pool, was trailing a banner that said Happy Birthday, Wilson Schmelski.

From where he stood at the pedestrian bridge that crossed into the city of Mason's most favored civic park, Pondview, Rory Adams counted eight ponies on the loose.

And only one person trying to catch them.

"You little monster! You beady-eyed ingrate!"

The woman lunged right, the pony left.

If it had been anyone else, he might have allowed himself to see the humor in her predicament.

Instead, he frowned. When he thought of Gracie Day,

somehow, even after speaking to her on the phone, he hadn't factored in the passage of time. She was frozen in his mind at fourteen or fifteen. All glittering braces and freckles, skinned knees, smart-alecky and annoying.

To him, six years her senior, Gracie, his best friend's little sister, had not even been a blip on his radar. He had not considered her a *girl* in the sense that he considered girls. And at that age? Had he ever considered anything but girls?

He'd been twenty-one when he saw her last. He and Graham mustering out, on their first tour of Afghanistan, and her looking at him with fury glittering in her tear-filled eyes. *I hate you. How could you talk him into this?*

Graham had started to argue—the whole let's-go-play-soldier thing had been his idea, after all—but Rory had nudged him, and Graham had understood instantly.

Let me take it, let me be the bad guy in your kid sister's eyes.

The memory made him wince. They had looked out for each other. They'd had each other's backs. Probably thousands of times since they had said good-bye to Gracie that day. But the one time it had really counted…

Rory shook off the thoughts, and focused on the woman chasing ponies.

That *kid* sister.

Gracie Day was small and slender, deliciously curved in all the right places. Auburn hair that had probably started the day perfectly controlled and prettily coiffed, had long since surrendered to humidity and the pitfalls of pony-chasing. Her hair was practically hissing with bad temper and fell in a wild wave to her bare sun-kissed shoulders.

She was daintily dressed in a wide-skirted cream sundress and matching heels that had probably been perfect for the children's birthday party her event-planning company had just hosted.

But if Gracie had worked at it, she couldn't have chosen a worse outfit for chasing ponies.

The dress was looking rumpled, one slender strap kept sliding off her shoulder, and not only couldn't she get up any speed in those shoes, but the heels kept turning in the grass. At first glance, the smudge on the delectable rise of her bosom might have been mistaken for part of the pattern on the dress. But a closer look—that was *not* the bosom she'd had at fourteen—and he was pretty sure the bright-green splotch was horse slobber.

"Do you have any idea what glue is made from? Do you?"

Something still in her, then, of that fourteen-year-old girl she had once been. That girl was closer to the surface than the cool, calm and collected Gracie Day she had managed to convince him she was when he had spoken to her on the phone.

"I need to talk to you," he'd said, when he'd finally made it home. By then Graham had already been gone for six months. He'd wanted to tell her the truth.

I failed.

"I can't see why we would need to talk," she'd responded, and the fact was, he'd been relieved.

Talking about what had happened to Graham—and his part in it—was not going to be easy. And while he was not a man who shirked hard things, he had been thankful for the reprieve.

Rory felt a shiver along his spine. They said it was

survivor's guilt, but in his heart he felt it *was* his fault her brother hadn't come home.

Somehow, instead of being a temporary diversion, playing soldier had turned into a career for both of them. Graham, on their third deployment, Afghanistan again, had taken a bullet.

Rory still woke almost every night, sweating, his heart pounding.

Two teenage boys. Something about them. He'd hesitated because they were so young. And then bullets everywhere. Ducking, taking cover. Where was Graham? Out there. Crawling out, pulling him back, cradling him in his arms.

Blood, so much blood.

But the dream woke him before it was done. There was a piece missing from it, words he could not remember though he chased after them once he was awake.

The dream never told him what he needed to know. Had it been those boys? Were they the ones who had fired those shots? What could he have done differently? Could he have shoved Graham behind him, taken it instead?

Check up on Gracie. Those words whispered, a plea.

You didn't take a dying request lightly. And especially not the dying request of the man who'd been his best friend for more than ten years.

So, back home for six months now, Rory had tried. He called Gracie twice, and admittedly had been somewhat relieved to have been coolly rejected each time. The dreams were bad enough without the reality of having to tell her what had happened, while at the same time sparing her what had happened.

And so, he had followed the letter of Graham's instruction and checked up on her. While he had been away, the company he and his own brother had started—they had begun with race-car graphics and were now taking on the world—had succeeded beyond his wildest dreams. Once home, done with the military for good, Rory Adams was amazed to find himself a man with considerable resources.

One of whom was named Bridey O'Mitchell. Officially, she was his personal assistant. Unofficially, he considered her his secret weapon.

Bridey, middle-age, British, unflappable, could accomplish anything. Some days, Rory entertained himself by finding impossible challenges for her.

Can you get ice cream delivered to that crew working on the graphics for those Saudi airplanes? I know it's short notice, but do you think you could find half a dozen tickets to the sold-out hockey game? I'd like a koala bear and two kangaroos at the opening of that Aussie tour company we did the buses for.

Checking up on Gracie Day? That had been child's play for Bridey.

And the ensuing report about Gracie Day had been soothingly dull. Gracie was no longer engaged to the fiancé Graham had disliked intensely, and she ran a successful event-planning company, Day of Your Life, here in Mason, in the Okanagan Valley of British Columbia. Hers was the "it" company for weddings and anniversaries and special events.

The company had just been chosen to do the major annual fundraiser for Warrior Down, the organization that helped wounded vets and their families.

But Gracie's bread and butter was birthday parties for the children of the well-heeled, politicians and doctors and lawyers and CEOs. She put together the kind of parties that had clowns in them. And bouncy tents. Maybe a magician. And fireworks. The ponies must be an added touch since Rory had received Bridey's very thorough report.

Gracie Day organized the kind of parties that he had never had. In fact, he didn't recall his birthday ever being celebrated, except on one memorable occasion when his mother had ended up face-first in the cake. How old had he been? Six? After that, he'd said no thanks to efforts at celebration.

There. He'd "checked up" on her. Even that little bit of checking had triggered a bad memory, so he wanted to let it go there. Grace Day was doing well.

Still, even as he tried to tell himself he'd obeyed the letter of Graham's last instruction to him, it ate at the honor he had left. Rory had needed to see for himself that Gracie was doing all right. His last call had been a week ago.

And there had been *something* in her voice.

Even though she had said she was doing fabulously.

He couldn't pinpoint what exactly he had heard in her voice. A certain forced note to the breezy tone? Something guarded, as if she had a secret that she was not planning on revealing to him?

Whatever it was, it wouldn't let him go. Over the past week, the need to see her had grown in urgency. Instinct had become such a big part of his life when he was a soldier, that he found he couldn't ignore that niggling little voice. When he tried, it was just one more thing that woke him in the night, that haunted his dreams.

A little lie to her secretary had sent him to Pondview. "My company is one of the sponsors of Warrior Down. I need to talk to her urgently. And in person."

Just as he'd suspected, the mention of Gracie's pet project got him all the information he needed. Did he feel guilty for lying?

No. Guilt was for guys of a sensitive nature, and he definitely did not qualify. In his house, growing up, later on the battlefield, that was how you stayed alive. You didn't let things touch you.

But Graham dying… Rory shook it off, chose to focus with unnecessary intensity on Gracie. She was sneaking up on a fat black-and-white pony, who, while seeming oblivious, was clearly watching her out of the corner of his eye. She was right on one count: the pony *was* beady-eyed.

And a whole lot smarter than he looked. Because when she made her move, the pony sidled sideways, out of her grasp. He turned and looked at her balefully, chewing a clump of grass.

Rory winced when her heel embedded itself in the grassy ground, spongy from a recent watering and Gracie pitched forward. The heel snapped off her shoe with a click so audible Rory could hear it from where he was standing.

What was left of her cool reserve—and that wasn't much—abandoned her. Rory found himself smiling when she pried her foot free, took off a shoe and hurled it at the pony, who kicked up its heels at her and farted as it dodged the shoe.

"Bad horses become glue," she shouted. "And dog food. How would you like to be breakfast for a Great Dane?"

"Tut-tut," Rory muttered to himself. "Your decorum doesn't match your dress, Miss Day."

The truth? He liked the Miss Day who would throw a shoe at a pony much more than the one who answered her phone with such cool reserve, or the one who ran perfect birthday parties in her designer duds.

But then, he knew enough about the *real* Miss Day that she would be appalled. That's how bored guys whiled away their time. Played poker. Smoked. Slept. Talked.

About girlfriends and family.

Graham had never been that successful in the girl-friend department, so Rory knew an awful lot about his sister.

Like: *Gracie just never lets loose. You know, ever since she was a little girl she's carried a picture of a candy-apple red Ferrari. How did she become such a stick-in-the-mud? And how is it she's going to marry a stick-in-the-mud accountant, least likely ever to own a sports car? He drives a car that would barely make the economy class at a car-rental agency!*

Then, as if to prove her brother had her all wrong, that there was nothing stick-in-the-mud about her, Graham Day's straitlaced sister, who didn't know how to let loose, took off the other shoe and hurled it after the departing pony. She said a word—loudly—that soldiers used with fast and furious frequency but that would have raised a few eyebrows at her perfectly executed rich kids' birthday party.

Rory felt a smile tickle at his lips. A long, long time since he had found much to smile about.

Still, it was more than evident it was a bad time to talk to her. Of course, the chivalrous thing to do would be to rescue her, to save the day, but he had given up any illusions of being a hero long, long ago. And more, Gracie would *hate* his catching her like this.

In a bad spot.

Vulnerable.

Out of control.

Needing his help.

Besides, he didn't know anything about horses of the large variety, and less about the tiny ones.

Still, just leaving her to deal with it seemed too hard-hearted, even for him, the man generally untroubled by guilt.

But there it was: the memory of Graham required Rory to be a better man. Even if she was not his sister, Graham wouldn't have approved of abandoning the damsel in her distress.

Rory remembered he had a step up on the other heroes out there. A secret weapon. He pulled his cell phone from his pocket and tried not to wince when Bridey answered, halfway through the first ring, with her chipper, "Mr. Adams, sir."

He had tried to tell her his preference was for a more casual form of address, but on that topic she would not hear him.

Her tone reproachful, she was fond of reminding him, "Mr. Adams, you are the CEO of a very success-ful company."

"Bridey, I need you to find me someone who can round up some escaped ponies."

If the request took her by surprise, she certainly didn't let on. She took all the details and assured him she was on it.

Rory made a decision to help Gracie Day save whatever pride she had left by sinking further back into the shadows of the park, to be an interested spectator, nothing more.

But just as he made that decision, Gracie froze. It reminded him of a deer sniffing the air, some sense alerting it that it no longer was alone, that it was being observed. Then Gracie turned her head slowly and looked directly at him.

He saw recognition dawn in her eyes, and then in the set of her mouth.

She folded her arms over the green smudge on her chest and lifted her chin, trying for composure, distancing herself from that woman who had been hurling shoes and shouting invective at horses.

Taking a deep breath, feeling a sensation in his chest that was similar to what he felt just before starting the mission, just before stepping into the heat of battle, Rory Adams moved toward Gracie.

And stopped right in front of her.

Had he ever known her eyes were that color? He thought it was called hazel, a plain word for such a rich mix of golds and greens and browns worthy of an exotic tapestry.

Had he ever known that her lips were lush and wide? The kind of lips that a man imagined crushing under his own?

Of course he hadn't.

She had been a kid. His friend's sister.

Now she was a woman. A beautiful woman, if not a very happy one!

He hesitated, picked up her shoe—who said he couldn't be chivalrous?—and handed it to her.

"Hello, Gracie."

Grace Day blinked at the way her nickname sounded coming off his lips. *So right.*

As if part of her had ached to be called that again.

And, of course, part of her did. But by her brother. Not by Rory Adams.

She grabbed her shoe from his hand, and accidentally brushed his fingertips. The shock was electrical, and to hide its shiver from him, she shoved the shoe on her foot, buying a moment to breathe.

It had been eight years. Couldn't he be bald? Or fat? Couldn't life give her one little break?

She straightened, trying for dignity even though she was distinctly lopsided, and the narrow strap of her sundress chose that moment to slide down her shoulder.

Grace could clearly see that Rory Adams was *better* than he had been before. Twenty-one-year-old lankiness was gone, replaced with a male physique in its absolute prime. He was tall—well, he'd always been that, standing head and shoulders above his peers—but now he was also broad-shouldered and deep-chested.

He was wearing a sports shirt—short-sleeved—that showed off rock-hard biceps, the ripple of toned forearms. Khaki shorts hugged lean hips and powerful thighs, showed the naked length of his long, tanned legs.

His face had matured, too. She was not sure she would say it was better. *Changed.* The mischievousness of a young man was gone. So was the devil-may-care light that had always burned like fire in the depths of those green, green eyes.

Around his eyes, now, were the creases of a man who had squinted into the sun a great deal. There was a set to his jaw, a firmness around his mouth that had not been there before.

There was something in his expression that was closed and hard. It was the look of a warrior, a man who had accepted the mantle of serving his country, but at a price to himself. There were new shadows in eyes that had once been clear.

Rory Adams had seen things—and done things— that made the tatters of the birthday party behind her seem frivolous and superficial.

Her eyes wandered to his hair. It was brown, glossy and rich as a vat of melted dark chocolate, shining with the highlights of the Okanagan early summer sun.

The last time she had seen him, that dark hair had been very short, buzzed off to a mere shadow, vanity- and maintenance-free in preparation for hard, hot work in inhospitable climates.

Now, Rory had returned to a style closer to that she remembered from when he was coming in and out of their house with Graham.

Rory's family had moved onto their block and into their school district in the latter half of Graham's senior year. And then in those carefree days after they had finished high school, they had both worked for the same landscaping company.

That was before they had decided it was imperative that they go save the world.

Rory's hair was longer than it had been even then, longer than she had ever seen it, thick, rich, straight until it touched his collar, and then it curled slightly.

She supposed that's what everyone who got out of the military did—exercised the release from discipline, celebrated the freedom to grow their hair.

And yet the long hair did not make him look less a warrior, just a warrior from a different age.

Too easy to picture him with the long hair catching in the wind, that fierce expression on his face, a sword in his hand, *ready.*

He was the kind of man who made a woman feel the worst kind of weakness: a desire to feel his strength against her own softness, to feel the rasp of rough whiskers against delicate skin, to feel the hard line of those lips soften against her mouth.

But Rory Adams had always been that. Even now Grace could feel the ghost of the girl she had once been. She could feel the helpless humiliation she had felt at fourteen because she loved him so desperately.

And pathetically.

She'd been as invisible to him as a ghost. No, more like a mosquito, an annoyance he swatted at every now and then. His best friend's aggravating kid sister.

She'd known from the moment he had first called her six months ago, that nothing good could come from seeing him.

There had been something in his voice, grim and determined, that had made her think he had things to tell her that she was not ready to hear, that she would probably never be ready to hear.

Besides, seeing Rory? It could only make her yearn for things that could never be. She had never seen Rory without her brother, Graham.

The brother who was not coming home. Hadn't she thought seeing her brother's friend would intensify the sense of loss that was finally dulling to a throbbing ache instead of a screaming pain?

Once she had blamed this man who stood before her for Graham's choices, but a long time ago she had realized her brother had been born to do what he was doing. It was a choice that he had been willing to give his life for.

And he had.

But if Rory wanted to think she still held him responsible, and if it kept up some kind of barrier between them, that was okay.

Because what shocked Gracie right now was that what she felt looking at Rory was not an intensified sense of loss. Rather, she was unprepared for how the yearning of her younger self—to be noticed by him, to be cared about him—had not disappeared with her braces and her first bra.

Not even close.

She blinked. And then again, hard. "No one calls me that," she said. "No one calls me Gracie."

She thought she sounded childish and defensive. She didn't want him to know he'd had any kind of effect on her.

Why couldn't she just have said, "Hello, Rory. Nice to see you"? Why couldn't she have just said that, all her years of hard-won polish and sophistication wrapped around her like a protective cloak?

Because he had caught her in a terrible moment. Running after renegade ponies, her shoe broken, her hair clasp lost, her strap sliding around and her dress stained beyond repair.

If she'd known he wasn't going to take no for an answer, she would have invited him to the office she was so proud of on the main street of downtown Mason.

Where she could have been in complete control of this reunion!

"What do they call you?"

His voice was deep and sure and sent unwanted shivers down her spine.

Miss Day would have sounded way too churlish, plus she was wobbling on one shoe, and feeling damp and disheveled and not at all like the cool professional woman she wanted him to believe she was.

"Grace."

"Ah."

She didn't like the way he was looking at her, his gaze probing, those deep green eyes feeling as though they were stripping away her maturity and success and exposing the vulnerable and gauche girl she was so startled to find was alive and well within her.

"Graham's the only one who called me that. Everyone else called me Grace. Even my parents."

"Graham and me," he reminded her.

Gracie-Facie, pudding and pie, kissed the boys and made them cry...

On those rare occasions when Rory Adams had noticed her, it had been to tease her mercilessly.

But that boy who had teased—the one with the careless grin, and the wild way—seemed to be gone. Completely.

Why couldn't her inner child be so cooperative?

"So, how's life?" he said.

As if he'd just been walking by, and happened upon her. Which she doubted. When she'd talked to him a week ago, she'd told him she didn't want to see him.

She should have guessed that would not have changed about him. He was not a man who had had to accept no for an answer very often. Especially not from those of the female persuasion. She should have guessed he would not accept it from her.

"The same as when I talked to you a week ago," Grace said stubbornly. "Fabulous."

This was not true. In fact, nothing could be further from the truth.

"Except for the ponies," he commented dryly, but he she had a feeling he wasn't buying it, and not just because of the ponies. Not for a second.

Couldn't he see that her dress was perfectly cut fine linen? That the shoe he had handed her was an expensive designer shoe? Couldn't he see that she was all grown up and that she didn't need any help from big, strong him to get her through life's hurdles?

Of which, at the moment, she had more than her fair share.

"Fabulous," she repeated, tightly.

"You look worried," he said after a moment.

And then he did the darndest thing. He took his thumb, and ever so gently pressed it into her forehead.

Where she knew the worry lines had been building like storm clouds for a whole week!

Ever since Serenity had arrived with her entourage. Ponies. Tucker.

There was a momentary sensation of bliss: a momentary desire to lean into that thumb and all it offered. Someone to lean on. Someone to talk to. Someone to trust.

Hopeless illusions that she, of all people, should have left far behind her. The end of her engagement really should have been the last straw.

Had been the last straw, Grace told herself firmly. Her business was everything now. Everything. She had laid herself out on the altar of romantic love—and had been run through by love's caprice—for the last time.

She was not leaving herself open to hurt anymore. She had made that vow when her fiancé of two years, Harold, had bade her adieu. Vowed it.

And then, as if to test that vow, Serenity had come.

And now Rory was here. This man appearing in her life, her entertaining the notion it would be nice to hear his opinion about Serenity—or feel his whiskers scrape her face—those were tests of her resolve.

When he had phoned, she had contemplated asking him a few questions, but in the end she had decided not to.

And the deep cynicism that permeated his expression should only confirm how right she had been in that decision.

Because he could lay her hope to rest. Dash it completely before it was even fully formed.

Hope was such a fragile thing for her.

Hope was probably even more dangerous to her than love. But still, not to hope for anything at all would be a form of death, wouldn't it?

She was not about to trust her hope to someone like him. And yet, there it was—the temptation just to tell him, to see what he thought.

Not to be so damned alone.

Recognizing the utter folly of these thoughts, Grace slapped his thumb down from her forehead. "I'm not worried."

No sense giving in to the temptation to share confidences, to tell him she'd spent years building up her business. One incident like this, and it could all crumble, word spreading like wildfire that she was unprofessional, that she'd had a disaster.

Thank goodness the party had been over, the last of the pint-size revelers being packed into their upscale minivans and SUVs when the ponies had made their break for it. Hopefully the park people—or the press—wouldn't come along before she got this cleared up.

But that was only the immediate problem, anyway, although all her problems were related at the moment.

"Didn't the ponies come with a pony person?" he asked.

Ah, that was the other problem. The pony person was exactly the secret she wanted to keep.

"The pony person is, um, incapacitated. Not your problem," she said, flashing him a smile that made him frown. She had been aiming for a smile that said, *This? Just a temporary glitch. Nothing I can't handle.*

And she had obviously missed *that* smile by a long

shot. Grace hoped he didn't catch her anxious glance toward the parking lot.

Thankfully, she'd had the trailer the ponies had arrived in moved way across the parking lot into the deep shade of the cottonwoods on the other side. She had not wanted the partygoers to bump right into it in its decrepit condition.

"Maybe we'll meet again under different circumstances," she said, hoping he would take the hint and leave.

But he did not have the look of a man who responded to subtlety, and he had caught her glance toward the parking lot. Now he was looking past her. She moved in front of him, trying to block his view, but it was no use. He looked over her head, easily.

Not a single person at the party had mentioned the trailer. It was as if they hadn't seen it at all.

But then, most people weren't like him.

And Rory Adams had become a man who saw everything, who missed absolutely nothing.

Of course, she knew from the few things Graham had said when he came home on leave that these men led lives that depended on their ability to be observant of their surroundings, every nuance of detail, every vehicle, every person, every obstacle.

Rory stepped around her, and headed right toward where the ramshackle horse trailer was. It was painted a shade of copper that almost hid the rust eating away at it around the wheel wells.

On the side, in fading circus letters, three feet high, it said, Serenity's Wild Ride.

He looked over his shoulder at Grace, his eyes narrow. "What's she doing here?"

He recognized the trailer. He knew Serenity. Was it what Grace feared? Or what she hoped?

CHAPTER TWO

"You know her," Grace said, scrambling to keep up with him on her one shoe. "You know Serenity."

She stopped and picked up the other on her way. Since one had a heel and the other didn't, she took them both off and dangled them from her fingertips.

"A chance encounter a long, long time ago." Rory glanced back at her, hesitated, and then waited. "Watch for pony poo."

"Oh!" Life was so unfair. Well, that was hardly a newsflash. But, if Grace had to see Rory Adams, wouldn't it have been nice if she had been sipping a glass of white wine and looking entirely unflappable, rather than chasing after him in bare feet, avoiding poo?

"What's she doing here, Gracie?"

She wanted to remind him she didn't want to be called Gracie, but something about the way Rory had stopped and was looking down at her made her feel very flustered.

The weak compulsion to share the burden won.

"She came by the office a week ago."

"She knew where your office was," he said flatly.

"I'm in the phone book. She said she knew Graham."

Grace did not miss how his eyes narrowed at that.

"She knew I had an event company."

"So, she's done some homework."

"You don't need to make it sound like she's running a sting, and she found an easy mark."

He raised an eyebrow. It said *exactly*.

"She just wondered if I could give her some work. She had ponies, I had an upcoming birthday party. It seemed like it might be win-win."

"What aren't you telling me?"

Hell's bells. She did not like it that he could see through her that easily. It meant she had to avoid looking at his lips.

Naturally, as soon as she told herself not to look at his lips, she did just that. Why did men like him have this kind of seductive power over people? Female people anyway!

"What makes you think I'm not telling you something?" she hedged.

"I was Graham's best friend for ten years and you refused to see me, but a complete stranger shows up who claims a passing acquaintance to your brother and you're forming a business partnership with her?"

"I rented her ponies for an afternoon. That's hardly a business partnership."

"It's not 'I can't see why we need to talk,' either."

Something crossed his face.

"I hurt your feelings," Grace said, stunned.

For a moment, he looked stunned, too. Then a shield came down over his eyes, making them seem a darker shade of emerald than they had before. A little smile tickled the sinfully sensuous curve of his mouth. His expression was not exactly amusement, and not exactly scorn. More a kind of deprecating self-knowledge.

"Gracie, honey—"

Gracie wasn't bad enough? Now he had to add honey to it?

"I don't have feelings for you to hurt."

That was what he wanted for her to believe. And she saw it was entirely possible that he believed that himself. But she didn't.

And suddenly Rory Adams was more dangerous to her than ever. Because he wasn't just handsome. He wasn't just the first man she'd ever had a crush on. He wasn't just her brother's best friend and fellow adventurer.

Because just before that shield had come down in his eyes, Grace was sure she had caught a glimpse of someone who had lost their way, someone who relied totally on himself, someone lonely beyond what she had ever known that word to mean.

"There was a complication," she admitted slowly. "That's why I agreed to have her provide ponies for the party."

"The thing about a woman like Serenity?"

She hated the way he said that, as if he knew way too much about women in general and women like Serenity in particular.

"What kind of woman is Serenity?" Grace demanded sweetly, though the kind of woman Serenity was was terribly obvious, even to Grace. Serenity was one of those women who had lived hard and lived wild, and it was all catching up with her.

The line around Rory's lip tightened as he decided

what to say. "She's the kind who used to own the party," he said. "And then the party owned her."

Grace suspected that he had sugarcoated what he really wanted to say, but what he had said was harsh enough, and it was said with such a lack of sympathy that the moment of unwanted—and weakening sympathy she had felt for him—evaporated.

Thank God.

"And what about women like Serenity?" she said, yanking her strap up one more time.

"There's always a complication."

Then he strode over to the horse trailer, and Gracie could not help but notice he was all soldier now, totally focused, totally take-charge and totally no-nonsense.

It felt like a terrible weakness on her part that she was somewhat relieved both by the fact his armor was back up and by the fact he was taking charge.

So she had to say, "I can handle this."

He snorted, glanced meaningfully at the pony in the wading pool, trampling what was left of the soggy Happy Birthday banner, and said, "Sure you can, Gracie."

I hurt your feelings. Really, Gracie Day couldn't have picked a more annoying thing to say to him.

Feelings? Weren't those the pesky things that he'd managed to outrun his whole life? Starting with a less than stellar childhood—no ponies at birthday parties, for sure—and ending up in a profession where to feel anything too long or too intensely would have meant he couldn't do his job.

No, Rory Adams was a man ideally suited for soldiering. His early life had prepared him for hardship. The little bit of idealism that he had managed to escape his childhood with had soon departed, too.

So, Rory Adams had *hated* the look in Gracie's eyes, just now, doe-soft, as if she could see right through him.

To some secret longing.

To have what she and Graham had had. Their house the one on the block that everyone flocked to, and not just because there were always freshly baked chocolate chip cookies, either. There was something there. That house was full of laughter. And love. Parents who actually made rules and had dinner on the table at a certain time.

Rory remembered calling Graham once about a party. And Graham saying, "Nah, I'm going fishing with my dad."

A family that enjoyed being together. That had been a novelty in Rory Adam's world.

Is that what he'd wanted when he'd called her? Had it been about him and not about her—or his obligation to Graham—at all?

No, he reminded himself. He'd been *relieved* by her rejection.

Rory shrugged off the thoughts, annoyed with himself. He was not accustomed to questioning himself or his motives. Except for the event that haunted his dreams, he moved through life with the supreme confidence of the warrior he was. The qualities that had made him an exceptional warrior also made him good at business.

So it flustered him beyond reason that a single glance from her had shaken something deep, deep within him.

He drew in a long breath, steadying himself, clearing away distractions, focusing on what needed to be done.

Poking out from underneath the horse trailer, near the back bumper, was one very tiny, suede, purple cowboy boot, with a fake spur attached.

He nudged at the boot with his shoe and then a little harder when there was no response. The boot moved away.

Sighing, he bent down and tugged. And this time he met some real resistance.

He felt under the trailer, found the other boot and pulled. Out came long, naked legs, and then short denim shorts, frayed at the cuffs, and then a bare belly, and then a sequined pop top with fringes. And then the face of an angel—if it weren't for the circles of black mascara under her eyes—and blond curls topped with a pink cowboy hat.

He studied her for a moment. Despite her prettiness, she was aging badly. He and Graham had partied—hard—with her and her rodeo crowd. They'd been a rowdy, rough bunch. It had been a brief interlude—a few crazy days before their unit had mustered out the very first time.

That made it eight years ago, about the same amount of time since he had seen Gracie in her braces.

But whereas Grace had come into herself, Serenity had deteriorated badly. She must have been in her twenties at that first encounter, which meant she was way too old now to be wearing short shorts and a pink cowboy hat. She was on the scary side of skinny, her hair had been bleached once too often, and she was definitely drunk.

Well, that part was the same.

"Leave me alone," the black-eyed angel mumbled, swinging at air.

"Yes, leave her alone," Gracie said. "Really, there's nothing here I can't handle."

He ignored them both.

"Look, Rory, you just don't understand the delicate nuances of this situation."

"Uh-huh," he said, but he was pretty sure he got the "delicate nuances" just fine. Serenity had probably come across the obituary for Graham somewhere, and zeroed in on the grieving sister.

It made him mad, but one thing that the military had been really good at was training him to channel aggression, control it, unleash it only as a last resort.

So he satisfied himself with giving Gracie a sour look that let her know he was not impressed with how she had handled this so far.

And he was rewarded with a look that had nothing doe-soft about it.

"There's nothing here I can't handle," she said, again.

"Given that this woman is bad, bad news and her ponies are devouring Mason's most prime real estate, you might want to consider the possibility you are in over your head."

Her mouth worked, but she didn't say anything. He could tell that Gracie had suspected Serenity was exactly what he said. Bad news.

And she had suspected that she was in over her head.

But there was something else, too, something glittering at the back of her eyes that gave him pause.

For some reason she *wanted* Serenity here.

What did Serenity have to offer that Grace had rejected from him?

Sheesh. His damn feelings *were* hurt. That was a stunner. A weakness about himself that he could have lived quite happily not knowing he had!

"Hey," he reached down and took Serenity's shoulder. "Wake up, get your ponies and clear out."

The attack came from the side. At first, confused, Rory thought it was Grace who had hurled herself at him, nearly pushed him over.

He stumbled a step sideways, straightened and felt a warrior's embarrassment at not even having seen the attacker coming, at having been caught off guard.

It made it worse, not better, that his attacker was pint-size.

The attacker aimed a hard kick with cowboy-boot-clad feet at Rory's shin. Still slightly off guard, Rory shot out his arm and held the child at arm's length. The kick missed but, undeterred, the kid tried again.

A boy. Rory had not been around children much, so he didn't know how old. Seven? Eight? Maybe nine?

Despite his size, the boy had the slouch and confidence of a professional wrangler. And he was dressed like one, too. His jeans had holes in both knees, his denim shirt had been washed white. A stained cowboy hat was pulled low over his brow. It was more than obvious this child had not been at the upscale birthday party that had just ended.

"Don't you ever touch my mama," he said, glaring up at Rory, not the least intimidated by the fact his opponent was taller than him by a good three feet and outweighed him by about a hundred and fifty pounds.

He was the kind of kid—spunky, undernourished, defiant—that you could care about.

If you hadn't successfully killed the part of yourself that cared about such things. Rory had seen lots of kids like this: chocolate-brown eyes, white, white smiles, spunk, and he'd learned quickly you couldn't allow yourself to care. The world was too full of tragedy. It could overwhelm you if you let it.

Rory let go of the boy, backed away, hands held up in surrender. "Hey, I was just trying to rouse her so she could catch her ponies."

"I'll look after the ponies," the boy said fiercely.

"It's okay, Tucker," Gracie said, and put a hand on the boy's narrow shoulders. "Nobody's going to hurt your mother."

The boy flinched out from her touch and glared out at her from under the battered rim of his straw cowboy hat with such naked dislike that Rory saw Gracie suck in her breath.

Rory looked at the boy more closely.

And then Rory looked at Gracie's face.

She was clearly struggling to hide everything from him, and she was just as clearly a person who had never learned to keep her distance from caring. Her tenderness toward that boy was bald in her face. And so was the hope.

But she hid nothing at all.

Rory Adams was a man who had lived by his instincts, by his ability to distance himself from emotion. He had survived because of his ability to be observant, to see what others might overlook.

Rory looked back and forth between the boy and Grace, and he saw immediately what the complication was.

He studied the boy—Tucker—hard.

"How old are you?"

Grace gasped, seeing how quickly he had seen the possibility.

The boy did not look like Graham. But he certainly looked like Grace had looked just a few years older than this: freckle-faced and auburn hair.

A million kids looked like that.

For a moment, Rory thought the boy wasn't going to answer him at all.

From Serenity, a moan, and then, "Come on, Tuck, tell the man how old you are."

"I'm seven," he said, reluctance and belligerence mixed in equal parts.

So, there it was. A little quick math and the complication became a little more complicated, a little more loaded with possibility. And Grace was clinging to that possibility like a sailor to a raft in shark-infested waters.

Serenity crawled back under the truck.

"I need to talk to you," he said, grimly, to Grace. He pointed at the boy. "And you need to go catch those ponies."

"You're not the boss over me," Tucker said.

The flash in his eyes and the tilt of his chin were identical to those of the woman beside him.

And the defiance was likable, if you were open to that kind of thing. Which, Rory reminded himself, he wasn't.

"You're the one who said you'd look after the ponies," Rory reminded him. Tucker left, making it clear with one black backward glance it was his choice to go.

When he was gone, Rory turned his full attention to Gracie, whose expression clearly said he was not the boss over her, either.

"Did Serenity tell you that kid was Graham's?"

"Don't call him that kid! His name is Tucker."

"Okay," he said, feeling how forced his patience was, "did she tell you Tucker was Graham's?"

"No." That very recognizable tilt of chin.

"Did she insinuate it?"

"No. I had them over for dinner the other night. She never said a word about Graham and Tucker. Not one word."

"You had them over for dinner? At your house?"

The you're-not-the-boss-over-me expression deepened. Rory had to fight an urge to shake her. All those years of discipline being tried by a hundred-and-ten-pound woman!

"Why wouldn't I have them over for dinner?"

Because it's akin to throwing a bucket of fish guts to seagulls. They'll be back. He said nothing.

"I actually enjoyed it. She's had a very tough life, but she's very interesting."

"You don't know anything about her!"

Her chin was tilting stubbornly.

"You can't save the whole world, Gracie."

"No? Isn't that what you and Graham were so fired up to do?"

He let that bounce off him, like a fighter who had only been nudged by a blow that could have killed had it landed.

His voice cold, he said, "That's precisely why I know it can't be done."

Instead of having the good sense to see what he was trying to tell her—that he was hard and cold and mean—that soft look was in her eyes again.

It made him wonder if maybe, just maybe, if she couldn't save the whole world, if she could save one person.

And if that person was him.

The thought stunned him. It had never occurred to him he needed to be saved. From what?

"You want desperately for that boy to be Graham's," he said softly.

"Don't you? Don't you want some part of Graham to go on?"

He heard the desperation, the pure emotion, and knew he could not rely on her to make any rational decisions.

"Look, the things that made Graham who he was are not exactly purely genetic. Those things are the result of how the two of you were raised."

He remembered her family. Off to church on Sunday mornings. Going to their cabin on the lake together. Playing board games on winter nights. Lots of hugs and hair-ruffling. Their parents had given them so much love and affection.

He was trying to tell her that the way that Tucker was being raised he didn't have a hope of turning out anything like Graham. Even if he was Graham's, which was a pretty big if.

"It's easy enough to find out," he said. "Whether he's Graham's or not."

She said nothing.

"A cotton swab, the inside of his cheek, an envelope, a result."

"Good grief, how often have you done that?" she said with scorn, but he knew it was to hide the fact it frightened her that it was that easy.

He didn't say anything. Let her believe what she wanted. Especially if it killed the soft look in her eyes, which it did.

"Don't you want to know the truth about Tucker?" he asked.

"Yes! But I want Serenity to tell me the truth!"

"You want Serenity to tell you the truth?" he asked, incredulous. Was it possible to be this hopelessly naive?

Grace nodded, stubborn.

"You know how you can tell Serenity is lying?"

"How?"

"Her lips are moving."

"That's unnecessarily cynical."

"There is no such thing as being unnecessarily cynical."

She glared at him then changed tack. "How well did you and Graham know her?"

"Well enough to know she'll tell you whatever you want to hear if there's money involved."

"You're hopelessly distrustful."

"Yeah. And alive. And those two things are not mutually exclusive. Grace, there's a woman lying under a trailer, presumably drunk. Her ponies are all over the park. If ever there was a call to cynicism, this is it."

Suddenly, the defiance left her expression. He wished

he'd had time to get ready for what she did next. Grace laid her hand on his wrist.

Everything she was was in that touch. The way she was dressed tried to say one thing about her: that she was a polished and successful businesswoman.

At least before her pony encounter.

But her touch said something entirely different. She probably would have been shocked by how her touch told her truth.

That she was gentle, a little naive, hopeful about life. She was too soft and too gullible. He was not sure how she had managed that. To remain that through life's tragedies, the death of her brother, the breakup of her engagement.

There was a kind of courage in it that he reluctantly admired even while he felt honor-bound to discourage it.

She looked at him, and there was pleading in her eyes. "I know you're just trying to protect me. But please, Rory, let me do this my way. Is it so terrible to want a miracle?"

Miracles. He'd never been a man with any kind of faith, and spending all his adult life in war zones had not improved his outlook in that department. He—from a family who had never set foot in a church—had said his share of desperate prayers.

His last one had been *Don't let this man, my friend, die*.

He both admired her hope, and wanted to kill it before it got away on her and did some serious damage.

Trying for a gentle note, which was as foreign to him as speaking Chinese, Rory said, "Gracie, come on. No one walks on water."

At that moment, a pickup truck shot into the parking lot, and pulled up beside the horse trailer. It had a decal on the side for the Mountain Retreat Guest Ranch. A cowboy got out of the driver's side.

He looked as though he was straight off a movie set. Booted feet, plaid shirt, Stetson, fresh-faced and clean-scrubbed. Three other cowboys spilled out the open doors.

"Slim McKenzie," the first one said. "I hear you're having a pony problem."

Gracie turned and looked at Rory, those amazing eyes dancing with the most beautiful light.

"Maybe no one walks on water," she said, quietly, "But garden-variety miracles happen all the time."

He wanted to ask her where the damned miracle had been for her brother. But he found, to his dismay, he was not quite hard-hearted enough to be the one to snuff out that light in her eyes.

And the light in her eyes was doing the strangest thing to him. He knew the arrival of the cowboys was no miracle, not of the garden variety or any other. It was the Bridey variety miracle, pure and simple.

But something was happening nonetheless. Unless he was mistaken, Gracie's light was piercing the darkness in him, bringing brightness to a place that had not seen it for a long, long time.

He did not allow himself to marvel at it. He thrust the feeling of warmth away. His darkness could put out her light in a millisecond.

And he'd better remember that when he was thinking about how beautiful Graham's kid sister had become.

CHAPTER THREE

GRACE watched with absolute delight as the angels who had arrived dressed as cowboys rounded up the ponies. How could Rory not believe in miracles?

In less than an hour the whole disaster was not just repaired, it was practically erased.

It also took less than an hour to become very evident to her that Rory Adams might not know a thing about ponies, but leadership came as naturally to him as breathing.

"How about if you just sit this one out?" Rory had suggested with a meaningful look at her damaged footwear.

She could have resented how he took over from her, but frankly she was sick to death of ponies, and though it was probably a crime in the career woman's manual, she reluctantly admitted it was somewhat of a relief to have someone take over. But not out loud.

Rory set up an impromptu command center, and she found, in her softened frame of mind, with him unaware of her scrutiny, it was nice to watch him.

Rory Adams was a force unto himself, pure masculine energy practically sizzled in the air around him. He came up with a plan, quickly, delegated, and then he pitched in. He was afraid of nothing: not ponies racing straight at him, not being dragged on the other end of a rope by a tiny pony that was much stronger than seemed possible.

From a purely feminine point of view, watching Rory was enough to make her mouth go dry. He was agile, energetic and strong. It seemed every muscle he possessed was being tested to its rather magnificent limits. Every now and then his shout of command—or laughter—would ring out across the field.

When a pony charged in her direction, he threw himself at it, glancing off its shoulder, but managing to change its direction.

And then he rolled easily to his feet—as if he had not just risked life and limb to save her—and kept moving.

It occurred to her that he protected in the same way he led. It came to him as naturally as breathing.

And it felt like the most terrible of weaknesses that it made her insides turn to jelly.

Within an hour the last of the ponies was loaded into the ramshackle trailer. The poop was scooped. The birthday banner was fished out of the pool. Serenity was installed in the backseat of her crew-cab truck, and Tucker, looking at home for the first time since she had met him, was sandwiched in between two large cowboys on the front seat.

"Clayton and Sam will drive their truck to wherever they want to go," Slim said, addressing Rory. "I'll follow in my truck."

There was something in the way he was addressing Rory, with a respectful kind of deference, that gave her pause. A suspicion whispered to life inside her, and

Grace could feel the pink cloud she had been floating on since the timely arrival of the cowboys evaporating beneath her.

"Anything else you need done, Mr. Adams?"

Mr. Adams? Grace tried to think whether there had been an exchange of names in the flurry of activity that had begun since those cowboys first rolled up. Certainly, she had not given her name.

She felt as if she was on red alert now, watching Rory even more intently than she had been when he was commanding the field. Maybe she didn't know him that well, and maybe many years had gone by since she had seen him, but he simply was not the kind of man who would introduce himself as Mr. Adams.

It was the kind of thing Harold might have done: trying to one-up himself over simple, working men, but Rory would *never* do that.

She told herself it was impossible to know that given the shortness and circumstances of their reacquaintance, but it didn't matter. Her heart said it knew.

Still, instead of feeling a soft spot for him, she reminded herself something was up, there was more going on here than met the eye.

Rory, catching her sudden intense focus on him, clapped the cowboy on the shoulder and moved off into the distance, where she couldn't hear what they said.

But she was pretty sure that was a wallet coming out of Rory's back pocket!

By the time he came back, any admiration she had felt about his camaraderie with the working man was gone. So was her pink cloud.

In fact, Grace felt as if she had landed back on earth

with a rather painful thump. She should have never let her barriers down by admiring him, not even discreetly! Now she had to build them back up. Why was that always harder than taking them down?

The trucks pulled out of the park, the horse trailer swaying along behind them, with great clinking and clanking and whinnying of ponies.

And then there was silence. And Rory standing beside her, surveying the park and looking way too pleased with himself.

"That wasn't a miracle, was it?" she demanded.

"I don't know. Eight ponies successfully captured in—" he glanced at his watch "—under eight minutes per pony. Might qualify. Did I mention I'm no expert on miracles?"

He was looking at her, his expression boyishly charming, though there was something in his eyes that was guarded.

"I meant the arrival of Slim and the gang."

He was very silent. And now he looked away from her, off into the distance. He wouldn't look at her.

"It wasn't even the garden-variety kind, was it?"

Silence.

"Why didn't you say something instead of letting me prattle on?" *Instead of letting me believe.*

"Aw, Gracie," he said, finally looking back at her, "you're too old to believe in stuff like that, anyway."

She blinked. "I'm *old?*"

"Not old as in decrepit." His look was intense, and then he said softly, "Not at all."

Grace recognized how easy it would to be charmed by him. And she recognized he was a man who had been charming his way past the ruffled feathers of the female species since he'd been old enough to blink that dark tangle of lashes over those sinfully green eyes.

And that after he'd been the one to ruffle the feathers!

"I just meant the last time I saw you, you were a little girl. You probably still believed in Santa Claus."

"I was fourteen! I certainly did not believe in Santa Claus." Though she had been hopelessly in love with the man who stood before her, imagining endless scenarios where he finally *saw* her. And that was probably exactly the kind of magical thinking he thought she was too old for now.

And he was right.

Somehow the hurt of being invisible to him all those years ago, and this moment of his debunking her desire to believe in miracles were fusing together, and she could feel her temper rising.

"What did you have to do with those men arriving?" she demanded.

"I saw you were having trouble. I made a phone call."

"What kind of man can make a phone call and have a truckload of cowboys delivered?"

"You needn't say it as if it were a truckload of bootleg liquor during prohibition and you were leading the group of biddies waving a sign saying liquor is of the devil."

"Old and prim," she said dangerously.

"You do have a little pinched look around your mouth that reminds me of a schoolteacher who has found a frog in her drawers."

She sputtered with outrage.

"Hey. Desk drawers!"

"Stop it! You're trying to distract me."

"Is it working?" he said silkily.

Yes. "No!"

"Because I have another way to take that pinched look off your lips. Not to mention distract you."

Rory Adams was threatening her with a kiss!

And it was far too easy to imagine the hard line of those lips dropping over the softness of her own!

She stared at him, and then felt the traitorous blush moving up her neck. She didn't blush anymore. Who blushed in this day and age? Oh God, she was acting exactly like the old biddy he'd accused her of being.

Then she realized he had no intention of *really* kissing her. He was teasing her the same way he had when she was a child. And she had the frustrating feeling he was still enjoying the result!

She drew in a deep breath, did her best to erase kisses from her mind. "Quit dodging the issue. What I want to know is how you happened to be here at the park as all this was unfolding?"

"Just as you found yourself in need of a white knight?" he asked.

He was baiting her. Wanting her to argue about his qualifications to be a white knight. Or maybe about hers to be a damsel in distress.

But she wasn't fourteen anymore, and she was not going to allow him to suck her into his teasing. Or to look at his lips and wish, in a moment of madness, that he hadn't been teasing about his ability to distract with *that*.

She folded her arms over her smudged chest and

tapped her foot. She told herself she didn't care if she looked like an old-biddy schoolmarm with a frog in her drawers.

"What were you doing here?"

"Your secretary told me where I could find you," he admitted.

Grace felt a moment's annoyance at her secretary, Beth, but it quickly dissipated. What woman would have a chance against Rory if he decided to turn on his charm? Including her. So she steeled herself against him, kept her arms folded and her foot tapping.

"And why did you want to find me?"

"We have some business to discuss."

"I already told you we didn't."

"Well, now we do."

"You're right. Send me a bill and I'll reimburse you for whatever you paid to have the ponies rounded up."

He looked scornful. "That's never going to happen."

"Then we have no business. I'd like to say it was nice seeing you again, but the circumstances overshadow the delight, I'm afraid. Good-bye and—"

"My company wants to be one of the sponsors for your fundraising event for Warrior Down. We're prepared to make a substantial contribution."

Now he had truly caught her off guard. Her arms dropped and her foot stopped tapping.

A stronger woman would have refused him outright. But Warrior Down was her baby. Of all the events she would plan this year, only this one would be so close to her heart. Its success meant everything to her. Everything.

As much as she wanted to, she could not put her own

pride in front of her cause. How could she say no to a man who could pull cowboys out of thin air? She was pretty sure any contribution he wanted to make to Warrior Down was going to be amazing, because he was not a man who would ever be satisfied with the ordinary.

Including an ordinary girl like you, she thought, and then pushed that thought away like a pesky fly.

She wanted to know right now what he considered a substantial contribution, but she also had the horrible feeling of the balance of power shifting to him, and she'd had enough of him having the upper hand for one day.

She was not going to address this situation while standing here in the growing afternoon heat of the park in a broken shoe and a smudged dress. She was not in any kind of frame of mind to make good decisions, never mind maintain absolute control over her baby, Warrior Down.

She could barely defend herself against his teasing!

No, she needed time to repair herself. And prepare herself for whatever he had to propose.

She was going to meet him on her own ground.

After she'd had a chance to regain her composure. Not to mention have her hair done and her best outfit on. The next time she saw Rory Adams she would have her best foot forward! She would not be a woman flustered by the insinuation of a kiss!

She smiled with as much professionalism as she could muster. "I'd be delighted to discuss that with you. If you'll call my secretary, Beth, she'll make an appointment for you."

He looked shocked that she was putting him off. He

wasn't used to not having his way, and that was just too damned bad.

She turned and limped away with as much dignity as she could muster.

"Hey, Gracie-Facie."

She looked over her shoulder and glared at him.

"You could say thanks for the help."

For a delicious moment, she thought she had gotten to him. That he had expected her to fall all over herself in gratitude for being rescued by him, that he was actually flustered by a woman who did not succumb to his charms.

But she saw, in that glance back, that he was not the least perturbed by her lack of gratitude.

That he was amused by it. And by her. The same way as he had been when she was that little girl he had tormented by calling her Gracie-Facie instead of falling madly in love with her.

Gracie-Facie, indeed!

Well, next time they were meeting on her turf, and everything was going to be under her control. She would be completely cool, calm, collected, professional. Completely.

But for a woman who wanted to be completely cool, calm, collected and professional, she actually had to bite down on her lip to keep from sticking her tongue out at him.

And his shout of laughter, as if he could see right through her, shivered along her spine.

Rory did not look as if he laughed like that very much anymore.

Grace recognized it as a dangerous weakness, that

after all the fun he'd had at her expense, she was actually glad she had made him laugh, glad she could pull from him, even for a second, a shadow of the carefree young man he had once been.

Rory watched her go, the smile still tickling his lips.

Given that he considered himself a man generally unencumbered by touchy-feely sentiments like guilt, he was just a little amazed by how relieved he was to be turning the little white lie he'd told her secretary into a truth.

Offering to do something for Warrior Down was the carrot Grace Day could not resist.

The fact was, he already knew it was not going to be that smart to tangle their lives together. She was sensitive, sweet, feisty, smart—in other words, way more complicated than the kind of woman he was used to.

She also was way more innocent than anybody he was accustomed to dealing with. Her face had turned the color of a fire hydrant when he had said he knew just how to wipe that prissy look off her face!

His own reaction to the thought of kissing her had been anything but playful.

On the other hand, she was in way over her head with the whole Serenity thing, and he was not cutting her loose to deal with it herself. Warrior Down would be the perfect excuse to keep tabs on her.

And he hoped she would never find out what he had just asked that cowboy.

She probably would have no objection to the fact he had asked to be informed about where Serenity and Tucker and their eight ponies were living and how, but it was the other part that would probably put her nose seriously out of joint.

Buy the kid a can of soda pop on the way to wherever they're going. Keep the can.

Grace wanted to play it one way with Serenity and that was okay *for her.* But Rory needed to have a backup plan in case hers didn't pan out, which he was fairly certain it wasn't going to.

Serenity was going to play her hand close to her chest and milk it for all it was worth. If Tucker was Graham's, wouldn't Serenity have said so already? Why wouldn't she have told Graham while he was alive? What would be the benefit to her of keeping the boy a secret?

Rory watched Grace toodle out of the parking lot in one of those big luxury cars you associated with an old person who was sending the message *I've made it.* She looked cautiously right and left, careful not to even glance in his direction.

Make an appointment with my secretary.

Grace thought it was all going to go her way next time, that she was inviting him into her uptight little world where she would have all the control.

The thing was, from everything Graham had told him about her, the last thing Gracie needed was more control.

Hey, he warned himself, *getting way too involved here.*

But what if Graham hadn't meant just check on her? What if that was too literal? What if he had really meant, check on her and if there is a little tightness around her mouth and still shadows of sorrow in her eyes, and if she's trying to control everything in the whole world, do something about it?

Rory sighed. He was the man least qualified to interpret a dying man's last words.

But he was pretty sure Graham would approve of him shaking up Gracie's world just a bit. And even if Graham didn't, a little part of Rory was looking forward to it. And so it just wasn't going to go her way.

And though she was unlikely to recognize it at first, that was going to be his gift to her, the kid sister of his deceased best friend. Maybe he didn't actually have to burden her with the details of his part in Graham's death. Maybe he just had to try to make up for it.

And, unreasonably pleased with himself, Rory was pretty sure he knew just how to shake up Gracie's tidy little world.

He took his cell phone out of his pocket and dialed the office of Day of Our Lives. He made his appointment for the next day. And then he called Bridey. His personal assistant would be earning her money today.

"Mr. Adams, *sir*."

Rory winced. "Great job on the cowboys, Bridey. How did you do that?"

"Thank you, sir. Mr. McKenzie is a nice young man. I spent a weekend at his guest ranch not long ago. I'm afraid it's not faring that well with the poor economy."

"I gave him another little job to do, so maybe that will help. And I've got another challenge for you. I need you to find something for me by tomorrow. It's not going to be easy."

Bridey sighed with rich contentment. "Not easy is my favorite," she told him.

He told her what he needed. He waited for her to gasp, for her to tell him that finally he had given her a task she could not complete, that it was impossible.

Instead, completely unfazed, Bridey said, "Italia or Spider?"

Grace had been slightly taken aback to return to her office and find Rory had already made an appointment to see her. Had she known he was going to be that prompt she could have forewarned Beth to put him off for at least a few days!

Still, by the next morning Grace felt as ready for Rory Adams as a woman could ever feel ready for a man like that.

She looked around her office with satisfaction. The space was not ostentatious, but it was tastefully decorated to welcome clients. Her desk was antique mahogany, the two chairs on the other side of it were deeply comfortable distressed leather. The art was local, the rugs were imported. Like her car, it all whispered, subtly, *arrived.*

Still, Beth had sniffed the air this morning and asked if she was planning on doing surgery in here.

"What does that mean?"

"I don't know. It looks sterile. It smells antiseptic."

Sterile and antiseptic weren't quite the impressions Grace was looking for, so she had ordered herself an arrangement of white lilies and placed them artfully on the corner of her desk.

When they'd asked her at the florists what to put on the card, at first she had said no card. But then it had occurred to her: what would it hurt for a card to be inserted amongst the fragrant blossoms? Just in case he happened to glance that way? He was a detail guy. The type who saw everything.

So, it would be good for him to see a lovely bouquet with a card addressed in masculine handwriting that said, *To Gracie, with love.*

When the bouquet had arrived she looked at the card and wondered if it foreshadowed things not going quite as per her plan, because there was nothing masculine about the handwriting. So she took out the card and tossed it.

Unnecessary attention to detail, maybe, but this was, after all, what she did for a living. Staged perfect events.

Though it was not completely lost on her that the fact she was going to all this trouble to manipulate his impressions of her already meant she was in trouble of some sort.

And it wasn't just the freshly cleaned office and the flowers, either.

No, a nearly sleepless night planning what to wear, in her tired mind trying on and discarding nearly every outfit she owned.

She had settled on the light wool Chanel suit in a shade of turquoise that reminded her of an ice-wine bottle. Secretly she called it her "sexy librarian" outfit. Which was exactly the look she wanted: looking sexy at the same time as looking as though she had made no effort to do so. Under the jacket she had on a navy blue silk blouse, very professional, even with the buttons undone one lower than normal.

"For the *very* sexy librarian look," she said.

The outfit was obviously way too warm for the hot

summer weather, but the office was air-conditioned, and observant as he was, Rory Adams wouldn't know wool from hemp.

So, unlike their last meeting, this time everything was perfect.

Her hair was pinned up, her makeup was subtle but flattering, the outfit was professional with the tiniest hint of sexy, and the atmosphere was one-hundred-percent successful businesswoman. Grace even had a script of sorts figured out.

So, what exactly did you have in mind for sponsorship? A cash donation would work best for us.

At precisely eleven o'clock, Beth came in the door, closed it behind her, leaned on it.

"Ohmygod, he's here."

There was no question who *he* was. Beth's faintly dazed expression said it all.

Annoyed at her secretary's easy capitulation to Rory's considerable charms, Grace was even more determined to remain as icy cool as the color of her dress.

"Who is here?" she asked coolly, hoping to prompt professionalism. Beth, naturally, ignored the coolness. They were a two-woman office, which over the years had made them so much more than employer and employee. They were friends and coworkers. Beth could—and had—run the business singlehandedly, especially in those awful weeks after Graham's death.

"Your date is here."

Grace felt her mouth fall open. She snapped it shut, annoyed at herself. She could not have predicted, after all this preparation, how easy it would be to become flustered.

"My date?" she squeaked and then pulled herself together. "I don't have a date. I have a business appointment."

"Grace, he's gorgeous. I'm thinking Hugh Jackman only a hundred times better. No! No! Tracker Tannison!"

Don't ask. She asked. "Who is Tracker Tannison?"

"The TV series, *Find Your Man*. He plays Special Agent Booth Bentley. He's dreamy. But not as dreamy as your date."

After all her careful preparation, Grace felt as though her head was spinning. She felt a desperate need to get this situation under control.

Aware of a certain tight note, of enunciating every word very carefully, Grace said, "I do not have a date."

"He says it's a date."

"It isn't."

Beth was looking at her closely. "Well, you look like it is."

"I don't. I've worn this suit dozens of times."

"I meant the blush."

"I am not blushing!"

"If you say so." Beth scrutinized her. "Isn't that wool? It's supposed to go to thirty-two degrees Celsius today."

"We have air-conditioning."

"That suit is extremely flattering. I've always loved that color on you," Beth said, soothingly, making Grace aware she was telegraphing her distress at the fact her plan for this meeting already seemed to be going awry. But at least it wasn't eight ponies on the loose, a broken shoe and a smudged dress.

"Make him wait. Until I'm done blushing." *Until I've collected myself.* "Ten minutes. Then show him in."

Those would be the longest ten minutes of her life. A date? How dare he say it was a date?

"He told me to send you out."

Grace allowed herself to feel flabbergasted by the pure arrogance of the man!

"Well, I'm not going out. You tell him to come in. He's not the boss over you. Or me." Oh, God. She sounded exactly like Tucker.

"Grace?"

She closed her eyes. She just knew something terrible was coming. She could feel it, like storm clouds building on the horizon.

"He's got a Ferrari sitting outside the front door. He said he's taking you for a ride."

She closed her eyes. She mustered all her strength, which was what it took to utter one little word.

"No."

"It's red."

"So what?" But her voice had a high, desperate note to it. The truth? She was beginning to wish for ponies!

"Well, I can't help but notice, when you open your wallet, you have that picture…" Beth's voice trailed away. And then stronger, she said, "Go, for God's sake. You might never have this opportunity again. That man is absolutely gorgeous. And even if he was a toad, you should go for a ride in that car."

Grace glared at Beth. Imagine that. The devil looked like her secretary today.

"No," she said.

"If you're going to tell him no, you do it yourself." Beth, loyal secretary and friend turned traitor, gave her a meaningful look and slipped out the door.

Before it shut behind her, Grace heard Beth say, "Can you just give her a moment?"

The door shut.

Now she had to go say no herself. She had to tell him their meeting was going to go just as she planned it, in the safety of her office, where he could admire her decor and her flowers and her outfit. Where she could erase any last vestiges of a woman throwing shoes at a pony. Where she could erase any last vestiges of a woman who needed the prissy look wiped off her face…with his lips.

Still, if she said no, and said it too vehemently, how was he going to read that? At the very least, control freak. At the very worst, fighting a terrible attraction to him. She had to prove to him—no, she had to prove to herself—that Rory Adams had no power over her.

None.

So, she would go out there, and she would not see going to him as any kind of defeat. No, living up to her name, she would do it gracefully. She would still say no, of course, but with no vehemence at all. She would say it with a reluctant smile. She would explain, *I'm just too busy today. A huge wedding coming up this weekend. So much to do.*

She got up. She went to the door. She flung it open. Is this how he had felt going into battle?

His heart pounding in his chest? His palms slicked with sweat?

She wished she hadn't thought of him like that, going

into battle. Because Rory Adams was sitting in a chair, leafing casually through a magazine, a man who, despite his aura of great power, had spent a great deal of his life waiting…for all hell to break loose.

There was something about him that was all warrior, despite the civilized backdrop of her office, despite his casual slacks, despite the sports shirt, despite the hair that was long enough to tickle the back of his collar.

Rory looked up at her, and smiled, and she thought of him threatening to kiss her. And wondered if even that was a distraction, something to keep her from seeing who he really was.

Because just behind the devastating charm of that smile she could see the warrior. And worse, she could detect a faint weariness, strength that had been tested to the point of breaking but that had not broken.

"Good morning, Grace."

Her whole prepared speech about how important and busy she was abandoned her.

This man had been her brother's friend. He was here trying to do something nice for her. Probably to honor her brother.

She could not treat him like the enemy.

Not even to protect herself.

"I hear we're going for a ride," she said. She cast a warning glance at Beth who looked as if she was going to stand up from behind her desk and clap.

"I was hoping you could squeeze it in."

He was offering her an out. It was her last chance to claim, yes, indeed, she was too busy. If she looked away from him, maybe her head would clear.

Maybe she would have a better chance of making the right and rational decision.

Her eyes moved beyond him, but unfortunately they drifted to the big picture window of her office that faced the front street. The car was parked at the curb, already attracting attention. Two teenage boys had their cell phones out and were taking turns taking pictures of each other posing with the car.

For as long as she could remember, Grace had carried a picture of a red Ferrari in her wallet. If you asked her why, she didn't even know. It appealed to some part of her that was deeply secret.

She was not sure how she felt about this secret being exposed to Rory Adams. Her brother must have told him. That link, her brother, connected her to this man in ways she was not at all sure she could handle.

And she liked having a handle on her life!

Instead, Grace felt the terrible loss of control. And she felt an equally terrible temptation just to surrender. She fought it.

"We are going to discuss Warrior Down?" she asked, trying for a stern note, trying to recapture at least an illusion of control.

"Of course," he said smoothly.

"All right. Beth clear my calendar for—" She looked inquiringly at him.

"A couple of hours?"

Impossible. But her control seemed to have abandoned her despite her attempt to fight for it. "All right."

But in one last ditch effort to salvage something of all that time wasted in an effort to manipulate his im-

pressions of her, Grace darted back into her office and
grabbed the flowers, hugged them to her chest.

She plunked them down on Beth's desk. "These need
water," she said, regally, and Beth, bless her heart, did
not say *But they just arrived.*

She said, "Oh, yes, I noticed that. I'll look after it
right away."

And before Rory could get a look at the water level
in that crystal vase, Grace marched by him, waited for
him to open the door for her, and then passed through
it, and waited for him to open the door of the car.

The car was red and low and so sexy it took her
breath away. It had a hard top that had been retracted.

She hesitated, feeling as if if she did it, if she actually
stepped into that car something in her life was going to
change irrevocably and forever.

Don't do it.

Do it.

Don't.

Do.

Do was winning. What was so great about her life
that it couldn't stand changing? She worked, she slept,
she worked some more. She did an important job. She
brought people joy. She made happy memories for them.

That's what dedicated career women did: they got
their sense of fulfillment from their work. That's what
women who didn't want to be hurt anymore did.

Yesterday it had seemed like a perfectly acceptable
life, she wailed a reminder to herself.

No, the day before yesterday. Before the ponies. Before him.

The door of the car whispered open. She could smell

the heat of the engine, Italian leather and Rory's cologne.

They were drugs that stole what was left of her resolve. Grace Day took one more step toward the car.

CHAPTER FOUR

"Hang on," Rory said as Grace moved by him to get in the car. She tried not to brush against him but the effort was lost when his hand went to her hair. He ran his palm along the side of her face, over her ear, until it rested on the delicate nape of her neck. With a gentle, firm tug he freed the clasp that held her hair up.

Grace felt her hair tumble, whisper against the sensitive skin of her neck where his fingers had just touched.

How dare you would be the appropriate response. To turn around and march right back into her office, and her perfectly satisfactory life, slam the door and turn the bolt would be the appropriate response.

Instead, she felt the shiver of his touch, of the strange intimacy of him releasing her hair, to the bottom of her toes. Instead, she stood there frozen, captured by the shimmering greenness of his eyes, and by the glint of hard, male appreciation in them.

"You can't ride with the top down without feeling the wind in your hair," he said, something in his voice faintly gruff. He held out the hair clasp to her.

And she took it and slid it into her pocket without one single word of protest!

Maybe another woman could be stronger. But the

combination of the sexy car and the sensuousness of his touch on her hair and her neck rendered Grace helpless. She could not resist the temptation. Taking a deep breath that she let out with a sigh, she put her leg in the car and then sank into the low seat.

Nothing could live up to a fantasy she'd held for so long, she told herself, trying desperately to regain some semblance of her sensible well-ordered life.

But when Rory Adams came around and took the seat beside her, and the engine started with a deep low purr of pure power, and his scent and the smell of leather both filled her nostrils, she had the awful thought that maybe some things could actually be better than a fantasy.

"Where are we going?" Grace asked him.

"Does it matter?" He shoulder-checked and pulled away from the curb so smoothly it was as if she was riding on air.

Whatever was left in her that wanted to be in control evaporated. She laughed. "No."

"I thought we'd take the back road around Lake Okanagan. Stop at the Blue Water Resort and have lunch."

"That resort is where the big fundraiser for Warrior Down is."

"I know."

She pondered that as they surged in and out of traffic, making their way through Mason to the head of the lake road. Did he know everything? Apparently he did. Even about her lifelong dream to ride in a Ferrari.

"Graham must have told you about my secret fascination with this car," she said.

"Is it everything you expected?" he said with a smile that did not distract her. He didn't want to admit he and Graham had discussed her.

"So far, it's more than I expected," she admitted, but got right back on topic. "I have to admit, it makes me uncomfortable thinking about you two discussing me."

"It should." He sent her a sideways look, and waggled his eyebrows, the villain in a movie. Despite the fact he was still trying to distract her, Grace laughed again, and enjoyed the sensation of laughing. Since Graham had died, and then her engagement had blown up in her face, it really seemed like there had not been much to laugh about. She was not unaware of the irony of the fact that she planned joyous, happy occasions for others, but rarely felt those things herself anymore.

"Do tell," she challenged him.

"Okay. I know just about everything about you. I know your favorite color is yellow. And your favorite book is *Anne of Green Gables*. I know you once punched a boy in your class for stealing a kiss."

"Something for you to remember," she said, pretending haughtiness.

"And that you were suspended for it. That's funny. *You* suspended."

"Despite the fact you think you know everything about me, I am not the Goody Two Shoes you think I am."

"Uh-huh." With utter disbelief. "Tell me something about you that would surprise me."

They were taking the exit now and she could see the dark blue waters of Lake Okanagan blinking under the sunlight in the distance.

She didn't just want to surprise him. She found herself wanting to shock him. So, feeling bold, she said, "I've skinny-dipped in this lake."

His laugh was derisive. "Oh, sure. By yourself at midnight."

"It wasn't! It was at a coed party."

"Oh," he said dryly. "Coed. Boys and girls at the same party. And how many beers did you have to have before you went in? I bet you're completely soused on two. And I'll bet it was completely dark and you raced down to the water's edge wrapped in your towel and didn't take it off until the last possible moment. And then you stayed in the water freezing, scared to come out and were in bed sick for a week after."

She stared at him, aghast at how accurate his portrayal of the one racy event of her entire life was. Obviously, he and Graham had talked about her way too much!

"So," he said, satisfied by her fuming silence, "I know just about everything about you, and you, on the other hand, know nothing about me."

But that wasn't exactly true. A memory of his house came to her mind. When he had moved in, the house his family had occupied had been the only rental on their block. Everyone else owned their properties and had been in them for years, forming a family as much as a neighborhood.

And then the Adamses had arrived and moved into a neglected two-story down the street from her own house. The neglect, as she recalled, was not improved by his family's possession.

Outside, paint peeled and fences sagged, and inside

curtains drooped and burnt-out lightbulbs were not replaced. The lawn sprouted weeds, an occasional motor-
cycle, newspapers tangled in the shrubbery. One old,
dilapidated car replaced another in the parking spot in
front of that house.

Somehow, even though he had challenged her that
she knew nothing about him, Grace could not bring that
up. She could not tell him that he was a long, long way
from his humble roots.

But he glanced at her face, and she was shocked by
what an open book she was to him.

"Oh, wait," he said, slowly. "You do know a thing or
two about me. Boy from the wrong side of the tracks."

"You lived on the same block as me!"

For a moment something in his face closed, he became intensely focused on driving the car as they entered the first of the twists in the road that ran in a
serpentine around this edge of the lake. When he finally
glanced at her, a small grin was on his face. "Don't kid
yourself, Gracie-Facie. Same block, different worlds.
The Cleavers meet the Osbornes. Only, the poor version."

The grin was a fake. It said it didn't matter. It said it
didn't bother him, but there was something guarded in
his eyes, daring her to judge him.

She wanted to tell him it didn't matter, but she remembered all too clearly the police cars arriving on
their quiet street, the shouting from inside their house, a
rather memorable occasion when his mother had stumbled out onto the street drinking straight from a wine
bottle.

And she remembered the dignity with which he had

handled that, the pride flashing in his eyes as he had retrieved his mother from in front of all her neighbors, walked her back into the house with straight shoulders, his hand on his mother's elbow, never glancing back at the assembled neighbors.

"You know something about growing up in a house like that, Gracie?"

She knew he was trusting her with something, and that this was not something he did often. The grin was completely gone.

"When you grow up in a war zone, you never expect anything good from life. That bred-into-the-bone cynicism made me a born soldier. And it always made me feel I had a leg up on those who did expect good things."

She had to admit, he had something there. Look at her, going through life like Pollyanna, her dreams broken at every turn!

But still, there was something about him not expecting good things that made her sad.

"When you expect the worst," he said, his voice grim, "you are rarely disappointed."

"And what happens when the best happens?" she asked. "What happens when the boy from the wrong side of the tracks ends up in the red Ferrari?"

"Don't forget the part about the girl next door being with him," he added, and the grin was back, devil-may-care, daring her to see beyond it. The thing was, she *could* see beyond it.

"I'm being serious!"

"Are you ever anything else?"

"Occasionally! But not now. What do you feel when the best happens instead of the worst?"

"Oh, that word again. *Feel.*"

"As uncomfortable as it makes you, could you answer the question?"

"When good things happen, I enjoy every second of them. Without any expectation that it will last."

He was telling her something, and she was aware she needed to pay attention. He wasn't the staying kind. He wasn't the lasting kind.

And what did she care? She would never think of Rory Adams like that.

Only, a secret part of her always had. And she was suddenly aware that secret part probably always would.

He would be such a foolish choice to fall for.

But he was right. She was being way too serious. She reminded herself it wasn't in her new life agenda to fall for anyone. The exact opposite, in fact.

Besides, Rory hadn't proposed they spend their lives together. He was giving her a day. And a dream.

And even if he was maintaining his own cynicism, she just needed to enjoy it, for this to be her *occasionally,* for this to be the day when she was not so serious.

When was the last time she had just had fun? A carefree day? A long, long time ago, certainly not since her brother had died.

She was accepting this as the unexpected gift it was. She was not even allowing herself to think that there might be a price to pay later.

"Rory?"

"Um?"

"Could you go a wee bit faster?"

He laughed and complied and she felt the thrill of both things: his laughter and the adrenaline of moving fast, a little closer to the edge. And Grace was aware his laughter brought that as surely as the power of the car did.

"Tell me about the car," she called over the roar of the engine and the wind in her hair.

"This is a 2011 Ferrari, a 458 Spider with a V8 rear engine."

"Somehow I don't think they rent these to just anybody," she guessed dryly. "In fact, where do you rent a car like this in Mason?"

"It's not exactly from Mason," he said, a little uncomfortably. "I had to make special arrangements to get it."

"First cowboys and now a Ferrari. If I ever need a rabbit pulled out of a hat, I guess you're my go-to guy, hmm?"

"If you ever need anything, Gracie," he said quietly, "I'm your go-to guy."

The simple statement, said so matter-of-factly, made her turn her face away from him so he could not see how deeply it affected her.

He was a man who said what he meant and meant what he said. And those simple words—that promise she could have someone to count on—filled her with unexpected emotion.

Dumb, since after Harold she had been so resolute in her intention not to rely on anyone for anything. Her plan now was to be one of those independent women who scoffed at *need*. She would hang her own pictures and refinish her own floors. When she came across a project she couldn't do, she would hire someone.

After Harold, she had been resolute in her intention

not just to be independent physically but also to be that way emotionally. Not to rely on anyone to make her feel anything anymore, and so the emotion clawing at her throat and stinging at her eyes because of his simple words, *I'm your go-to guy* felt as if it could swamp her whole plan for her life!

But riding in the car was a much-appreciated distraction from the unexpected meeting with her own secret longings, and she made herself focus on that. She might never, after all, experience something like this again!

She took off her jacket and threw it behind her seat.

And, after a while, she allowed herself to appreciate these moments with Rory. She liked the way one of his hands rested, light and confident on the wheel, the other on the gear shift. She liked the look on his face, relaxed but alert. Ready.

And she liked the way he drove. Many men would have gone crazy driving a car like this, but Rory drove without aggression, playing with the power but not unleashing it totally. It was as if he was riding a high-strung horse and he was in perfect control.

He put a CD in and the raspy tones of an old rock-and-roll band that had stood the test of time and could still fill stadiums filled the car.

The choice of music. The way he drove. The house he had come from. *If you ever need anything, Gracie, I'm your go-to guy.* How could he think she did not know anything about him?

She leaned back into her seat, felt the wind play with her hair. And surrendered.

* * *

Rory sat across the white linen tablecloth and watched Grace. The view of the lake from where they sat on the marble outdoor terrace of the Blue Water Resort's restaurant was amazing. Grace had already told him, her eyes sparking with excitement, the transformations she planned for this space when the Warrior Down fundraiser was to be held here in the last days of August.

He had talked her into a glass of wine from a local winery, while refusing one himself.

"You're not going to have one?" she asked.

"No. You don't drive a car that powerful and that sensitive with anything in your system that could impair your judgment."

He could tell she liked that, that his attention to safety appealed to her.

But there was a deeper truth behind his refusal to join her for a drink—and it wasn't just that he wanted to prove himself right that she would be soused on two.

He had long ago come to rely on his instincts. There were times his survival and the survival of others had depended on that. Now, he rarely ever did anything that made those instincts fuzzy. He had not had a drink in at least five years.

Was it just about his instincts being muddied? Or was part of it about his family's history with alcohol, trying to divorce himself from that completely?

And he was acutely aware there was already something about being with her that had impaired his judgment.

He didn't talk about his family, *ever,* and he tried not to think about them. What had made him bring it up? Just the fact she already knew? The fact she had grown up just down the street from the ongoing circus that had been his family life?

No. More than that.

He had trusted her with something about himself he did not trust everyone with.

"What happened to your fiancé?" he asked. For a guy who prided himself on his instincts, it was probably the wrong question. The door of camaraderie that had been opening between them snapped shut.

Or maybe that was exactly what he wanted to happen.

"What do you know about my fiancé?" she asked warily.

"Graham talked about your engagement when it happened. He didn't much care for, um, Herbert."

"Harold."

"So, what happened?"

She was so silent that for a moment he thought she wasn't going to tell him. She looked out at the lake, where children were playing on a float. Pushing each other off it, their splashing and laughter shivering on the air.

But when she looked back at him, he saw she was struggling to contain her emotion.

He was not good with emotion.

He wished he hadn't opened this kettle of fish. That door of camaraderie that had squeaked shut, was suddenly flung open, wider than before.

"He left me," she said bravely, tilting her chin up as if she didn't care. Her eyes told a completely different story, and he was aware he was seeing Gracie at her most real and her most raw.

And that she was trusting him with that.

Just as he had trusted her.

He waited.

"He left me because he couldn't stand the grief. He said it was time to get over it. He said it was time to be who I was before."

Rory felt a ripple of pure fury that he was very careful not to show her. In fact, his voice was very measured when he spoke. "Gracie?"

She looked at her hands.

"He was wrong. You never get over it. You're never who you were before."

She looked up at him, and the gratitude in her eyes was so intense it shook him. But he understood then, that the death of Graham was a bond between them. Unbreakable. They, alone, understood what it was to lose a man like that, how it changed the world forever for the worse.

"I hope I never meet old Herbert," he said, getting the name wrong deliberately, letting her know the name was not important. The character of a man was important.

"Why is that?" she asked.

"Because I won't be responsible for what happens next."

He thought she would reprimand him for his insinuated violence. Maybe he even hoped for it: to close that open door again. That something about showing her this little flash of who he *really* was, how quickly he could go to the dark side, would frighten her just a little bit.

He was not sure he was ready for her trust.

Yes, she could rely on him to be her go-to guy; no,

she could not rely on him to handle things her way, which would be all sweetness and light.

He was aware, again, of having darkness in him that could snuff her light.

But instead of her seeing that, instead of her being properly wary of him, she said, ever so softly, "Thank you."

Still, the intensity of that moment must have shaken her nearly as badly as it shook him: how fiercely protective he felt of her, how joined to her.

Grace changed the subject abruptly. "Tell me about your business, and what you'd like to do for Warrior Down."

Or maybe it was the most natural of segues, thoughts of her brother turning to ways that they could both honor his memory.

Rory was more an action guy than a talker, so it surprised him how easily he opened up to her.

"When I first enlisted, my brother, Sam, was just getting out of high school. He was a really talented artist and he wanted to get into graphics. I didn't have much to spend my money on, so I invested in him. In his education, later in his idea for a company.

"He got his big break doing graphics on a car for Saul Bellissimo. Do you know that name?"

"A race-car driver?" she ventured.

"*The* race-car driver of the past few years. Anyway, he did Saul's car, and that got him all kinds of other jobs and publicity. Sam just kept pushing the envelope, first graphic wraps for race cars, then he got the contract to do some buses.

"He's an artist, and to everyone's surprise I'm good at business."

"I'm not surprised," she said. "Tell me more."

It was another moment where something shivered along Rory's spine. It was as if Grace saw things in him that others didn't. And her interest in him was genuine. He should not allow himself to be flattered, but he did.

"Because of good access to the internet most of the time, I could even keep involved while I was overseas. When I decided to leave the service, I was a little astonished to find myself the CEO of a pretty viable company. In the past couple of months we completed our first contract for an airline company, graphic-wrapping their planes. In the next month or so, we're going to do our first graphic wrap on a building."

"A building?" she said. "Where?"

"Melbourne, Australia."

"My goodness, Rory, you're an international mogul!"

He felt the danger zone he was in. Boy from the wrong side of the tracks basking in the admiration of the wholesome girl from next door.

Enjoying her admiration in no way meant it was going any further.

He scrambled to keep it impersonal. "It all puts us in a pretty good position to sponsor something for Warrior Down."

"What did you have in mind?"

"I went on the internet and looked at your outline for the event. It sounds great. Dinner. Dance. Silent auction, everything set up here on the edge of the lake. I thought we might contribute something to the silent auction."

"Like?"

"What if we thought outside the box? Something like 'A Perfect Day.' A helicopter ride to the top of a mountain for a champagne lunch, something like that? Or maybe a ride in Saul's car, a turn or two around the track. Or maybe both."

"That's fantastic."

It was wrong to be so darned pleased that she was so darned pleased. It was wrong to want to bask in her admiration all afternoon. Still, a man was allowed a few weaknesses, wasn't he?

"What's your perfect day?" he asked her. "Because we could do anything—an elephant ride in Thailand, bungee-jumping... Literally if you can think of it, we can do it."

Now he was just showing off, plain and simple. He thought he'd better buy Bridey some flowers tomorrow, since she'd be the one executing whatever scheme they came up with.

"Oh." Grace looked flustered. "I thought I was a bit of an expert on perfect days, but my mind doesn't even begin to work like that. Elephants in Thailand?"

"Just close your eyes, then, and tell me what comes. Your perfect day."

And suddenly he wanted to know very, very badly, because it seemed like it would tell him secret things about her.

"Nothing so grand as elephants or helicopters," she said tentatively, not closing her eyes, but taking a fortifying sip of her wine before she bared her soul to him. She gazed out at the water, and then said, "You see those kids playing over there? Swimming out to the float and jumping in the water? That looks darn near perfect to me."

It had become quite hot in the last hour. Her blouse was sticking to her in the nicest places, and the skirt, which was about the most flattering straitlaced outfit he had ever seen, seemed to be causing her grief. He probably should not have suggested lunch outside.

He'd given her a chance to choose anything, and she had chosen that? It did tell him just about everything about her.

Except for her one Ferrari fantasy, she was just as she seemed. Wholesome. Without airs. Why did that seem kind of refreshing instead of just boring?

"That's too easy for a perfect day," he chided her. "We could have that today."

"I've already had days like that," she said, a little wistfully. "We used to have the cottage on Mara Lake. Not the multimillion-dollar kind you see today. A real cottage—ramshackle, falling down, no power, an outhouse. And all I remember there are perfect endless summer days."

"I remember your family heading out to that cottage, your station wagon packed to the roof." He did not say anything about that funny little twist of envy he would feel when he watched them depart, the longing to be part of something like that.

And, oddly, at the same time he had longed for it, he had refused every invitation Graham had offered him to join them there.

He'd felt as if he had to resist ever tasting something he knew he could not have.

People from perfect families matched up with other

people from perfect families. He had known that before he'd gone away to war and become even more hard and more cynical than he had been back then, and that had been plenty hard and cynical for a kid.

It suddenly seemed that this was a demon he needed to face: punch a hole in that illusion of a perfect life or a perfect day.

"Let's have it today," he said. "We'll put on some swimsuits and jump in the lake before we go home."

And he would find the wholesomeness of it hokey and boring, and somehow break free of the spell she was weaving around him.

"No. It's perfectly all right. I've already had a perfect day. Thank you for the car. It really was an incredibly sweet thing to do."

"Ah, I'm a sweet guy," he said, and wagged his eyebrows at her fiendishly.

But she didn't buy it. "What *do* you think you are?"

He could distract her with charm. Why ruin a light moment? But something overtook him, had been overtaking him ever since he remembered the perfect Day family leaving for their cottage, had been overtaking him ever since he had seen her again herding the damn ponies.

It was as though he was driven to show her what was real about him, driven to see if she could handle it.

It was the perfect time to tell her how he had failed her brother, but somehow he was not ready for that.

"Who I really am? Cynical. Dark. Aggressive when the situation calls for it."

He hated that he had said that. It made him feel as vulnerable as if he had told her the whole truth about her brother. He had exposed a wound to her that he had succeeded in hiding from the whole world. And so he finished with just a touch of sarcasm, "In other words, Gracie, not your type. At all."

As he had hoped, she was insulted. "Whoever said you were my type?" she said with a bit of heat.

"No one. Just to keep you from getting ideas."

"I would not ever get an idea about you!"

"Great. Let's go swimming before you sweat to death in the skirt you didn't put on for me."

"I don't have a bathing suit." Her voice was stiff with indignation. So, she *had* picked out that delectable, sexy and too warm suit just for him.

"Is that wool?" he said leaning over the table to get a better look. It was sticking to her, and she tugged it away.

"Very lightweight wool," she said, annoyed. "We should leave now."

"We should go swimming. What are you afraid of?"

"I'm not afraid of anything! I just don't happen to carry a bathing suit in my purse. Though I'm sure *your type* would."

"And what is my type, Gracie?"

"Bimbo," she said, without any hesitation at all.

He lifted his water glass to her. "Touché."

She gulped back the rest of her wine. Her cheeks had pretty red spots on them. He was right. One glass and she was practically soused.

She tossed the glossy wave of auburn hair that he had been dumb enough to set free, looked him straight in the face and said, "There are all kinds of stores here at the resort. I guess I could find a bathing suit."

He could tell it was not in her plan for the day, and that it did not come naturally to her to be spontaneous.

And maybe spontaneity between them had some dangerous overtones, given the startling intensity that had unfolded between them.

She wanted to move away from it.

And so did he.

And at the same time, he wanted to see if he could be immune to her. If he could burst the myth that he had always had surrounding her family.

He supposed she'd buy a one-piece suit, about as sexy as the uniforms of the East German girls' swim team, pre-Wall collapse.

And even though that was exactly what he wanted, he goaded her.

"When you buy that bathing suit? Be the girl in the red Ferrari," he suggested, "not an old stick-in-the mud."

Instead of looking offended, she looked suddenly sad. "Graham used to accuse me of that."

"I know," he said softly. "Break loose, Gracie."

And then he wondered what the hell he was playing with, and why. He looked after the check, and they separated in search of swimwear. He purchased a pair of trunks from one of the hotel stores in about two seconds, left them on, and went and sat on a bench where she would see him when she came out of the store she was in.

He had turned off his phone just before picking Grace up this morning, and now he turned it back on and sorted through his incoming messages.

Only one interested him. From Slim McKenzie, the cowboy who had accompanied Serenity home.

Rory glanced toward the store. Through a plate-glass window he could see Gracie holding up a very Gracie bathing suit. It probably had a matching bathing cap with a flower over one ear.

He listened to Slim's message and taking one more glance at the window to make sure Gracie would not materialize while he was in the middle of the call, he called back.

"Sorry, Mr. Adams. The kid tossed the soda can out the window before I could grab it."

"Never heard of littering?" Rory asked.

There was a pause. "Littering? I think that kid would laugh at the concept that that was a bad thing to do. He's pretty streetwise. Anyway, they were camped in an area off Bixby Road about six kilometers this side of Grumbly. The property was clearly marked No Trespassing. I don't think they had permission to be there. There was a creek to water the horses, but I didn't see much in the way of grass, and I didn't see any hay."

"The ponies looked fat to me."

"Yeah. Unfortunately, horses who aren't on a proper parasite-control program can look fat. That's called worm belly. Also from eating poor-quality feed. That's called hay belly."

"You're telling me the horses were hungry." Or full of worms. Way more than he'd ever wanted to know about an equine's belly.

"I think they were hungry. That's why they broke loose at the park and were so hard to catch."

Rory did not want to get involved in this. And yet how could he not be involved? If the horses were hungry, chances were the kid was, too.

He hung up the phone, frowning, and not just because his soda-pop-can plan had failed, either. He glanced at the window. Grace had disappeared from sight.

He could just call the authorities. There were people whose job it was to look after things like this and he was not one of those people. But even though he couldn't see Gracie, it seemed like just being around her required him to be a better man.

He sighed and called Bridey.

"Mr. Adams, *sir*."

"I need some good-quality hay delivered to some ponies. And a couple of days' worth of groceries for a kid and his mom. I need you to track down a landowner and get permission to use his land. Offer him whatever it takes to get that permission. You can use Slim again to deliver the food and the hay. He knows the situation and the location."

He hung up and glanced again at the window. Gracie was back in view, wearing a huge white robe, and peering at a rack of bathing suits as if it were the enemy. Her tongue, as she flipped rapidly through hangers, was caught between her teeth in fierce concentration. Obviously she was torn between being a stick-in-the-mud and shocking the hell out of him.

He hoped she would be a stick-in-the-mud and at the same time he didn't hope that at all. He was not used to being a man divided. He was used to being a man who knew exactly what he wanted.

Rory sighed, aware he did not want Gracie Day to know anything that he had just found out about Tucker and Serenity. If ever there would be a sucker for starving ponies, it would be her. Throw in the kid and that remote possibility that Tucker was Graham's, and she'd be mortgaging her business to save them.

He had no choice. He had to protect her. And the catch? She could never know he was protecting her.

Break loose, Gracie.

Those words echoed in Gracie's head as she studied the bathing-suit rack. How could a girl back down from a challenge like that? How could any woman in the world not rise to the bait? She *needed* to show him he had it all wrong.

That she was no stick-in-the-mud.

She selected a navy-blue tank-style, planning to defy his instruction to break loose. She held it up, studied it, silently declared it perfect. The matching bathing cap, with its huge plastic rose over the ear was a little silly, but the bathing suit would definitely do.

Except that it wouldn't. As soon as Grace took it to the change room and tried it on, she knew it was all wrong. The bathing suit, on, while definitely practical, made her look about as sexy as a refrigerator box. Just the kind of suit a stick-in-the mud would choose in a pinch!

So, going way out of her comfort zone, she wrapped herself in the robe provided by the shop and peeked out of the change room.

She could see Rory sitting on a bench on the open-air walkway, talking on his cell phone, comfortable in his new swim trunks, looking at the lake.

Life was so unfair sometimes! When a guy needed a bathing suit, he just went and grabbed one off the rack and put it on. There was no twisting and turning and looking at it from this angle and that, no self-doubt, no feelings of not being perfect!

While she watched, he hung up the phone, put it back in his pocket. He gazed out over the lake, and she was taken by his stillness while he waited, a man who had learned to appreciate quiet moments—that lull before the storm—when he could get them.

What he wasn't expecting was that she—little Gracie-Facie Day—was going to be his storm!

She looked back at the rack of suits, and this time refused even to look at the huge offering of one-piece suits. Taking a deep breath, she picked a half dozen of the skimpiest she could find!

A few moments later, she stared at herself in the change-room mirror.

Somehow, without planning it, maybe even against her will, she had become a totally different woman from the one who had walked into her office this morning.

"Not too late to put on the blue tank," she whispered to herself.

But she knew she wasn't going to.

CHAPTER FIVE

"My, my," Rory said, rising to join her as she came out of the shop, "Could you have found a bigger towel?"

He looked wickedly amused and Grace realized the huge towel she had purchased to wrap herself in only confirmed what he had suspected earlier when she had shared her skinny-dipping experience with him.

Goody Two Shoes. She was in a no-win position. If she dropped the towel now, she would feel like an idiot, displaying herself to him. If she didn't, she would feel like the prude he so clearly thought she was!

"My skin is sensitive to the sun," she said. "I haven't been on the beach yet this year." Shouldering her freshly purchased beach bag with her turquoise suit crumpled up inside it, she moved by him onto the flagstone pathway that wound down to the beach.

"You're going to have to take it off sometime," he said. "I wonder what you have on underneath it?"

She wished fervently for the blue suit that she had hung back up with a certain pride in the new her. She was not feeling nearly so bold now. In fact, she was feeling well out of her league.

"I have on the kind of suit a girl who rides in a

Ferrari would wear," she said with as much sophistication as she could muster.

"Ah, here's the rub, my Gracie, the girl in the Ferrari wouldn't have bothered with the towel."

My Gracie?

"Unless she burned easily," she retorted stubbornly.

"Tanning beds have a way of eliminating that problem."

"Hasn't your fictional Ferrari girl ever heard of melanoma?"

"Mel-a-nom-a. Is that three syllables?"

"Four."

He laughed. "That would be a no, then."

"Bimbo."

"Touché," he said, and somehow she found herself smiling.

They reached the hotel beach and she shuffled through the hot sand to the water's edge.

"Not going to lie in the sun and heat up a little first?" he asked smoothly.

She decided not to share with him that the wool suit she had so foolishly worn for precisely the reason he had guessed had heated her up quite enough for one day.

Sending him a little sidelong glance, she unhooked the towel from where it was clamped under her armpits. Unnerved by his frank anticipation of the towel dropping, Grace plunged into the water before the towel was even done slithering to the ground.

She couldn't help the little shriek at the cold, but still she did not stop until the water was up to her neck.

"Come in," she said. "It's beautiful."

"Liar. Your teeth are chattering."

"Chicken."

His eyes narrowed. "No one calls me a chicken and gets away with it, Gracie."

"Bok-bok-bok-bok-bok."

He hit the water running, dived cleanly, was nearly at her in one powerful stroke.

But she had grown up swimming and playing in these ice-cold waters, and she turned quickly from him and swam with expert strokes for the float.

She made it to the float a breath ahead of him, and clung to the side, scared if she got out of the water, the bathing suit might not come with her.

"Some suits," he growled in her ear, "are not exactly designed for swimming are they, Gracie?"

She pulled an errant strap back on her shoulder. This was turning into a repeat of yesterday!

He began to hum *Itsy Bitsy Teeny Weeny Yellow Polka-Dot Bikini*. Deliberately defiant, trying to find a red Ferrari girl in herself somewhere, Gracie hauled herself up, thankful the children who had been there earlier had departed and did not catch a glimpse of all the parts of her slipping from her suit. She quickly adjusted and then turned back to face him.

He was laughing so hard he was having trouble treading water. That was not exactly the effect she had intended.

"I'm coming to get you, Gracie. Nobody calls me a chicken." He switched from his *Yellow Polka-Dot Bikini* humming to a much more sinister tune, which she recognized as the theme music from *Jaws*.

Then he launched himself at the float. When he tried to pull himself up on the water-grayed wooden planks, she waited until he was precariously balanced on his forearms, placed all her weight on his shoulders and shoved.

He fell back in the water with a splash, and she barely had time to register how lovely his shoulders, skin and muscle had felt under her touch. She bounced on the balls of her feet, waiting for his next attempt.

He trod water for a moment, and she became aware he wasn't laughing now. She fought the urge to cover herself. With what, after all? Why not just enjoy the gleaming appreciation in his eyes? Why not play with it? Why not be the fun and flirtatious kind of girl who would wear a suit like this and ride in a red Ferrari?

"I'm giving you one chance to surrender," he told her.

"No. I hold the high ground and I intend to keep it."

"Ha. You haven't a hope, Gracie-Facie."

"Maybe you haven't a hope."

He came again, lifted himself up. She placed her foot solidly on the slickness of his wet chest and pushed. He fell back again, but this time he grabbed at her ankle and she slid forward before shaking free.

He came again, and this time she went for his head. She leaned out precariously, shoved and he went under the water easily.

Too easily, because just as she was congratulating herself on repelling another attack, a hand snaked out of the water and locked on her wrist. He tugged and she flew off the float and over his head, landing with an ungracious splash.

Now he clambered up on the float, and repelled her efforts to get up on it. Soon, the air was shimmering with their shouts and their laughter.

She forgot to be self-conscious. She just became immersed in the playful sensuality of the moment: cold water, wet bodies, a perfect summer day and a perfect man to enjoy it with.

She finally managed to get her hands locked around one of his knees and refused to let go, hanging on like a terrier to a bull.

He plunged into the water beside her. Surfaced, shaking droplets of water from his hair, shouting with laughter.

"Okay," he said, finally, when they were both gasping for air, breathless from laughing, as sodden as half-drowned puppies. "You've worn me out. I'll share the float with you."

"May I count that as a surrender?"

"You may count it as a truce."

She pretended to be thinking about it. "All right."

He pulled himself up on the float, held his arm out and she took it. He yanked her from the water with amazing strength, and they stood there in the bright sun, dripping water and staring at each other, something as sizzling as the sun in the air between them.

Rory Adams was as perfect as God had ever made a man. His features were chiseled, masculine, glorious. His muscles, beaded with water, told a story of easy, self-assured strength. And his eyes were the most intense shade of green she had ever seen.

His gaze moved with frank appreciation to where the water slid from her hair down in between the minute protection of the two tiny scraps of fabric that hid her breasts.

And then they moved to her lips.

And for a moment, while they rested there, she felt the heat of it, wanted what he wanted.

But then he turned, flopped down on the deck and patted the worn boards beside him.

She flopped down and felt the delicious heat of the sun on her cold skin.

"How come you never came home, Rory? Graham came when he could. For Christmas at the very least."

He was silent, she sensed debating how much of himself to trust her with. And she felt a little thrill when he spoke, knowing intuitively she had passed a test not many had passed.

"I was so glad to get out of my house that, except for my brother, I never looked back. The military was heaven for me. Routines, rules. Meals."

"You could have come home with Graham. I know he asked you."

"I tried to spend holidays with my brother. We both liked to pretend it wasn't Christmas at all. We went skiing, sometimes. California, once. France, another time."

Despite the fact he tossed that out casually, she hurt for him. "How are your parents, Rory? They moved out of the neighborhood shortly after you left."

"They're both gone. My mom first, cirrhosis, my dad a few years later in an accident."

"I didn't know," she said. "Graham never said anything."

"They lived hard. People who live like that die young."

She scanned his face. It was closed.

"I'm sorry," she said. Not for the deaths of his parents, but for him. For growing up like that, for the loneliness of having nowhere to go at Christmas, for being so alone in the world he had not shared his pain with his best friend.

He closed his eyes. For a moment, she thought he had shut down completely.

"How are your parents, Grace?"

He obviously wanted to move on. She could tell he did not like it that he had revealed so much of himself to her.

But she felt deeply honored by his trust. And somehow, despite the fact she was nearly naked beside the most glorious man in the world, it suddenly felt easy to be with him. In so many ways it was as if he was brand-new to her, but there was also a sense of knowing him. He had been in and out of her house with her brother for a couple of years.

She told him about her parents, and then ventured into the territory of old haunts: the park at the end of the street where she'd caught him and Graham smoking cigarettes and threatened to tell.

"You were a sanctimonious little brat."

The high school and mutual acquaintances, what childhood sweethearts had married and who was now divorced. He closed his eyes and it gave her a chance to study him, to breathe in the just-out-of-the-water purity of his skin, to marvel at the thick ropes of his hair where they touched the broad perfection of his shoulders.

When she had gotten up this morning, could she have predicted a day like this? When was the last time she had allowed herself to be surprised? When had she developed this death grip on life, feeling as if she ever let go of control things would spiral wildly toward chaos and destruction?

The sun dried the water on their skin, and she became aware of how good she felt. Relaxed. Did she dare say happy?

Yes, happy.

"I'm happy," she said it out loud, with the wonder it deserved.

"I'm glad," he said, and he opened one eye and looked at her.

"Are you?"

He closed his eye again, seemed to feel the rough boards of the float under the roughening whiskers of his face, seemed to contemplate the question with a deep seriousness.

He opened his eyes and stared at her, and the surprise showed in his eyes and then ran in a grin across the beautiful curve of his mouth.

A real grin, a grin that lit the darkness of his eyes like sun being filtered through a glass pot of steeping tea.

"Yeah," he said, "I am."

"It's been a long time since I felt happy," she admitted.

He was silent. She was aware of his dark eyes on her, aware that something in him was guarded, was aware of it giving way.

"Me, too," he said slowly.

And again some delicious tension built between them. He reached out and traced a drop of water that fell from the thickness of her hair, trickled down the curve of her face to her neck.

He's going to kiss me, she thought.

* * *

I'm going to kiss her, Rory thought with amazement.

Being with her was amazing. What was it about her that made him feel powerless over what was going to happen next?

He didn't talk about his family. And yet he had. And instead of feeling as if he should have kept his mouth shut, he felt unburdened.

Accepted.

And so his sense of amazement increased as his hand traced the droplet of water down her neck, felt how delicate her skin was, possibly the softest thing he had ever felt.

He leaned toward her. He could smell the water on her skin and feel the temperature of her skin changing as it heated under the sun.

Happy.

The thing about happiness for him? It had always felt like a challenge to the gods, something that could be taken away with remarkable swiftness.

He had never gone for Christmas at the Day house because he had known how it would be. Happiness. Closeness.

Him on the outside, looking in, knowing he couldn't have what they had.

He pulled back from the temptation to taste her, looked into her eyes, saw the light, that miraculous light that seemed able to pierce all his shields, that seemed to be able to reach right inside him and pierce the darkness, too.

Having allowed her to make him happy made him feel vulnerable. Open. If you opened yourself to happiness, what other feelings slipped in? He didn't want to be open.

He carried too much with him that he didn't want to let out of the bag. He had lives on his head. From both sides. Brothers who haunted his dreams. Men he called enemy, but that did not make doing what had to be done in any way easier.

He had formed an attitude of survival that involved no attachments.

Except to Graham.

He could not kiss Graham's sister. Or maybe he could. That's what happiness did. It was like wine. It impaired a man's judgment.

A splash broke just off the edge of the float, and there was enough warrior left in him that he was annoyed with himself for not having noticed the approach of the boys.

This was the second time with her that his guard had been broached—yesterday Tucker had caught him off guard.

Today it was young men, teenagers, maybe sixteen or seventeen, three of them.

They hauled themselves up on the float, and began a rambunctious shoving match that was punctuated with some very foul language.

Was he faintly relieved to be exchanging one kind of intensity for a much more familiar kind?

In one move, lithe and silent, Rory found his feet. He crossed his arms over his chest, placed his feet wide, *presence* was second nature to him.

"Enough of the language," he said quietly. He said

nothing else. They could clearly see there was a woman here. He wouldn't point that out to them.

For a moment he saw all the things he'd seen too many times before: boys on the cusp of becoming men, thinking of challenging him. Their expressions were momentarily belligerent, sullen. There was a moment, right here, that he felt, wearily, he had visited a thousand times.

Two teenage boys. Something about them.

It was that microsecond of decision when a bright day could suddenly be marred by darkness. Rory was aware of being completely relaxed, and completely alert at the same time, like a large, predatory cat. He altered his stance only slightly, ready.

The boys saw it. He had sculpted boys their age into men, that he had then sent to die, and they read that history in his stance and his eyes as if he had spoken it out loud. The belligerence fell away.

They mumbled apologies and in a flash had slipped into the water and were gone.

But even so, the magic was completely gone from the day. This was what he carried inside him.

Grace in her world of perfect Christmases and planning birthday parties, did not need it.

Gone, too, was the moment when that kiss had shivered in the air between him and Grace. When he looked at her, he was aware there would be no returning to it. He was not so sure if he saw that as a blessing or a curse.

Grace's eyes were on his face, and he knew she had seen precisely what those boys had seen.

History. Mess with me at your own risk.

Looking at her, suddenly self-conscious again of her

skimpy bathing suit, he was very aware it was not what she needed out of life. Grace Day did not need someone like him.

No, she needed someone solid and dull, who would give her afternoons like this one unmarred by the shadows of what they had seen and who they had become.

Not that being with her and playing in the water had been as dull as he had hoped it would be.

No, instead it had been pure. He had been refreshed. He had felt carefree and young.

It had given him a moment of purity, connection, happiness that he had not experienced for a very long time.

And then those boys had come along and reminded him that this kind of life belonged to someone else.

Rory was aware of needing to get away from her. From the sunny perfection of the day, from her wholesomeness.

From the feeling in his chest—what was that feeling? *A heart heavy with yearning.*

The thought astounded him. He eyed the water, looking for escape from the unexpectedness of that thought.

"You didn't have to do that," she said.

That's where she was wrong. "Yeah," he said. "I did."

"I don't need you to protect me," she said. "I would have told them myself if they were bothering me."

"Right." She could have handled it, just like she was handling Serenity.

He felt himself drawing away from her, forming another plan. He suddenly didn't like the way Grace made him feel.

As if he could tell her anything. Worse, as if he wanted to.

After he dropped her off, he'd head out to that land Serenity had set up camp on. He'd ask her point-blank what she was doing, demand answers, a DNA sample.

Bridey could look after his contribution to Warrior Down. On the way home he would confirm with Grace that his company would provide the perfect day—of her choosing—for silent auction.

And then, with relief, he would turn over the details of making that happen to Bridey. She could do a better job on it than him anyway.

Their roads—his and Grace's—could part right here. He had a million ways to deal with the astonishing discovery of the yearnings he harbored without involving her.

Melbourne, Australia, seemed to be calling his name.

He looked at her, her flawless skin, the bathing suit showing off her perfect womanly curves, the wide eyes, the tangle of her wet hair, the droplets of water pebbled on her skin.

He wondered if Melbourne was going to be far enough away.

"It's getting late," he said. "We'd better go."

He didn't like the way she was looking at him. As if she could see everything about him that he didn't want anyone to see.

What she didn't seem to be seeing? That he would never be worthy of a day like this or a girl like her.

The drive back was sadly silent. He answered her questions with monosyllables. Pulling away. Saving her. Protecting her.

From him.

Finally they pulled up in front of her now-darkened office windows. He got out of the car, held open her door for her.

She didn't hurry by him as he had hoped.

"Thank you," she said.

"Sure."

"We didn't talk much about Warrior Down."

"Just let me know what you consider a perfect day." He gave her a business card. "Call me at this number, and I'll make it happen."

"There couldn't be a more perfect day than the one I just had."

He wasn't getting sucked into her gratitude. He wasn't even going to look at the warmth spilling out of her eyes. Why couldn't she respect the fact he was pulling away for the good of both of them?

"Well, try and think of something that someone might part with a few thousand dollars for. Helicopters. Yachts. Caviar. You know."

And even though she dealt with what people thought was the perfect day all the time, aggravatingly, she did not look like she knew.

Then she did what he least expected. She refused to accept that distance he was trying to put between them.

She reached up, stood on the tips of her toes. Her hair was dry now, but it had dried in a rumpled pile of curls that made him want to touch it. She had put on her uptight suit again, but it was rumpled to the point of ruination, and it didn't hide the woman she had been on that float.

He thought he had never seen a more beautiful

woman. And maybe that's what made him helpless to pull away from her, to do what needed to be done.

He saw it coming. He could see it coming from a mile away. Her half-closed eyes, her deeply inhaled breath, the bow of her mouth drawing into the most adorable little pucker.

He had plenty of time to get away.

But he didn't. He let her.

He let Gracie Day kiss him.

And it was everything he knew it would be. Her lips touching his contained a sweetness he had never known, a delicious innocence.

But when her kiss deepened he detected something else in there. Her hidden Ferrari dreams, her passion, the place in her that old Herbert or Hoover or whatever the hell his name had been would have killed for good.

He pulled back from her, touched his index finger to her chin.

He fought the temptation to take her lips again, to tangle his hands in her hair, to pull her to him, to coax her wild side to the surface.

He'd done hard things his entire life. But nothing quite as hard as walking away from Gracie.

"Don't settle," he said.

"What does that mean?"

It meant not to settle for someone boring and stupid like Harold. But he didn't say that. He said, "It means get rid of that gas-guzzling old-people car you are driving and get something a little spiffy. Don't settle for anything less than your dreams."

Rather than looking appreciative of his advice, she

looked annoyed. A good note to leave her on. He went to turn away.

And stopped. Something caught his attention, something not quite right. In the darkness of her door stoop a paper was fluttering on the window of her office.

Cars parked where they shouldn't be. Teenage boys with a certain look on their faces. Papers fluttering on windows. Things out of place unnerved him, and he went and yanked the paper off, and scanned it briefly.

It should have made him relax, it should have allowed him to register, *no threat, stand down.*

No phone, it read, *Did you still want me and Tuck to come for supper at your place tomorrow? Love, Serenity.*

Love. As if Serenity had a clue what that was.

Of course, neither did he.

Instead of standing down, he felt he was on red alert. Wordlessly he handed Grace the note, and saw the little smile tickle her lips when she read Tucker's name.

"You invited them over to your place? For supper?" He folded his arms over his chest and glared at her. Melbourne seemed to be fading by the second.

"Yes." She looked defiant, having correctly read by his tone he did not approve of Serenity and Tucker being invited to her house.

"I don't think you should."

The last of the dazed look left her face. "Don't think that just because you gave me a perfect day and an okay kiss, you can boss me around."

An okay kiss? "You didn't have to invite them to your house, for God's sake. If you're worried about the kid being hungry, you could have taken them for a pizza."

Shoot. He had not played that one very well. He could
tell by the stricken look that crossed her face it had not
occurred to her that Tucker might be hungry.

That's what you got when you grew up in a perfect
world. Despite what she wanted to believe, Grace had
been sheltered. A home where there wasn't enough food
on the table had never crossed her mind. And never
would have if he hadn't opened his big mouth.

The stricken look was quickly replaced with one of
pure stubbornness.

"I'll invite whomever I please for dinner. And what's
more, Rory Adams, I am not looking for anyone to run
my life. I would only be interested in a relationship of
equals."

"A what?" he sputtered.

"Never mind."

"A relationship?" he said, incredulous.

"I didn't mean it the way you are taking it."

"You're blushing."

"I'm sunburned."

"You should know I am not a guy who is interested
in a relationship of any kind. Not equals. Not unequals."

For a moment she scanned his face, and he steeled
himself, daring her to see the yearning that had nearly
swallowed him earlier.

"I'm not looking for a relationship, either!" she pro-
tested.

"You just said—

"That just slipped out. I meant it generically, as in no
kind of woman with any sense of her self would toler-
ate being bossed around."

"Directed," he inserted.

"Whatever! Personally, I'm not looking for a relationship of any kind. I'm done with that sort of thing. I'm a career woman. And a very successful one."

"That's not true, Grace."

Her jaw dropped. "It is. I can show you my financial statements!"

"I wasn't referring to your success at business. I don't believe you're done with that sort of thing, the big wedding followed by the cute house followed by a baby. And then another one. Three. I bet you want three."

"I don't. I'm done with those dreams!"

"I can see in your face that you're not. I can see in your face exactly what you're looking for. What you'll always look for—what your mom and dad had. A perfect family to go with your perfect days. The cottage in the summer. The Thanksgiving turkey. The big Christmas hoopla."

"After the breakup of my relationship I've decided none of that is for me."

"I can clearly see what is making you such easy prey for Serenity."

"I am not her prey! What an ugly thing to say!"

Ugly. Raw. Cynical. That's what he was. It made him unworthy of her kisses, but maybe it also made him the perfect one to deflect Serenity.

"You think you've given up on your hopes and dreams, but you really haven't."

"I have!"

"They've just gone underground. Serenity knows what you want. You'd give your right arm for Tucker to be Graham's. A substitute for that baby you thought you and Henry were going to have."

"Stop it!"

He could see angry little spots of color on both her cheeks. Good. He had succeeded at nipping any attraction she was feeling for him in the bud. So he shrugged. "Okay."

Just as suddenly as it had come, her anger was gone. "Don't you want Tucker to be Graham's son?"

The truth was it was much easier to contemplate Tucker *not* being Graham's, and that's how he was playing it until he had cold, hard proof that showed him differently.

"I'm coming for dinner tomorrow," he announced.

"You're not! I haven't invited you."

"I'm not letting you deal with Serenity on your own. You're naive. You're way too innocent."

"I am not innocent," she sputtered. "What on earth would give you that idea?"

The fact you could barely wear that bathing suit. Your kiss.

"Let me help you deal with it," he said quietly.

For a moment she looked stubborn. But then she looked at the note in her hand and he saw the doubt on her face.

"I won't say anything to Serenity," he said, playing that doubt. "I'll let you handle it. But I'll be there, gauging what she says, running it through the meter of my cynicism. I'll offer you my opinion after, but I won't force it on you."

And if I pocket a spoon with a little saliva sample on it, who's that hurting?

"All right," she said, clearly unhappy with the surrender, unhappy that she was accepting what she needed most and wanted least.

Not to do this alone.

"Where do you live?" he asked.

"I bought the house from my parents when they moved, so I live where I always lived," she said with stiff pride, as if the fact she had never left her family home proved everything he had just said about her.

And it did, didn't it?

He sighed. "What time should I be there?"

"Fiveish?"

In the world he had started moving in, dinner didn't happen at five. It happened at eight or nine. After cocktails. And hors d'oeuvres. After endless small talk, and sometimes a little careless flirting with people who were no more interested in relationships than he was.

The banality of it all suddenly made him feel like his world had become unbearably lonely.

He was being pulled into her little world. And he didn't like it. But he was just going to have to suck it up until this Serenity situation was cleared up.

And then nothing, but nothing—not even the memory of the way Grace's lips had tasted crushed beneath his own—was going to keep him from personally supervising that job in Australia.

CHAPTER SIX

"Mr. Adams, are you all right?"

"Huh?" Rory had been staring aimlessly out his office window. He'd had the dream last night. Worse than normal. The two teenage boys, the bullets. This time, he had ducked, as if he could see the bullet coming, as if he had deliberately let Graham get it instead of him.

And still, there was a sense of having awoken too soon. There was still a piece missing, something important. Words.

Not that it mattered. There were no words that could make him feel better, that could take away this feeling of tremendous guilt. There were no words that could make the realization of a man's powerlessness over life and death any easier.

Sometimes, you couldn't protect the people you cared about. His mother. Graham. Was the dream more intense because he had spent time with Gracie? Because he was seeing how his inability to stop bad things from happening had gone out like a wave and swamped other lives?

If he could protect Grace from Serenity would it make up for all his past failings?

"I'm fine," he said gruffly to Bridey. "I've been invited out for dinner tonight. Could you get me something to bring?"

"The regular?"

"Yeah, whatever." What was the regular? A bottle of good wine, exquisitely expensive, roses in the same price range. "No, wait."

He didn't want to bring wine if Serenity was there. She'd probably swig it all back and then try to drive herself and the kid somewhere.

And he actually didn't want wine with Grace again, either. Because after one glass at lunch, she'd lost her inhibitions enough to put on a bikini.

And kiss him.

A kiss powerful enough to send a man packing to Australia!

"Uh, no wine," he said. "And not roses for the flowers, either." Somehow, Grace wasn't a rose kind of girl in his mind. "Something less, uh, formal. Less, uh, ostentatious."

"Got it," Bridey said.

He arrived at Grace's feeling foolishly like a boy on his first date. He wished he hadn't brought the flowers at all, because the bouquet was quite large, a colorful explosion of daisies and daffodils, mums and lilies.

There was no sign of Serenity's decrepit old truck yet.

He looked at the house—Graham's house, really—and waited for the sadness of the memories of them together here to hit. They didn't and he felt thankful for all that Grace had done to it. She had made the house her own, painted, changed the facade, added colorful plantings beneath the windows and up the walkway.

She came to the door, and he found himself steeling himself—not against memories of him and Graham, but against memories of him and her.

And the way her lips had tasted: the hint of passion in them, the faint eagerness. And the way she had made him feel.

As if he could trust her. As if he could trust her with things he had told no one.

She opened the door and looked over his shoulder. "No Ferrari today," she said. "Hello, Rory."

"I traded it in on something a little more me."

"The Ferrari was you." She studied the 1965 Chev truck parked at the curb, and said, "That's you, too. Ah, a man of many faces."

She meant it lightly, but he didn't take it that way. He *was* a man of many faces, and some of them would probably terrify her. That would be a good thing for her to remember. That he was not always what he seemed.

She took the flowers with such genuine delight that he was glad he'd brought them after all.

"Daffodils in July!" she said. "Imagine that! Come in."

The house, too, was completely changed and he felt some stress he had been holding leave him.

"You've fixed this up," he said.

"I love my house. I'm afraid my idea of a good time is hanging out at the hardware store mooning over engineered flooring and cabinet pulls."

So, it was exactly as he had guessed. She wanted to pass herself off as a career woman, but she was pretty solidly invested in the whole concept of home.

And she had it so right. The living room he was looking at was a relaxed space, but everything from the furniture choices to the paint colors invited you to feel at home, to relax, to sit and maybe to stay for a long, long time. There was even a teddy bear nestled among the couch cushions that didn't look the least ridiculous. It added to the cozy feeling of just coming home.

There was a feeling here of safety.

He frowned at that. He felt safe. Why wouldn't he feel safe? He wasn't in the land of blood and sand and tears anymore. And he was never going back there.

Though, standing in her living room, he was acutely aware maybe he had not totally ever left that land.

Because a place like this—cozy, inviting—was foreign to him. The whole concept of home was foreign to him. His own houses growing up had always been temporary. Sooner than later, his family would be moving all their broken furniture and chipped dishes. No nice touches like those yellow-shaded lamps or the Finnish rug on the floor.

And his place now?

A showpiece of modern design. All black leather, steel, shiny surfaces, hard angles. It had a temporary feel to it. And it *was* temporary. He bought real estate as an investment. He did not attach to it.

He had not known he wanted "homey" until he saw this.

"Come through to the kitchen," she said. "I'm peeling spuds. I thought Tucker might like homemade fries. I hope you don't mind. The menu is pretty kid-friendly tonight. Burgers. Fries. Milkshakes."

"Mind? That's a menu out of every man's dream."

That earned a smile, and then she led him to the

kitchen, which also reflected more changes to the foot-print of the old house. A wall had been dispensed with, the kitchen, dining room and living room were all seam-less, one harmonious space.

She set him down on a stool at a granite countertop island that gave a hint of separation between the kitchen and the other spaces.

He picked up a knife and tackled a heap of potatoes while she ripped lettuce into bite-size portions for a salad.

He was aware of feeling at home here. Not just the setting. But with her.

He pursued that sense of safety. Music was play-ing softly in the background. A cat wound around the leg of his chair. Everything was in order, but not in an uptight way. This was a space where a person could relax. Where there would rarely be a raised voice. Or the sound of dishes breaking in anger. And maybe that, alone, made it one of the most dangerous places he had ever been.

Rory Adams was in her space. He put down the knife after cutting the potatoes into fries. He was looking as at home here as if he had been born to this space.

She glanced at the clock.

"They're late," she said.

"The thing about a girl like Serenity?"

Grace truly hated it that he was such a self-proclaimed expert on girls like Serenity, but she man-aged to bite her tongue. "Yes?"

"They're always late."

"How do you know so much about girls like

Serenity?" She tried for a teasing note, but was pretty sure she failed. She was scared about his answer, but when he was silent for a long, long time, she wasn't sure he would answer.

"She's like my mother."

And she remembered him again, out on the street that night long ago, taking his mother's elbow.

He was concentrating fiercely on the potato, as if what he had just said didn't matter.

But she knew it did. She knew it mattered that he told her things like that.

"Tell me how you and Graham came to know Serenity."

"*Know* is stretching it a touch," he said. "We had ten days leave before we were shipping out. I think it was that first time, Afghanistan. We were shipping out from Edmonton, and the Calgary Stampede was on. None of us had ever been to it, so we decided to go. Calgary is only a couple of hours drive from Edmonton.

"Guys being guys, we had to make a few pit stops along the way. Quite a few, actually. Finally, we stopped in this rinky-dink little town not far from Calgary, and they were having their own little second-rate Stampede and rodeo.

"Serenity was running her ponies as part of the midway, plus riding a horse in the barrel-racing competition. Somehow, we got partying with all those rodeo and fairground people, and we never quite made the Calgary Stampede. And never had any regrets about it, either."

She read his face. "Until now."

"You know, when you're shipping out and facing the very real possibility you might not be coming back, life has this intensity to it. It's a kind of a high. But it does not involve consequences. Not one of us—including Graham—ever glanced back at those few crazy days before we left."

"So, there is a very real possibility that Tucker is Graham's?"

"Well, it's one possibility. But it doesn't add up, Grace. Why would she wait until now to let you know?"

"I'm going to ask her, point-blank, tonight if Tucker is Graham's. And if he is, why she didn't let Graham know that."

"I think that's a good plan."

She recognized it as a weakness that she liked having his approval. But like many good plans it had a flaw: it relied on Serenity showing up, and by six, Grace was beginning to acknowledge maybe she wasn't going to. And also acknowledging how eagerly she had wanted to see Tucker again, searching his face and his mannerisms for traces of Graham.

And the part she hadn't admitted to Rory? That she was finding more evidence all the time. The crooked way he smiled, the way his hair grew in a little swirl at the crown of his head, the stubborn set of his mouth, the way he walked.

"Are you starving?" she asked.

"I don't mind waiting."

But by six-thirty, she knew they had waited long enough. "I'll cook some for us, and leave some, just in case…"

Cooking with him almost took away the pang that Tucker and Serenity had not arrived.

It was fun having a man who knew what he was

doing at the grill. It was a cozy little scene: one she had imagined a million times when she was laboring over this little space.

Imagined it with Harold. Cozy evenings of cooking together, an easy companionship, a sense of home that she had never one-hundred-percent achieved by herself, much as she had tried.

And now this. Rory Adams in her kitchen, peeling potatoes, taking charge of the hamburgers, laughing at her concern that the flames were leaping too high in the grill. The problem with having a man like this in your space?

Would it ever feel totally like your space again, or would it always seem slightly lacking, no matter what you did?

There was no way a cat, a career and a penchant for decorating magazines was ever going to make her feel like this: zingy with an electrical energy, suffused with laughter, *so aware.* Certainly she had seen a man standing at a grill before, but had she ever noticed the small details of that experience? The smell in the air, the way he did little things with such a supreme confidence in himself?

She had imagined an evening like this with Harold, and they had even had evenings similar to this. So why had it never felt like this? Always a faint discontent between them, something that stifled instead of invigorated.

For the first time since her engagement had ended, Grace could truly see it as a blessing, and not just pay lip service to the whole concept of "if it was meant to be, it would be."

It was seven-fifteen by the time they had finished eating and cleaning up. He had cheerfully buried himself up to his elbows in suds, cleaning her difficult grill, flicking soap with playful threat in her direction when she tried to help.

Without warning, the elation left her. It felt as if it hissed out of her like air out of a punctured balloon. And in its place was disappointment.

It was disappointment that Tucker and Serenity had failed to show up.

Disappointment that this was not really her life. Rory Adams wasn't here because he wanted to be with her. Because he'd found her kiss impossible to back away from. No, he was here to protect her.

And the thing he thought she needed protecting from wasn't coming. The dishes were done. They had eaten. There was absolutely no reason for him to stay here—or for her to want him to.

"Well," she said, trying to inject a note of cheer into her voice, "I guess they aren't coming. I took out my favorite board game for nothing."

"You have a favorite board game?"

"I do. And everyone should. Tucker looks like he's never played a board game in his life. Can you imagine?"

"Actually, I can."

"You've never played a board game?" She was incredulous. At first she thought he must be pulling her leg. Then she read in his face, that he was not.

Girlfriend, she told herself sternly, *send him home. Something is happening here. You are getting in way too deep.*

But a person who had never played board games? It was practically like saying you had never had a childhood.

She thought of his house, that night he had walked out to rescue his mother. Not very old then, already a man.

Rory Adams was the man least likely to need rescuing. He was all easy confidence and male grace. He was all sensual appeal. No doubt women had been throwing themselves at him since he had learned to blink.

She had not been a blip on his radar eight years ago, and she was only a little more than that now. He was the CEO of a big company. He could conjure cowboys and cars out of thin air.

What about that would make her think he would enjoy a silly board game?

"Would you like to try it?" She tried for careless aplomb, she sounded shy and faintly strangled.

Was she desperately holding on to this, her perfect evening? A matched set. Her perfect day yesterday, her perfect evening tonight.

The thing about having achieved perfection? Did you ever want to go back to just normal again? Ordinary? Could you? Or did you crave it now? A person who had slept in silk sheets did not want to go back to burlap sacking after all!

He studied her, and she had the horrible feeling he knew what it had cost her to ask him, that a frightened fourteen-year-old waited for rejection, a sneering laugh.

"Sure, I'll play with you. Don't give up yet, in Serenity's world, fashionably late could mean midnight."

Suddenly playing a silly game, intended for children, seemed ridiculous. He'd told her about his company. He wasn't playing for entertainment. He was rubbing shoulders with race-car drivers and the jet set. He probably couldn't wait to get out of here, was being held here by some sense of obligation.

"You don't have to stay, you can go."

"Nah. I'll stay."

"Because you don't want me to deal with Serenity by myself if she does turn up?"

"Well, if she turns up at this time of night, you might want someone around who can wrestle her truck keys from her."

"That poor kid. Poor Tucker."

"That's why I'll stay. Because you seem sad. It's no fun being sad by yourself."

"No, really."

"No, really. Haul out the game."

Don't, she told herself. But she did.

"I think you can play with two," she said, getting her game off the sideboard, and putting it on the kitchen island. The box was faded with age, and all the corners were held together with tape that had turned dark yellow. "But it's more fun with four."

"We'll be two people each then. I'll be Nasty Ned and Roaring Rory and you be Goodie Two Shoes Grace and Sideswipe Sally."

"I am not going to be Goodie Two Shoes!"

"Okay. You pick who you're going to be." He had already retrieved the instructions and, after a quick skim, began setting up pieces.

"I'll be Racy Gracie!"

"Good one. No stealing kisses from me, though."

"That wasn't really a kiss," she said, flustered.

"It wasn't? You could have fooled me. And I would have thought I kind of knew a kiss when one was planted on my lips, but if you say it wasn't…"

She could feel the heat move up her face. "It was just a thank you, for such a nice day."

"Uh-huh. You be careful about thanking all the boys that way, or you really will be Racy Gracie."

"Oh!"

"What are we playing for, by the way?"

"You don't play a game like this *for* anything. You just play it for fun."

And this was fun for her, damn him. The light teasing, the familiarity, his willingness to do something dumb.

"For fun?" He snorted. "Soldiers don't play anything for fun. They'll bet a week's wages on which spider is going to cross the room first. There has to be something at stake."

"What would you like to play for?"

"How about that teddy bear on the couch?"

"I got that out for Tucker. I don't still have a teddy bear."

"Gracie, that kid is not a teddy-bear kind of kid. Or a board-game kind of kid, either."

"Well, you didn't strike me as either of those things, either, but here we are, playing a board game for my teddy bear."

"I knew it was yours," he said triumphantly.

"Well, maybe you're not quite the tough guy you seem, either, since you want to take him home."

"It's not really about the teddy bear. He must mean something to you. So it would be fun to take it away."

"That's awful!"

"I know," he said happily.

"So, what's at stake for you? What am I going to take from you when I win?"

He eyed her lips for a moment. "You choose."

She eyed his lips for a moment. No, too dangerous. Akin to playing strip poker. Over a board game. That would be degenerate!

She snapped her fingers. "The CD we listened to going up the lake."

"Ouch."

"Perfect," she purred happily.

"This has become a high-stakes game, Miss Day."

"My favorite kind," she said, and then they were both laughing at the absurdity of her ever having played high-stakes anything.

She won three games in a row. With great grumbling he went and retrieved his CD. It was now closing in on nine.

Time to send him home. Because something was happening to her heart. She was realizing she could fall for this man so fast and so hard it would make anything she had ever experienced before seem as lackluster as porridge congealing in a pot.

"Can I listen to it one more time before I surrender it?" he asked.

He couldn't possibly think Serenity was still going to show, but part of her was so hungry for more time with him that she didn't care, she threw caution to the wind.

She knew, after all, she had to walk away from this.

For her own self-preservation. Only yesterday he had told her in no uncertain terms what he thought of relationships.

And she had agreed with him. But she might have been lying. Even to herself. So, after tonight, she would keep her distance. She would.

But she felt like someone who loved chocolate being told they could never have it again. Except for one last taste.

Who could resist that?

And so Grace made them milkshakes and they sat on the sofa, side by side, listening to the CD.

He was so relaxed, sprawled out on her sofa. She had not been aware of some finely held tension that was intrinsic to him until now that it was gone.

It seemed to her the whole evening had been so filled with simple things, and yet it had felt suffused with light.

She wanted to kiss him again.

She was pretty sure he wanted to kiss her, too.

She leaned toward him, and the tension was back in him.

"Don't, Gracie. There's things you need to know. About me."

But she didn't want to know those things if they would stop her from wanting to kiss him, and she had the sense that that was why he wanted to tell her. She wanted the barriers ripped down, he wanted them up.

"I need to tell you about Graham. When I'm done you'll know who I really am."

Unspoken, she heard, *And you won't like it.*

Strangely, when Rory had first contacted her, Grace had heard this very moment coming.

She had thought she was not ready to hear what he had to say. She had thought she would never be ready. That was why she had said, *I can't see why we need to talk*.

But suddenly she could see exactly why they needed to talk. Suddenly, she was ready.

Somewhere, somehow, she had become less interested in protecting herself. Somehow, more was being required of her. She needed to hear what he had to say. To save them both.

Rory was silent for a long time. Finally, working past the lump in his throat, he managed to say, "I was with him when he died."

When he had contacted her when he got home, this is precisely the conversation he had been determined to have. He wanted her to know he'd been with her brother when he died. That he had not been alone. That he had not been afraid. That Graham's last thought had been of her.

Why was it so hard to do it, then?

Because he wasn't expecting that moment—fear and chaos and ultimately death—to be superimposed over this one—laughter, safety, feeling relaxed.

Happy again.

And because all that—that Graham had not been alone or afraid—was only part of the truth. The real truth was his failure, and she needed to know that before they traded kisses.

She needed to know it all before she offered him her lips.

"I'm ready," she said, and he saw the bravery in her and saw that she was ready.

He closed his eyes. He could feel the heat and smell the dust. And other smells. Garbage. Sewage. Death.

"It was a pretty ordinary day for over there. Too hot. We were on patrol. It was average. You're always alert, scanning, but none of the signs were there.

"Then I saw these two teenage boys. I felt like something was wrong, but I didn't react right away. I'm not sure why. Maybe because it was so hot. Maybe because they just seemed so young. Maybe because they hadn't done anything. It's not as if they were reaching under their robes to pull out submachine guns.

"But I knew something was off, and I didn't react fast enough. One of them glanced up, touched his nose. I guess it was a signal. And the next thing I knew there were bullets flying everywhere.

"I ducked behind a wall. And I looked for Graham and was shocked that he wasn't right with me. He was always right with me. We always had each other's backs. Always. He was out there in the street. He'd already been hit.

"I went and got him, dragged him back to cover. He was alive, but it was already too late."

He frowned. Just like in the dream, he knew there was a part of this missing, a part his mind refused to remember. Important words.

But what could be more important to Grace than the fact she had been one of the last things on her brother's mind?

"I just wanted you to know that he wasn't alone. That I was there. And I wanted you to know that he wasn't afraid. I wanted you to know his last thoughts were of you. He wanted you to be okay."

He glanced at her. She was crying.

"I'm so sorry, Grace."

"No. I'm so glad you told me. I needed to know, even though I was scared to find out. I needed to know that he wasn't alone. I needed to know he wasn't afraid. And I know it will bring me great comfort that his last thoughts were of me."

She wasn't getting it. He obviously had not been plain enough. She seemed to be looking at him with a graver sense of connection instead of less of one.

"Grace, I didn't have his back. I failed him."

It couldn't be more plain than that.

The tears came harder. "Oh, Rory," she whispered. "Don't do that to yourself. Please."

Now, she was right over beside him, her arms were around him, her warm tears were spilling down his chest.

"No," she said. "I will not allow you to carry that burden one step further. It was not your fault."

"I saw the boys."

"And what should you have done when you saw them? What should you have done differently?"

"I don't know," he said, and it was a terrible admission, that he did not know how he could have changed things. Even now, looking back, even visiting it every night in his dreams, he did not know. He suspected he could have done something.

And that he had failed to do it.

And that was the part that was missing from his dream and from his memory.

And he hated that feeling more than any other.

And himself, for not knowing.

"I should have pushed Graham out of the way. I should have been the one who took it. Jesus, Gracie, why not me, instead of him? Your whole family torn apart. I don't have a family to be torn apart."

This was going all wrong. All wrong.

He had planned for this to be his secret weapon. His way to stop the growing attraction between them.

He was the man responsible for her brother's death. That should make her pull away and fast.

But the effect seemed to be the exact opposite.

She was doing what he had never been able to do. She was forgiving him. She was accepting that he was just a man who had not been able to stop the unfolding of destiny.

She was scanning his face.

"You're not really doing okay, are you?"

Why was it that she could see that? Everyone else, even his brother, thought he was the successful businessman. They didn't know he was running.

And he didn't want her to know, either. He didn't want to burden her.

And yet, he could not stop himself, he could not hold the words back.

"I have dreams. In every single dream I am responsible."

"How often do you have those dreams?" Her voice was so soft, and the tenderness in her eyes was making him *want* to tell her. Why? What earthly good could come from sharing this terrible burden with her?

"I have them every night," he said. "Sometimes half a dozen times a night."

"So, what are they telling you that you won't admit during the day?" she asked.

He closed his eyes. He recognized the million-dollar question when he heard it. He made one last desperate effort to make her understand.

"I know it's my fault," he said, his voice hoarse. "We looked out for each other. I let him down. I let him die."

He waited for her to say something patronizing that he could hate her for, that would allow him to rebuild this wall that had tumbled down. He waited for her to say something about survivor's guilt and it wasn't his fault at all.

She didn't say anything. He dared to look at her, and saw the tears still sliding down her face.

Only now, they were not for her brother.

They were for him.

It felt as if she was reaching inside him and taking the pain. Sharing it. Understanding it. It wasn't pity.

It was compassion so pure that it stole his breath and what was left of his strength.

He reached for her, took her wrists, marveled at their delicacy and pulled her into his chest. She came to him easily, and he rested his chin on the top of her head, and felt her surrender, melting into him like warm putty.

He breathed in her scent and held her.

"Do you think we'll ever be okay again?" she asked after a long, long time.

"Right now I am," he said, and was surprised how much he meant it. "Right now I am."

She thought about it, changed her position so she could tilt her head up and look at him. "Me, too," she decided.

And then she pulled away from him, and scanned his face, saw something there that reassured her and she tucked herself back into him.

And it just was.

Her breath rising with his breath.

Her heart beating with his heart.

Her warmth melting into his warmth.

Her softness feeling so good against all in him that was unyielding.

Rory had just told Grace the worst thing about himself. He knew he'd been saving that confession as his out, as his way of driving her away if things got too complicated between them.

He could not have predicted that the exact opposite would happen. She seemed to trust him more, not less.

And he did not feel deserving of that.

The courageous thing to do would be to tell her good-bye.

But he didn't feel courageous. This house, and Gracie, had been chipping away at his armor.

And he felt, without his really being aware, he had been stripped of it completely.

He wanted to hold her, just like this, for as long as he could make this moment last.

But he of all people should know that moments like this one, filled with unearthly quiet, moments of nothing that held everything, were way too rare.

And always brief.

And the calm before the storm was called that for a reason. There was always a storm.

And it came.

They heard the truck coming from a long way off, the boom-boom of the untuned diesel engine, the shriek of a corner taken too fast.

They were both up and at her window when Serenity's very distinctive truck veered in behind his own, jumped the curb and came to rest in the very center of Grace's front lawn.

CHAPTER SEVEN

"If she's driving like that with the kid in there with her—" Rory didn't finish the sentence, and he didn't have to. He bolted for the front door and went out, bypassing her front staircase in a single leap. Grace was hard on his heels.

He arrived on the passenger side of the truck, its engine off but the headlights eerily illuminating the yard while making it impossible to see the vehicle's interior.

Rory yanked open the passenger door. Serenity must have been leaning hard against it, because she didn't so much fall as spill out. Despite his surprise, Rory dived and managed to catch her before she hit the ground.

He straightened, staring down at the woman in his arms, shocked to find her there, more shocked by her slightness. Holding Serenity was like holding a wounded sparrow.

Her body was completely limp, and there was no warmth to it. She was unnaturally pale. When he bent and put his nose close to her slightly parted lips there was no smell of alcohol, but she was barely breathing.

He glanced up. "What the hell?"

It was Tucker, wide-eyed with fear, behind the wheel of the truck. Astonished, Rory saw the boy had used duct tape to fasten blocks of wood to the brake, gas and clutch pedals. Ingenious? Or not the first time he had driven the huge vehicle?

"My mama's so sick," Tucker said, his voice choked with fear. "I didn't know what to do. We don't have a phone."

"You did exactly the right thing," Rory said. "Come on. Get out of the truck. Grace, start your car. We're going to the hospital."

"Mama said no," Tucker said plaintively. "We ain't got no money. We don't have no medical insurance."

"I'll look after it," Rory said, adjusting the slight weight he carried, moving toward where Grace had her vehicle going. He glanced over his shoulder.

The boy looked at him suspiciously, and then he drew in a deep breath, and his face crumpled. He hid his face in his shirtsleeve.

Rory knew by pure instinct that he could not acknowledge those tears from a boy who had probably spent his whole life trying to be tough and hard and strong.

"Go get in Grace's car, now. Your mama's going to be okay," Rory said. Of course, he had no idea if that was true, but he knew he had to be both calm and firm.

He was a man who could claim a lot of experience dealing with men who were young and who were frightened. Maybe not this young and maybe not this frightened, but it was all the same thing.

He could not show a flicker of doubt, even if, feeling Serenity's limp form in his arms as he went to Grace's car and got in the backseat, that's exactly what he felt.

Grace was already in the driver's seat, and she

glanced back at him, and he saw something in her face. That she was counting on him, too, to somehow make this all right. The truth? He did not want to be counted on to be anyone's hero.

And yet, at the very same time, a man could come to live for the look on Gracie's face.

All night, Grace had felt herself falling.

Falling for Rory Adams.

All over again. Just as she had been foolish enough to do at fourteen.

The sensation of falling had only increased when he had told her about her brother, when she had sensed the enormous burden he had shouldered by himself for way, way too long.

Now that sensation increased again as Grace watched Rory in the emergency room of the hospital. It was obvious he had become an expert on crisis. His demeanor was one of complete calm.

The emergency room unnerved her. She could hear a child wailing, a man in a chair in the waiting room had blood seeping through the white dressing that was wrapped around his head. A mother paced and made reassuring noises to the quiet baby in her arms. A woman slept in one of the chairs, oblivious to the drama around her.

But Rory, his hands full of Serenity, was not distracted. He paused only for a moment in the doorway, scanning, and he seemed to know by pure instinct where to go and who was in charge. He found a nurse, followed her through swinging doors that said No Admittance. Tucker followed.

That left Grace to deal with the thorny issue of admittance. Beyond Serenity's name Grace knew little about her.

But after a while Rory was back at her side, Tucker stuck to him like an orphaned pup looking for a pack leader.

Between him and Tucker they were able to provide the admitting clerk with Serenity's birth date and some other basic information.

When the question of health insurance came up, Rory didn't even hesitate. He guaranteed payment and backed it up with a credit card that made the admitting clerk raise her eyebrows.

Finally, he led Tucker to one of those hard plastic chairs, sat him down, went to a vending machine and got him a soda and some potato chips.

Grace and Rory both watched as the boy wolfed down the food.

"When do you think he ate last?" Grace asked.

"Don't ask," Rory said, nudging her. They moved away from him a bit.

"They're going to have to admit Serenity," he said. "What are we going to do about him?"

We.

Even in this chaotic, somewhat frightening situation, she allowed herself to savor that.

We. As if they were a team. And if she were on a team? Wouldn't she pick his? He was a leader. He could be counted on to make hard decisions in difficult circumstances.

He was the kind of man everyone wanted on their side when the chips were down. If you were in a hotel that was on fire and saw him coming through the smoke, you would know you were going to be okay. If you were on a ship that was going down in rough seas, he was the one you would follow to the life raft.

And he knew he was that kind of man, so no wonder he felt so acutely responsible for Graham's death.

And so it was time for her not to let him take the lead, not to accept him taking full responsibility. She had to be worthy of him.

And that meant she had to be as strong as he was, as responsible for the decision-making process.

"What do you mean what are we going to do about him?" she asked.

"I think we should call the authorities," he said in a low tone.

"The authorities? No." She said it firmly, his equal.

Something in her tone made Tucker look up from licking salt and chip crumbs off his fingers. He regarded them both with deep wariness.

"Shh. If he catches wind that we're going to turn him over, he'll run like a rabbit."

"Well, we aren't turning him over," she said, stubbornly. The problem with these alpha types? They always thought they knew what was right. They relied only on themselves.

It was too lonely. She was not going to let Rory be that lonely anymore.

"Look, you can't just take somebody's kid because you want to. It's not like we're his family."

"We don't know that yet. I might be his aunt."

"That's a big *might*."

"Let's just ask him if he has anyone we can call for him," she asked, hearing the leadership in her voice.

Rory looked doubtful. "If he had anyone to call I don't think he would have driven a truck that he couldn't even reach the pedals on to your place in the middle of the night and parked in the middle of your lawn."

"I am not sending him with strangers."

"Grace, *we're* practically strangers to him."

A nurse came out and beckoned to Rory. She was young and extraordinarily beautiful, despite a certain no-nonsense look about her. Grace could not help but notice the respect shown to Rory. It was as if people who dealt in crisis recognized each other, belonged to a secret club.

The nurse put her hand on Rory's arm.

Grace felt a little shiver of shocking jealousy, though the gesture was no more than casual contact.

Still, she felt herself bracing for his reaction. Despite the situation, would he wink? Smile that disarming smile? Touch her back ever so lightly?

But Rory did not reciprocate in any way. If he had noticed the beauty of the nurse it did not show. In fact, with a slightly curt nod, he slid his arm out from under the nurse's touch and came to Grace.

"They are admitting Serenity," he said in an undertone. "They have no idea what's wrong. She's in and out of consciousness, not well enough to give them any clues."

"I'll tell him," Grace said, and went to Tucker. She squatted on her heels, not wanting to intimidate him by looking down at him.

"Hey, buddy," Grace said quietly. She saw he didn't like her calling him buddy.

In her peripheral vision she was aware of Rory standing close, waiting to take it if she needed him to, but letting her have the lead.

She was not quite sure what she had done to earn Tucker's animosity, but it made her aware they were strangers, that maybe Rory was right. There were people trained to deal with these situations.

But this child, this frightened, hungry, brave little boy might be Graham's. She might be his aunt. She could not abandon him. She could not. He, a little boy, had driven a truck, that he had no business driving, to her house. Trusting her, overcoming his mystifying dislike, believing she would do the right thing by him and his mother.

"They're going to keep your mom here for a while," she said.

"Is she okay?"

"She's in very good hands. They'll look after her."

Tucker looked at her, searching her face for truth. She could tell he was trying very hard not to cry, "What do you want to do, Tucker?"

He looked suddenly frail and exhausted. "I gotta look after the ponies. They never got fed tonight."

The answer nearly broke her heart. So small, so much weight on his shoulders.

"I'll look after them," Rory said. "I think you should go with Grace. She's got a spare room. You can stay with her tonight and we'll see how your mom is doing in the morning."

"You don't know nothing about looking after ponies," Tucker said, managing a note of scornful pride despite his fear and exhaustion. "And I'm coming back here after, to be with my mama."

"How about Slim McKenzie?" Rory said, down on his heels now, too, not missing a beat. "Would you trust him to look after your ponies?"

Something shifted in Tucker's face at the mention of Slim.

"Yeah, Slim could do it. And then I could stay here with my mom."

"Here's the thing, Tucker," Rory said, his voice tempered with the most exquisite patience, "I don't think they're going to let you stay with your mom. But I'll give you my cell phone, and I'll tell that nurse over there you're going to be checking in, all night long if you want to. Is that okay?"

"I don't want to stay with her," Tucker said, jerking his chin at Grace.

Again, Grace wondered what she had done to deserve his animosity, tried not to take it personally.

"If you don't want to stay with me, I'm sure you can stay with Rory," she said soothingly.

Rory glared at her, came off his heels and took her elbow. He took her off a bit from where Tucker was watching them. "No. That's just weird. Men do not take little boys they don't know home with them."

"I'll come, too, then." She could feel it again. Doing this with him. Not leaving him to the loneliness of making every decision by himself, being so responsible. "Do you have two spare rooms?"

"Unfortunately. Why do I have the feeling you're

going to get us all arrested? Or leave us wide open to being blackmailed by Serenity?"

"I think she'll be nothing but appreciative."

He snorted, but if she was not mistaken, he was taking to the novelty of having someone share the decision-making process with him.

"Unless you have a better idea?"

But he didn't. Still glaring at her, he fished his cell phone out of his pocket. "Slim. Sorry. I know it's late. I have a bit of an emergency I need your help with." He outlined it, listened to Slim's calm reply. "Thanks. Okay. Ponies looked after. Let's go."

And that's how Grace found herself at Rory Adams's super-posh bachelor pad in a condo on the shores of Lake Okanagan.

"Wow," Tucker said from the backseat when they drove up to the building. "You're rich."

"Don't tell your mother," Rory muttered under his breath, and Grace gave him a little kick.

They got out of her car, and she tried not to be too overawed by the building. She dealt with wealthy people all the time. But still, this was probably the most sought-after address in the entire Okanagan Valley.

The Monashee was an exclusive building engineered right into a cliff that overlooked the night-blackened and restless waters of the lake. They pulled up at the front entrance; the building looked like ten stories of nothing but glass.

"Holy…" Tucker said, getting out of the car and staring up at the architecture. The *holy* was then followed by a word that shocked Grace, not because she had never heard the word before, but because she had never heard it come from a seven-year-old boy!

"You don't say that word in front of a lady," Rory said, but without heat, without that kind of frightening firmness he had shown those teenage boys on the float. It was obvious Tucker was beyond exhaustion, and Grace appreciated Rory for knowing intuitively how to deal with him.

A valet came and took her car, and Rory ushered them through a lobby that reminded Grace of a very expensive hotel. Deep leather couches sat on handwoven Armenian carpets on highly polished marble floors. A black granite wall had water sliding silently down it.

They got on an elevator that opened directly into Rory's apartment.

It was an open space, but as different from hers as a camel was different from a kangaroo. Everything was muted opulence: white sleek furniture, Brazilian-cherry flooring, art that was obviously not from the poster bin at the discount store. The entire back wall was a sheet of glass that overlooked the lake.

"Holy…" Tucker said again, but this time, with a glance at Rory, excluded the second word.

"Do you want something to eat?" Rory asked.

The little boy contemplated this, but then shook his head. Rory showed them through to a guest wing: two beautiful bedrooms that shared one extraordinarily glamorous bathroom.

Within minutes, without even taking off his clothes, Rory's cell phone in his hand with the hospital on speed dial, Tucker was fast asleep in between pure-silk sheets.

Unwrapping a toothbrush in the guest bathroom to brush his teeth seemed to be all he could manage.

Grace gazed at him tenderly for a moment. He looked so small in the huge bed. She resisted the impulse to brush his hair back from his pale forehead and plant a kiss there, and backed out of the room with a whispered good-night.

She recognized her own exhaustion and how vulnerable it made her. When she came out of Tucker's room and saw Rory silhouetted at his floor-to-ceiling living-room window, she wanted to go to him.

To cast the last of her caution to the wind.

But he sensed she was there and turned to her.

She wanted to say, *Come hold me, let's go back to that moment before that truck ended up parked in my front yard.*

Instead she said, "Poor kid was done. He could barely brush his teeth."

She wanted to comment on the availability of toothbrushes, but suddenly it just seemed like a symbol of all that was different between them.

Who kept a dozen brand-new toothbrushes in the event of unexpected guests, after all?

Exactly the kind of man who lived in a space like this. The kind of man who had nurses touching his arm on the basis of a few seconds acquaintance.

"You must be done in, too." There was something faintly cold in his voice when he said, "I'll show you the other guest room."

And she could understand that completely. She had just hijacked the man's life. Those spare toothbrushes weren't for stray little boys, after all.

She had just shown him he didn't have to be alone with it all.

He needed some distance from that, and so did she.

"Thank you," she murmured. And she didn't just mean for the room. No, she meant for letting her look after Tucker.

For letting her have her opportunity to play auntie before all the evidence was in. Though in her heart, she felt she already knew the truth.

Rory listened to Grace's bedroom door close and felt as if he had been holding his breath and now it was safe to breathe.

Grace in his space.

When he had seen her coming out of Tucker's room, he had turned and looked at her, and known how easy it would be to take it a step further.

Known that she wanted to.

The hunger in her eyes had almost slain his strength.

But it was just wrong.

She was exhausted emotionally and physically. He couldn't take advantage of that.

Plus, Gracie was not the kind of woman he had become accustomed to, not at all. Those women were sophisticated and fast, they had no use for attachments anymore than he did.

When you took things a step further with a woman like Grace?

You better think things all the way through, starting with this thing: she was a forever kind of girl.

The kind that you waited for at the end of an aisle prepared to vow your whole life for her. The kind who harbored dreams of white picket fences and cottages on the lake and children squealing with delight.

And if you weren't prepared to provide a life like that you weren't worthy of her.

And added to that? She was Graham's kid sister. There would be a special place in hell for the man who took advantage of the look he'd seen on her face tonight.

Rory stood by the window until the last of the sounds had died, water running, bed creaking slightly as she got into it.

He let his mind stray. What was she wearing? Her clothes? Nothing at all? One of the old shirts he hung in that closet?

He made himself stop.

They had already waltzed way too close to the danger zone tonight. And he had something he had to do that would not make him Grace's favorite person when she found out.

On stealthy feet, he moved to the guest wing, to the bathroom that Tucker had used, and that Gracie had just exited moments before.

He looked at two toothbrushes that lay on the counter, side by side, for a long time. It was perfect, really. Better than the soda can, because for the soda-can idea to have worked, he would still have needed something of Graham's, or of a member of Graham's family.

He doubted whether, if Grace knew his intentions, she would have volunteered anything in either of those two categories. She had already told him she wanted Serenity—and not science—to deliver the truth.

And would Grace accept whatever Serenity said as the truth? Without verifying it? Surely not. Surely no one was that naive. But then he remembered the cowboys showing up and her determination to believe in a miracle.

Rory wasn't going to take a chance that she could be that trusting. He wasn't going to do it her way. He wasn't leaving it up to her. She would want to just let things unfold, he on the other hand liked to make things happen. He was going to protect her from herself.

Because opportunities like this did not come at every turn. Two toothbrushes. Both, presumably, would hold the genetic code that would prove or disprove if the two people who had used them were related.

He picked both toothbrushes up by their handles, careful not to touch the bristles, took them to the kitchen and bagged them in separate bags.

It was funny how he felt, a familiar feeling. A soldier who had been given an unsavory assignment, who had no choice but to do his duty.

Still, it felt sneaky, and he knew Grace would not approve of sneakiness in any form, even if it would speed up their arrival at the truth.

But from the shape Serenity had been in tonight, Rory knew something he had protected Grace—and Tucker—from.

It was possible they would need the truth sooner than later.

He looked for his cell phone, remembered he had given it to Tucker.

He went into his den, picked up the landline.

If Bridey had been sleeping, nothing in her tone indicated it.

"I need two things," he said. "And I need them fast.

I need a DNA test, I have the samples here that I need tested. And I need a private detective. To find out everything there is to know about a woman named Serenity Chambers." He gave the birth date and the other information that he had gleaned from Tucker for the hospital admittance desk.

He hesitated and then added softly, "I'm particularly interested in the birth of a child, a boy, seven to eight years ago."

"I'm on it."

"It's not about me," he said.

"That was unnecessary, sir. I already knew it wasn't about you."

"Now how would you know that?"

"You just know things about people after you've been around them for a while. And you are not a man who shirks your responsibilities."

"It could have been an accident," he said, enjoying playing devil's advocate to Bridey's complete loyalty to him.

"Or the kind of man who has those kinds of accidents."

"Thanks, Bridey." But as he hung up the phone it seemed to him if Graham, the most decent of men, could have had that kind of accident, then anyone could. A lot of life was luck or lack of it.

Rory allowed himself to feel his own exhaustion. He went back into the guest bathroom and unwrapped two new toothbrushes and put them side by side on the counter. It seemed unnecessarily sly, but really confirmed he was not quite the man Bridey thought he was.

Or the man Gracie seemed determined to believe he was.

And then he went to his own bedroom and felt the unpleasantness of what he had just done.

But despite the fact he had left war zones behind him, despite the fact his bedroom was one designed for a king, Rory had never been more aware he was a soldier. He could be counted on to do what needed to be done.

He could be counted on when no one else had the stomach for it.

He thought of that moment when he had just held Grace tonight. After he had told her about his dreams, shared the burden of his tremendous guilt

When his armor had been down, when he had let go of his need to be strong.

And he cursed himself for the longing that pressed against his chest and felt like fifty tons of steel. He thought he wasn't going to sleep at all, knowing Gracie was just down the hall. Knowing he had confessed his weaknesses to her. Knowing there was a little boy here that he had to figure out what to do with.

But in the morning, Rory awoke, refreshed and amazed.

No dreams.

Gracie was already in the kitchen and he tried to steel himself against how he felt about Grace in the morning: tousle-headed and makeup free, she had slept in a man's shirt that she must have found in the guest-room closet.

She was gorgeous as she snooped through his fridge, making herself at home, making that weight on his chest even more impossible to ignore.

A smarter man would be on his way to Australia.

But Tucker's arrival in the kitchen served as a reminder. Rory was in this now, and he was determined to see it through to the finish.

So, he took them for breakfast at a place that kids liked, though Tucker showed nothing but surliness as he gobbled down enough food to feed a small army. And then they went to the hospital.

Serenity, to everyone's relief was sitting up in bed, looking pale and wrung-out, but as though she would survive. She wanted out, but the doctor would not release her.

Tucker's whole demeanor changed after they had seen his mom. He insisted they drive out to the ponies so he could check on them. Slim was there.

"You know, Tucker," Slim said, "I have a whole pasture out at my place that needs eating down. Why don't I take the ponies out to my place for a while? It would be doing me a favor."

It was put in such a way that Tucker could give in without feeling as if he had absconded on the responsibility he took very seriously.

"I guess that would be good," he said with dignity that was way too grave for a seven-year-old.

Grace must have noticed that, too. As they watched the ponies being hauled away in Serenity's old trailer she looked around the camp with troubled eyes.

But she didn't let on she was troubled to Tucker.

"Want to spend the day with us?" she asked him.

Us.

"I guess," Tucker said, without any real enthusiasm.

"What would your perfect day be?" she asked him.

Tucker looked annoyed by the question. But then, reluctantly, he said, "Never having to go to school. That would be a perfect day."

"Well, it's summer so you already have that. If you could do anything you wanted, Tucker, what would it be?"

His look of annoyance deepened, but then he sighed, and seemed to give in to the frivolous temptation to dream a little.

"My perfect day," he said, "would be riding a horse up into the mountains. I'd set up a camp by a lake. I'd cook hot dogs and have as many as I wanted. Probably six or seven of them at least. And I'd have six sacks of potato chips all to myself. I'd drink a whole gallon of hot chocolate."

He looked like he wanted to stop, maybe even tried to stop, but the dream had taken hold of him. "I'd go to sleep lying right under the stars and I'd feel really full, like I couldn't eat another bite. Not even one more potato chip. I'd listen to the horses grazing, and the water moving and maybe a screech owl.

"I'd be with people who loved me more than anything else. I'd be away from problems. It would be a place where I never worried about anything, ever. And I'd feel safe, like nothing bad could ever happen."

He shut up suddenly, eyed them defiantly, clearly believing he'd revealed way too much of himself.

Rory slid Grace a glance. He could see tears in her eyes.

And he could feel the lump in his own throat. What kind of seven-year-old boy had dreams like this?

Didn't they dream of acquiring the newest toy? If they were offered a perfect day didn't they want to go play with their friends at the swimming pool? Or spend a day at the amusement park? Or go to hockey camp? Meet a sports hero? Or a rock star?

What kind of seven-year-old boy's best dream was being out in the middle of nowhere with a full tummy and feeling safe?

Rory Adams knew exactly what kind of seven-year-old boy dreamed those kind of dreams.

He met Gracie's eyes over Tucker's head. There was that look again, asking him—no, expecting him—to be some kind of hero. He had to walk away from this thing: from her and from this kid before what was left of his heart felt as if it had been ravaged by wolves.

But running away from what scared him most?

That had never been in his nature.

And running away was not even close to the vow he had made to see things through to the end.

He took a deep breath, recognized the irony of both surrendering and preparing for battle.

"Have you ever driven a Ferrari?" he asked Tucker.

CHAPTER EIGHT

IT WAS called Automotion, and it was a go-cart track Grace had driven by a thousand times without giving it a thought.

Now, choosing her go-cart, she wondered what she had been missing all her life. They had a huge selection of all the great high-performance cars in miniature.

Grace watched as Tucker and Rory debated the features of each car as if it were real before they decided which one to drive.

She wasn't just falling for Rory anymore.

No, she had seen on his face the exact moment when he had decided to give Tucker a normal little boy's dream of a perfect day. She had seen on his face the exact moment he had decided to give himself over to this: a sense of being a family.

And she had gone from falling to the ugly part: *splat*. *Splat*. As in Gracie Day loved Rory Adams. *Splat*. As in she couldn't stop herself. *Splat*. As in it could have all kinds of messy consequences. *Splat*. As in there was every chance this would not end well. *Splat*. As in Rory would no more reciprocate these feelings than he had when she was fourteen.

Grace had always had a gift for exactly this: seeing

all the things that could go wrong, seeing the potential for disaster everywhere. It was part of what made her such a good event planner. While her customers were doing nothing but having fun she was anticipating every single thing that could go wrong and putting out fires before they roared to life.

So she was astonished to find that after careful evaluation of all the things that could and probably would go wrong as a result of her very foolishly giving over her heart to Rory, she simply didn't care.

She liked the way she felt right now, sliding behind the wheel of her miniature Ferrari.

Alive.

Aware that if you let go of control a little bit, life had crazy potential to go in directions you never expected, and that that wasn't necessarily a bad thing.

She was awake, and being awake made her realize that she had the potential to feel and experience things that she never ever would if she was too cautious.

So Grace vowed she wasn't going to be cautious. She wasn't going to weigh every possibility and every option. She wasn't going to squint toward the future with fearful eyes.

No, she was going to be alive, aware and awake to her own life.

No, she was going to accept with open arms and an open heart the unexpected gift this day had given her. She was going to acknowledge the unexpected gifts she had been given since the day those ponies had broken free and ransacked Pondview.

Wasn't that one of the strangest things about life?

Sometimes the greatest gifts were going to come as a result of an event that you had originally judged as bad.

The Ferrari she chose was yellow and not red. Now she was at the starting line. The track was packed, at least eight little cars were revving beside her.

The pistol went off.

Rory and Tucker took off like they had been shot out of cannons.

It took Grace a little longer to get the hang of it. It was hard to lose that cautious habit, and this activity seemed decidedly dangerous once she was actually moving. People were racing around the figure-eight-shaped track with reckless abandon!

They had lapped her twice when she saw Rory glance back at her, faintly mocking, faintly challenging.

She couldn't have possibly heard him over the roar of the engines. But she must have read his lips.

Let loose, Gracie.

And then, she did. She let go of her need for absolute control. Hadn't the universe been showing her for days that its plan for her was so much better than anything she could plan for herself?

She let go. She pressed down on the accelerator and surged forward. She loved the feeling of power. She pressed down a little harder.

After the final lap, she was still dead last, she couldn't make up for the lost time—and maybe that was another lesson in life. You could not make up for the lost time.

But as she got out of that car, she felt tingly with excitement.

"That was fun!" she said with amazement.

"Tucker and I are going to go again. How about you?"

She looked at the two guys watching her and felt her heart swell. Just like some sort of surrender had happened to her, so had one happened to Rory.

Right now he was the carefree boy he had never been. Even when her brother had brought him home, he might have seemed careless and carefree, but he hadn't been, not totally. Something in him never quite letting go. Something in him watchful and a bit wary even as he had teased her to distraction. Of course, she hadn't seen that at the time. She'd been fourteen! All she had seen was how handsome he was.

And the truth was he was still handsome enough to rattle her world.

She shifted her focus to Tucker. He was shining with happiness.

"Are you coming again?" Rory asked, already heading over to select his second car.

Despite having managed to overcome her cautious nature, she had to acknowledge, secretly, she had been happy when it was over. Secretly, she had felt overjoyed to have survived her own recklessness.

Which meant she hadn't quite learned the lesson yet!

"Of course I'm coming again," she said.

She chose the Ferrari again. Who could resist? And she relaxed a little more this time. Let loose a little more. Came in third instead of dead last.

But what she loved most was watching them, Tucker and Rory, fiercely competitive, both giving themselves over, both learning to play.

Grace knew Rory had probably never had anything approaching a childhood. Not as she thought of childhood.

And so, as with most gifts, as he gave this one to Tucker he received it himself.

"I'm starving," Rory said when they had finally exhausted themselves. She had given up after the third race, but they both had tried every car on the track.

"Me, too," Tucker said approvingly.

"Wanna eat hot dogs till we puke?"

"Yes," Tucker said with soft reverence. "But first we need to go see my mom."

"Absolutely," Rory said, throwing his arm around the boy's scrawny shoulders. Tucker didn't even flinch away.

Serenity was sitting up when they arrived, cursing out a nurse and telling her she'd leave if she wanted to.

But she stopped as soon as they came into the room. Stopped and stared, first at Tucker, then at Rory, then at Grace and then back at Tucker.

And suddenly her fight was gone. There was something in her face that was about the saddest thing Grace had ever seen. Serenity pulled the blanket back over her skinny legs, and said to the nurse. "Okay, then, run your damned tests. But I'm not paying for them."

Tucker scooted up on the bed. "Mama, guess what I did?"

"What did you do, Yucky?"

"Drove a race car!"

She smiled, but Grace could see she was exhausted and that her genuine happiness for Tucker's happiness was mixed with something else. "Fun, huh?"

"The most fun ever," Tucker said.

"Well, they're gonna keep your mama here for a while. I don't want you to worry. I'm tough as an old mama grizzly bear and harder to kill."

"You don't have to worry, either. Slim is taking the ponies to his pasture."

"Slim, huh?" Again, there was some expression, deep in her eyes, that Grace could not completely understand. "You go have fun. I'll be back to my rootin-tootin' self in a couple of days. Enjoy your auntie."

"My auntie?" Tucker said.

"Pretty sure that lady right there is your daddy's sister."

Tucker turned and eyed Grace; she saw that dislike again, naked in his face. Or maybe it wasn't dislike. Fear. Why would he be afraid of her? Why would he be afraid that she was his auntie?

She glanced at Rory to see how he was taking the news. He looked like thunder.

He obviously wanted to say something, skepticism was stamped on his features. But he looked off for a moment, glanced at Tucker, marshaled himself and then he turned on his heel and left the room.

"I gotta go with him, Mama. We're gonna eat hot dogs till we puke." Tucker stopped and went very still. "Unless you want me to stay. I'll stay right here if you want me to."

"Nope. I already told you. Go have fun with your kin."

Guilt and desire warred on his face. "Can we bring you a hot dog?"

Serenity made a face. "Maybe, later, if you think

of it, smuggle me in a little ice cream cone, the kind dipped in butterscotch."

Grace could clearly see Serenity was not up to eating an ice cream cone, she had given her son a little chore to do for her to relieve his guilt. And it worked.

"Hey, Rory, wait up," he called and darted from the room.

But Grace was not so quick to follow. She sat on the edge of the bed.

"You do think he's Graham's," she said softly.

Serenity closed her eyes. "Oh, yeah. I do."

"But why now? Why tell me now?"

"Why not?" Serenity said, something angry in her tone. She opened her eyes, challenging Grace.

"But why didn't you tell Graham?"

"Do I look like the type of person your brother, Mr. Squeaky Clean, would have been happy to know he had a kid with?"

Grace was silent.

"He probably would have tried to take him away from me if he knew. I'm tired now. Just go away."

The words seemed harsh, but there were tears shining behind Serenity's eyes.

When Grace didn't move, she closed her eyes again. Softer, she said, "Please?"

Grace got up and left the room without another word, aware that even as she was troubled, something was blooming inside her.

Hope.

And love.

Tucker was Graham's baby, and it was like the light flickered back on in her world.

She skipped down the hall to find her nephew and Rory. Rory took one look at her face and his look of displeasure deepened.

But she didn't care.

"This is a moment to celebrate," she told him.

"Don't be so sure, Grace."

"Don't spoil this moment with your cynicism."

He drew in a deep breath, as if she had slapped him across the face. But then he smiled, the smile she had come to recognize as the one that hid what he was really feeling.

"Gracie-Facie, that's what I do. I put out the sunshine in girls like you."

"Well, I'm not a little girl and I don't believe you have power over light and darkness."

He sighed, ran a hand through the thick silk of his hair. "Don't count on that," he muttered.

"I've said before that you are unnecessarily cynical," she said. She was aware they were bickering. This was how badly she had fallen: she *loved* bickering with him.

"I told you there's no such thing."

"Are we going to eat hot dogs?" Tucker demanded.

"I guess we are," Rory said. "I guess we are."

And for some reason, he backed off on his cynicism. He looked at her long and hard, and then at Tucker. "I happen to know where the world's best hot dogs are."

She recognized it as a surrender, even if Rory didn't.

"You do?" Tucker asked, reverent.

"Yeah, I do."

Rory watched Tucker eating hot dogs. The little boy claimed he would eat six, but he was petering out after three.

The kid obviously had not had a decent meal in a long time. And then there was Grace. That little smile hadn't left her face since Serenity had announced she was Tucker's aunt.

So everybody was happy.

Why did happiness make him so deeply suspicious? He had a feeling of waiting for the other shoe to drop.

And the thing was? He didn't believe Serenity. Even after Grace had taken him aside and told him Serenity's reasons for not telling Graham that Tucker was his, Rory had serious reservations.

But he'd have an answer in a few days. He wouldn't have to take Serenity's word for it and that filled him with relief.

It occurred to him, he'd had the perfect opportunity to tell Grace about the DNA test. But he hadn't. He had let that moment pass. Why? Because she believed he would not bring darkness to her world, despite the fact she had been properly warned.

And maybe he wouldn't have to. Maybe that DNA test was going to prove exactly what Serenity had said, and he could relax.

And until then, was there any way of preventing Grace from getting completely attached to that kid?

He doubted it. He was already feeling kind of attached to the spunky little fellow himself.

So, he couldn't prevent her from getting attached, but maybe he had to stay near. Watching. Waiting. Being there when that other shoe dropped.

She had asked him not to spoil everything with his cynicism. Okay, then. He'd do his best to hide how he really felt.

Maybe he'd even give himself permission to enjoy giving that kid a few things that he'd never had before.

But unlike her, he would expect the worst, and he would prepare for that. It was how he'd gone through his whole life. It was what had protected him from the disappointment he could see Grace headed toward at breakneck speed, as if she had her foot down hard on the gas pedal of that little yellow Ferrari.

The truth was he had a million things to do today.

The truth was he was losing a bit of control here. Because he *wanted* to be with them.

"Do you want to go to the beach this afternoon?" he heard himself asking.

"I don't have swim stuff," Tucker said, not enthused.

"We can go out to where you're staying and pick it up," Grace said.

"You don't get it. I don't have that stuff. Swim trunks. A beach towel." This was said with a certain defiant pride.

He saw Grace absorb that. Felt himself absorb it.

"That's easy to fix," Rory said. "Ask Grace."

She actually blushed. Rory found himself hoping that if they went to the beach, she would wear her new bikini again.

A little more of that control felt as if it was slipping away from him.

"I don't know how to swim," Tucker said.

"It's not rocket science," Rory said. Unlike Grace, he could feel the pressure of a time line. Within days they would know the truth. Was that enough time to give this kid a taste of a childhood? Something he could hold inside himself when it all went to hell in a handbasket?

Rory wondered if he was kidding himself.

Was this about Tucker, or was this about him?

Since he was Tucker's age he had yearned for normal things. For a normal family. For a normal Christmas. For a normal dinner around the family table. To go to bed at night and not hear raised voices and things breaking, his mother crying. Not to feel that sense of helplessness as he watched his mother unravel; not to feel that sense that he was failing her every single day. Failing to protect her from his father's temper, from her own impulses, from the life that she seemed so disillusioned with.

All his life, he had fought that yearning just to be normal.

Especially when he had met the Day family. He'd liked hanging with Graham, but he had steadfastly refused the invitations to the cottage, for Christmas dinner, the invitation to experience this thing called home too deeply.

At some level he feared that if he ever got what he wanted most, it would destroy him. It would make him weak instead of strong. It would make him squander his moments chasing after something he couldn't have.

And so he had scorned it instead. Held himself aloof from it. Told himself other men *needed* home, family, but he did not.

Every marital breakup among friends, every Dear John letter, Rory had taken as evidence that he lived in reality.

He had congratulated himself on seeing through the illusion, on walking away from it.

And so Rory Adams was startled to find he had no

strength left to fight this thing. Ever since he had told Grace the truth—that he had failed her brother—and she had refused to see it that way, he had felt this weakness growing in him.

And wasn't that his greatest fear, that love made a man weak instead of strong?

Love. Where had that word come from? The word he had avoided his entire life? That he had rarely spoken, and when he did, only in the most casual of contexts, as in *I love pizza with feta cheese on top of it.*

But the truth was what he was feeling for Grace was a whole lot different than what he felt for a pizza, even with feta cheese on top.

Stand down, soldier, he ordered himself.

But his heart wouldn't listen. His heart was prepared to mutiny.

"You're going too fast," Grace called, gasping. "You have to slow down."

She was breathless with laughter and the effort of pedaling her bike up a huge hill. Now Rory and Tucker were swooshing down the other side, speed demons, both of them.

"Tucker, stop it! You just learned!"

But he was already too far away to hear her, and maybe that was a good thing. The last thing he needed was to have the enjoyment of the moment overshadowed by her sense of caution.

She stopped to catch her breath and to watch them.

She acknowledged it had been the best week of her entire life. She loved being with Tucker. She loved being an auntie. It was as though she had lived for this.

But, of course, it was more than being an auntie to Tucker.

Far more. It was the magic of all of them being together. She had let Beth take over the whole office for the past days. Rory must have done the same. Because they were like a family on holiday.

She had lived in the Okanagan Valley her whole life and she felt as though she had never seen it before. She felt as if the scales had dropped from her eyes.

She lived in a state of discovery as they explored and went on picnics and discovered new beaches.

She must have seen sunsets before, but had she ever felt their warmth shimmering along her skin like a living thing?

In the evenings, after the days jam-packed with sightseeing and the headlong pursuit of fun, Tucker's favorite thing was playing video games at Rory's apartment on a state-of-the-art gaming system.

Even she had to admit it was way more fun than board games. She particularly liked the one where you could virtually go bowling, or golfing or play baseball. The laughter they shared at her ineptitude at each of those sports would live with her forever.

They were managing, two or three times a day, to get to the hospital. After that first butterscotch-dipped cone, they always brought Serenity something, made her part of the circle. They gave Tucker a camera and he took a zillion pictures, would climb onto the bed with his mom and share them all. Once they sneaked the gaming system in, and laughed so hard that a nurse came and banished them for the evening and the machine for good.

But, despite a softening in Serenity, at a deeper level, Grace could feel something haunted her? What was it?

Somehow, they were becoming a family. Not a family that met any kind of definition of family, but a family all the same. Grace and Tucker were still staying at Rory's apartment, living in separate rooms, but still, how could you not feel like a family when you were sharing the same space, eating off the same dishes, arguing about what television show to watch, what game to play, thinking about what surprise to cook up for Serenity that day? They were becoming wonderfully good at dreaming up ways to make her smile.

Even Rory seemed to be overcoming his suspicion of her. It was his idea to bring one of the ponies to the front lawn of the hospital where Serenity could see it from her window. Slim delivered it in a trailer. Tucker stood outside waving and grinning. The pony wore a banner that said, Get Well Soon.

But, as exquisite as each day was, and as much as Grace enjoyed every moment of laughter and discovery and togetherness, there was a moment in each day that she looked forward to like no other.

That was when Tucker fell into bed, exhausted. He would call his mom on the cell phone Rory had lent him, and then fall into a deep, deep sleep.

And then Grace and Rory were alone.

There was always one suspended moment when it was suddenly silent. When they would look at each other as if they were thirsty people drinking cool water.

That moment would pass, but the awareness would continue to sizzle softly between them.

It was there as they decided what music to listen to,

or what drink to share as they sat out on his deck watching night claim the lake.

It was there as they talked, the comfort level between them constantly growing, evolving, becoming. They remembered Graham, now, not with pain, but with affection, and those memories brought them comfort and drew them yet closer together.

Without either of them saying a word, somehow Grace and Rory had become a couple. It had started with his hand resting casually on her shoulder or around her waist on some of their excursions.

Encouraged by his easy familiarity she had started taking his hand in hers.

In the evenings now, they shared the couch, closer and closer, together, legs brushing, shoulders touching.

Finally, they had kissed.

It was an intentional kiss, the sun setting, bathing them both in golden light, her shoulder touching his.

And then he had turned and looked at her.

And moaned low in his throat, a sound of surrender, of almost animal wanting.

He had dropped his head over hers, sought her lips and then her throat and then her eyelids, and then she had drawn him to her lips again, hungry for his taste.

And he had tasted of everything he was: strength and power, masculine self-certainty, confidence.

But underlying that, she had been amazed by the pure sweetness of him. That was the taste that lingered after all the others were gone.

In his kiss, he had revealed finally, holding back nothing, who he really was.

And that was a man so genuinely good it brought tears to her eyes.

It was a kiss that there was no mistaking the intention of. It was not *Thank you for a lovely day*. It was not a casual brush of lips where either of them could go *oops, how did that happen?*

No, it was a kiss that said, *I see you*.

It was a kiss that said, *I know you*.

It was a kiss that said, *My heart and yours have begun to beat together*.

It was a kiss that said, *I loved today. I cannot wait for tomorrow*.

In other words it was a kiss that embraced the future.

But then, as if to deny everything that kiss had just said, he had broken away from her, vaguely troubled.

"Good night, Gracie."

And she had been left on the deck, standing in the dying light, so aware that things were not defined between them. It was as if they had become a couple by default, without a conscious decision.

She was afraid if she asked for a conscious decision, if she did anything to disturb the balance, it would end as quickly and casually as it had started.

Now, watching Rory ride his bike down the hill, his hair tangling in the wind behind him, she felt breathless again. Not from riding her bike but from knowing her own heart.

She loved Rory's easy strength, his laughter, his camaraderie with that little boy. She knew she had to find the courage to tell him the truth. She would tell him soon, waiting for the perfect moment.

She would tell Rory Adams she loved him.

It wasn't the cautious thing to do.

But in the past few days, she had become the girl she always wanted to be. A girl who had carried a picture of a red sports car in her wallet without knowing why.

Now she knew.

The car represented the contradiction that was her: she loved home. She loved family. She loved playing games and canning peaches.

But with Rory, she was becoming more whole, more herself, embracing another side, the side that she had always repressed.

The side that was willing to take the lead. The side that was bold. The side that loved adventure.

The side that made her his equal.

The side of her that made her brave enough to say yes to the greatest risk and the greatest adventure of all.

Falling in love with another person. Deeply and truly. Wanting, always, what was best for them.

Even if that meant consequences to herself.

Even if there was the potential there for pain.

Telling Rory Adams she loved him was going to take more courage than anything she had ever done.

And she felt ready.

And somehow it was love that had made her this courageous and this ready.

And wasn't that exactly what love did? Made you better than what you had been before? Made you better than you had ever imagined you could be.

Was he feeling the same way? The very thought made her insides quake, made her tremble with anxiety.

No, she would not let fear into it. She wouldn't. She would be the girl who had dreamed Ferrari dreams.

She kicked off from the top of the hill, took her hand off the brake and kicked free of the bicycle pedals. She had not a single thought of falling.

CHAPTER NINE

Rory stared down at the envelope in his hands. Grace and Tucker were both fast asleep in his guest bedrooms. It was the last night they would be here together like this, the little makeshift family that he had taken such unexpected and fierce pleasure in.

Once they were gone—Serenity was being released from the hospital in the morning—and things got back to normal, how was he going to be able to stand this apartment? It would be as if the light had gone out of it. Even now, glancing around, he realized the place had become a home.

There was a beach towel tossed over the couch, and a remote-control car wedged underneath the coffee table. There were two pairs of tiny sneakers at the front door, Grace's and Tucker's. There was a bowl of potato chips left out on the counter and a tin of hot chocolate and three mugs in the sink.

There was a clumsily wrapped gift on the table, a new blouse that Tucker had picked out for his mother's homecoming.

It felt as if a family lived here.

And over the past week, isn't that what they'd become? A family.

It was what Rory had longed for his entire life. And avoided at the very same time. Now, it had been thrust upon him.

Rory was aware he should not have let his guard down. He should not have been sucked in so completely.

But that's what love did. It impaired a man's judgment as surely as wine. As he thought back over the last week, it occurred to him, maybe even more than wine.

He thought of everything they had done: driving minicars and having picnics, riding bikes, teaching Tucker to swim. He thought of overcoming his deep suspicion of Serenity to honor Tucker's love and devotion for her.

He thought of the evenings in the apartment playing video games, eating chips, sipping hot chocolate.

And he thought of the best moments of all: when Tucker had gone to bed and he and Grace sat out on the deck, sipping hot chocolate and watching the sun set over the lake.

He thought of last night when he had kissed her so thoroughly it felt as if they had exchanged souls.

He let the shock of that ripple along his spine.

He loved her. He loved Grace Day as much as he had ever loved anyone in his whole life.

And love filled a hole in him that he had tried to outrun his whole life.

The envelope had been delivered earlier, and he had put it aside, not wanting to know what was in there, stealing as many moments of this sense of family as he could. He had wanted to have this last night. Of what?

Being a family.

But he had not gone out on the balcony tonight, and

had not kissed her. He had steeled himself against the longing he saw in her face, and his own.

Taking a deep breath, Rory slid the papers from the envelope.

A few minutes later, he set them down, leaned forward and put his elbows on his knees, covered his eyes with his hands.

That's what hope did. Left you open to being broken like this, like a shattered piece of glass.

He hadn't been part of a family. He'd been part of an elaborate pretense, and he of all people should have known better.

He heard her before he saw her, opened his eyes and gazed at Grace. She was in one of his shirts, her hair tousled, her long legs naked.

He had never seen a woman look so sexy.

So beautiful.

"Rory, what's wrong?" she said. "What time is it?"

"It's late."

"You couldn't sleep? Are you having the dreams again?"

He had not had the dreams all week. He had slept soundly. Now, he realized he had failed all the way around.

He had failed to protect his mother.

He had failed to protect Graham.

And he had failed to protect Gracie, too.

When it should have been him being pragmatic, what had he been doing? Throwing himself into the fantasy she had been creating.

"Grace, he's not Graham's."

"What?"

"Tucker isn't Graham's."

She stood there, sleepy and vulnerable, and looked stunned. "What do you mean? How do you know?"

"He's actually not seven. He's nine." Rory thought of that first meeting with Tucker, asking how old he was, Tucker's hesitation, Serenity's voice coming from under the truck.

Tell the man how old you are.

Tucker was small for his age. They'd accepted without question he was seven.

"Given his age," Rory said, "it goes without saying that the DNA was not a match."

"What DNA?" she asked.

"I collected a sample," he said, and then found he could not fudge the truth. Hadn't he been doing that all week? Pretending? Pretending it could all be true. It was enough now. "I collected a sample from each of you."

"Without telling me?" she whispered.

"Grace, you never wanted to know the truth. That's why you didn't want a DNA test from the very beginning. Part of you knew it could end like this and you wanted it all to match your little fantasy."

"I wanted Graham to go on," she said, shrilly.

"Well, he doesn't," Rory said harshly. "Life doesn't always go the way you dream. In fact, it rarely does."

She began to cry.

He got up. He wanted to close his arms around her. He wanted to protect her from the world and from any kind of pain.

But when he began to move toward her, she stepped back from him.

"How could you do this to me? Eventually, I would

have been ready to do a DNA test. How could you collect a sample without telling me? It's a betrayal!"

"I tried to warn you I could put out your light, Grace. I tried to warn you."

She stared at him, then turned on her heel, ran into her room and shut the door firmly.

He stared at the closed door for a moment, and then went to bed. The dreams came back with a vengeance.

At dawn he admitted there would be no more sleep. He got up, a man who had been assigned an unpleasant mission, a man with a job to do.

He went to the hospital.

Serenity was sitting on the edge of her bed, already dressed, ready to go. It would be hours before they released her, but she already was ready. He stood in the doorway for a moment, watching her. He waited for the anger to come at the deceit she had visited on them, on how she had deliberately hurt Grace.

But what he saw in her face in the early morning light was not deceit. It was weariness and fear.

She glanced up and saw him, scanned his face, seemed to sag.

"You know," she said tiredly.

He came and sat beside her. "I took a DNA sample. I put a private detective on it."

"Ah."

"Why would you do this?" he asked. "Why would you cause such a good woman so much pain?"

"In case you haven't figured it out, Sherlock, I'm really sick," she said. She tried for defiance and somehow failed. "I knew before I came in here. I've got Hepatitis C. I'm going to die from it."

He searched her face for the con, and found none.

"I'm sorry," he said. And he was. He was sorry for her, heartbroken for Tucker. But he had to know. "But why visit your troubles on Grace?"

The tears came then.

"In my whole life, one man was decent to me. One. What does that tell you about a life?"

"Graham," he guessed.

"Those few days we were all together. It was a crazy party. He could have done anything, but he never even tried. He never treated me like a whore. He never showed me anything but kindness and respect I didn't deserve."

Rory felt a pang for his friend.

He'd always been like that. Even over there. Keeping his pockets full of candy for the kids. Everyone treated with love and respect. Everyone.

Suddenly, the missing words, the missing part of his dream when he always woke up slipped into his consciousness, but it was gone before he could capture it.

"I saw his picture in the newspaper," Serenity said. "I hadn't seen him for what, eight years? But there was a whole bunch of pictures of Canadian soldiers who had been killed over there. I'm a tough girl," she said, "but when I saw that picture I cried like a baby.

"I guess I started thinking about it right then. What's going to happen to Tucker when I die? I've been in foster care. I didn't want that for Tucker. I thought what if that decent, decent man had a family?"

"What about Tucker's real father?" Rory asked.

"He wasn't a good person. I was never with him, except for a night or two. He died. He never even knew about Tucker. I don't think he would have even cared."

"So, you were looking for a home for Tucker?"

"He doesn't know how sick I am. I mean, I guess he does, 'cause he's seen me not feeling well lots and lots, but he doesn't know I'm going to die.

"Though he must have suspected something was up, because he didn't take to Grace. Almost like he sensed I was choosing who to leave him with and hated her for it. Instead of me.

"But then that first day you guys had him, and he drove the race car, he came in here and he was shining.

"I've never given him that. I want him to have a shot at life. I want him to have what I never had."

Rory felt his own *want* for those very things claw up his throat. Wasn't this what it was to be human? Wanting a family, a place to belong, a place where you felt safe and loved, as basic a need as eating or having a roof over your head? He felt something in him softening toward Serenity.

"There's no hope on the diagnosis?"

"There's an experimental treatment for it. It's the same way they treat cancer. If the treatment doesn't kill you, it can actually get rid of the Hep C permanently."

"And you aren't a candidate?"

She snorted. "I don't even have health insurance."

"If you had health insurance?"

"It wouldn't matter. I still wouldn't have a place to live. Who would look after Tucker on those days I couldn't move away from the toilet I was so sick?"

"What if those weren't issues, either?"

Something flickered in her face—a moment of

hope—and then she tried to kill it. "You won't get this, 'cause you got pure courage coming out your pores. But, Rory, I ain't got no kind of courage. I can't suffer like that."

"Here's the thing, Serenity. It's not really about you. It's about that little boy. And you can't give up without a fight. You can't. Love won't let you. Love is going to ask you to be stronger than you have ever been, and braver than you have ever been. Not for yourself. If it was for yourself, you couldn't do it. But for him, you can. For Tucker you can."

Serenity eyed him, and then the hope flickered back to life in her eyes. And there was something else there too, a startling kind of knowing.

"Well, look at you," she said. "An expert on love. Who would have ever thunk that?"

"Yeah," he said, "Who would have?"

He left the hospital.

Who would have thought he'd be an expert on love? He remembered the look on Grace's face.

How could you?

He'd known all along he had to protect her. He'd known all along what she would need protecting from most was his cynicism, his darkness, his ability to snuff out her light.

He left the hospital. He felt as if cinder blocks were attached to all his limbs. He fished his cell phone out of his pocket.

"Bridey? I need you to find out everything you can about Hepatitis C treatment programs. I need you to find a place for a woman, a nine-year-old boy and eight ponies to live."

"Is that all, sir?"

"No, then I need you to book me a flight to Australia."

Grace was furious at Rory for three days. She could not think of him without feeling that surge of anger. How dare he go behind her back? How dare he take control like that?

And underneath that: How dare he expose the truth? That she was so vulnerable to her dreams?

In a way, those three days of fury helped her cope with the fact that Tucker was gone, too. And that he was not Graham's.

When Serenity had confessed to her how she had been looking for a home for her son because she was ill, Grace had realized she did not need Tucker to be Graham's to love him.

Serenity had gone to live in one of the little guest houses at Slim McKenzie's ranch. Grace had helped them get settled, and between that and getting caught up at work, especially on planning for Warrior Down, she had been grateful to be so busy.

Still, through all the busyness of her days, a part of her waited. She had thought Rory would call. They had been so close. Their lives had become so interlinked.

She missed him so dreadfully. It felt like a physical ache.

How could he not be missing her in the same way?

When she saw his office number on her caller ID, her heart went into triple-time. But it was not Rory.

It was a woman named Bridey. She needed to start putting together The Perfect Day package for the silent auction at Warrior Down. Mr. Adams had suggested a helicopter ride to the top of Silver Lining Mountain, a table set for two, white linen, a chef.

Grace had had perfect days. Seven of them in a row! That was so far from what she'd had!

But she heard herself saying, "Yes, that's fine."

And then, "Is Rory there? Could I talk to him?"

"Oh. I'm sorry. I thought you must know. Mr. Adams is in Australia supervising a job."

She could ask for a number to reach him at. She could leave a message for him. But somehow, she didn't.

He was pulling away from her.

And if she listened closely, she was pretty sure she could hear the sound of her own heart breaking.

But then, she remembered that night long, long ago, when she had seen Rory standing over his mother, fiercely protective.

And in a flash of light she got it.

He saw himself as a protector. The go-to guy. The one who called the shots. The one who maintained control.

He had told her he carried the burden of feeling he had failed to protect her brother.

And he was probably also feeling as if he had failed to protect her, Grace, from Serenity's lie.

All along, he had tried to warn her that he was dark to her light.

Was he trying to protect her from himself?

And who protected him? Where did he rest? Who was his equal?

I am, she thought.

His time with her had made her more than she had ever been before: stronger, more confident, more able to cut loose. She had become more herself than she had ever been before.

And if she could not use those things: if she could not take the biggest risk of all to rescue Rory from himself, then were all the lessons lost?

Wasn't what he needed to know most—and what she needed to know most—that love triumphed?

That love triumphed over deceit? That love triumphed over weakness? That love triumphed over darkness?

That love triumphed, yes, even over death.

Because, somehow, it was her brother who had brought all these events together. Even though he wasn't here, the bigness of his heart had gone on.

Not to live up to the bigness of her brother's heart would be a disgrace to his legacy. To say no to love would be to scorn everything Graham had stood for.

She was going after Rory. And not as Gracie-Facie, either.

No, it was the girl who dreamed of red Ferraris who would find the boldness needed to rescue Rory Adams.

From the terrifying loneliness of the world he had made for himself. Where he had to be in charge of everything and everybody.

And where, because of the hugeness of the task he had set for himself, he was doomed to failure.

The music swirled around Rory. Lights reflected off the lake, and the laughter filled the soft evening air.

He did not want to be here, even if it was for Warrior Down, and he tugged uncomfortably at the bow tie that seemed too tight. He felt alone in the crowd, disconnected. Of course, he had felt disconnected from the moment he had made the decision to leave Gracie and go to Australia.

Now he fingered the piece of paper in his pocket.

I need you. Please come.

The words had been written on an official invitation to the Warrior Down fundraiser. And Rory could not resist them. Not even to protect himself.

Grace needed him. And he had vowed to her he would be her go-to guy.

He had to separate that vow from what he was feeling.

Ever since he had left and gone to Australia it was as if the hole in his heart had grown a little bigger.

The missing part of the dream had come on his second night in Australia.

Two teenage boys. Something about them. He'd hesitated because they were so young. And then bullets everywhere. Ducking, taking cover. Where was Graham? Out there. Crawling out, pulling him back, cradling him in his arms.

Blood, so much blood.

Graham telling him to check up on Gracie, and then a flicker of movement. Those teenage boys, who were responsible for this, for his friend lying dying, had appeared, trying to slink past where he and Graham were hidden.

And he'd snatched up his rifle and pulled it in tight to his shoulder, seen the boys freeze and fear dawn in their eyes through his rifle sights.

And with whatever strength Graham had had left, he had reached up and yanked the barrel down.

"Don't. Not for me. I want my legacy to be love."

Lowering the rifle, the boys slithering away, his chance at retribution gone even as the light winked out in Graham. Forever.

Rory had wanted to phone her after he had had that dream. Had been desperate to talk to her.

And when the dream had not come back at all, he wanted it even more.

But he fought that wanting.

Now, watching her event unfold gloriously, success-ful beyond what she could have planned, he was deter-mined not to let Gracie see his weakness. His wanting. But the truth was he was growing increasingly annoyed. Considering the urgency of that note, he had barely seen Grace.

She was flitting around like a beautiful butterfly, in a gown spun from golden gossamer. She looked gor-geous. Hair up. Makeup perfect.

Not like a woman pining for him at all!

In fact, she had given him a tiny kiss on the cheek when he arrived, introduced him to some people and then she'd been gone.

Well, it was her night, and obviously she took being in charge of it very seriously. And what a night it was.

The Warrior Down fundraiser had been a great suc-cess, a gala on the edge of the lake. The Perfect Day his company had sponsored had been the second-highest moneymaker at the function.

The first highest?

An idea he had scorned when he had first seen it.

Grace had hatched a plan to have people sponsor vacations for military families: four-day excursions into the mountains on horseback.

Rory had thought, cynic that he was, that no one would go for that. They would want a perfect day for themselves. But to give it to someone else? A stranger? Nothing in it for them?

He hadn't thought that would be a big hit.

But it was. The last time he had looked at the list more than thirty families had been sponsored for the mountain horseback holiday.

And all of this was well and good, but where was Grace?

Except for the occasional little wave from the distance, he had barely seen her.

He was beginning to wonder if this whole thing was a joke. A way of her getting back at him for shattering her hopes and dreams, a way of punishing him for abandoning her and everything she stood for and going to Australia.

A note had been slipped to him by a waiter a few minutes ago.

Wait for me. Trust me.

Sure, but finally, the endless evening was drawing down. The crowds were all gone. Now, even the tables were being packed away. The lawns had grown quiet. The dancing and revelry that had happened here were gone, like night evaporated before the morning.

He stood out on the empty lawn, wondering if he should wait any longer.

And then he heard a splash in the dark water.

"Rory! Come in. It's gorgeous."

He squinted out at the water. He would know that voice anywhere. It was too dark to tell.

Was she skinny-dipping?

He cast a look over his shoulder. Sheesh. Anyone could see her.

"Grace, get out of that water. No, don't."

"You come in."

"You're being crazy."

"I know. Quite a departure for an old stick-in-the-mud like me, but you have no one but yourself to blame."

He walked down to the water's edge. She was swimming toward the float. He tugged off the tie, the suit jacket, the shirt, the pants. He left his skivvies on.

"Oh," she called, taunting. "Shy!"

He dived into the water, caught up with her in a few strokes.

"What the hell are you doing?" he asked. He couldn't see through the dark water. Was she naked?

"I'm drowning," she said. "I need you to save me."

"Stop it. You swim like a damned fish."

"I'm drowning in loneliness. I'm drowning in need. I'm drowning in my love for you."

"Gracie—

"No," she said fiercely. "Enough of you being in charge. Enough of you thinking you have to run the whole world. Enough of you thinking you need to protect me. Enough. Come home, Rory. Come home to me."

He stared at her.

"Do you have anything on?"

"Not a stitch," she said without an ounce of shame.

And then he laughed. This was the Gracie he had come to love: spontaneous, willing to embrace the adventure, bold.

This was the girl who had carried a picture of a bright red sports car in her wallet her whole life.

This was her secret side, the side that was for him.

And she was holding it out like a gift, and he could not resist anymore. He could not.

He reached for her, and she came into his arms.

"You have a bathing suit on," he said. He didn't know if he was relieved or disappointed.

"I know. But thinking I didn't got you into the water, didn't it?"

"Diabolical," he said, but gently.

He gave in to the temptation. He pulled her water-silky body close to his. He touched the wetness of her nose with the wetness of his.

"What are you doing?" he whispered.

"I never want you to forget this moment. Not ever. I love you. I want to marry you. I want to have your children. I want to swim naked with you and touch the stars with you.

"I want to be the best I can ever be, and I can't do that without you."

"I'm supposed to ask you to marry me, not the other way around."

"The days of you running the whole world are just over, Rory."

He thought about that. And felt something like relief. Still, he made one last halfhearted effort to show her the error of her ways.

"Grace, you don't know what you're getting into. You really don't."

She took his lips and he found the truth there. She knew exactly what she was getting into. Exactly. She knew him as well as he knew himself, possibly better. She knew his every strength and, even better, she knew his every weakness.

And she was still doing this.

"Actually, I really do," she said. "It might be you who doesn't have a clue what you're getting into."

He laughed and drew her yet closer, nuzzled the curve of her neck with his lips, felt the sensuality of her wet hair on his shoulder.

"You may be right, Gracie-Facie."

"Is that a yes?"

"Oh, yeah, baby, that's the biggest yes of my entire life."

EPILOGUE

RORY lay on his back and watched the stars wink on, one by one in a perfect indigo sky.

A loon called off the lake, that haunting, beautiful sound like no other.

Grace sighed beside him, nestled deeper into the crook of his arm.

A horse nickered softly, another stamped its feet. The bell of the lead mare jangled.

And then the sound of Slim's guitar.

"We should go back," she said. "The campfire is starting."

He twisted slightly, and sure enough sparks were beginning to shoot up behind them as the sky grew darker.

"We will. In a minute," he said.

"This is a good group," Grace said. "Maybe the best yet."

He laughed softly. "You said that last year."

It was the third year they'd been invited to join one of the Mountain Retreat Guest Ranch's excursions for the military families sent by Warrior Down on these adventure camping trips far, far from everything. This year, the schedule was so packed there were hardly enough days of summer. Slim would lead these wilderness adventures, day in and day out, until they could not squeeze one more ounce of time out of summer.

Serenity's voice rose, pure and true above all the others.

"Maybe it's because this is the first time she's been well enough to come that it feels so perfect," Grace said.

No, perfect would be when there were no more devastating illnesses.

No, perfect would be when there was no more war, no more families so in need of this respite from an uncertain world.

But he didn't say that.

Instead he contemplated the miracles around him. Once, he'd been a man who didn't believe in miracles.

But in the face of so much evidence?

Serenity for one. The doctors had not held out much hope for her when she had begun the treatment.

And they had nearly lost her a dozen times in that perilous year. Rory and Grace had been there for her and for Tucker, growing closer and closer, a family of the heart. When his mother was ill, Tucker lived with them, moving seamlessly between their houses.

And to Serenity's credit, she had dug deep and she had never given up. Rory had redefined courage when he had seen her Herculean struggle.

And somehow, through that terrible year of hardship, the real Serenity had emerged. Not hard. Not wild. Sensitive. Sweet.

Slim had fallen madly in love with her, but for the longest time she would have none of it.

Not because her health offered no guarantees, but because she couldn't believe a guy that squeaky clean, as she called him, wouldn't get tired of her.

Her extraordinary efforts to get rid of her suitor reminded Rory of him and Grace at the beginning.

Just like him, Serenity had not really believed that she deserved love.

And just like Grace, Slim had refused to let her believe it.

And so Slim and Serenity had married last year in a simple ceremony with just a few people and a whole lot of horses.

Tucker came now, out of the darkness, sighed with relief when he found them. He was twelve, stretching up the way twelve-year-olds do.

Tucker was not a normal twelve-year-old and Rory had come to understand he never would be.

He was a serious kid, always worried. He monitored his mother's wellness program with the tenacity and fierce devotion of a pit bull.

Now, he settled down on the ground beside Grace.

"Auntie, are you all right?"

Auntie.

Grace had wanted so desperately for her brother to go on. The funny thing was, that he had.

Even though this boy was no relation to them, Graham went on.

In Grace. In Rory. In every single person he had ever touched. In a tiny chance encounter with Serenity years ago, Graham went on. Who could look at this, all of them together, the stars in the night sky, Serenity's voice soaring higher than the stars, and not be convinced of the existence of miracles?

"I'm fine, Tucker, honey."

Out of the corner of his eye Rory saw her reach out and give Tucker's hand a quick hard squeeze.

"What if the baby comes tonight?" Tucker asked, not reassured.

She didn't tell him not to be silly, or that the baby was still more than a month away.

"Uncle Rory has his satellite phone set on speed dial for the helicopter."

Rory could sense the tension ease from those skinny shoulders.

"Remember, a long time ago when you asked me about a perfect day?" Tucker said.

"I remember."

"Who knew it could be better?"

Rory smiled to himself. It was true these mountain days were pure delight and the nights were so intensely beautiful your soul stood still.

But perfect?

Rory's perfect Day was lying beside him and, much as he enjoyed things like this, he had no sense of needing them.

No, perfect was glancing up from the newspaper to see her curled up in a chair engrossed in a book. Perfect was when she made a small fist with her hand and smacked his shoulder with mock annoyance. Perfect was her breathing beside him at night.

Perfect was that moment, nearly three years ago, when she had looked at him with shining eyes and said, "I do."

Perfect was this woman as his wife.

And now a baby, not completing their circle, expanding it.

That secret longing he had always had to belong to something, to find a purpose larger than himself had been found.

Once he had served war.

Now, he served love.

They could hear voices now, raised in song. The songs would begin like this; fast and rowdy, but as the evening grew chillier, the songs would grow more quiet, softer, slower.

Serenity's voice rose up above all the others: pure, perfect and impossibly angelic.

Rory turned his head slightly so that he could see Gracie's gorgeous profile silhouetted by the night.

Just as he had known she would be, Grace was crying, the tears trickling down her cheeks.

And he understood perfectly. He had long ago told her about the end of the dream that did not haunt him anymore.

This was Graham's legacy. Tucker was not his flesh and blood, but this was how he went on, nonetheless. What he had wanted more than anything had come true.

He had asked that his legacy be love.

And against all odds, it was exactly that.

Graham went on in the love.

Rory had a thought, reassuring to a man who had long since realized his power only went so far. He took Grace's hand more firmly.

And this is what he thought: *This is how we all go on, long after the light is extinguished, long after the last breath is drawn. In the love.*

* * * * *

"Gabby?" Caitlin stood behind her desk, leaning towards her young pupil. **"You know how I feel about notes being passed in my class."**

She watched confusion cross Gabby's face as she put the neatly folded piece of paper on her desk. "But it's for you."

Caitlin's eyebrows rose. "For me?"

Gabby giggled and ran back to her seat.

"Ten more minutes to finish your writing," Caitlin instructed, before sitting back down herself. "Then you can all share your stories with the class."

She carefully unfolded the paper and looked to the end of the letter as soon as she had it unfolded. *Tom*. His name was printed neatly, his handwriting bold and uniform, as she imagined he was at work.

For the first time since he'd walked out on her his name made her smile.

Caitlin looked up to make sure all the children were busy before letting her eyes rove back to the start. Her pulse started to race, her body tingling with…anticipation. She'd never been sent a letter by a man before.

Dear Caitlin

Gabby came home with a note in her bag last night and it made me think of you. I'm sorry for the way I behaved. Thank you for a lovely dinner and please don't think I'm some rude idiot with bad manners. My mum would kill me if she found out.

Meet me Saturday afternoon? I'd like to make it up to you if you don't mind giving me a second chance. Let's go hiking. I'll pick you up around 2 p.m.

Tom

Dear Reader,

I've always been fascinated with Navy SEALs. Their discipline, dedication and mental strength makes them perfect hero inspiration, and when you meet Tom Cartwright I'm sure you'll agree! He has all those attributes and more, although with a traumatic accident having ended his career he's also deeply troubled.

Finding an equally inspiring woman to complement Tom was no easy task. However, as soon as Caitlin Rose appeared on the page I knew she was the one. Caitlin is an upbeat woman who hasn't let her past hold her back— except when it comes to love.

I hope you enjoy reading about my gorgeous Navy SEAL as much as I enjoyed writing about him, and if you've read my previous book, *Back in the Soldier's Arm*s, you're in for a nice surprise. Tom made brief appearances as the hero's brother in that story, and I was so excited to be able to give Tom his own book! It's with a very heavy heart that I say goodbye to the Cartwright brothers.

Don't forget to visit me at my website www.sorayalane.com for more information about upcoming and past releases, and for behind the scenes "sneak peeks" of your favourite characters.

Enjoy!

Soraya

THE NAVY
SEAL'S BRIDE

BY
SORAYA LANE

First published in Great Britain 2012
by Mills & Boon, an imprint of Harlequin (UK) Limited,
Eton House, 18-24 Paradise Road, Richmond, Surrey TW9 1SR

© Soraya Lane 2012

ISBN: 978 0 263 89446 2
ebook ISBN: 978 1 408 97121 5

23-0712

Harlequin (UK) policy is to use papers that are natural, renewable and recyclable products and made from wood grown in sustainable forests. The logging and manufacturing processes conform to the legal environmental regulations of the country of origin.

Printed and bound in Spain
by Blackprint CPI, Barcelona

Writing for Mills & Boon® is truly a dream come true for **Soraya Lane**. An avid book reader and writer since her childhood, Soraya describes becoming a published author as "the best job in the world", and hopes to be writing heart-warming, emotional romances for many years to come.

Soraya lives with her own real-life hero on a small farm in New Zealand, surrounded by animals and with an office overlooking a field where their horses graze.

For more information about Soraya and her upcoming releases visit her at her website, www.sorayalane.com, her blog, www.sorayalane.blogspot.com, or follow her at www.facebook.com/SorayaLaneAuthor

This book is dedicated to two very special women. Firstly, my mom, for looking after my young son so I can write every day. Your love and support are invaluable, and I can't imagine how I'd ever find time to write without you! This book is also for Natalie, who is the most amazing friend. Where would I be without our daily chats? You are a talented author, a wonderful mother and the most inspiring friend. Thank you both for being such an incredible support team.

SAVE UP TO 25%

Subscribe to Cherish today and get 5 stories a month delivered to your door for 3, 6 or 12 months and gain up to 25% OFF! That's a fantastic saving of over £40!

MONTHS	FULL PRICE	YOUR PRICE	SAVING
3	£43.41	£36.90	15%
6	£86.82	£69.48	20%
12	£173.64	£130.20	25%

As a welcome gift we will also send you a FREE L'Occitane gift set worth £10

PLUS, by becoming a member you will also receive these additional benefits:

🌹 FREE Home Delivery

🌹 Receive new titles TWO MONTHS AHEAD of the shops

🌹 Exclusive Special Offers & Monthly Newsletter

🌹 Special Rewards Programme

No Obligation - You can cancel your subscription at any time by writing to us at Mills & Boon Book Club, PO Box 676, Richmond. TW9 1WU.

To subscribe, visit
millsandboon.co.uk/subscriptions

MILL
BOON

S2GI

CHAPTER ONE

TOM Cartwright sat slumped, his head bracketed by his palms. The hallway was oddly familiar, took him back years to when he was a schoolkid. All the times he'd sat outside the principal's office, trying to figure how to talk himself out of trouble.

He stifled a low groan.

The principal's office might be better than a room full of six-year-olds. How he'd been talked into doing this...

"Uncle Tommy?" Gabby's sweet, pure voice pulled him from his thoughts. She was standing in the doorway only a few feet away. She skipped over to him and tugged on his arm, her tiny hand dwarfed by his biceps. "Come on."

That's how.

Tom dropped a kiss to his niece's head before dragging his feet out from beneath him and standing. She didn't even reach his waist, but she slung her arm around him anyway.

"You look sad." Innocent eyes locked on his, looking up, and he did his best to convince her with a smile.

"Are you sure you want me to do this?"

Gabby rolled her eyes. "You're *way* more exciting than Mom and Dad. I've told the others *all* about you."

Tom found her hand and followed her to the classroom. He tried not to laugh. If only she understood what she was saying. "Gabby, your mom's a retired soldier and your dad was a Navy helicopter pilot. They're hardly boring."

She dismissed him, shrugging as only a kid could.

And just like that, after years of staying quiet about his career, of so fiercely protecting his identity, not wanting to put those he loved at risk, he was about to address a roomful of kids. To tell them a little about what he did, or what he used to do, all because a girl no taller than his hip had insisted he had to.

But he no longer had to keep his career close to his heart. He was free to talk about some of what he'd once done.

He leaned forward to open the door, waiting for Gabby to walk through before doing the same. Tom swallowed as he surveyed the room, looked at all the little kids sitting on the mat, waiting, fidgeting.

"What do we say?"

Tom turned his body to see where the voice was coming from.

Oh. He sure hadn't expected the woman standing behind her desk, the smile on her face so open and wide he was sure she must be directing it at someone else. Not at him.

"Good morning, Mr. Cartwright," the children sang out.

Gabby still held his hand, squeezing it as though she was trying to wring water from it.

They all sat looking back at him, cross-legged on the mat, curiosity plain on their faces.

"Ah…good morning," he said, prising his gaze from the woman before glancing at the class again.

She didn't make it easy though, his eyes, as if with a

mind of their own, being drawn back in her direction. The teacher's hair was drawn up into a swishy-looking ponytail, almost-black locks with a slight curl at the very end. Blue-green eyes seemed to smile at him, wide and happy.

Tom looked away. He wasn't used to being distracted, to finding his attention so easily diverted.

"Thanks for joining us, Mr. Cartwright," she said, her voice low and filled with warmth. "Gabriella's told us a lot about you and what you do."

Now it was he who fidgeted. Not because of the woman crossing the room toward him, but because it went against all his instincts to talk about his work. He tried to settle his rapidly racing heartbeat. Gabby was only six. How much could she even know about what he'd done?

"You must be Gabby's teacher," Tom asked, even though the answer was obvious, needing to say something before she thought he was mute.

There went the megawatt smile again.

"Miss Rose," she said before closing the distance between them and touching her hand to his forearm, leaning in ever so. "Or Caitlin, just not to the class." Her voice had dropped to a whisper, barely audible, as if she was letting him in on a tightly held secret.

Tom fought the urge not to take a step back, was conscious of all the little faces turned their way. He wasn't used to someone being in his space, had been trained to keep a distance in most situations. Had craved this kind of contact for so long that he'd forgotten what it felt like.

All the same, he was pleased that she was Miss Rose and not Mrs.

"Tom, please," he said, forcing a smile and wishing

it had come naturally. "Mr. Cartwright reminds me of my father."

And that was not something he liked to be reminded of.

"Well, Gabriella, I think it's time you introduced your uncle to the class."

Gabby beamed up at Tom as he touched his open palm to her hair, before scurrying off and standing tall and proud before her classmates.

"I did my project about my Uncle Tom because he's so interesting," she began. Tom nodded when she looked at him, as if needing his support. "He works for the United States Navy, but he doesn't go away anymore because now he teaches new…" Gabby's face flushed. She paused, clearly stuck.

A warm, soft breath touched close to Tom's cheek.

He jumped as it was followed by a gentle squeeze of his arm, words whispered near his ear. "I think she needs some help up there."

He thrust his hands in his pockets and crossed the room in four strides, wanting to rescue his niece from embarrassment but needing to put space between him and the pretty teacher, too. He'd spent too many years almost exclusively in the company of men to deal with that kind of sensory overload. She looked too good, smelled too good…hell, she even sounded too good for his liking!

"Recruits," he said, smiling at the children, pushing any thoughts of women aside. "I teach new recruits."

Gabby leaned into him and he let his arm fall around her. It didn't matter what happened, what *had* happened, she grounded him. Made everything right, showed him what was important. Made him realize that he had to suck up his pain and push past what was holding him back. What had stolen his career from him.

Made him want to stay strong.

"So," said Gabby, confidence returned, "Uncle Tom was a Navy SEAL, like as in a seal in the ocean!" She giggled and the other little people did the same. "But really it means…"

Tom took over again when she floundered, wanting her to enjoy her school project rather than be nervous.

"A SEAL is someone in the Navy's Sea, Air and Land team for special operations." The room went silent. Gabby plopped down to listen, and suddenly Tom felt like a fraud standing there, not knowing what to say or do.

He glanced at Caitlin, the teacher, with her kind smile. She leaned forward a little from where she stood against the wall, as if to encourage him.

Suddenly he was back in the classroom as a kid again, wanting to act out and be naughty because he didn't know what else to do.

Silly, because the man he'd become knew how to behave, how to take orders, do what was expected of him. And whether he was on active duty or not, he had no intention of letting the side down.

"Do you guys have any questions for me?" The last thing he wanted to do was stand up and talk about being a SEAL. Only the people closest to him had ever known his role, and even then he'd been selective about what he told them.

Now he'd retired, talking about it didn't come any easier.

A confident boy's voice piped up. "Is it true that most of you don't pass the training?"

Tom blew out a breath. He could have guessed the boys would have most of the questions, and that they'd want to know about the physical stuff. He rocked back on his heels, head turned slightly to the right in case the kid asked another question.

"All Navy SEALs have passed a tough training test," he said. "If you don't pass, you don't get in, simple as that. About eighty per cent of the guys who try out don't make it."

"What about the girls?"

Tom wasn't sure where that question had come from.

"Unfortunately there are no women in the SEALs yet," he said, "but that might change one day."

He watched as Gabby shrugged her shoulders. The girl next to her was pouting as though she was personally offended by his response.

"How hard is it?"

The same little boy again. Tom grinned at him, he couldn't help it. He would have been just like that at the same age, full of questions and curiosity. He'd dreaded coming today, but this was doing him good—making him feel less like a failure, as if he no longer held any value, and more like a worthwhile member of society. So long as he could keep his eyes off the brunette on the other side of the room.

Tom cleared his throat then crouched down on his haunches, at the same height as the children watching him. Gabby was cute, but this little guy had spunk and he liked to encourage kids.

"The toughest challenge is when you train for five days on no more than four hours sleep. Your body is so exhausted you don't know how you're going to keep putting one foot in front of the other. But you do. That's what makes a SEAL."

The boy asking the questions shuffled closer. It made other kids do the same; they were hanging on his every word.

"So it's kinda like being a superhero?" the boy asked.

Tom laughed, shaking his head and resisting the urge

to ruffle the boy's shaggy mop of blond hair. "Yeah, I guess. Only it's like you're going to die and you feel like…" He tapered off before saying the expletive that had nearly spilled. "Rubbish."

Temporary silence filled the room and Tom looked up. Miss Rose had remained quiet, to the side of the room, but now she walked toward him, smile still firmly in place.

And suddenly he couldn't take his eyes off her all over again.

"I think we should thank Mr. Cartwright for coming now," she said, gaze firmly on those in her charge.

A groan rang out around the room, but not obeying her clearly wasn't an option.

"Children?"

"Thank you, Mr. Cartwright," they said in singsong unison.

Except for that one little boy again. "What about the trident?"

Tom's head snapped up. "The trident?"

"Yeah, is it true you get one? Have you got it with you now? What's it look like?"

The kid sure knew his stuff. Tom had no idea how he knew so much.

"No," said Tom, before clarifying. "I mean no, I don't have it with me now, but I was given one."

He didn't know why, didn't know what made him do it, but he sought out Caitlin's eyes, locked his focus on her. "Most of the men I know have given their trident away with their heart. When they get married, they've given it to their brides on a gold chain."

Tom swallowed. Wished he wasn't looking at the woman who'd taken his mind off everything yet put his brain on high alert at the same time. He shouldn't have looked at her like that, didn't know why he'd even disclosed the importance of the trident. Not in that context.

"How sweet," she said, hands clasped together.

But Tom didn't miss the gentle pink blush that had crept up her neck and was curling toward her cheeks.

He should never have said it, not like that. Didn't know what had come over him.

He had nothing to offer a woman, not now. He didn't know who he was, how he would ever cope with what had happened to him, what he'd had to give up. He was lost.

Before, he'd have done anything to meet a woman as sweet and kind as he imagined Caitlin to be. Now, he was damaged, and he didn't want anyone else drawn into that web of pain with him.

No matter how darn cute her smile was.

Caitlin Rose faced her class and gave them her most serious of looks. "Gabby's in charge for a moment while I see our guest out," she instructed, knowing full well they'd erupt into chaos the minute she stepped out the door.

The truth was, she'd probably be better saying goodbye here, in front of the children. It was silly to walk out of the room with him.

But regardless of her worries, she was more polite than that. He'd volunteered his time and been sweet with the children.

She only wished she didn't have to look into those dark brown eyes that seemed to have caught on hers from the moment he'd walked into her classroom.

"Thanks for taking time out to talk to them," Caitlin said as she threw a final, stern look over her shoulder at the children. "It was very sweet of you."

Tom held the door and she ducked beneath his outstretched arm to emerge into the hallway. She wasn't used to that. To manners like that.

It had been a long time since she'd been in the company of a man, and even longer since one had treated her in that way. *With courtesy. Kindness.*

She felt him behind her, could sense there was something else he was waiting to say.

"It's weird for me, talking about the Navy like that." Honesty laced with uncertainty. "But Gabby wasn't exactly taking no for an answer."

Caitlin smiled—she couldn't help it. She might not be attracted to the whole tough-guy persona, but she could appreciate a man acknowledging that a kid held all the power. She liked his manners.

"I'm sure they loved having you here. It beats most of the other parents we've had," she told him, leaning against a locker as she stood facing him. He was at ease, feet shoulder-width apart, back effortlessly straight. "We usually have the odd doctor or even a lawyer, but a real-life Navy hero? Not often."

Caitlin felt the smile flee her face as soon as the expression changed in his eyes. They turned stormy, the brown suddenly looking like the black of a raging thundercloud.

"I'm not a hero." It sounded as though he had to bite down on his words to force them out. He didn't look at ease any longer, his stance appearing fierce, displaying the edge of a temper.

Goose pimples sent a trail across her skin. "I can tell Gabby's very proud of you," she said, changing the subject and ready to back off. This wasn't a situation she was prepared to be drawn into. "Thanks for coming in, I hope we meet again sometime."

Caitlin turned before he had a chance to answer.

He might be handsome and kind to his niece, but she'd sensed something in him then she didn't ever want to be witness to again.

She'd grown up with a military man for a father. Her one and only serious boyfriend had been a Marine. And they'd both known only one way to prove their point, to get what they wanted.

As far as she was concerned, big strong men had one thing in common, and their *strength* wasn't something she'd ever fall for. Not again.

Caitlin stole a quick breath before pushing the door open and facing the kids again, knowing it would take her twice as long as she'd been out of the room to quieten them down.

Caitlin glanced over her shoulder to find Tom still standing there, his shoulders bearing the faintest droop.

But his eyes were still on her. Blazing.

She averted her gaze and walked into the room.

He might be attractive, but she wasn't interested. Not in the least.

She was a teacher. She was happy on her own. *Satisfied* on her own.

And the last man she'd want if she did decide to let someone in was a Navy SEAL. Even a former one. Because his height, the breadth of his shoulders, the darkness of his eyes…it told her enough.

He just wasn't her type. Period.

It took Tom a moment to kick into gear, but it was a moment of hesitation that took him by surprise.

He never hesitated.

But the look on Caitlin's face had been like a blade through his stomach, had repulsed him. *Because he wasn't that guy.*

He never snapped at women. Never let his emotions get the better of him.

But ever since he'd been back, he hardly even recognized himself. If it weren't for Gabby he'd have sunk into a darkness that was still lingering on the edge of his mind.

Because all he could think of whenever anyone called him a hero or made him remember his last days as a SEAL was that he'd failed. That he'd turned into a man he'd never wanted to become.

Never leave a man behind. That was their motto, words that were so true to him they were like the beat of his own heart.

And not only had he been forced to leave one of their own behind, he'd left his career behind, too. Because he'd put himself in the line of fire and it was a risk he should never have taken. Something he'd pay for for the rest of his life.

The acrid smell swirled around him, made him drift back to consciousness. He tried to lift his head, tried to shake it, wanted to know why there was a high-pitched scream echoing through his head.

His hand shook, but his head wouldn't move. When it did, when he regained control of his body, what he saw made him wish he'd stopped breathing and never had to witness the carnage that surrounded him.

Tom shuddered.

He hated the word *hero* more than a tomboy hated a dress.

Even when it came from the lips of a woman so beautiful, so obviously genuine and all things good.

Tom whirled around and stormed down the hallway,

back the way he'd come in. Right now, he had to get back to work. Had to do *something*. Because the busier he kept himself, the easier it was to forget.

CHAPTER TWO

CAITLIN stretched, watching herself in the mirror as she went through her routine. The movements were as natural to her as walking, but she never tired of them. In less than ten minutes her class would arrive, tiny girls full of chatter and squeals, but for now the studio was quiet and she could indulge in a moment of silence.

There had been a time when she'd imagined ballet would be her life, but now it was like a long-lost love. Movements her muscles would never forget, a craft she'd always respect for the self-discipline it had taught her.

"Sorry we're a little early."

Caitlin turned, her stretches forgotten. A mom was standing with her perfectly attired daughter beside her. "No problem, I was only warming up."

She ushered her student in and took a deep breath as she glanced out the window and saw the other cars pulling up. But the outline of one parent made her fingers curl around the blind, holding it in place so she could keep watching the road.

Only he wasn't technically a parent.

Mr. Navy SEAL himself was leaning against the hood of a large 4x4. Long denim-clad legs stretched out, arms folded to show off golden skin and eye-raising biceps protruding from a crisp white T-shirt. She could see

Gabby jumping up and down, holding hands with a little friend.

Caitlin let the blind go and stepped back. What the hell was she doing ogling him?

"Miss Rose?"

A shy voice made her turn, distracted her, but her eyes were still begging to flick back to the window, no matter how much her brain tried to argue.

"Miss Rose?"

"Two minutes class, then we'll start," she instructed, beaming smile locked in place as she addressed the girls. "You may start your stretches."

Caitlin surveyed the room and touched a child on the back as she passed, trying to keep herself busy. She didn't know why she was giving the man even a second thought, but something about him was pulling her like a magnet to metal. The flicker of kindness in his eye when he looked at his niece, the determined fix of his jaw as he'd stood listening in class today.

But there was a very valid reason she didn't date tough guys, and he definitely fell into that category. Because she knew firsthand that physical strength didn't necessarily mean the guy was built only to protect you. She'd already learned that the hard way.

Tom ran his hands over his hair, still surprised to feel the length of it. He'd always kept it close to buzzed off, but now that he wasn't on active duty, he'd let it grow out.

"Are you going to stay?" Gabby's face was turned up to him.

He dropped his hand to her hair, stroking her forehead with his thumb. "Sure thing, kiddo."

She skipped off and into the building, and Tom was left walking on his own. There weren't many other parents there, just a few moms standing in clusters inside, no doubt gossiping, so he headed for the door. Thought he might watch for a…

Wow.

The tiny ballerinas in a sea of pink surrounded their teacher. She was dressed in skintight black leggings and the palest of pink tops crossed over her breasts and tied at the back. She was pointing her toes, asking the giggling girls to do the same.

He'd had no idea that she was the schoolteacher *and* the dance teacher.

And he might have sat in the waiting area and kept his eyes off her had he known.

"I haven't seen you here before."

Tom turned, dragged his gaze from the all too distracting Miss Rose. "Sorry?"

He locked eyes with a middle-aged mom sipping from a paper coffee cup. "I just said that I haven't seen you here before, and we don't get many dads, so I'm sure I'd remember."

"Ah, I'm Tom," he introduced himself, still fighting the pull to glance back into the studio. "I'm looking after my niece."

The woman held out her hand and clasped his warmly. "Then that's why I didn't recognize you."

He rocked back on his heels, wished he'd dropped Gabby off and come back to collect her instead of waiting. He didn't exactly enjoy small talk.

"Not married, or do you just not like to wear a ring?"

Oh, hell. This was definitely the kind of small talk he didn't like to engage in.

"Single," he said, the smile leaving his face. He didn't take kindly to being interrogated. Never had, never would.

The woman didn't look at all as if she'd picked up on his *leave me alone* signs, either.

"Well then, I guess you're allowed to check out the teacher."

Heat hit Tom's cheeks before he could fight it. Jeez, had he been that obvious?

"You must be mistaken," he said, voice cool. "I was watching my niece. She asked me to stay within sight."

The mom looked confused, but Tom didn't change the expression on his face. He'd been trained not to betray a hint of weakness, and here he was mooning over a pretty girl as though he'd never seen an attractive member of the opposite sex before. Sure, she was beautiful, but he wasn't in the market for a relationship, and he didn't want to be called out like that again. The last thing he needed was to hurt the feelings of a fragile paper ballerina who doubled as his niece's teacher.

"Nice to meet you," Tom said, turning his back and putting an end to the conversation.

He crossed the room and sank onto a chair, but he still couldn't look away. Because even from there, he could see through the door to the happiness and laughter in the studio. Gabby danced around as if she couldn't think of anywhere better to be in the world, and the mesmerizing Miss Rose twirled about amongst the girls as if she was loving every minute of it.

And she probably was. Darkness clawed its way into his chest and threatened to sink its teeth into him, but he steeled his jaw and fought it, pushed the haunting clouds of memory away.

Just because he was troubled didn't mean everyone else around him had to be miserable. He'd gone through hell, but he'd emerged alive, and he wasn't going to let anything drag him down.

Or at least he wasn't going to be pulled any further into the web of emptiness than he'd already allowed himself to be.

Tom was struggling not to zone out. He'd never tried so hard in his life to focus, had never paid anyone so much attention in his life, but still…Gabby was talking a million miles an hour and it was hard to keep up.

"So, did you see me? Did you see how fast I can twirl? Were you watching when…"

He didn't hear another word. Lost the fight to stay tuned in to what she was saying.

Because a slender frame, braced against the cool autumn wind with only a flimsy coat around her, appeared in his rearview mirror. Ankles bare and peeking out from skintight black leggings, but with her hair out and wrapping around her face; a contrast to the tight bun she'd had it pulled back in before.

"Tommy?" Gabby had just figured out he wasn't listening. He had no idea what she'd been saying. All he could focus on was the slim figure retreating from view.

And he didn't like it. Didn't like it one little bit.

"I'm sorry, honey, hold that thought." He gave her a quick smile, not sure whether he was trying to reassure her or himself. "Buckle up, there's something I need to do."

Tom thrust the key into the ignition, waited until he heard Gabby's belt click, then checked in his mirrors before doing a U-turn. Caitlin hadn't gotten far, had just turned the corner into the next block.

He ran his tongue over his teeth. His mouth was dry. And he couldn't figure out what the hell he was going to say when he pulled over. Didn't want to appear to be a sleaze-hanging-out-the-window-and-trying-to-convince-the-girl-to-get-in kind of guy.

"Is that Miss Rose?" Gabby burst through his thoughts again the way she always did.

"She looks cold. Don't you think she looks cold?" Tom asked, needing the kid to agree with him.

Gabby met his gaze, the smile in her eyes settling him. "I guess."

"I think she does. How about we offer her a ride home?" Tom asked her.

His pint-size passenger shrugged. "Okay."

Tom didn't need any further encouragement. He slowed the car to a crawl and pulled up to the curb, lowering his window at the same time.

Caitlin looked back, a frown line creasing the smooth skin of her face, and picked up her pace.

Damn. He'd done exactly what he'd hoped not to do. Tom leaped from the car and called over the hood, not wanting to frighten her any more than he already had.

"Caitlin!" he called. "You need a ride home?"

This time when she turned the beaming smile was back. Tom hadn't realized he was holding his breath until he saw that, was pleased she'd recognized him straight away. She held her bag clutched under one arm, was holding her hair with the other to keep it from her face.

"You scared me before."

He walked around the front of the car and gestured to the passenger side. "Can we give you a ride? It's too cold to walk." Tom could tell she was thinking about it. "Please."

He'd negotiated enough to know when someone was about to say yes, but he still didn't take it for granted. Tom turned his back and opened the door.

"Scoot, kidlet," he said to Gabby.

She obliged, scrambling into the backseat and leaving the front free.

He rocked back on his heels and smiled. Didn't find it so hard to do this time because it came more naturally. "Jump in."

Caitlin nodded, before walking briskly to the car. She paused, looked nervous, before slipping past him and onto the seat. "Thanks."

Tom shut the door behind her and walked around the back of the car this time. Took a moment to touch the cool metal of the trunk as he sucked back a breath and prepared to get in the car with a woman who was doing strange things to him. Making him yearn for things that weren't within his grasp any longer.

But this was just a car ride. This was just him taking his niece's teacher home. Nothing to get all hot under the collar about. Even he wasn't capable of screwing this up.

Tom jumped behind the wheel and buckled up. "Do you always walk home in the freezing cold?"

She responded with a laugh that settled every bone in his body.

"No," she said, leaning back into the headrest and angling her face to peer back at Gabby. "My car's at the shop and I thought the exercise would do me good. Are you sure it's no problem to drive me?"

He took his eyes off the road for a beat and glanced at her. "No problem. The last thing I need is Gabby coming home and telling me her teacher is off sick because I was too careless to stop and offer her a lift."

Caitlin grinned at him before brushing her fingers over his arm in the most casual of ways. As though she was used to touching him, as though it was something she did often.

Tom kept his eyes on the road and wrapped his right

hand tighter around the wheel. He wasn't used to contact like that. Aside from Gabby, and maybe his sister-in-law, no one usually touched him. Almost all his adult life he'd had to be strong, physical, brave—and with that came a solitary life most of the time.

"Well, it was very kind of you to stop."

He'd stopped in more way than one. Her skin against his had near stopped his brain from processing.

Caitlin tried to relax but her heart was skipping erratically. She hoped Tom didn't pick up on it.

Hadn't she heard something about guys like him, trained so carefully for special operations? That they could feel a heartbeat and know instinctively whether someone was lying or not? If they were dishonest? That's what the kids had told her, years ago, in one of her past lives. She'd moved so much as an army kid that she found it hard to remember sometimes.

She wasn't lying about anything, but the thumping of her pulse racing was signaling that something was affecting her. And she didn't want him to know her nerves were on edge.

"So tell me how you ended up staying with your uncle Tom?" Caitlin decided it was safer to direct questions at Gabby. She'd be in less risk of getting hot and bothered.

"Mom and Dad are away." Gabby's voice was like a lullaby, a soft melody that spoke only of happiness. Caitlin loved teaching children like Gabby, when she knew instinctively that they were happy at home, that they were safe and loved.

Tom caught her eye, before he was focused on the road again. "They're on a second honeymoon."

Catlin laughed at the way he rolled his eyes. "Did they renew their vows?"

Gabby piped up then. "Daddy gave Mommy her rings back, plus a special new one that's all sparkly, and they keep kissing. *All the time*."

Tom and Caitlin both laughed out aloud.

"Okay, *what?*" she asked, suddenly not quite so nervous of making eye contact with Tom.

"Believe me, it's a long story, but the short version of it is that Penny came back from serving overseas and Daniel did everything he could to prove that he was worth coming home to."

Caitlin had questions, but she wasn't going to ask now. "Sounds romantic."

She watched as Tom flicked the fingers of his left hand against the wheel. "Yeah, they're kind of cute."

Caitlin watched him, suddenly unable to stop staring at him.

"If they don't make you sick first with all the loved-up antics," he added.

She laughed. Truly laughed, liking the way his mouth kinked up when he grinned back at her, as if he was trying to be serious and struggling.

"So that's why you're looking after Gabby?"

She watched as Tom's lips parted, only to be interrupted by his niece. "Grandma is away already and so they weren't going to go, but then Tommy came home and he said he'd have me."

Caitlin got the feeling that Tom didn't mind being spoken for. He was friendly, sure, but he wasn't exactly bursting to talk. Was probably more comfortable being the quiet guy.

"Well, aren't you lucky having an uncle to look after you?"

Tom looked serious, but she could tell he was comfortable in his role as uncle. Probably liked playing protector. Maybe she'd lumped him into the same category as other military-type tough guys too quickly. Perhaps he *was* kind, and didn't misuse his physical strength or abilities. He sure seemed fond of Gabby; that kind of behavior was impossible to fake. She'd been around children and parents enough to know that for sure. Not to mention the way Gabby treated him, as if he was her placid Labrador puppy, jumping to her every command.

But still, it didn't change the way she thought. There was no room in her mind or her heart to take any risks where men were concerned.

"Hey, Tommy?" Gabby asked from the backseat.

Caitlin watched as his eyebrows rose, waiting for the question that was sure to follow.

"Yeah?" he asked back.

"I think you promised that I could have ice cream before dinner tonight." Gabby was giggling now, looking at him in the rearview mirror.

Tom put on a stern face. Gabby was still laughing, but Caitlin wasn't convinced, and didn't know what was going on.

He pulled over, before turning in his seat and staring long and hard at Gabby.

"Did I or did I not tell you to keep that a secret?" he demanded, voice low and gravelly. "Gabby Cartwright, answer me this minute!"

Caitlin's heart started to pound in fright; her hands became clammy. She was trapped, felt that she couldn't move, wasn't in control. Wanted to do something and was paralyzed from action.

"Gabby?" he growled.

A high-pitched trill of laughter filled the car, verging on squealing. "Tommy!"

Tom pulled a face before opening his door, but not

before he grinned at Caitlin. "I know you're her teacher and you're probably going to tell me off, but I did promise her ice cream before dinner. You know, trying to be the favorite uncle and all."

"You're my only uncle, Tommy," Gabby piped up.

Caitlin nodded, it was all she could do. Tried to make her relieved smile appear stronger than it felt, needing a moment to let blood pump back through her leeched-dry veins.

Gabby and Tommy got out of the car, but it wasn't until he opened her door that she followed—prised her fingers from the seat and forced her legs to cooperate.

They were at the ice cream shop. She turned her head slowly, could see the pink lettering glittering in the near-dark. But her heart was still pounding.

She knew it was stupid—she could see them holding hands, was watching as Tom poked at Gabby and had her leaping around and laughing, but for a moment there she'd almost lost it.

Because she hadn't known they were joking around. Had thought she was about to witness something she didn't ever want to see again.

Because she knew firsthand what it felt like to be spoken to like that, only without the laughter and jokes at the end.

When it had happened to her, that kind of seriousness, that type of conversation had never ended in ice cream.

"Caitlin?" Tom looked concerned. Gabby was watching her, too. "You all right?"

She closed the car door and fixed her smile again. "Sorry, I was a million miles away."

Tom slung his arm around his niece and waited for her to catch up. "My shout."

And just like that, Caitlin found herself having ice

cream before dinner with a man she'd thought this morning that she'd never see again, and one of her favorite little students.

Tom passed Gabby her ice cream before reaching for the single scoop of chocolate Caitlin had ordered. "Enjoy."

Her fingers brushed his as she took it from him. "I can't believe you two talked me into this."

Tom liked her smile, liked the fact that nothing about her seemed put on. "Believe me…the things that this girl makes me do."

Gabby was licking furiously at her ice cream, completely ignoring him.

"It's nice that you're so close to her."

That made him look up. "She's pretty special to me, to all of us."

Caitlin waited. He liked that about her, too, that she didn't feel the need to press for information like some people did. He hated being quizzed when he didn't want to talk about something, but he was finding with her that he was opening his mouth and spilling his stories before he even had a chance to think about it.

That needed to stop.

"We kind of made a pact, the three of us, when Gabby was born," he told her. It wasn't something they ever spoke about, had never needed to talk about again, because they were all committed to making sure she was the happiest little girl around. "There was a time when Gabby's mom and dad both had to serve at the same time, and I was always there to step in, although her grandmother, my mom, she's great with her, too."

"Were you scared something would happen to them? That she could end up with—" Caitlin paused and lowered her voice, although Gabby was walking far enough ahead not to hear their conversation "—no parents?"

Tom felt a catch in his throat. "Yeah."

Caitlin's fingers fell over his forearm, rested there for a moment as they walked. "You're very brave, Tom."

He forced himself to look up. Not to shrug away the contact until she let her hand fall away of its own accord, not to recoil at her words. He sure as hell didn't feel like he deserved the *brave* tag.

"Do you mean for serving in the Navy or for looking after her?" He had to ask, had to know what she was thinking.

Caitlin's eyes met his, her gaze fluttering as if she found it difficult to hold the contact. "Both. But what I meant was that not many men are that committed to a child, especially to a niece or nephew." She blew out a breath. "Hell, half the dads I meet seem to be less committed to their own children."

Tom relaxed, was pleased they were still talking about kids, that she hadn't tried to flip the subject back to his work. *To that kind of bravery.*

Caitlin looked fragile enough to snap beneath the weight of harsh words, and he didn't exactly find it easy to bite his tongue these days. Not when it came to his work or what had happened to end his career.

"There was always the chance that one of us wouldn't make it home," he told Caitlin, suddenly wanting to talk, wanting to get the words off his chest. "I wanted my brother to know that I'd always step in, wouldn't hesitate to fill his shoes if I had to. And Penny—" He paused, not able to help but smile. "Penny's like the sister I never had. She's pretty special to me."

His eyes darted back to Caitlin, to see the look on her face, needing to see her reaction. The response was warm, a soft acknowledgment by way of a gentle blink, a curve of her lips in one corner, before she turned her attention back to her ice cream.

Tom didn't know why, or how, but there was something about Gabby's teacher that was pulling him in, reeling him like a fish resigned to being caught on a line. Maybe it was just because she was so good at her job, was skilled at playing the kind, caring teacher, at getting people to open up.

But something else, some whisper of a voice in his mind, told him that her being a teacher had nothing to do with it.

That he needed to back off now if he ever wanted a chance of escape.

Caitlin didn't like to be confused. Ever. And tonight she was more confused than she'd ever been.

Tom was being sweet, kind…verging on downright charming, but she had no idea where he was going with it. Was he trying to impress her? She didn't think so. Or maybe she just didn't *want* it to be so.

There was something about him that unnerved her, that was rattling her like a key chain blowing in the wind, but she couldn't put her finger on it. He was troubled, sure. There were things he was obviously holding tight to his chest. But he was honest, she'd give him that. From the expression she'd seen more than once in his eyes, from the way he looked at Gabby, she doubted he was any good at lying.

Although maybe that was just a by-product of his special-forces training. After all, she didn't exactly have a great track record when it came to judging men.

"Penny for them?"

She laughed at his old-fashioned saying. "You caught me dreaming again."

He opened the back door for Gabby, and then the front one for her. Caitlin wasn't even sure a guy had ever opened a door for her before and yet Tom was already making a habit of it.

"You sure it's okay to take me all the way home?"

His eyebrows nudged together as he frowned. "Like I'm gonna buy you an ice cream then make you find your own way to your place?"

Caitlin laughed. His expression was so comical she couldn't do anything *but* laugh. "Okay, okay. I don't like being a burden, that's all."

From the look on his face, he didn't think she was a burden.

And from the look of it, he was struggling with what to say, how to behave, as much as she was. Could he honestly be as unused to attention from the opposite sex as she was? Caitlin sure doubted it. She'd perfected her look, a *back-off* way of staring at guys who so much as threatened to show interest in her. Tom's body language was closed, but he sure didn't have a *stay-away* vibe, not in that way.

"Miss Rose, do you have a husband?"

Caitlin coughed, tried not to inhale ice cream up her nose as she spluttered. Where the heck had *that* question come from?

"Gabby!" Tom scolded. "That's not a polite question."

Caitlin didn't turn to look, couldn't even brave a glance at Tom. But she wasn't going to let Gabby get in trouble for being inquisitive. Didn't she always tell her class the importance of asking questions? Maybe she needed to remind them of what types of questions were appropriate, though!

"It's fine, Tom. It doesn't matter."

"So *do* you?" Gabby asked.

"Gabriella!" Tom's voice boomed through the car.

No, thought Caitlin. No, she didn't. But the thought of saying that in front of Tom scared her, made her want to wrench the car door open and run. Because she'd built a fort around herself, never made herself available in any way, and she sure as heck wasn't ready for that to change.

"Sorry," Gabby said, sounding unsure why she had to apologize. "It's just that Tommy doesn't have a wife and Mommy is always saying that he needs a 'nice girl to settle down with.'"

Caitlin fought the urge not to laugh at Gabby's put-on voice and failed miserably. One look at Tom and he was in hysterics, too, laughter ringing through the car. Jokes she could handle. Jokes were safe.

"A nice girl, huh?" She couldn't stop the smirk that settled on her face when she found her voice again.

Tom glared at her, but that only made them both laugh again. "Don't kids say the darnedest things?" Only this time his gaze hinted at a seriousness below the surface, and she wondered if Tom was after a nice girl, or if it was just his sister-in-law wanting him to find one.

Either way, it meant nothing to her. She wasn't interested in a relationship, and Tom wasn't her type.

What she couldn't understand was why talking about Tom like that had sent an itch under her skin that she couldn't dislodge.

CHAPTER THREE

"So you're telling me that nothing happened?"

Caitlin sighed into the lukewarm coffee she was nursing. "Correct."

Her friend and fellow teacher sighed dramatically. "Look me in the eye and tell me," Lucy demanded.

Caitlin wasn't lying. She was dreadful at keeping secrets, but she was guilty of one thing.

"I promise nothing happened," she said, raising her eyes and shrugging. "Seriously."

Lucy tucked her legs up beneath her, curled like a cat on the sofa. "But you *wanted* something to happen, right?"

Heat burst onto Caitlin's cheeks as she sipped her now almost-cold coffee, trying to avoid Lucy's gaze. "I agree that he's kind of cute, but he's not really my type. And seriously, Lucy, what was going to happen in a class full of six-year-olds?"

The groan she received in response told her she'd given the wrong answer.

"He's every girl's type, Caitlin." Lucy stood up and stretched. "Either you've got rocks in your head or you've gone blind. I saw him leave your class yesterday and he's hot, hot, hot." Lucy waggled her eyebrows suggestively. "Don't give me that rubbish about being in a classroom either, because I know you walked him out. It's about time you gave a guy a shot. One day you might just surprise yourself."

Okay, so Tom was hot. Gorgeous in fact. Sexy as hell. But it still didn't mean she was capable of liking him in that way. And if he'd been interested in her, surely he'd have made a move by now? Guys like Tom were used to playing the game, knew how to attract a girl and how to reel her in.

Which was another reason she wasn't interested in him.

"I've got to get back to class," Caitlin said, raising her fingers in a wave and scurrying toward the door. "And *nothing* happened, okay? I mean, jeez, I only just met the man. I was hardly going to jump him in the hall!"

"Admit it, Miss Rose," Lucy called out, voice all prim and proper. "There's nothing about him not to like and you know it."

She ignored Lucy and kept on walking. That part her friend was wrong about. Caitlin had perfectly good reasons for not being interested in Tom, for wanting to keep her distance from him, she just had no intention of sharing them. Of delving into the past and letting those feelings resurface.

Not now.

Besides, she was happy. Liked her life the way it was. If a man came along to tempt her, he'd have to be perfect husband material. And Tom Cartwright sure as heck didn't fit the bill.

"Miss Rose, Miss Rose!"

She looked up to find a little girl from her class jumping up and down in the hallway. "Honey, what's wrong?" Caitlin bent to talk to her, preferring to be on the same level as the children.

"Sarah fell over in the playground and hurt her knee. She's crying."

Caitlin took the girl's hand and let herself be led outside. "You did the right thing, sweetheart, let's go find her."

Tom found it hard to indulge in the simpleness of guzzling water on a hot day. He'd spent so long rationing every sip, being so careful to preserve what he'd come to think of as his lifeline. Yet here he was, back on American soil, gulping water as though he had an endless supply of it.

He stopped and wiped his mouth with the back of his hand.

It suddenly hit him as if he'd been slammed into a wall—a solid, massive brick wall.

He *was* back for good. There were no more rations, no more missions. *Nada.* He was back now and he had to lump it or leave it. Or however the hell that saying went.

"Sir?"

Tom turned, bottle almost squashed in his hand, the plastic pressed tight between his fingers. He paused, wanting to calm down before he risked snapping unnecessarily at his pupil. Just because he hadn't been able to sleep last night didn't mean he could take it out on anyone else.

"Yes?" He fought not to glare. The poor kid was suffering enough through his training without him being an ass, as well.

"Sir, I saw your name on the board and the guys wanted me to ask if it was you."

Tom nodded, a tick starting to pulse at this temple. He could feel it, like a pressure point, thumping away. "Yes, that's me."

He'd taken the top honors in the water for his year. Had been in the top five percent consistently, one of the strongest of the bunch in all their training. Tom raised a hand to his ear as he so often did these days, rubbing, worrying it. Self-conscious of his hearing, he angled his body further to make sure he could hear the young man without having to ask him to repeat himself.

If he hadn't been so close to the explosion, hadn't suffered such damage to his eardrum he'd still be in the water instead of being on the sidelines with nothing to do other than coach others, encouraging them to do the same.

"You sure set the bar high, sir."

Tom smiled as the young man walked back off to his buddies. A giant's fist clenched around his throat, squeezing the lifeblood from him as he watched the group of men bond, knowing how close they'd become, those that made it.

It was something he'd miss for the rest of his life, but he was going to have to get used to it.

Because the doctor had been pretty clear about his prognosis. He could still go permanently deaf in one ear, and he'd never be able to get in the water again. Or at least not in the way he had to be able to in order to pass his physical.

It was over. Period. Something else he'd have to get used to.

"Okay, boys, break's over. Back in the pool," Tom barked. He also needed to stop playing Mr. Nice Guy. If these men were going to make it, they had to be the toughest of the tough. He knew that firsthand. "Unless you're prepared to break my record or come damn close, you can expect a long night."

Groans echoed out.

"Do I hear a 'Yes, sir'?" he boomed.

"Yes, sir!" came an even louder response.

"That's more like it. Now get in the water!" Tom ordered.

Tom folded his arms and fingered the whistle hanging around his neck. If he couldn't be out there himself, he was going to make darn sure he trained the best Navy SEALs ever to graduate from the academy.

Tom was starting to wish he hadn't been such a demon to his training team when they were still in the water two hours later. He was also starting to think that perhaps none of them were going to make the cut. Because they hadn't left the pool yet and they still had hours to go.

"Come on!" he ordered. "Push yourselves. You can do this!"

He waved over another training officer over who'd clearly finished for the day. "Can you watch these guys for me? I have to make an urgent call."

Tom gave his colleague a quick pat on the back and jogged into the office. He looked up the school number, glanced at his watch and dialed.

But all the bravado in the world wasn't helping his nerves any. The hand holding the phone went clammy, he couldn't stop fidgeting.

He didn't know what the hell was happening to him. Why his usual nerves of steel and unflappable attitude were failing him now. But he wasn't going to let a woman rattle him.

Not a pretty wisp of a teacher who could be blown off her feet in a strong gust of wind, who'd looked so vulnerable the other night that he'd struggled not to soften. Found it hard not to let her in.

Because he wasn't that guy anymore. He didn't have

the strength to deal with his own problems, so he certainly didn't have anything to give a woman, and he didn't want to have to explain himself. Or hurt anyone else, let anyone else close, and then expose them to the demons that kept him awake at night.

"Brownwood Elementary School."

Tom cleared his throat and made a fist, pressing it hard into the desk. "I'm sorry to call during school hours, but I need to speak to Miss Caitlin Rose."

Caitlin nodded to the office lady and walked quickly down the hall. It wasn't often she had to disrupt her lessons to take a phone call.

"Hello?" she pressed the telephone to her ear, dread crawling in her belly.

"Caitlin? It's Tom."

She didn't know whether to be relieved or terrified! A ripple of goose pimples tingled across her skin. "Hi, Tom. Is…ah, everything okay?" Why was he phoning her during school hours?

There was silence, followed by the deep rumble of his voice. "Yeah, everything's okay, it's just that I'm not going to make it to pick Gabby up and I don't have anyone else to phone."

Oh. Caitlin ignored her feelings, kicking herself for hoping, even for the tiniest of seconds, that he might have been phoning her for something else. He'd hardly call her during class time to ask her out on a date!

"Caitlin?"

She had no idea what he might have said. "Sorry, Tom, I was listening to one of the children." Caitlin cringed. She was a dreadful liar, surely he'd know she was fibbing?

"You wouldn't be able to watch her for an hour or so,

would you? I'm not going to be able to get away early and I don't know what else to do."

Caitlin relaxed, forced her shoulders to fall from their hunched position. "Of course. It's no problem at all."

"Are you sure? I hate having to ask you."

She started nodding before realizing that he couldn't see her. "Honestly, don't even think about it." She paused, knowing she had to end the call yet reluctant to say goodbye. "I'll take her home with me if that's okay? Save me hanging around here, then you don't have to hurry."

"I really appreciate it, Caitlin. I owe you."

They said goodbye and she placed the receiver down carefully, before leaning against the wall and shutting her eyes, needing a moment to herself. Needing to think about what she'd said yes to, about the fact that she'd just invited Tom to her home. Sure, it was only to collect Gabby, but home was…well, until now it had been private. Sacred.

She'd never, ever invited a man there. Yet right now, without even being pushed into it, she'd told Tom to collect his niece from her place.

And there wasn't a doubt in her mind that she'd be asking him in. No matter how hard her heart was pounding at the thought of it.

She'd always known the day would come, but it still troubled her. Her privacy—being alone—had been her sanctuary, the only way she knew how to protect herself, to stay out of harm's reach.

CHAPTER FOUR

CAITLIN peered out the window, then berated herself for doing it. There was no point waiting, mooning around. He was coming to collect his niece, not to see her.

She looked up as the timer on the oven rang out.

So if she wasn't trying to impress him, thinking of ways to lure him in, why had she scooted home to make lasagna as if her life depended on it?

So much for being committed to keeping guys out of her domain.

"Miss Rose, look at him now!"

Caitlin crossed the room and fell onto the sofa beside Gabby. "I think he likes you."

She watched her patient, kind-natured Burmese cat as he stretched out in Gabby's arms, paws swatting at the little girl but meaning her no harm. She knew he'd never show his claws.

"I'd love a pet." Gabby sighed dramatically.

"They're a lot of work you know," said Caitlin, reaching over to stroke Smokey. "You need to feed them and love them every day, and if you get a dog you need to walk it, too."

Gabby rolled her eyes, but she didn't let the cat go and she was still smiling. "You sound just like my mom."

"Well then, your mom must be a very smart woman."

A knock echoed through the living room and Caitlin jumped. Jeez, just when she forgot that she was waiting for someone. The loud knock rang out again.

"Coming!" she called.

Gabby stretched out on the sofa, Smokey curled up against her belly. "Tommy *always* knocks like that. My mom says it like he's always in a hurry and can't wait for even a moment."

Caitlin didn't turn around when Gabby spoke, was too busy rushing to the door and running her hands over her jeans to answer.

Because no matter what Gabby's mommy said, Caitlin guessed *she* never felt like this when Tom was knocking at the door. And Caitlin didn't want him to be in a hurry, she wanted him to stay.

She didn't know why, she just did. Even if she was nervous as hell.

Caitlin pulled the door back and found a rumpled-looking Tom standing on her porch.

"Hey," she said, as though seeing him there was the most natural thing in the world.

"Hey," he replied, running a hand through hair that looked as if he'd just fallen out of bed. "Sorry I'm so late."

Caitlin took a step back, gesturing with one hand. "Come on in."

He hesitated, shoved his hands in the pockets of his jeans. "I don't want to put you out, Caitlin, so we'll head straight home."

"But Miss Rose made us dinner," Gabby called out.

Caitlin shut her eyes for a beat before forcing a smile on her face, trying to stop her hand from shaking, from trembling. She'd never been so pleased for a child to interrupt a conversation in her life, and she'd never felt like she'd held her breath for so long, either.

Tom raised an eyebrow, his head on the slightest of angles. "You cooked for us?"

Caitlin swallowed. "Yeah," she said softly, "but it's just lasagna…"

"*Just* lasagna?" Tom was grinning now, one hand falling from his pocket to rest on the doorjamb. "On second thought, I'd love to come in."

Caitlin stood back as Tom passed her, his frame dwarfing her as he moved toward Gabby, grabbing her around the waist and planting a kiss on her head before following her to the sofa.

She paused, just for a second, knowing she'd taken a big step, but feeling as if it was the most natural thing in the world.

Just like that, she'd invited a man to step over the threshold and into her home. And she had no regrets whatsoever. Maybe if he'd been on his own she'd have thought otherwise, but with Gabby here, too, it comforted her. Made her feel secure.

"Tommy!" Gabby squealed.

Caitlin followed and stood, watching them play, seeing the look on Tom's face as he pulled his niece onto his knee. Even if it was only one dinner with the pair of them, she was going to enjoy every moment of it. After years of wanting to live alone, to keep a distance from others, suddenly she was pleased to have company. No, more than pleased, she was *happy*.

"So, tell me about being in the Navy, or is that a taboo question?"

Caitlin nursed her glass of red wine, taking a slow sip before turning her attention back to her meal. She watched as Tom swallowed before pausing, his knife and fork hovering an inch above his plate.

"If I tell you I'll have to kill you." His voice was deep and dangerously serious.

Now it was Caitlin who was swallowing, or more like gulping furiously. He was joking, she knew he was, but those kinds of flippant comments still made her teeth rattle.

"Kidding," he said, raising his eyebrows, smile hitting his eyes.

Caitlin laughed nervously and blew out a breath. "I didn't mean to pry, I'm only interested, that's all."

Tom kept eating, focused on the food, before raising his head and setting the cutlery down. "It's not that I don't want to talk about it. It's— I don't know, complicated, I guess."

Caitlin understood complicated. "Honestly, Tom, I was only making conversation." The last thing she wanted to do was pressure him into talking about something he'd rather keep private. "Don't feel like you have to answer me."

"Tell her one of your stories!" Gabby called out from the living room, cross-legged on the floor and leaning against the sofa, eating her dinner in front of the television. *Please.*

Caitlin waited, not wanting to stare at Tom but finding it difficult to look away. She'd thought he was too similar to her father and her ex because he was military, and because he was physically imposing, but she could see from the look on his face that she'd been wrong. He was different. At least he seemed to be.

Tom didn't have the hard edge to his profile, the cocky, self-assured aura that she had expected. Maybe when she'd first met him she'd wanted to think he did, but he was so far from that she didn't know how she could have been so judgmental. When he'd found out that she'd made dinner for them tonight, his face had lit up like hot embers being coaxed back to flame.

The last thing Tom wanted to do was talk about his career, that much was obvious, but he never snapped at Gabby, and seemed to want to shield her from any hurt. "Maybe another night, okay?"

Caitlin could see the pain, see how troubled he was behind those deep, dark eyes. But if he didn't want to talk she wasn't going to push him. Because she'd been there herself.

"How do you feel about dessert?"

Tom grinned at her, his face breaking into the most genuine smile she'd seen in a long while. "I think that's the best question I've heard all night."

"It's not much, so don't get too excited. Some ice cream and a chocolate brownie," she told him, clearing their plates and leaving them in the sink to do later. "And before you ask and make me feel guilty, they're store-bought brownies. I'm not the world's best cook."

Tom laughed. "You could have fooled me. I'd never have known."

She was pleased he was still at the table. Having him here—it was different. Ever since she'd been single she'd kept home as her private place, only ever inviting girl-friends over. She'd been on dates every now and again, but she'd never let a man collect her or come back to her place, so Tom being in her private space was…not uncomfortable, but something she was going to have to get used to. Slowly. Just like ever learning to trust a man again would be a huge leap of faith for her.

Caitlin ran her wrists under the cold water she had

running; she was nervous, jangling like a bunch of jittery wind chimes. He was just a parent. An acquaintance.

Argh. Who was she kidding? He wasn't a parent and that's not why she'd asked him in.

She turned off the faucet and served up dessert.

"Can I help?"

Caitlin spun around and pressed a plate into Tom's hands. "Here we go, this is for Gabby."

His gaze held hers, eyes questioning, but he took the plate and took it to his niece.

Caitlin bit the inside of her mouth and finished serving the other two brownies.

Lucy had been right. She *was* interested in Tom. And the first step in the right direction was admitting it to herself. Even if she had no intention of acting on her desires. She was a bad judge of character when it came to men, and she still didn't trust her instincts. Not yet, and maybe not ever.

Tom scooped up the last of his dessert before sitting back in the chair. For the first time in as long as he could remember, he felt content. Full, happy and oddly satisfied. And it wasn't just the food. It had been a long time since he'd enjoyed an evening without thinking about work or what he could or couldn't do in the future.

"I think she's asleep," Caitlin said.

Tom looked up and followed her gaze, angling his body slightly. Gabby was tucked up on the sofa, cat curled into the curve of her belly, sound asleep, and he used her being there to reposition himself properly so he could make sure he'd be able to hear Caitlin without her realizing what he was doing. "She looks so peaceful, don't you think?"

"She looks happy." Caitlin's voice was soft, caring.

"I like that she feels safe enough to curl up and drift off to sleep."

Tom didn't ask but he almost did. The way she spoke… it made him wonder if she knew what it felt like not to feel safe, or whether she was simply referring to children in general. She was an elementary teacher, after all, and had probably seen plenty of situations that had upset her.

"I'm sorry I cut you off like that earlier. When you asked about my work." His voice was low, gruff. The words hard to expel.

"Don't be sorry." Caitlin turned her attention back to him, her aqua eyes echoing the smile that traced across her lips.

Tom blew out a breath and folded his hands together, pressed them into the table.

"My entire adult life I've had to keep quiet about my work, pretend I had a normal job and that it wasn't that big a deal." Tom kept the burning fire, the anger, perfectly contained within him. Exercised every ounce of restraint he possessed.

Caitlin was listening intently, leaning forward, encouraging him. He watched her hands, long, elegant fingers, as they played with the edge of a napkin.

"And now?" she asked.

"If I'd met you a year ago and you'd asked what I did, I'd have made up some ludicrous story instead of telling you the truth." Tom laughed. "The truth is that we have to be so careful to protect our families, and sharing where in the world I was at any given time, or why I was away, had the potential to put those I loved in danger."

"And family is super important to you, right?" Caitlin's voice was so soft, unassumingly gentle. As though she understood implicitly what he was trying to explain.

"Family is everything to me. Without…" Tom paused,

cleared his throat and looked at Gabby's tiny sleeping form. "Let's just say that without Gabby I don't know how I would have dealt with everything that's happened over the last few months. It's been tough."

"It's amazing how much little people can help." Caitlin's hand skimmed his, the lightest of touches. "They seem to understand so much but at the same time they're so innocent."

"It sounds stupid, but Gabby seems to put everything in perspective for me," he told her. He'd never said it to anyone else, but it was true. "I made a career for myself in the Navy. My brother always knew he'd leave— he only joined to get his qualifications, a means to an end, but the Navy was my life. It was everything I'd ever wanted, and it still is."

Caitlin squeezed his fingers beneath hers before reclaiming her hand and wrapping both arms around herself as if she was cold, only it was warm in the room. Tom touched his plate then crossed his own arms and leaned back. Part of him wanted to change the subject, but there was something about talking, about getting his thoughts off his chest and being able to be honest to someone other than family that felt good.

"What happened?" Her voice was so soft he could have missed that she'd even asked a question.

Tom took a deep breath. He didn't have to tell her, could make something up or avoid the question entirely, but he *wanted* to tell her. Liked that she cared enough to ask. Enough to sit up late talking about him, what had happened to him, when they hardly knew each other. And it was different than trying to talk to his family or Navy buddies. Because in them he saw pity. With Caitlin he could hold things back, could keep parts to himself, and share snippets of what he wanted, *needed*, to get off his chest.

"We were on a mission." His mouth went dry, every drop of saliva gone, his tongue struggling to move. Tom ran a hand through his hair, tugged at the end, then dropped his hands to his side. Stood up because he didn't know what else to do.

He looked at what remained of the man he'd been so close to. Of the brother he'd served with, the life gone from his body, other guys he knew so well lying injured.

Remembered the screaming pain in his chest, the truest of heartaches, as he'd realized his friend was gone. Remembered how the pain in his ear was nothing like the pain he felt at knowing he'd failed him.

Tom forced his eyes up, made himself connect with Caitlin as she watched him.

"Everything seemed to be under control. We were so careful, like we always were. We all trusted each other so much, knew we were the best at what we were doing, and then it all went wrong."

Caitlin didn't say anything. She didn't have to. The look on her face, the open expression and concern in her eyes, told him she wanted to know more. That she was waiting for him to continue. And for the first time in as long as he could remember, he wanted to talk.

"The explosion took us all by surprise. One minute we were focused on our mission, the next I was flying through the air."

Caitlin leaned forward and touched his hand again, but this time her grip was firm. She locked her fingers over his, shaking her head gently. "How could you survive an explosion like that? What happened to you?"

Her eyes were darting across his face as if she was trying to see where he might have been harmed. Trying to figure out what had happened. Wanting to know how it had ended for him.

Tom raised his other hand, trying to ignore the soft, warm touch of her palm over his. He tapped his ear. "I'm almost completely deaf in this ear." A burst of pain exploded from his chest—the pain of admitting he wasn't strong enough, that he had failed. "I can't pass the physical anymore, so it's all over for me."

Now she knew. He watched her, really watched her, waited for the look of pity that he dreaded, was becoming so used to seeing.

But it never came.

Tom's breathing slowed. He relaxed.

Caitlin was nodding, the expression on her face hadn't changed. "So that's why you're teaching at the moment?"

Tom sighed. "That's why I'm teaching for the rest of my working life."

Caitlin's eyebrows knotted. "When you say the rest of…"

"My ear could get worse but it'll never get better, and that means I can't do my job. Ever. End of story."

Tom wished he hadn't snapped that last part out so harshly, but it was true. His career as a SEAL was over and he had to come to terms with it. And the fact that they'd lost one of their own when they were usually so careful, usually so precise. The operation had gone from as routine as could be expected for their kind of work to bad and then to worse before they'd even known what had hit them.

"I'm so sorry, Tom. I don't know what to say."

He gave her what he knew was a sad smile because it hurt just forcing it. "There's nothing anyone can say that'll make me feel any better, so don't beat yourself up about it."

Caitlin stood up and walked over to check on Gabby, bending over her, running a hand over her forehead—the same gentle way of moving her fingers that she'd done to him, comforting him with one soft stroke, and he watched her openly while she did it.

She scooped up her cat before walking back toward him, snuggling her pet to her chest.

"I know what it's like, Tom," she said, sitting down across from him again. "I know exactly what you're going through."

Her voice was low, tense, but it didn't soften the blow any.

Tom shut his eyes, clenched his fists and tried to push his anger away. Why the hell did everyone always think they could understand! He restrained himself, fought not to explode.

"I don't think that's possible, Caitlin." He kept his voice as even and calm as he could, but he jumped up, ready to leave, all the same. He should have kept what had happened to himself. This was why he didn't tell people about what had happened, because no one *could* understand and no one ever would.

"You're wrong, Tom," she insisted, eyes wide. "I've been there and I know how it feels."

"You have no idea what I've gone through, okay? No one does." There was a sharp edge of finality to his voice.

The cold, bitter tone sent a ripple of nervousness down Caitlin's spine. She went ice-cold herself. Didn't know how to respond, what to do. Other than tell Tom to get the hell out of her house for speaking to her like that. But she was scared. Nervous about the change in him, how he could go from so earnest and gentle one moment to looking as if he was going to erupt like a long-dormant volcano the next. Opening up to her so genuinely then shutting down as if the conversation had never taken place.

She wanted him out. *Now.*

"I do actually," she said, forcing herself to be as frosty to him as he had just been to her. Not prepared to quiver beneath his sudden show of strength, of power. Because if there was anything she hated, it was a man trying to assert his dominance like that. She could fall into a heap later, but right now she was going to stick up for herself.

Tom glared at her before striding over to the sofa and bundling Gabby into his arms, scooping her up like a rag doll. He held her tightly to him, his big hands firm to her tiny body, mouth touching her hair in the gentlest of ways, so at odds with how dominant, how intimidating she felt he was being.

"Thanks for dinner," he said, walking straight past her. "I appreciate you helping me out this afternoon."

Caitlin stood dead still, cat still in her arms, trying to stop her mouth from hanging open as Tom swung open the door and walked out. Left as though they'd shared nothing, as if tonight had never happened.

Good riddance.

"Good night," he called over his shoulder before shutting the door and disappearing into the dark.

The beast, she thought, anger pumping like adrenaline through her veins. Rude, arrogant, cold son of a…beast. She corrected her thoughts. There was no way she was bringing herself down to his level.

So she'd thought he was nice, that he deserved a chance. That maybe, just maybe, she could have been attracted to him. That he could prove her wrong, that it was time to trust her man-radar again.

Caitlin put Smokey down, locked up and made herself walk into the kitchen to start loading the dishwasher.

She'd been way wrong about Tom Cartwright. He was *exactly* like she'd originally expected him to be, and she'd been a fool to think he could be anything else. There was a reason she didn't let men into her life so easily, and he was only making her see that more clearly.

CHAPTER FIVE

Tom pushed himself to run faster, punishing his body with every pounding footfall. He lived for the adrenaline of exercise. For the way he could lose himself so completely from his thoughts, push so hard, make his body hurt and scream out from exertion. Sometimes it was his only savior, the only thing he could cling to when his thoughts were at their darkest.

Tom slowed, wanting to keep his control while he trained the young men working hard to keep up with him.

What had happened to him could at least help him produce the most elite of SEALs. He doubted any of the men he was training would struggle with their physical exams. Not if he had anything to do with it. So long as he stayed focused instead of acting as though the demons troubling him were literally hot on his heels.

"Keep going!" he commanded. "Let me hear you!"

The recruits' feet hit the pavement in time with his as he started the running cadence, singing for them to follow the beat, trying to pick his mood up and encourage the young men. "Hey buba-louba SEAL team baby."

"Hey buba-louba SEAL team baby," they chanted back.

"I joined up for this, now people think I'm cra-zy." Tom ran backward, watching the men, pleased to see them sweating hard. "I shaved my head, make me pretty for the *la-dies*," he bellowed out.

"I shaved my head, make me pretty for the *la-dies*," they sang back.

Tom kept up the song along to the *thump-thump* of their footfalls, but he couldn't help reaching up to run a hand quickly through his too-long-for-his-liking messy hair. Maybe that was his problem. He needed to cut his hair again.

Not that he wanted to be "pretty for the ladies" but he sure wanted to feel like a SEAL still. At least he wanted to look like the team leader he sorely wanted to be, no matter how much he moaned about his new role.

Because training the young recruits was important; the Navy was nothing without them.

Only it didn't feel anywhere near as important as being out there in the field, and he doubted that for him, personally, it ever would be. No matter what anyone said or how much he tried to convince himself.

"Anyone who do this just ain't *right*," he continued, pushing their pace to make them work even harder. "Left, left, left-right-*left*."

Tom tried to focus on the constant of each foot thumping down, the sounds of all their feet hitting in unison as they ran in rhythm, but there was only one thing he could see, no matter how hard he pushed himself.

Black hair caught up in a ponytail and aqua eyes looking at him as though he'd just run over her cat as he turned before leaving her house last night.

He shouldn't have walked out like that, not when she'd been so kind to him, but he couldn't deal with people trying to pretend that they knew how he felt. Because no one did and no one would.

Not his brother, not his sister-in-law, and certainly

not a pretty little teacher with not a care in the world. The darkness that he'd lived through was hard enough for him to talk about without people pretending they'd ever understand, without seeing others pity him for what he'd lost.

"Let's go, boys," he ordered. "Hit the pool as soon as we get back. And don't you dare even *think* about stopping for a rest."

A groan echoed out from behind him. Tom kept his face straight as he ran backward again, pleased that at least his general fitness was better than any of these kids'. He could run for hours without stopping, and before his injury he could easily have stayed as long in the water, too.

"Do you want to be Navy SEALs or not?" he barked, waiting for a *Yes, sir*. "So let me hear you or it'll be a double run next time!"

"Yes, sir!"

"I wanna be a Navy *SE-AL*," he sang, "run with *me-e* if you *dare*."

Tom clamped his jaw tight and gritted his teeth. He wasn't used to being distracted, and he didn't like it one bit.

Caitlin pulled off her trousers and replaced them with her black leotard, wriggling in the confines of the teacher's bathroom.

"You definitely need a night out." Lucy was waiting for her on the other side of the door. "Seriously, it'll do you good."

At least she hadn't said *I told you so*.

"I don't know…" Caitlin finished getting dressed, folding all her things back in her bag.

"Did I mention I wouldn't take no for an answer?"

Caitlin flung open the door, hair tie in her mouth as she fingered her hair into a bun. "Did I mention how bossy you are?" she mumbled as she plucked out the tie and twisted it into her hair.

"I don't care." Lucy picked up the bag for her and swung it over her shoulder. "The best thing to get your mind off a guy is to go out and have fun. Believe me, I know from experience."

Caitlin laughed, Lucy's attitude was contagious. "I'm not having any problems getting my mind off him, Lucy, I just wanted to tell you what a jerk he ended up being." She was lying. The way Tom had behaved had upset her, cut her up inside, but she didn't want anyone knowing that. Not even one of her closest friends. Men never rattled her, not anymore, and that was the way she wanted it to stay.

"Yeah, yeah." Her friend swatted her hand in the air as if what Caitlin was saying was completely irrelevant. "I don't need more details right now, what I need is for you to say yes to coming out tomorrow night. Okay?"

Caitlin grabbed her bag back and bumped shoulders with Lucy. "Okay."

"Okay?"

She laughed at Lucy's surprised expression. "Pick me up on your way," she said as she walked toward her car.

"Don't go all miss prissy ballerina on me, either, okay? I want sexy Caitlin!" Lucy called.

Caitlin cringed, hoping no one else had heard their conversation. But the truth was, she *did* need a night out, and Lucy was the perfect playmate. She was confident, engaging and loads of fun. Exactly what Caitlin needed to make her feel better. It was one of the reasons she'd been drawn to Lucy in the first place.

She started the car and made her way to ballet. Her

only hope now was that Tom would drop Gabby off outside. The last thing she needed was to bump into him and get herself all tangled in knots again.

Tom went through Gabby's schoolbag, fishing out some uneaten lunch and her school books. "Is there any homework in here?"

Gabby called back at him from her room. "Nope."

He seriously doubted that. "Gabby, come on out here."

She didn't call back. Tom dumped her lunchbox on the counter and put her books beside it. He was sure there'd be something in there they were meant to be addressing. He checked to make sure there wasn't an uneaten banana or anything else lurking, but found a note instead.

Hmmm. Tom unfolded the tatty piece of paper, recognizing Gabby's handwriting and an unfamiliar child's writing. He wondered how long it had taken the little girls to write the note when they were meant to be listening in class.

Miss Rose asked us for dinner last night.
Why?
Don't know. But my uncle kept looking at her all funny.
Like what?
She made nice food. Like my mom does.

Tom put the note down, unable to stop smiling. It didn't seem to matter how hard he tried to ignore the woman, she kept popping back up in his thoughts. Or right now on paper in front of him. He hadn't even known six-year-olds could write that well.

"Whatcha doing?"

Tom dropped the note and cleared his throat. Caught out. "Oh, nothing, just emptying out your bag."

"Were you looking at my things?" Gabby had her hands on her hips.

"Nope," he said, shaking his head as he pushed her books forward. "But I've been trying to find your homework."

"But Tommy, it's my last night," she whined. "I don't have to hand it in till Monday. Can't we have fun?"

She sure knew how to work him. Her parents were back in the morning and it did seem stupid not to have fun on their last evening together. "Okay, I'll make you a deal."

Gabby looked up eagerly, eyes alight.

"You read some of that story to me we started the other day, then we can watch a movie together. Eat some popcorn or something."

"Yay!" She ran around to him and flung her arms around his hips, holding on tight. "Thanks, Tommy."

He gave her a pat on the head as she stopped squeezing, watched her skip back off to the spare room she liked to call her own.

But as soon as she was out of eyesight he rustled up a piece of paper and started to write a note of his own.

Maybe Caitlin couldn't ever truly understand what he'd been through, but he liked her and he'd been rude.

If he wasn't man enough to apologize to a woman for his behavior, then he wasn't worthy of the position he'd held as a SEAL. He needed to suck it up, be a man and say sorry.

"Gabby?" Caitlin stood behind her desk, leaning toward her young pupil. "You know how I feel about notes being passed in my class."

She watched confusion cross Gabby's face as she put the neatly folded piece of paper on her desk. "But it's for you."

Caitlin's eyebrows rose. "For me?"

Gabby giggled and ran back to her seat.

"Ten more minutes to finish your writing," Caitlin instructed, before sitting back down herself. "Then you can all share your stories with the class."

She carefully unfolded the paper and looked to the end of the letter as soon as she had it unfolded. *Tom.* His name was printed neatly at the end, his handwriting bold and uniform, just as she imagined he was at work.

For the first time since he'd walked out on her, his name made her smile.

Caitlin looked up to make sure all her children were busy before letting her eyes rove back to the start. Her pulse started to race, body tingling with...anticipation. She'd never been sent a letter by a man before.

Dear Caitlin,

Gabby came home with a note in her bag last night and it made me think of you. I'm sorry for the way I behaved. Thank you for a lovely dinner and please don't think I'm some rude idiot with bad manners. My mom would kill me if she found out.

Meet me Saturday afternoon? I'd like to make it up to you if you don't mind giving me a second chance. Let's go hiking. I'll pick you up around 2:00 p.m.

Tom.

Caitlin could feel the heat in her cheeks, flushed from reading the words he'd penned. She scanned the letter again before tucking it into the top drawer of her desk.

A note, huh? Almost cute, and he was right, he had been a brute. But she was always telling her pupils that sometimes all a person needed was a second chance, so she'd be a hypocrite to say no. Right?

Caitlin pulled out a clean sheet of paper and picked up her pen, toying with it, playing with it between her fingers and chewing on the end while she figured out what to write.

She worried the edges of the paper of the paper until they were creased after she'd scribbled her reply before folding it into a square and standing. She walked to Gabby's desk and crouched down, tucking the note into the front pocket of her bag.

"This is for your uncle. Would you mind giving it to him?"

Gabby giggled, looking at her little friend, before biting her lip. "Sure."

Caitlin tried to give her a stern look back but their smiles were infectious. "Tell Tom that he's not to write notes anymore, do you hear me?"

But the girls were already laughing again, schoolwork forgotten.

Caitlin could hardly tell them off. She was more than a little distracted herself.

CHAPTER SIX

"THANKS so much for looking after her."

Tom leaned into his sister-in-law as she hugged him. Penny wrapped her arms tight around him and squeezed.

"I see where Gabby gets it from," he said drily.

Penny swatted him before getting into the car. "She said she had a great time. I really appreciate it."

Tom leaned into the open window, pulling a face at Gabby as she sat beside her mom and angling his head to make sure he could hear his sister-in-law properly. It was strange how quickly he was becoming used to it. "She's a pretty good kid, Pen. You know I love having her, even if she is a rascal."

Gabby poked her tongue out and Penny scolded her.

"Do you want to come around for dinner tonight?" Penny asked, putting the car in gear.

Tom shook his head. "No, I'm heading out for a few drinks." He fingered the carefully folded piece of paper in his pocket, eager to open it. Gabby had given it to him with a big grin on her face, but he'd managed to bribe her with chocolate promises not to tell her mom.

"Hot date?" Penny waggled her eyebrows suggestively.

"I wish." He thrust his other hand into his pocket, too,

and stepped back onto the pavement. "Just Friday-night drinks with the guys from work."

Penny threw a smile his way before waving. "If things change, come on over. You're always welcome."

Tom waved to Gabby as she turned in her seat, watching until they disappeared around the corner. He sighed and walked back into the house.

He wasn't even in the front door yet and he knew how it would feel. *Empty.* He'd get use to it, but there was something nice about sharing his home with someone else. Even if that someone else was a pint-sized kid.

But at least he had something to read.

Tom opened the paper, smiling as he paused to look at the big red love heart Gabby had drawn on one side. Damn it, that kid was making him way too soft.

Tom
You're forgiven, but only just. I appreciate your apology and I'm not one to hold a grudge. Hiking sounds like fun, but you'll have to be easy on me, okay? I'm dance-fit, not outdoors-fit!
See you Saturday, and stop encouraging Gabby to write notes.
Caitlin xxoo

Tom dropped the note, stepped into the bathroom and turned the shower on hot. He would have a quick rinse off, get dressed and head to the bar. If there was one thing he needed, it was a drink. Or maybe a cold shower before he started worrying over whether he'd done the right thing asking Caitlin to join him tomorrow. He usually trained hard on the weekends. Ran fast and long, went to the gym, ran some more. But instead he was volunteering to spend his time with a woman.

Hiking wasn't new to him, but it sure wasn't something he usually did with company. It was another way he liked to push himself to make sure he spent more time forgetting than remembering.

Tom stepped under the water and let it blast him.

He couldn't help but smile, no matter how he fought it. *She said yes. Yes.*

If he'd had a buddy beside him he'd definitely have had his hand up for a high-five. Because that was the effect Caitlin was having on him and he didn't know how to stop it.

Or maybe he didn't want to stop it.

Tom turned the water to cold and steeled himself for the sudden change in temperature. The icy blast chilled every inch of his skin, but he stood, not moving a muscle. This was nothing compared to his Navy SEAL training, but right now it felt like *torture*.

He had no idea what he was going to say to her, why he'd felt so compelled to ask her out even, but what he did know was that he wanted to see her. That something was pounding away at him, telling him to let her in, to be in her company, and he wasn't strong enough to say no.

No, he *was* strong enough. He just didn't *want* to say no, not yet. As much as he didn't want to get close to anyone, didn't want to hurt anyone, especially not a woman, he wasn't quite ready to back off.

The music was starting to pound a little too loud for Tom's liking. His right ear was taking the brunt of it, and for once he was pleased not to hear through his left properly, if at all. He took another swig of beer and leaned back deeper into the seat. It wasn't that he hadn't had a good time—he had, but nothing seemed the same anymore. He was used to enjoying his down time because he never knew when he'd be off overseas again, loved being home before the adrenaline of a new mission.

Now he didn't have that edge any longer. Wasn't waiting for the hit of excitement the way he used to. Right now, all he wanted to do was kick back and relax; he wasn't in the mood for a big night out.

"Check her out," Sam said, whooping and slapping him on the back. "Now *that's* what I'm talking 'bout!"

Tom grinned at him and downed the rest of his beer, turning so he could hear his friend. Even if he hadn't been able to hear, it wasn't exactly difficult to figure it out. He was usually the first to spot beautiful girls, would have been the first to go over and say hi to a single woman in a bar, weaving together a story about what he did to avoid admitting he was a SEAL.

"Where're we looking, boys?" he asked.

His buddy pointed, not bothering to be discreet. "The one dancing. I reckon she'll be up on the bar next. Wow!"

Tom laughed…but it died in his throat like a final, choking gurgle. He slammed his beer down on the table. *No way.*

Caitlin?

She was gyrating as though she didn't have a care in the world, as though she had no problem with every hot-blooded male in the room watching as she sashayed back and forth, around and around.

Tom saw red, blurs of color flashing fast before his eyes. He squeezed his beer bottle, in danger of smashing it between his palm and fingers.

"Hot or what?" Sam asked, laughing with the other guys.

"Off-limits," Tom forced out through gritted teeth. "Way off-limits."

"But hot!" he faintly heard someone else call out.

He didn't care who it was checking her out, he only cared about stopping anyone else from leering at her. Tom pushed past the guys and tried to calm down, focus on his breathing. He knew better than to let his emotions show, but staying sane over the way she was moving right now was a real struggle. What the hell would have happened to her if he hadn't been here to protect her?

He fought not to glare at Caitlin as he approached. She was meant to be a ballet teacher, not a stripper!

A guy with a cheesy grin stepped out, eyes on Caitlin.

"Back off," Tom ordered, ready to thump the guy if he so much as looked at her like that again.

The guy went to open his mouth then thought better of it, holding his hands up and walking backward.

"Hey, handsome."

Tom almost ran smack-bang into a pretty blonde when he spun back around. The girl was laughing as she watched Caitlin. He didn't reply, stormed past her and grabbed hold of Caitlin's arm, harder than he meant to.

"Ouch!" He heard her squeal even over the loud music. "Tom?" Now she looked confused, but even drunk she was gorgeous. Annoyingly, irritatingly gorgeous.

Tom fought not to tell her off. He needed to get control of the situation now. He could tell her what he thought of her antics later when he'd calmed down. And when she wasn't so annoyingly drunk, so she could comprehend what he was saying.

"Come on," he commanded.

She shook her head, grabbing hold of the blonde, who was now standing, very seriously, beside her with hands on hips. She looked angry. Not as angry as he was, but angry enough to make him to feel imaginary prickles rise along his back as he watched her reaction. It was as if they were both being possessive of Caitlin.

"Mr. Navy SEAL," the blonde said, shaking her head as she laughed at him. "Well, I'll be."

Tom tried his hardest to keep his face impartial, not to show how much seeing Caitlin like this infuriated him. Or how much he hated being teased, *goaded,* by a woman he didn't even know.

"What do you want with the lovely Miss Rose, huh?" the blonde asked.

Tom glared at her companion and touched Caitlin gently on the arm. "I didn't mean to hurt you, Caitlin, it's just…"

"What?" she asked, all innocent and wide-eyed, as though she had no idea what she'd been doing. He could have sworn he'd seen tears pooling in her eyes, as well as an expression in them that made him fear she'd actually been scared of him.

Tom groaned. Jeez, she really didn't have any idea. About how gorgeous she was, how she looked, how she affected him…

Her friend stepped closer. "I need a word with Caitlin," Tom said, trying not to growl. "In private."

The friend shrugged. "Those your handsome Navy friends over there?" she asked, waggling her fingers in their direction, suddenly looking a whole lot less angry and a whole lot more interested.

Tom looked over his shoulder, not wanting to let go of Caitlin. "Ah, yeah," he said, shaking his head as the guys hooted with laughter, cat-calling and whistling. "I'm sure they'd love to meet you."

He looked at Caitlin, pleaded as best he could with his eyes. "Please, just a minute?"

Caitlin rocked, a little unsteady on her feet before nodding at her friend. "Luce, I'm fine. Go have fun." She hiccuped and clamped one hand over her mouth.

Tom watched the other woman go before circling his arm around Caitlin's waist and leading her away from the bar. She pressed into him, cuddling against his frame, turning big eyes up at him.

He fought not to turn his head away, forced a half smile, trying to ignore how good she felt tucked against him. How soft her body was, how warm she felt, *how right it seemed.*

"Mmm, you smell good," she said, face still upturned, eyes bright.

She's drunk, Tom reminded himself. *She has no idea what she's saying and she sure as hell won't remember it in the morning.*

"Caitlin, what are you doing?" he asked, pushing her gently down into a seat and sliding in beside her. He'd always hated modern booth seats, but now he wasn't so quick to moan.

"Um, having fun, dancing, you know," she said, voice slightly slurred. "But my head's starting to hurt." She let her forehead fall into her hands, suddenly looking as weak as a wilting flower in the sun. "Tom, you're not going to hurt me, are you?"

She was watching his hand where he was resting it, clenched on the table, as if it were a cobra ready to bite. Tom shook his head. Was she actually scared of him? He was used to being the protector, was used to his role being so clearly defined.

"Caitlin, I'm the good guy here." He tried to soften his voice, tried to eliminate the anger that was like an itch beneath his skin. "You have to believe that I would never, *ever*, lay a hand on *any* woman unless she wanted me to, okay?" He'd been angry before, sure, but enough to scare her? Surely not...

Tom watched as she slowly, nervously nodded her head.

"See those guys I'm with over there?" Tom hooked a finger in their direction. "You'd hate to know what they were saying about you when you were dancing."

"Like what?" she asked, all innocent-looking again.

Tom swallowed hard and reached for her hands. He didn't know why, what made him do it, but his fingers closed over hers, drawing her skin close against his. Slowly, so as not to alarm her.

He hadn't touched a woman like that, in that way, with that kind of purpose, in forever. Since his high-school sweetheart, in fact.

"What about Lucy?" Her eyebrows suddenly shot up.

"Sweetheart, I think Lucy can handle herself," Tom said, shaking his head at how sweet she was. At how genuinely in the dark she was about how sexy she'd been before and what all the guys in the bar had no doubt thought of her.

Caitlin pulled her hands away and leaned into him, fell against his shoulder so quickly he didn't see it coming. "I don't feel so good."

He braced her with one hand as he stood, before pulling her up with him. "I'm gonna get you a coffee then take you home, okay?"

She nodded, leaning into him, heavier than before. "You'll look after me, right? Please look after me, Tom."

Tom squeezed her shoulder, resisting the urge to drop a kiss to her inky-dark hair. It seemed like the natural thing to do, *the right thing,* but he knew it wasn't.

She was a sweet girl. His niece's teacher. That was all. And for some reason she was bringing out the primal, manly desire in him to protect and serve.

"I'll always look after you, don't worry." He was only glad she was asking him that and not some other guy in the bar.

"Always?" she asked, eyes swimming.

Tom gulped. That had come out all wrong. "How do you take your coffee?" he asked, changing the subject.

"Hot chocolate," she murmured, tucking in closer to him and wrapping one arm around his waist as if she had no intention of ever letting him go. "I need chocolate."

And I need you.

He'd wanted to fight it. Had told himself he was only meeting her tomorrow because he had to make up for being rude at her place. But he was lying.

He wanted to see this girl again because she was the kind of girl he'd always imagined a life with. The kind of girl who made him want to take her home to meet his mom. The kind of girl who deserved to be cared for and protected, to be kept from harm and carefully nurtured.

The kind of girl he'd once hoped to marry.

He stopped resisting her and tucked her firmly to his side. It was only one night. Nothing was going to happen. She was drunk and he was going to take her home. He could fight his feelings for her tomorrow.

"Come on, sweetheart, let's go," Tom said, waving to his buddies and receiving a whoop from the group in reply. Caitlin's friend was there and she raised her eyebrows and laughed.

He looked down at Caitlin wrapped around him, cuddled close.

Tom gulped.

She was the kind of girl he wanted to call his sweetheart, that's what she was.

Tom drew her closer again as they walked toward his car, ignoring the cool night air and wanting to keep her warm. He opened his car by remote and kept Caitlin by his side.

Thank goodness he'd nursed that one beer for so long. Tonight was one night he was sure glad he could drive.

"Come on, let's get you into bed."

Caitlin laughed. Tom had to remind himself that she was drunk. Not just mildly drunk or a little tipsy, but in the kind of state he hated to see a woman in, out on her own.

Sure, she'd been with a girlfriend, but it still worried him.

If they'd been out together and she'd drunk too much, it wouldn't have mattered, because he'd have protected her. But he didn't want to imagine who could have taken advantage of her with so many men openly leering at her earlier on.

"Are you getting into bed with me?" she asked, still giggling to herself.

Tom sighed. Thinking about *her* and *bed* in the same context was not something he wanted to do. Especially not when she was tucked so close to his body again.

"Is it down here?" he asked, leaving her keys on the counter and guiding her down the hall. "I'm going to lay you down then lock up the house, okay?"

She leaned into him before steering them both through a door and flopping down onto the bed.

"The room is spinning. Tom, why is the room moving so fast?" she asked, one hand flung over her eyes.

Tom trained his eyes on Caitlin. He didn't want to look around her room, see her pretty things all around him or want to stay here with her. He was putting her to bed, making sure she was safe.

He wasn't here because he'd been invited back.

"Will you be all right if I leave you?" he asked, trying to force the huskiness from his voice as he looked at her lying on the bed.

Caitlin's dress had risen up to expose perfectly shaped, toned lower legs silhouetted in the light of her bedside lamp. They were golden, smooth, feet in pointed shoes with heels that had made her way taller than she was.

Tom looked around the room again instead. Looking at her things instead of *her* suddenly felt a whole lot safer.

"Tommy?"

He grimaced. Only Gabby ever called him Tommy.

"I'm sooo hungry."

"That I can help with," he said, backing out of the room. "Stay put and I'll make you a sandwich or something."

Tom tried to think of something else, of work, of *anything,* but it wasn't easy. Caitlin was gorgeous, a knockout, in the sweetest, most appealing of ways. Not overconfident or brazenly attractive, but soft and gentle-looking, beautiful like a perfectly proportioned doll.

And she was tiny. His little ballerina was tiny and breakable-looking…

Hell.

Tom rushed into the kitchen and rustled through the fridge. He had to get out of here. She wasn't *his* anything, and the quicker he got out of here, the quicker he could come to terms with the fact that she wasn't ever going to be his anything, either.

He found a turkey breast, sliced it, and slathered some mayo over the bread, starving hungry himself but wanting to get out of her house. He didn't even pick at the meat, cutting the sandwich in half and looking for a plate.

Whoops! He almost dropped the plate as a loud *meow* made him jump.

"Do you mind?" Tom glared at the cat.

It only meowed louder.

"Seriously, feline, you're killing me here." Tom opened the sandwich to retrieve a piece of turkey for the cat, before closing it up and walking determinedly down the hall.

He was going to pass her the food, say good-night and walk out the door.

Or not.

Caitlin was out for the count, sound asleep. Snoring ever so softly and passed out on the bed.

Tom placed the plate on her side table, carefully slipped her shoes off and pulled up the comforter. She was so peaceful, so beautiful lying there that all he wanted to do was cuddle up right beside her. He craved the idea of closeness, of holding someone and being held, of having a warm, loving body beside his to comfort him.

But that wasn't in his future now. Or at least not for a long while. He was dealing with too much, felt too much like a failure, even to make himself available to someone. Even to want that life he'd once wanted so badly. Too afraid that he'd pull someone else down and into the fears and pains that haunted him every day.

"Good night," he whispered, hovering above her, waiting, before dropping a slow kiss to her forehead.

Tom looked down at her and smiled. He doubted she'd even be able to squash a spider, this pretty little teacher who'd made him go all protective tonight.

Tom grabbed half the sandwich and ate it as he left the house, flicking the catch on the door as he walked out.

He stood outside in the chilly night air, swallowed, then stretched his legs. What he needed right now was to run.

A cold shower might have helped, but running was

what he did. How he coped with things. Right now his mind was scrambled and he didn't like it one bit.

Tom ignored the fact he was wearing dress shoes and broke into a slow jog. He inhaled deeply, in and out, clearing his mind, focusing on the pull and release of his muscles, the burn of cool air as it entered his lungs.

Sometimes when he ran it exhausted him enough to stop him from dreaming, too. *Sometimes*.

Tom stepped up a gear and ran faster.

He hoped tonight was one of those nights.

CHAPTER SEVEN

CAITLIN shut her eyes tight before opening them slowly, one at a time.

Ow. The sunlight felt as though it was burning her. She was like a vampire exposed to daylight when she should have been bathed in darkness instead. She tried to sit up and stuttered back down flat.

A hangover. She had a hangover. She never had a hangover!

She could hear her phone ringing, but it hurt too much to move. Caitlin leaned as far as she could off the bed without falling, eyes still shut, groping for the phone.

"Hello?" she croaked.

"Morning, sunshine."

Lucy. "What… I mean how?" She rubbed at her eyes and gently tried to sit up again before slumping back down. "How can you be calling me this early?"

Lucy laughed. It sounded like glass being shattered to Caitlin. "It's not early, silly, it's after lunch."

What? Caitlin groaned, looked at her bedside clock. No way. "Why do you sound so cheerful?" She was grumpy now.

"Why don't you? I thought you went home with Mr. Navy."

Caitlin flung herself back down again, stomach flip-flopping some more. Only it wasn't the alcohol making her queasy this time.

"Caitlin?"

"I left with him. I mean…" She paused, trying to remember. It was like trying to see through thick fog just thinking about the night before. Or the latter parts of it anyway. "He brought me home."

Lucy laughed again. "Maybe next time I won't let you have so many shots."

"Let me?" Caitlin shut her eyes again as her head started to pound. "You practically forced those drinks on me. It's your fault I feel like this. I *never* get drunk!"

Partly because she didn't like to be vulnerable and partly because she hated feeling like this.

"So where is he? Did he stay over?" Lucy asked. "I need details here."

Caitlin gripped the phone tighter, her hand clasping it hard. "No, he didn't stay over." She had no idea what had happened, could only remember flashes of being with him, of arriving here with him and somehow ending up in her bed. A bead of sweat touched against her forehead. She was always so careful never to put herself in that kind of predicament with a man.

She sat up, let her feet touch the carpet, moved slowly to stop her head from spinning. She had no shoes on— they were neatly on the floor beside the bed, and there was half a sandwich on the bedside table. Next to a glass of water. She definitely wouldn't have been in the right state of mind to put a sandwich together like that. Which meant that…

Caitlin gulped down a few sips of the water, her mouth so dry it hurt. Tom must have been in her bedroom. Last night. With her.

She stifled another groan and put Lucy on speaker

phone so she could start to shuffle slowly toward the bathroom.

"You still there?" Lucy asked.

She shook her head before realizing that Lucy couldn't see her. "I have to go take a shower." Caitlin wasn't completely lying, she did need to do something to wake herself up. To make herself feel like a human instead of a brain-dead zombie again. "I'll call you later."

She hung up and walked carefully across the room. Turned on the shower and started to strip.

What if… She wrapped herself in a towel and walked slowly out and across her bedroom, peeking into the lounge.

No. He wasn't there. Just Smokey curled up on his favorite chair.

She'd had a funny feeling that Tom might have stayed on the sofa, but she'd been wrong.

But he'd been here. She knew that. He'd brought her home, he'd put her to bed and he'd been careful with her. She couldn't remember exactly what had happened, but she knew he'd looked after her. Because her clothes were still on, there was food beside the bed, and her front door was locked.

Tom had made sure she'd gotten home safe, that no one had taken advantage of her.

Without her even knowing it, without her asking for it, Tom had entered her home and kept her safe. So no matter how much she'd embarrassed herself the night before, drinking as if she'd never drunk alcohol in her life before, she needed to give the guy a chance. To be there when he arrived this afternoon for their hike instead of flaking out and canceling the way she wanted to.

Even if her head was pounding so hard she could hardly put one foot in front of the other, she owed him that. Because him bringing her home was the first time a man had gone out of his way to protect her. And she hadn't even asked for his help. Even if she still never trusted a man again, Tom had taken care of her. She at least owed him a thank-you.

Caitlin went back into the bathroom and found some aspirin. She swallowed two tablets with a swig of water and dropped her towel, stepping into the shower.

She didn't know how she was even going to keep her eyes open or stop the earth spinning when she moved, but she was going to. Because Tom was arriving soon.

The thought set a tickle up her spine that had nothing to do with the hot water pounding against her skin.

An hour later, Caitlin was sitting on her front doorstep, head cradled in her hands, sunglasses pressed firmly against her eyes. She gulped some more water from her bottle, but it didn't help.

"Hey, stranger."

Caitlin looked up slowly, squinting into the sun. She hadn't even heard the car pull up through the pounding in her head.

"Hi," she said back, wishing it had come out all deep and sexy instead of croaky.

"I'd ask you how you're feeling but…"

"Like death warmed up," she replied, at least able to smile this time. "While you look like you had a full night's sleep and then some."

Tom chuckled before holding out his hand. She took it, grateful he was hauling her up to her feet.

"I, um, well." She looked him in the eye, deciding to do it now instead of avoiding the subject. "I appreciate you bringing me home last night."

She wished he didn't look so darn chipper though.

"You do?" he asked, walking back to his car then leaning on the hood, legs crossed at the ankle as he watched her. "Because you were pretty sure you didn't want to leave the bar last night."

Caitlin groaned again. She couldn't seem to stop doing it. "Please don't rub it in."

"Oh, but I have to," he said, smirk back on his face. "You see, you were sure that you knew what you were doing dancing like that."

She ignored him and yanked open the passenger door. "Can we not reminisce about last night? It really wasn't me at my finest. *Please*."

"You sure about that?" Tom teased, standing on the other side, looking at her through the open windows of the vehicle.

She was pleased it was a 4x4; it meant she didn't have to bend down and risk another head spin. Part of her liked this more-relaxed guy; she only wished she didn't feel like hell and that they were talking about someone else.

"Look," she said, getting in as he did the same. "I don't usually drink, in case that wasn't obvious from my antics. So can we please forget it ever happened? That was not the real me you saw last night, and she won't be out on the town ever again. I can promise you that."

Tom laughed, shaking his head and putting his hands up in surrender before starting the car. "If you say so. But I can't stop thinking how cute you looked when I tucked you up in bed last night."

"Tom!" She was going to die of humiliation if he didn't stop.

He just kept laughing, as if it was the most amusing thing he'd ever talked about.

"I didn't, well, say anything embarrassing, did I?" Caitlin cringed at having to ask the question, but she was terrified of what she might have said or done. This was *exactly* why she didn't usually drink!

"Sweetheart, you're the size of a grasshopper, no one's going to judge you for not being able to hold your liquor."

Now it was Caitlin who was laughing. "A grasshopper? Couldn't I at least be something a little more, I don't know, elegant?"

"A butterfly then," he joked. "Hell, I don't know, but you're a ballerina, right? You don't exactly have the build of a woman built to knock back tequila."

Caitlin's head was starting to feel better, the distraction helping her from focusing on the constant thud she'd felt before.

"Why are you so perky, anyway, after such a late night?" she asked.

Tom cast a quick glance at her. "I'm a perky kinda guy," he said. "I've had years of having to get up at dawn, so I'm used to not having much sleep."

Oh. That figured. "So it wasn't exactly hard for you to roll out of bed to pick me up, then?"

"Did you only just get out of bed?" he asked incredulously.

Caitlin nodded and pointed to her head. "Hangover, remember?"

Tom turned up the radio a touch and tapped his fingers against the steering wheel. "I got up at 6:00 a.m.," he told her. "I've already been for a two-hour run, had breakfast, read the paper and stopped by to see Gabby."

Caitlin stared at him. "You're serious, aren't you? Who the hell are you and where did you come from?"

Tom shot her another of his gorgeous grins. "It's all about discipline, Caitlin."

She shut her eyes and tried to block him and his annoying perkiness out. Oh, she got it. When she'd been a professional dancer it wouldn't have mattered how late she'd been out, her commitment to her dance had been absolute. Unwavering. But that was another lifetime ago, and right now, she could hardly even remember that girl.

The car slowed and she had to see where they were.

Huh. "You don't strike me as the fast-food type," she said drily.

"I'm not," Tom said, putting his window down to order at the drive-through. "But if we have any chance of actually doing some hiking today, you need something greasy to get rid of that hangover."

Mmm. Greasy sounded good, even if she wasn't about to admit it to him. "I thought you'd be a health nut, given your interest in training so early in the morning like a crazy person," she said sarcastically. She could have told him that she understood, that she got it, but he was teasing her and she had to give him something back.

"Oh, I am, don't you worry." He reached into the backseat and pulled out a bottle of green sludge. "Here—down this and it'll make you feel better."

Yuk. Green gunk. "Can I hold my nose while I drink it?" She'd definitely be sick otherwise. She was almost gagging just looking at it and she hadn't even smelled it yet. She might understand the exercising, but she'd never been into veggie drinks.

"If you have to." He moved up to the next window and collected the paper bags. "If it makes you feel any better I'm going to grease up, too. We can work it off later."

Tom passed her a bag and waited for her to open it before driving off. "Bacon-and-egg burger," he told her, taking a bite of his own, other hand on the steering wheel. "I promise it's good."

Caitlin unwrapped hers and inhaled the delicious

smell of melted cheese and bacon. She went to take a bite but Tom stopped her.

"Uh-uh." He nudged her with his elbow, already eating his burger. "Juice first, otherwise you'll never drink it."

Caitlin scowled at him, not liking being bossed around. "Where's yours then?"

He shrugged. "I don't need it. I had a homemade vegetable juice before I collected you."

Caitlin tried not to laugh. He made her look like a sinner, when she'd always thought she was the good girl. "Well, I guess you're not exactly a bad influence, are you?"

"I'm no bad boy. Workaholic, sure. Fitness freak, maybe. But I've never been accused of being a bad influence."

Tom had no idea where that had come from. Not a bad boy? It was a wonder she wasn't laughing at him.

"So, what're we doing today? You did get my note, right? The one that said I wasn't really hiking-fit."

Tom made the turnoff and put his foot down on the accelerator. "I've already had my morning workout so don't worry, I'm not going to push you too hard."

She stayed silent as he drove, but he couldn't ignore her. After last night…he had no idea what had happened. How he'd ended up storming across a bar and marching her home, but right now she didn't seem to be holding it against him. Maybe she'd liked his stupid alpha routine, or maybe she just couldn't remember.

Last night her hair had been out, hanging straight as silk down her back. Now it was caught up high in a ponytail, sitting across one shoulder. She'd put on sunglasses so he couldn't see her eyes, but he didn't need to. He could still see the way they'd looked at him last night when he'd helped her onto her bed.

Tom cleared his throat, focused on where he was driving. They were almost there.

"Why did you send me that note, Tom?"

The question took him by surprise. He had no idea why. Not when he'd spent so many hours trying to forget about her, trying to tell himself that it didn't matter if he'd been rude or annoyed her. She wasn't *his* daughter's teacher and he wasn't interested in her. *Couldn't* be interested in her.

And yet here he was in a car with her, on a Saturday afternoon, going for a hike. He usually ran these tracks fast, but now he was about to volunteer for a walk.

"Tom?"

He made the turnoff and drove slowly into the parking area. "I wanted to say sorry, that's all." It was a half-truth; he wasn't completely lying. "I was rude the other night and I shouldn't have been."

She kept staring out the window, before looking back at him, slowly taking her glasses off.

"Feeling better?" he asked.

"Much." She blinked a few times as if she was trying to adjust to the bright light. "So where exactly are we?"

"San Pedro Valley Park," he told her, pulling into a vacant lot. "We're going to do the Valley View Loop."

"Sounds hard," she complained.

"It's just over two miles," he told her. "I could bring Gabby here and she'd make it around without a break."

Caitlin punched him in the arm, her fist connecting with his T-shirt and biceps beneath. It didn't hurt, but it sure made him stop moving, made him still as a statue.

She flushed, cheeks pink, as though she hadn't realized what she was doing until it was too late. "You're the one comparing me to a kid." She was trying to be confident, but Tom could see she was as rattled as he felt. "And why would she need a break anyway? That girl has a never-ending supply of energy, like most of the other six-year-olds in my class."

Tom got out of the car, standing in the sun and stretching lightly, waiting for Caitlin to do the same. He was trying not to laugh, to keep a straight face, but he was struggling.

"She'd probably want to look for wildlife, knowing her."

Caitlin was suddenly in front of him, closer than he bet she wanted to be. He wasn't going to pretend that he didn't like it. No matter how much he tried to convince himself not to go there, to ignore her and move on, he couldn't. Because she was beautiful and interesting and she fired something within him that he'd thought he'd lost before he was shipped back home.

"When you say wildlife…"

He reached out and touched Caitlin on the arm, liking the feel of her warm, soft skin beneath his hand. Liking that he had an excuse to connect with her. "It's nothing, honestly. You must have been hiking before?"

She looked worried now, didn't try to move away from him. "Tom? What wildlife?"

"Look, it's nothing to be worried about. I'm talking rabbits, moles, gray foxes." He put his hands in the air, shrugging at the same time. "Coyote and bobcats sometimes, but…"

Caitlin's eyebrows shot up. "Hold up. *Bobcats?*"

Tom took her by the arm again and pulled her closer. He gave her shoulders a squeeze, tried to make it friendly even though his mind was screaming out that it should

mean something more. "I come here all the time, honestly, we'll be fine. I was just trying to rile you up."

She looked relieved. "Phew, you had me there."

Tom stayed close, tried not to chuckle again. He liked
how innocent she was, how her eyebrows arrowed when
she was worried. "I wasn't kidding about the wildlife,
but I do promise I'll keep you safe."

Caitlin looked at him as though she wasn't sure
whether to jump back in the car and refuse to move, or
to thump him for scaring her. She did look a little pale
though.

"You okay?"

She nodded, but didn't move away from him, stayed
close. And he liked that.

"Let's limber up, then get going. You'll love it."

Caitlin didn't look so sure, but she followed his lead,
checking her shoelaces, doing a few stretches, then grabbing her water bottle from the car.

"Ready?" he asked.

She gave him a sideways look before joining him,
taking two steps to keep up with his one long stride.
"As I'll ever be."

Caitlin was feeling better. Not about the wildlife, but
about the fact she could put one foot in front of the other
without her head pounding.

"Pace okay?" he asked.

She glanced at Tom and couldn't help but see the smile
etched on his face. "Too slow for you, huh?"

"There's nothing wrong with a stroll."

Caitlin stepped it up a bit, not wanting him to go too
easy on her. "So tell me about coming home," she asked,
wanting to know more about him. "Are you doing okay,
honestly?"

His face clouded over, darkened, like a storm brewing where before there had been sunshine. "What do you want to know?"

She watched the scenery as they walked, liked the fact there was hardly anyone else around and they could relax. It wasn't often she was away from the city. "I just thought you might have a story or two to share, that's all. It's no big deal."

He didn't say anything. She listened to the calls of birds she'd never heard before, scanned the trees as they passed. If he didn't want to talk it was up to him. She had plenty she didn't like to talk about, so she wasn't going to press him.

"There's more to it than me messing up my ear."

His flat, morose tone made her slow down and look back at him. She'd known there was more, that there had to be something else for him to have reacted the way he had the other night. It was why she'd wanted to ask him. Even if a part of her was scared of his response.

"What happened?" she asked, wishing she could touch him, comfort him, as she would a friend.

He pushed a hand through his hair and stopped walking, bending to pick up a rock and turning it over and over in his hand as if it were something interesting, something that he'd been looking for. "We lost a man when the bomb went off," Tom said, a hard edge to his voice that she hadn't heard before. "I hate that I'm not doing my job still, but we lost one of our own that day and SEALs don't *ever* lose one of their own." His voice had gone from deep to impossibly deeper, the muscles in his arms flexing as he started to squeeze the stone as if he was trying to kill it.

Caitlin didn't say anything. She stood on the spot, watching him, knowing he wanted to talk. That he had to get it off his chest. *And she wanted to be the one to listen.* Even if her pulse was starting to race. She tried to drag her eyes from his hand.

"Whenever I think about it I want to…" He started to walk again.

Tom didn't need to finish his sentence. It scared her anyway.

"I should have been able to do something. I should have been… Damn!" He hurled the rock through the air, hefting it with all his might, his big frame rising and falling with every breath he sucked back.

"I'm sorry," she said, trying hard not to whisper, not wanting him to see how much he was frightening her. Caitlin tried not to let her mind go *there,* but she wasn't strong enough.

She hid among her mom's clothes, hands over her ears, not wanting to hear what he was doing to her. Not wanting to hear her mom whimper as her dad hit her, aiming his punches low where no one would ever see the bruises.

She'd tried so hard to make him happy, to deflect the attention from her mom, but no matter what she did, it never seemed to work.

Caitlin fought to keep her feet planted, resisting the urge to run blindly down a track she'd hardly taken any notice of. She needed to trust in Tom, to try to believe that he wouldn't hurt her.

Tom's angry gaze met hers. "I'm sorry, too. I think about it every day and I don't know what we could have done differently, but there must have been *something.*"

"And your ear?" she asked, forcing her fear away, pushing through the barriers she'd had up for so long.

"I have another specialist appointment next week, but it's not looking great," he said, blowing out a breath.

His voice softened, returned back to normal, and Caitlin started to relax. "I just have to get over it and move on, right?"

Caitlin frowned. "Tom, I…"

He shook his head and stepped up the pace, body all rigid again. "I don't want to be rude, Caitlin, but I don't want to talk about it anymore. I find it hard enough dealing with it all inside my own head without talking about it and making it all real again."

She bit her lip and kept walking. He was more restrained now than angry, but she still felt that she needed to keep her distance from him. *I know how you feel,* she wanted to say. *Because I've lost what I love, too.* The words were there, in her throat and waiting to be shared, but he'd stopped her. His anger had made her falter.

"Come on, let's stop being morbid and have a good look around. See if we can find us some bobcats."

Caitlin blinked away a tear, pleased he was looking ahead and not at her. Because she never spoke about what had happened to her, what she'd been through, *to anyone,* and she'd been so close to opening up to him. To telling him about her past to try to help him deal with his future. He'd scared her, but she'd still been so close to braving up and telling him.

"Sure," she said, putting on a bright face. "I bet they'd eat you first though, given that you're bigger than me."

Tom chuckled, smiling at her over his shoulder as he held his hand out, completely at odds with how they'd been only moments before. "I'd disagree, but you're probably right."

She gingerly reached for his hand as they went off-trail, liking that he wanted to help her, but terrified of his touch all the same. The thought of how those hands could hurt her.

"Tom…ow!" Caitlin scrambled to stop her ankle from turning over, flung her arms out, but she was too late. Tom caught her before she completely hit the ground, his big hand clamping over her wrist.

"Jeez, Caitlin." He dropped to the earth beside her, gently pulling her ankle out from under her.

It hurt. Like hell. Tears burned in her eyes.

"Are you okay? Where does it hurt?"

She grimaced as he touched her foot, as much from pain as seeing his hand against her skin. "My ankle," she said, trying to be brave. "It hurts real bad."

Tom frowned as he undid her shoelace. "It'll be fine, I'm sure it's only a sprain."

Caitlin shut her eyes as he gently guided her shoe and then her sock off, his hands touching her as if she were a breakable doll that needed the most careful of attention. His touch was soft enough that it almost calmed her.

"It's starting to swell a little already," he said, pushing up the leg of her pants.

Caitlin started to heat up and it had nothing to do with the burning sensation in her ankle. She watched as Tom ran his fingers over every inch of her foot and ankle. He was inspecting her, checking her as he might a patient had he been a doctor, and it was making her flush. Then his hand went to slide higher. Caitlin fought the urge for a moment and then quickly brushed his hand away. "I'm fine."

"Did that hurt?" he asked, confusion crossing his face.

She shook her head, mute. Maybe it did hurt, she didn't know anymore. All she did know was that the way his fingers were playing across her skin could make even the most painful of broken bones feel healed. And at the same time she couldn't bear them getting any closer to…

"Where did you get this scar?"

Caitlin looked down. Oh. Her face burned as though it was being licked by flames.

He was crouched in front of her, inspecting the now-faint scars marring her skin, translucent against her light tan. She pulled at her trouser leg, covering the marks.

"Oh, them," she stuttered. "An accident, a long time ago." A few minutes before, she'd been ready to open up to him and tell him what had happened to her. But she didn't want to open up to him now, not injured and thinking about him the way she was. Not when he was already feeling sorry for her. The only reason she was going to tell him was to help him through his problems, not because she wanted him to feel sorry for her.

And besides, she didn't want to go there. Wasn't brave enough.

She'd spent years proving to herself and everyone around her that she was strong, and she had no intention of changing that now. What was she going to say? *Yeah, I don't want you touching me because I'm scared you're going to hurt me. Oh, and those scars are from my psycho ex-boyfriend, who was just like my dad.*

"Do you think you can walk?" Tom asked, still frowning, looking at her with *way* too much intensity.

Caitlin looked up and into warm brown eyes that stopped her from thinking. Or maybe they didn't, because she could think plenty about the way he looked, the way he was looking at her, as if she was the most precious thing in the world. At least it took her mind off her past, which all of a sudden seemed to be haunting her like a nightmare all over again, the way it used to.

Caitlin cleared her throat. "Yeah, I'll try to walk."

She took Tom's hand and tried to rise, held on to him and pulled herself up, knowing it'd be stupid not to accept his help.

"Take it slow," he instructed, hands firm against her body, holding her tight.

Tears sprang into Caitlin's eyes, but she fought them, tried hard not to show it, because she didn't want him to think she was weak.

"It hurts like hell, doesn't it?" Tom asked, voice gruff.

When she didn't respond, couldn't get the words out through the pain even with her teeth clenched, he took one hand from her waist and cupped it beneath her chin. "Doesn't it, Caitlin?"

"What?" she whispered, staring into his eyes, trying to stop her body from shaking.

"Hurt?" he asked again, but this time his voice was lower, as though he was distracted, too. Tom's gaze moved to her lips. He hesitated, but only for a heartbeat.

Caitlin hardly even had time to think before Tom dipped his head, lips brushing against hers in the most delicate of motions, touching her so gently she wondered if she'd imagined it.

He pulled back, watching her, seeming to want to give her the chance to pull away, to push him back. But she didn't. As flushed and hot and scared and in pain as she was, Caitlin had no intention of pulling away, of telling him no.

She couldn't. Because after so long keeping her distance from men, Tom's lips on hers felt so darn *nice*.

Tom bent, his big frame curved to bring his face to her level. He pressed his forehead against hers, looking into her eyes, before tugging her closer with his hand to her waist, the other tangled in her hair as though he didn't want to let her go.

Caitlin scooped her arms around him, catching them at the back of his neck, not caring that her ankle was burning and throbbing or that her fear was trying so hard to strangle her. Because Tom had taken all her weight and was holding her to him, mouth moving over hers as if he were hungry, lips caressing hers over and over again until they felt bruised. Plump from all the attention.

And she wasn't going to complain.

Tom pulled back, but he didn't let go of her. "I didn't plan this," he said softly, forehead pressed to hers again, eyes looking at her as though he'd never looked at anything so important in all his life.

Caitlin was breathless. Absolutely, ridiculously out of breath.

She fought not to wriggle away from him, braved his gaze. "Good, because my ankle's killing me."

Tom dropped another quick, gentle kiss to her lips before scooping her up and cocooning her against his chest. "Better?" he asked.

Caitlin shut her eyes and tucked her head against the warmth and breadth of him. She couldn't deny that being held by Tom felt great. As if she was finally, truly safe, when before she'd only ever felt safe on her own. "Much."

"Well, let's get you out of here," he said, walking back to the trail and carrying her as if she weighed no more than a child.

She nestled her body in, liking feeling weightless, enjoying the way his arms curled around her shoulders and supported her legs. "Are you sure I'm not too heavy? I mean, it's a fair walk back," she asked.

Tom placed his chin to the top of head but didn't slow his steady, even pace. "I've trained half my life for situations like this," he said with a chuckle. "Believe me when I say I'd rather carry you for a mile than some of the things I've had to haul for ten or more."

"Seriously?"

"You're a ballerina, not a heavyweight wrestler," he

joked. "And besides, it's about time I practiced what I preach. I make the recruits do stuff like this all the time, only they don't get to carry anyone near as pretty as you."

Caitlin blushed. "Do you have a favorite running cadence?"

He laughed, looking down at her as he moved. "How did you know it was called a cadence? Most civilians just call them running songs."

Caitlin hadn't meant to let anything slip. Had had no intention of telling him she'd been an army brat, that her dad had been a Marine. "Something I must have heard somewhere," she lied. "So, do you have one?" Caitlin pressed, forgetting all about her sore ankle again.

"Ha, I sure do." Tom started to run, feet thumping on the trail. "Hey Baba-lou-ba, SEAL team training."

He kept running before stopping and staring down at her.

"The whole purpose of this is for you to repeat after me," he said, his expression serious.

Caitlin laughed at the stern look on his face. "Me?" She wasn't going to let on that she knew a *thing* about them.

Tom rolled his eyes. "Well, it'll just sound stupid if *I* have to repeat it."

She went to laugh again but his mouth caught hers, took her by surprise before she had the chance. Caitlin wriggled in his grip before relaxing into the possessive way his lips moved over hers. It still made her heart pound from fear as much as excitement, but she was starting to get used to it.

"Ready?" he asked, breaking away and looking all serious again.

"Ready," she answered, forcing her face to be as serious as his.

"Hey Baba-lou-ba, SEAL team training," Tom chanted.

"Hey Baba-lou-ba, SEAL team training," she sang back.

"I joined the Navy now people think I'm *cra-zy*."

Caitlin started to giggle and then laughed so hard she had tears streaming down her cheeks. She looked up to see Tom's big smile.

She tucked her head back against his chest and sighed in between hiccuping bursts of laughter.

She was being carried through a trail after a failed hiking attempt, singing as though she didn't have a care in the world, in the arms of a man she'd never dreamed she could be attracted to. She was facing her fears head-on, and she liked it.

It was quite possibly one of the best days of her life.

CHAPTER EIGHT

Tom put Caitlin gently on her feet beside the car. He almost kept hold of her, but after nearly twenty minutes of walking with her against his chest, he had to give her up. Any longer and he'd have to start explaining himself.

He didn't remember the last time he'd held a woman like that. Wondered if he ever had. It was like learning to touch again, to feel, to connect with another human being. He'd been close to the men he worked alongside, but he hadn't had *contact*. Holding Caitlin against him was like reigniting someone he used to be, stirring the flailing embers of a fire and slowly coaxing them to flame again.

"How you feeling?" he asked.

Caitlin turned her face up toward him and smiled. "Okay. I think maybe it's not as bad as I thought."

He resisted the urge to bend down and touch the delicate skin at her ankle again. She'd flinched earlier, had looked almost panicked, as if she'd thought he was going to hurt her.

Tom pulled his thoughts away from earlier. It was stupid, he must have been mistaken. There was no way Caitlin could have actually been scared of him. Maybe she was jumpy, but she couldn't be *scared*. Could she?

Tom tried to change his focus, dragging his eyes from

her mouth and trying to forget all about what had happened back there. Or at least he wished he could. Because that kiss had his mind spinning.

"Do you think I should get it checked out?" Caitlin asked.

Tom opened the door for her and guided her down to the seat so she didn't have to hop on one leg. "I'm sure it's fine. I had a pretty good look at it. But I bet you'll need some crutches for the next few days."

Caitlin pulled her hair tie out and ran her fingers through her long hair, before tying it back up into a more orderly tail again.

His throat ran dry.

She had no idea what she was doing to him. No idea how her every action was affecting him.

"Tom?"

And he had no idea what she'd just said. "Sorry?"

Caitlin gave him a curious look. "I was asking if I should just ice it when I get home."

"No," he blurted.

"No? Should I put heat on it? I thought I'd need to ice it, but then you'd know."

"I don't want you going home alone. How about you come over for dinner so I can keep an eye on it for you?"

Caitlin's eyebrows raised. "You cook?"

"Well, no. I mean yes, I do cook, but I'm not cooking tonight," he corrected.

Now she looked even more confused. "Take-out's fine. I mean, if you're sure you want me to come over. I kind of ruined your fun last night and now I've ruined your hike, so I don't mind if you want to run and never see me again!"

Tom's mouth went dry. She had no idea. Seriously *no idea* how beautiful she was or how cute she was being all chatty and innocent. She'd made him wild last night, sure, but ruined his night? Been on his mind all night, more like. And today couldn't have been more enjoyable if he'd planned it, aside from her being in pain over her fall. Today had been exactly what he'd needed.

"We're actually all having dinner tonight, my whole family, so it'll be my mom's cooking and I can definitely vouch for it being great."

Caitlin visibly relaxed. "So you're asking me to your family's get-together…" Her sentence trailed off. "Are you sure they won't mind?"

Tom chuckled as he leaned in toward her, arms folded over the door as he looked at her. "Mind? I've never taken a woman to my mom's house for dinner in my life, so I'd say their reaction would be the complete opposite of *mind*."

Caitlin stared at him, didn't say anything. But a gentle smile did make her lips curve.

"I didn't mean to freak you out," he apologized. "It doesn't have to be a big deal at all. We can go out to a restaurant instead if you'd like?"

Her smile widened. "I don't mind either way. I'd love to come."

Tom was relieved. "Well, alrighty then."

Caitlin was still smiling when he got in beside her. "Maybe you should phone ahead, text your mom or something to tell her that I'm coming. I'd hate her to freak out at the thought of you bringing a date."

Now it was Tom trying not to laugh. A date, huh? If she wanted it to be a date, then he had no problem with that. At all.

"Are you sure you don't mind?" he asked, just to be sure.

"I don't have any family, Tom, so it'd be kind of nice

to spend time with yours," she told him, cheek against the headrest as she wriggled in her seat to face him, watching him. "It'll be fun."

"You don't have any family?" How could he not have known this already?

Caitlin kept smiling at him, but it was sadder this time, the happiness not reflected in her eyes. "Nope, just me."

"Can I ask what happened?" How could she have *no* family at all?

"Nothing to tell," she said, her upbeat words at odds with the look on her face, too forced.

Tom nodded slowly, trying to gather his thoughts. What he needed was to change the subject, give her an out. He understood all about needing to keep some things close to his chest, so he wasn't going to pry.

"So you survived your first hike, huh?" he said, instead of questioning her further.

Caitlin held up her ankle, propping it on the dash. Her smile was grateful. "Only just."

"Well, it was better than being attacked by a bobcat, so count yourself lucky."

Tom grinned at her before focusing all his attention on the road as he pulled out of the parking lot. Yesterday, he'd been feeling down. Now, he felt invigorated, the way he only ever usually did after a serious workout session or a mission when he was a SEAL. Even if he was itching to know more about Caitlin and why she was so totally alone.

He was under no illusions. Caitlin was the cause of his euphoria and he wanted to be in her company. There was something about the pint-sized ballerina that intrigued him, made him feel alive as he hadn't in a long time.

When he'd left his unit, he'd felt as if his future was

over. As if he'd never find even a blink of happiness ever again.

But Caitlin had changed that. She'd made him see that he was capable of smiling again, of feeling happy, and for that he owed her big-time.

"So why did you become a teacher?" Tom called out as he sat in Caitlin's living room, running one hand up and down her cat's back as he waited for her to get dressed. He'd never heard a cat purr so much in his life, but it wasn't helping to distract him. All he could think about was the fact that she'd been naked, only a room away from him, while he sat trying to pretend she wasn't.

He was behaving like a sex-starved teenager. It had been way too long since he'd been with a woman, and now it was a particularly beautiful woman that he was craving.

Tom stifled a laugh. His SEAL buddies would be hooting with laughter at him if they could see him.

"Caitlin?"

"Sorry," she called back, sounding breathless. "Getting ready without being able to walk is kind of trickier than I thought!"

Tom leaned back into the sofa and shut his eyes, thinking about all the ways he could help her. He seriously needed to think about something else.

"So tell me," he asked again, trying to keep his mind from the gutter and only just succeeding. "What is it you like about teaching so much?"

"Did I say I liked it?"

No, but she sure as hell looked as if she loved it when he'd seen her with the children. "I already know you like it, but I need to know why."

She hopped into the room before leaning against the

door frame. "I love it because the kids are like little sponges, and I get to help them soak up everything they need to learn."

Tom nodded, ignoring how cute she looked in her jeans. "So you like them because they're small and impressionable?"

"I guess, but I like the fact that I'm helping them, too. You know, that it's me they look to for guidance."

He patted the cat some more instead of running his eyes up and down her body. Even in bare feet she looked perfect, all tiny and delicate, her hair still pulled up into a high ponytail that fell halfway down her back.

"Are we talking about me or you right now?" she asked.

She was smarter than he'd given her credit for.

"I'm struggling with the whole teaching thing," he admitted. "I guess I'd never really thought about being the teacher. I've never had a problem learning, pushing myself to do better, but being on the other side is…"

"Different, I know," she finished for him.

"You do?"

Caitlin hopped some more and fell into the chair beside him. "Once you realize how important your job is, you'll make peace with it."

Tom doubted he would ever prefer teaching over being in the field, but right now he didn't have much choice. "So you think I'll like it better than the real thing one day?"

She shook her head, a gentle smile telling him no. "I doubt it. But without great teachers, no one succeeds, so whatever you're teaching you have to make sure you're the best leader your pupils can have."

Tom laughed at her words of wisdom. "Are you sure you haven't been attending some U.S. Navy training courses? Because you sure seem like you're giving me a formal pep talk."

Caitlin tucked her good foot up beneath her body and watched him. He liked that she was relaxed. Sometimes he got the feeling that he made her jumpy.

"Once you come to terms with it, I'll put money down that you'll love it."

"How much?" he joked. "I'll match you dollar for dollar on that bet."

Caitlin waved her hand at him and hauled herself to her feet again, looking the least graceful he'd ever seen her as she tried to keep the weight off her sore ankle. "Come on, let's go. I don't want to make a bad first impression on your mom by being late."

Tom leaped to attention, taking her by the elbow to help her walk. "Once she sees you, there'll be no checking the time. She'll get all flustered and flap about in the kitchen like she's a bird about to take flight."

Caitlin rolled her eyes. "Even more reason for you to have phoned ahead and told her," she insisted.

Tom just grinned and opened the door before flicking the lock and pulling it behind them. But he couldn't stop thinking about what she'd said.

First impression. Jeez. Did that mean she wanted to make another impression on his family? That she was thinking about seeing him again?

Had he been too quick to ask her over? Tom stilled his fingers even though they were itching to tug through his hair, ignored the part of him that was freaked out.

When they'd lost a man in the field, when the ringing in his ears wouldn't stop and when it had been replaced with almost silence, he'd thought his life was permanently dislodged onto the wrong track. Like a train veering off on the wrong line, with no hope of being pointed back in the right direction.

But he felt as if Caitlin was changing the rules, tugging at those invisible boundaries. As if she was testing him, pushing and pulling him in different directions, and he wasn't disliking it. Wasn't sure what the hell was happening, but not disliking it. He'd overreacted the other night, and he still felt bad about that. After so many months of everyone around him trying to pretend that they understood loss, as if they could comprehend how much he'd lost this last year, he'd snapped. He should have kept his feelings in check, but he hadn't and Caitlin had borne the brunt of it.

But not again. She deserved to be treated better than that, he'd just had to figure out where exactly he was heading and what his intentions were.

There was a chance here that he could move on. That he could go back in time to when he was at peace with his life, when demons weren't chasing him in the night. To have a normal future. So no matter how hard it was, he had to at least try to move on. To move forward. To figure out how to change things.

Because if he didn't, he had a feeling it was something he'd live to regret forever.

Caitlin was more nervous right now than she'd have been if she was about to perform. Her preshow jitters had always made her jumpy, but walking up to the front door of Tom's mom's house was even worse. She had no idea why she'd agreed to come. Or maybe she did. Because after years of dreaming of a proper family, of one where parents sat down to nice family dinners and didn't argue or scream at each other or worse, any chance to be part of a real family made her yearn for that type of childhood. Even just to be part of a snapshot for one night.

"I'm not convinced this was a good…"

The door swung open and Caitlin swallowed her words.

"Tommy!" Gabby stood on the other side of the door, a huge smile lighting her face.

He bent to scoop her up for a quick cuddle and a kiss, before putting her back down and reaching for Caitlin instead.

"Look who I brought with me, kiddo." He waited for Caitlin to brace her arm around his shoulder so he could help her inside and she obliged. "Injured but okay."

Gabby's head was on an angle as she looked at the pair of them. "Why is Miss Rose here for dinner?" She didn't even ask about the fact Caitlin's ankle was bandaged or that she was only wearing one shoe.

Caitlin gave her a grin, relieved that she hadn't met Tom's mom yet. "Because you have the best uncle in the world and he wanted me to join you."

Tom gave her a strange look and she wished she hadn't said anything.

"What happened to you?" Gabby asked, as though she'd finally noticed.

"Tom, is that you?"

"Yeah, it's me, Mom."

Caitlin gulped, back in panic mode again. Tom turned his head and looked at her, his gentle smile and quick wink making her nerves rattle for a completely different reason.

She could stare at him all day and not tire. His dark brown eyes, the way his gaze had the power to put her at ease and excite her at the same time… She looked down at Gabby again, needing to break the connection.

Her being here didn't mean anything. It was just dinner between friends, and Tom had been kind enough to ask her to join his family so she wasn't in pain and alone. But still, maybe she should have declined.

"Tom, I was wondering…"

His mom was calling out, talking to him as they followed Gabby down the short hall and into the open-plan living and kitchen area.

"Oh!" The words died on his mom's lips. "I see we have company."

Caitlin's face flushed warm and she was as nervous as a teenager meeting her boyfriend's parents for the first time. Tom's mother's expression went from surprised to happy all at once.

"Hey, Mom." Tom let go of Caitlin briefly to envelop his mom in a hug and kiss her on the cheek. He waved to an equally surprised-looking woman sitting at the table, chair pushed back and Gabby tugging at her arm. Caitlin recognized her instantly.

"Everyone, this is…"

"Miss Rose," announced Gabby.

It made them all laugh, Caitlin included. Tom stood beside her again and took her arm, helping her forward.

"Yes, *Miss Rose*. Otherwise known as Caitlin," Tom corrected.

"How lovely of you to join us," his mom said, holding both hands out to clasp one of Caitlin's. She kept herself steady by holding on to Tom still, letting her hand be squeezed by his mom's warm palms. "I'm Vicki."

"Nice to meet you," Caitlin said back, not having to force her smile. She'd gone from nervous to welcome within seconds. "I'd let go of your son but I'm not exactly capable of standing on my own right now."

His mom looked surprised and Gabby's mom frowned before pushing her chair back to walk toward them.

"Please don't tell me that Tom had something to do with this," Vicki said, shaking her head at her son. "It looks like a Tom kind of accident. Please don't tell me he made you go hiking?"

Caitlin laughed. "Does he take every girl he meets hiking?"

"Every woman? I doubt it. I've never met anyone who's said yes to one of his expeditions yet!"

Caitlin let her hand be squeezed again. "We have met before. I'm Penny, Gabby's mom. You must meet so many parents that I'm sure it's hard to keep track."

"I remember you. We don't have any other moms who are soldiers, so you're kind of hard to forget." Caitlin relaxed as Penny took her by the elbow, ushering her away from Tom.

"Come and sit down," Penny said, giving Tom a nudge. "You can pull her chair out. Make Caitlin comfortable," she bossed.

Tom jumped to attention, and Caitlin couldn't hold back her laugh.

"What?" Tom asked.

"I'm just realizing that maybe if I'd been a bit more bossy with you I could have avoided this sprained ankle completely!" That made the other two women in the room laugh, too. "I was intimidated by the whole Navy thing when I should have stuck to my guns."

Tom didn't look impressed as he glared at his sister-in-law before looking back at her. "I thought you wanted to go?"

She reached out a hand to touch his arm, smiling up at him. Instead of worrying, of feeling out of place, Caitlin was relaxed. Content with being at his family dinner, at being around a family again after so long on her own. It was comforting even though they were strangers.

"I did like it, Tom. If this hadn't happened," she gestured to her ankle, "it would have been the perfect afternoon."

His mom appeared across the table, leaning forward on the back of a chair. "Well, let's make this the perfect evening," she suggested, smiling with a warmth that instantly reminded Caitlin of Tom. "Let's get Caitlin a drink, Tom, and then you can help me in the kitchen."

He looked down at Caitlin, and she grinned up at him, propping her leg up on the chair he'd shuffled closer for her. "You okay for a minute?"

"I'm fine. Absolutely fine," she replied. And she was. It had been a long time since she'd been relaxed around a man, but for once, she wasn't lying.

Tom brushed his hand against her hair, barely connecting with her cheek beneath, but Caitlin felt it. It almost took her breath away, the casual way his fingers skimmed against her, reminding her that he was there. That he was aware of her and wasn't going to leave her for long.

She looked up to see Penny watching. Smiling, but watching.

"I think I'm starting to see why Tom was so keen to look after Gabby while we were away."

Caitlin met Penny's gaze, pleased to see only kindness there instead of any animosity.

"I promise I'd never even seen Tom before," Caitlin confessed. "But he did make quite a first impression on me when he visited my classroom."

"To collect Gabby?" Penny asked.

"Ah, I'm guessing your daughter hasn't told you that she dragged Tom to school for show-and-tell, then?"

Penny roared with laughter. "Are you serious? Tom actually did that?"

Caitlin had liked Penny the moment she'd met her at a parent-teacher meeting, but now she was convinced about the other woman. "I think you're underestimating the effect that little girl has on her uncle."

Penny held up her hands. "You're right, Gabby could get any of the men in her life to do anything for her."

"Who're you talking about?"

Caitlin looked up at the same time as Penny to see Tom and another man standing together, side by side. There was no mistaking they were brothers, all dark hair and even darker colored eyes, both close to filling the doorway they'd just passed through.

"Hi, I'm Daniel," the man announced, walking closer and standing behind his wife. "And I know *exactly* who you are." He grinned at his brother, and Caitlin watched as Tom scowled back.

"Play nicely, boys." Tom's mom came back into the room, carrying a huge dish of food.

Caitlin watched as both men moved toward their mom, Tom getting there a step before his brother and ferrying the dish the rest of the way to the table. Daniel followed her back into the kitchen and came back out with another huge plate. It was nice seeing grown men so eager to assist the woman who'd raised them.

"This looks delicious." Just as she'd imagined it would be.

"So Caitlin, I think I missed the part about how you and Tom met, and how he's going to make it up to you for getting that ankle sprained," Daniel asked.

Caitlin grinned at Tom as he carved the huge roast chicken on the table. "Funnily enough, we met in my classroom, and given that he carried me a mile or so back to the car today, I think we're about even."

"Why, what did you have to get even over?"

Caitlin felt the flush hit her cheeks, but she wasn't about to share stories from her drunken night out. "Ah…"

"Caitlin teaches ballet, too, and I helped her out with collecting some stage sets for her class's next performance the other day." Tom's lie rolled easily off his tongue and she was grateful.

"Ballet?" His mom asked. "Do you teach Gabby's class?"

"Yes," Caitlin replied, pleased to busy herself with the food before them. Everyone was helping themselves and she was happy not to be the complete center of attention. "Gabby's one of my favorite little students at ballet and at school," she praised.

Gabby wriggled in her chair, clearly excited. "Do you want to see what we learned last week?"

Caitlin watched as all the other adults nodded their heads, clearly used to Gabby's enthusiasm, liking to watch and praise her.

While they sat, dinner getting cold in front of them, Gabby twirled and danced and giggled until they were all laughing. But it felt right. It didn't matter that they were sitting there watching a child instead of eating, because to Caitlin it felt like being part of a real family. If only for a moment in time.

And she loved it.

Caitlin looked over at Tom and quickly lowered her gaze when he grinned at her. His smile was genuine but it held more than just happiness. It was a smile filled with meaning, and it sent a shiver down the length of her spine.

Because, after all this time of turning down almost

every man who had asked her out, after years of focusing on herself and building a life as a single person, being happy on her own, she was starting to wonder if she could build a different kind of something with Tom. If she could open up to him, if they could slowly build on what they had, maybe, just maybe, she could figure out how to trust again.

Tom reached out and brushed a hand over Caitlin's. He'd been wanting to do it all night, had been watching her, smiling at the way she interacted with his family. And he couldn't stop thinking how sad it was that she didn't have one of her own.

"You okay?" he asked her.

He liked the way Caitlin tipped her head back and met his gaze. "Yeah, I am. Better than okay, actually."

He didn't know if he'd ever seen her looking so relaxed.

Tom ran his fingers carefully up her arm before standing. "I'm going to help with the dishes. I don't want Daniel showing me up in there."

"Always competing. Trying to outdo one another," Penny said, leaning back in her chair with an almost empty glass of wine resting in her hand.

Tom looked down at Caitlin one last time before joining his brother and mom in the kitchen. He didn't want to leave her, had a feeling that he should stay by her side, but he ignored it. She was sitting with his sister-in-law and he needed to stamp out his sudden urge to protect her, because Caitlin wasn't his to protect.

"So," he asked his brother once they were both in the kitchen. "What do you think?"

Daniel shrugged, not bothering to turn from his position at the sink. "I have no idea how you convinced such a beautiful woman to go out with you. No idea at all."

Tom grabbed the tea towel and flicked Daniel hard around the back of the legs. "Like I've always wondered how you managed to convince a girl like Penny to marry you." He went to do a lock-hold around the neck, to hold Daniel until he begged for release. He didn't bother to tell his brother that he wasn't actually "seeing" Caitlin. That they weren't technically more than just friends.

"Boys!" Their mom's call made Tom step back, stop instantly. "You can leave the fighting until you're alone. We have a guest and I don't need any blood to clean up off the floor."

Tom blew his mom a kiss from across the room before he slapped his brother on the back. They'd always rough-and-tumbled, fought hard and fast, tousled whenever they could. And their mom had always joked about having to clean up after them if things got nasty. Like the time he'd accidentally broken Daniel's nose, or the time his brother had wrestled him a little too hard and knocked him out cold.

"So how did you ask her out?" Daniel asked, passing him a plate to dry.

"It was more…" Tom stopped, decided not to attempt to explain what it was that was happening between them because he actually had no idea. "Anyway, I'm just glad she said yes."

His mom smiled at him again from across the kitchen, her eyes showing her happiness. He didn't want her getting all excited, but he liked that she so obviously approved of Caitlin. He'd never brought a woman home with him before, even after months of dating in the past, yet for some reason he'd wanted to introduce her to his family and he'd never even taken Caitlin on a real date before. The look in his mom's eyes right now was the same look he'd seen her give Penny, her daughter-in-law, countless times.

Maybe he shouldn't have brought Caitlin here when he didn't even know yet if he was capable of letting things go any further between them.

"You know you can't hurt her, right?"

Tom looked up. He had no intention of hurting her. What the hell was Daniel even talking about? "I'm not planning on it."

"Good, because if you did you'd have Gabby to contend with. And she's always telling me how much she loves her teacher."

Penny held up the bottle of wine and gestured toward Caitlin. She shook her head no and Penny set it back down on the table. The other woman looked at her, head to the side slightly, a friendly expression on her face.

"I have to ask you, Caitlin," she said, making it sound more like an apology than a question. "Do you *really* like Tom?"

Caitlin couldn't help the surprised expression she was sure took over her entire face.

"I'm sorry, that was rude of me," blurted Penny before Caitlin had time to answer. "Don't feel like you have to answer that. I tell Gabby off all the time for shooting her mouth off, and there I go doing it myself."

Caitlin sighed. She didn't mind answering, but… "Can I ask why you want to know?"

That made Penny laugh. "Fair call," she said, leaning in a little closer. "I probably shouldn't be telling you this, but in all the years I've been part of this family, I don't recall Tom ever bringing a woman home for dinner."

"Maybe he did when you were away serving," she

replied, in reference to Penny's years as a soldier that she'd heard all about.

Penny laughed again, just a short chuckle this time. "No, I think I'm right in saying you're the first girl he's ever brought home to meet his mom."

Caitlin didn't know what to say. She hadn't known Tom long and it wasn't as if they'd even been out properly before, on a real date even yet. But she wasn't going to bring that up, not now. "I'm pleased he did," she told Penny. "Brought me here, I mean. It's nice to be part of a family for an evening."

Penny looked relaxed as she pushed her chair back and watched Caitlin. "I'm guessing you don't have a family?"

Caitlin hardly ever spoke about what had happened to her, what her past held, but sitting here with Penny seemed different somehow. "I have no idea where my dad is these days—he could be dead for all I know, and my mom passed away when I was a teenager."

She omitted the part about her secret fantasy, how she hoped her father had died. Wished that he was long dead so he couldn't hurt anyone else.

Caitlin could see the compassion, the feeling, shining from Penny's eyes before she spoke.

"My father left before I was born and my mom died a few years back."

So Penny understood. Maybe not everything, but a lot of what she'd experienced herself then. "So you're pleased to be part of this family then, right?" Caitlin asked her, an unfamiliar pang of jealousy tickling the back of her throat. Being here, seeing the way they all interacted and the love that was so clearly shared within the walls of this home, made her wish it for herself. For her own life.

Penny looked thoughtful before she spoke, as though

she was deciding whether to share her story. "When my mom died, I was so lost, but Daniel's mom became like my own, and this family meant everything to me. They still do."

"I can see that," Caitlin replied.

"Tom has been like a brother to me for years. If I'd met him instead of Daniel I think I would have married him, they're so similar. But don't be jealous," Penny said in a rush, as if she was worried how her words had come out. "I don't mean that I'm attracted to him, because Tom's a brother and nothing else to me. But the way they are, the way they treat their mom and everyone else around them, it's refreshing. They goad each other and fight like toddlers all the time, but they'd give their own lives for those they love, and the way they treat Gabby is…"

"Incredibly special," Caitlin finished for her, the words leaving her mouth before she could stop them. "I know what you mean. When I saw Tom with Gabby that first day, I wasn't even interested in him romantically, but I could see the kind of man he was when I watched how he looked at her. How much love he had for her."

"And now?" Penny asked, clearly wanting to gauge Caitlin's feelings for her brother-in-law.

Caitlin hesitated. She didn't know. Hadn't asked herself that question yet, figured out what they meant to one another or what might happen between her and Tom. Whether she could forget enough of her past to move forward. But then maybe what she really needed to do was confront it.

"I don't know," she replied, talking with honesty and from the heart. "I really like him, but I'm not sure what exactly is happening between us."

Penny's soft laughter made her look up. "I don't think you have to worry about how Tom feels, if that's what you're worried about," she said. "Whether he knows it yet or not, the look in those puppy-dog eyes of his and the fact he brought you here tells me all I need to know. Usually, I'd be telling him not to break a girl's heart, but somehow I don't think that's the case here."

Caitlin kept her eyes down. She didn't know where to look or what to say, but she did know one thing. Her heart was pounding and there was a dizziness in her head making her giddy, and it had nothing to do with the half glass of wine she'd consumed.

Caitlin took a deep breath for confidence. "This is going to sound weird to you, but…" She stalled, couldn't follow through.

She jumped up from the table, pushed her mom to one side and tried to deflect the attention from her. But her dad was too strong, swatted her aside so he could reach his favorite target.

Her mom.

"Caitlin?" Worry lines creased Penny's face.

Caitlin pressed her fingers to her temple, forcibly trying to push the memories back from where they'd emerged.

She shouldn't have brought it up. "I'm sorry, it's nothing."

Penny's hands met hers, intertwining their fingers as she might comfort a sister. "I'm good at keeping secrets, in case that's what you're worried about. I'm not going to go blabbering to the boys if you want to ask me something in confidence."

Caitlin shut her eyes, and when she opened them she locked her gaze on Penny, drew strength from her. "Would Tom hurt me physically? Can you tell me, hand on your heart, whether he would ever hit a woman? Whether he's capable of losing his temper like that?"

Caitlin had tears in her eyes, couldn't believe she'd so openly asked the one question that terrified her.

Penny's gaze didn't waver, but her grip on Caitlin's fingers tightened.

"I would trust Tom with my life," Penny told her, tears reflecting in her eyes now, too. "I would let Tom raise my daughter in my absence, because I can promise you, from the bottom of my heart, that Tom would rather die than raise his hand in anger to a woman. He would protect those he loved with force if he had to, but he will never hurt you. Not like that."

Caitlin was trying her hardest not to cry, but she couldn't control the quiver of her bottom lip. Penny didn't ask her *why,* didn't question her, but there was something unsaid between them, an understanding, that told Caitlin Penny knew what she was asking. Knew why she'd had to ask the question.

"You ladies need anything else? A drink or something?"

Tom's deep voice made her look up, her hands jumping from Penny's. The sudden loss of contact made goose pimples play a trail across her skin. She watched as Penny got up and left the room, smiling at her as she left, honesty shining from her eyes, telling her she could trust her even though they didn't exchange words. Penny called out to Gabby as she moved, but all Caitlin truly saw now was Tom standing before her. He was so tall that she had to tip her head back to meet his eyes from where she sat, and it wasn't hard to look at him. To run her eyes over his broad shoulders or down his tanned forearms, showing from beneath the rolled-up sleeves of his shirt.

"No," she said, voice low as she watched him, tears forgotten.

He crossed the room in a few strides and sat down beside her, close enough for his leg to brush against hers, thigh to thigh, pressed together. She couldn't help the smile that caressed her face when he watched her.

"Are you sure everything's okay?" he asked. "You looked kind of sad when I walked in."

Caitlin shook her head. "I'm fine."

Her body was on the verge of trembling, but she had to push past it. Because she owed it to herself to try, to believe that she could move forward and trust in another human being, in a man, again. At least to give him a chance.

"Shall we get out of here?"

Caitlin wanted to say yes, but didn't all at the same time. It was nice being here, but being with Tom, alone, would be…

"Caitlin?"

"Yeah," she answered. "Yeah, that'd be nice."

Tom took her hand on one side and cupped under her armpit on the other, helping her up. He pressed a soft, barely there kiss to her cheek, close to her ear, sending a tickling shiver down her back. "Let's go," he said.

Caitlin was proud of herself, felt an inner surge of confidence that she'd thought was long lost.

And what scared her even more than her earlier fears was that she wanted to trust him. She no longer wanted to push him away more than she wanted to pull him closer.

CHAPTER NINE

Tom refused to look at Caitlin, not wanting to take his eyes off the road, but he could feel her next to him, was so aware of her that it was hard to focus on doing *anything*. He had no idea if he was doing the right thing; all he knew was that he wasn't sure he could walk away from her.

He pulled up outside her house. Tom couldn't believe that a couple of weeks ago he hadn't even known she existed, had never even driven down this street, but in the last week he'd been here repeatedly.

At least he didn't have to make a move now. Because he had no intention of saying goodbye to her without walking her to the door and helping her inside. He'd kissed her earlier today, but it already felt like a lifetime ago and he needed to show her how he felt. That he wanted something to happen between them even if he wasn't sure what that something was yet.

"Here we are," he said, pulling over. "Stay put and I'll help you out."

Caitlin didn't disagree and he didn't hesitate. He opened her door and bent to pick her up, not wanting her to put any unnecessary weight on her ankle.

"Tom, you really don't have to…oh!" She half squealed

as he swept her off her feet and held her tight against his chest. "Twice in one day, huh?"

He smiled down at her, still not sure what to do. Or quite what to say to convey how he felt. All he knew was that he was good at being the protector and what he wanted right now was to be protecting Caitlin. He might not have been able to protect the men he'd lost, but he'd be darned if he wasn't going to protect her.

"It's not exactly a chore," he said, wishing he'd come up with something wittier.

Caitlin giggled. "You mean I'm not too heavy so it's bearable?"

Tom tried to stop himself from staring at her too seriously, tried not to look as fierce as he knew he must have looked. Because she was like a fragile bird, Caitlin was. There was something scared within her, something he couldn't put his finger on, that told him she'd be too easy to break. And he wanted to be the one to make her strong.

It was now or never.

"I don't mean it's easy because you're light." Tom's voice was gruff, rough around the edges in a way he hadn't heard himself speak before.

Caitlin leaned back a fraction to look up at him. "You don't?"

Tom gulped, swallowed hard and moved his fingers to cup more closely around her. "I would carry you all day if it meant I could be near you."

She looked surprised. Taken aback. He was, too, couldn't believe what he was saying.

Then a shy smile spread out over her face, lighting her cheeks a bright pink that he could see even in the half-light.

Tom didn't wait for her to say anything. Instead, he walked the last few steps up her porch, put her down gently to her feet and pressed her firmly against the door, back hard up against it. He didn't take his eyes off her, pinned her with his gaze, placing a hand on either side of her head against the timber, leaning in close until his mouth was only inches from hers.

"Caitlin," he said, voice low.

He watched her swallow, his body tensing as her tongue darted out to moisten her lips, as though she was nervous and didn't know what to do or where to look. Afraid, perhaps? He hoped not—she had nothing to be afraid of.

He let his hands drop lower, conscious that he didn't want to make her feel trapped, even if a tug within him wished he could hold her firmly in place and not let her go.

He kept his hands locked still, touching her instead with his body, pressed to hers before he kissed her. Tom touched his lips lightly to Caitlin's, pulled back to put the smallest of spaces between them, giving her the opportunity to say no, to push him away.

But she didn't.

Caitlin closed the distance between them herself, kissing him shamelessly, pressing her warm, tiny body into his. Tom kissed her back more fiercely than before, took her mouth hard against his own and touched his tongue intimately against hers, teased her with his lips. He dropped his mouth to her neck, caressing her with his hands, too, no longer able to keep them raised above her, needing to run them down her body, skimming her slender curves.

"Tom," she gasped, her voice barely audible as she put a hand to his chest and pushed him back.

He was breathing hard, adrenaline pumping through

his veins as though he was about to attack a foreign enemy. Was preparing to launch an assault.

"You want me to stop?"

Caitlin looked at him shyly, as if she didn't know what she wanted. "I need you to be gentle with me," she said.

Tom didn't need to be told twice. He'd already sensed she was fragile and it was time he trusted his instincts again. He scooped her up carefully, holding her in his arms as she fumbled with her keys and unlocked the door to let them in.

He kicked it shut behind him and walked down the hall, stopping only to cup her chin in his fingers, with all the care in the world, to tilt her face up, teasing her lips in a barely there kiss as he walked.

Caitlin's heart was racing, as if all the blood in her body had transferred to her mind, sounding like the rush of the ocean roaring through the room.

But it wasn't. The only sound was her gasping for air and Tom's silent breath as he walked the rest of the way down the hall with her in his arms. Suddenly she couldn't feel the thud of pain in her ankle. Instead, it was replaced with a warmth from being in Tom's arms that she couldn't describe. *Because she'd never been held like this before.*

She'd never felt safe in a man's arms before. Never felt cherished and cared for in a man's arms before. And she'd sure as hell never felt so attracted to another human being before, either.

Tom's lips murmured against her hair and she tilted her face up to him. "Your bedroom?"

She tucked her head to his chest, nervous, not sure how to look at him when there was such fire in his gaze. "Yes," she half choked out.

"Are you sure?" he asked, his eyes searching hers out, connecting with her. "You say stop, I'll stop."

"I'm sure," she managed to croak back.

Embarrassment fired within her when she remembered why he knew the way, but deep down she no longer cared. All she cared about was being in Tom's arms, being carried like a featherweight, as if he could walk to the end of the earth with her in his arms and not pause until he had her to safety. It wasn't because Penny had told her to trust him, that he wouldn't hurt her; it was because she'd known it all along. Although the confirmation had been what she needed to make her trust her own instincts.

He paused at the door to her bedroom, eyes touching hers again, looking at her with an intensity she didn't think she'd ever seen before. She smiled, the only thing she could do in response to the question in his eyes.

Tom walked her toward the bed, cocooned in his arms. "Has anyone ever told you how beautiful you are?" he whispered against her cheek. "Because you are so, so beautiful."

He ran his hands down her back as he lowered her onto the bed, placing her down as if it took no effort at all. As if she were weightless. Now he stood above her, watching, waiting. Not saying anything.

"Tom," she said his name but she didn't know what else to say, what to tell him. In her mind she did, inside she was screaming out to have his hands on her body, but they were words she'd never said to a man before.

"I don't want to hurt you," Tom said, his eyes shining with honesty, with kindness. "Do you want me to…"

"Stay," she said, finishing his sentence, finding her voice. "I want you to stay."

She watched as his gaze traced down her body, slowly, before resting on her ankle. "Are you really sure?"

Caitlin smiled with a bravery that didn't come naturally. "Be careful with me and I'll be fine."

Tom pulled off his T-shirt, tugged it over his head and stood bare-chested at the foot of her bed. Caitlin couldn't help it—she stared at him as though she'd never seen a man with his shirt off before. His shoulders were wide, strong, and his torso lean. Tom's skin was tanned, smooth and flawless. What would he think of her scars, the marks on both her legs when he saw them up close again? If he knew how she'd gotten them and what secrets her past held?

Caitlin pushed the thoughts away, refused to let them ruin this moment. The accident and her surgery, the weeks she'd spent not being able to walk, let alone dance, were not going to hold her back. Not now. She'd had to sacrifice enough because of what had happened, but that was in her past and it was time to leave those memories behind for good.

He still looked worried that she was going to change her mind and regret asking him to stay. "Kiss me," Caitlin told him, being the woman she wanted to be, making herself sound more confident than she felt. "Kiss me," she repeated.

Tom lowered himself down gently beside her, stroking his hand up her leg as he did so. Caitlin tensed at his touch, couldn't stop her hand before it brushed his away.

Tom responded immediately, hand hovering above her skin. "Is there something you need to tell me?" he asked, voice husky.

He wants me but he's still in control, she told herself. *It's Tom. Tom can stop.*

"No," she forced herself to say, making her body relax. "No."

Tom slowly touched her again, his fingers staying lower, not tracing up her leg this time.

With one hand he pulled off her sock instead, carefully taking it from her foot before bending to press a flutter of kisses against her swollen, tender skin.

Then he trailed his fingers slowly, so slowly up her body, giving her every opportunity to stop him. Even through the denim of her jeans she could feel his touch, was covered in goose pimples at the way he was caressing her, torn between pushing him away and making him touch her more.

Tom edged down, closer, lower, to kiss her on the mouth. Caitlin arched her back into his hold, tried to tell him how willing she was by the way her body moved. Encouraged him the only way she knew how.

And when he kissed her, when he slipped his fingers beneath her top and edged it down to show her skin, she sighed into his mouth and hoped he'd touch her all night. Because she needed this. Her attention-starved skin had been craving this more than she'd ever realized.

"No!"

Caitlin leaped up as the shout echoed around the room, dragging the sheets up to cover her naked body. Fear ran through her like a raging current, tore through her body as she fought the scream building in her throat.

Stop.

"No!" he yelled again, even more bloodcurdling than before.

Tom. It was Tom.

It wasn't anyone who was going to hurt her.

Caitlin bent to cradle Tom's head, to push the damp

hair from his forehead. She hadn't known where she was or what was happening, had immediately thought she was the one in danger. But it wasn't her who needed taking care of, who needed protection, not right now.

"Shhh, it's okay." She pressed kisses to his wet skin, pushing the sheets off him as she did so. He was hot and sweaty, terror making his body shake. Making him whimper like a child scared of the dark. "Tom, you're okay."

His eyes fluttered open, she could make them out even in the near dark. Frightened to begin with and then slowly relaxing.

"I'm here for you," she whispered, cradling his head and keeping her lips against his skin.

Tom didn't say anything, didn't need to, but his breathing became less shallow, his body relaxing beneath her touch.

"Shhh," she whispered again, as if she were comforting a baby.

Caitlin tucked her body more possessively to his and shut her eyes.

They both had their demons, she knew that, and the one thing she could do for Tom was to hold him. Because when she'd been in her most darkest of places, it had been not having anyone with her that'd made it that much harder to live through.

"Caitlin?"

She sighed as Tom's lips closed over hers, clumsily in the dark.

"Thank you."

She didn't need to say anything back, drifting off to sleep with him in her arms.

CHAPTER TEN

CAITLIN stretched out gingerly, needing to move her stiff limbs and be careful of her bandaged ankle, but at the same time desperate not to wake the man sleeping beside her, not after the way he'd woken in the night.

Tom.

She slowly shuffled back onto her side and curved her leg gently against his, molding her body to him. He was lying on his back, one hand thrown over his face as if he was trying to block out the light, the other by his side. Caitlin ran her fingertips up his chest, letting them fall over his heart.

He was perfect. So flawless that he looked like a model torn straight from a magazine, only bigger and stronger. More rough around the edges and *real*.

He reminded her of what she'd once been, an athlete, but she didn't begrudge him his fitness and discipline. Tom knew hurt, on a different level, as acutely as she did.

She stilled her fingers again, stopping the casual back and forth motion on his bare chest. Just because she'd spent the night with him didn't mean he wanted a relationship with her, even if it did mean something deeper to her. He was the first man she'd trusted in so long. After her only serious boyfriend had been sweet in the beginning before slowly revealing himself to be just like her father, she'd been too scared even to put herself out there to be hurt again. But now…

"Morning, beautiful."

Caitlin pressed her lips to the soft curve of his neck. "Hey."

Tom's grin lit his face, and he raised his elbow so he could look down at her. "I can see your lips moving but I can't hear you."

She shut her eyes, giggling. "I forgot you had a bad side." She reached up to stroke his ear, tickling her fingers over it. Caitlin nipped at his earlobe, tucking her body tight against him. Letting herself touch him, be natural and uninhibited with him.

"Come here," he said gruffly, catching her around the waist beneath the sheets and making her squeal.

"Tom!"

"I warned you," he said, pulling her down low on top of him. "I specifically told you that you were on my bad side, and yet you failed to move."

Caitlin wriggled, trying to escape his grasp yet not really wanting to. He had hold of her, tight, but she wasn't afraid. She slid down on top of him, pulling the sheet with her, trying to keep herself covered, and trying not to wince as she put too much pressure on her still-sore ankle. "Is this what you do to all your enemies?"

"Baby, you're not the enemy."

His voice was silky, sent ticklish ripples trailing across her skin. He was gorgeous, breathtakingly gorgeous, and it was sending the blood pumping through her body like liquid fire.

Tom kept hold of her but let her slide across him, his arms forming a tight circle around her as the length of their bodies touched.

"I could hear you just fine," he said, voice low. "I just

wanted an excuse to have you wriggling around on top of me again."

This time Caitlin's blush burned her face. Even her ears felt as if they were tingling with embarrassment. She hadn't been intimate with a man in so long, and Tom was so open. Talked from his heart and spoke the truth. And she liked it.

He kissed her on the mouth, his lips warm, before trailing soft kisses across her face and down her jaw. "What do you want to do today?" Then he looked alarmed, as though he'd forgotten she'd been injured yesterday. "Your ankle?"

"Is fine since you bandaged it. I don't think it's as bad as I thought," she whispered back, before adding bravely, "And today I want to stay in bed."

Tom snuggled into her tighter, his body hard against hers, strong in her arms, protecting and loving her at the same time. "I think I can help you with that, Miss Rose."

She tilted her head back, inviting him to kiss her neck, sighing as he fulfilled her wish as if he knew exactly what she was thinking. "I thought you'd be up running already. Exercising."

Tom shook his head and trailed kisses lower, his focus unwavering. "Wrong."

She flexed her fingers against the taut skin on his back. "Well, good."

Tom tickled her stomach as he kept wriggling farther down. "The run can wait for later," he said, as though he had all the time in the world, wasn't in any hurry to explore her body. "Afterward, I want to introduce you to someone, but right now—" his hand skimmed her breast "—you're my morning exercise."

Caitlin relaxed in Tom's arms, refused to worry about him touching her in the daylight, the fact that he could see her. Because she could see him, too, and she wanted to watch him. To let her eyes rove across his skin, to watch the way he touched her and see the expression on his face as he spoke to her, as he caressed her.

"Have I told you how incredible you are, Caitlin?" Tom was looking at her now, had paused to stare at her.

Caitlin shut her eyes again, not believing that she was lying in her bed, with a man like Tom, and that he was showering compliments on her. She hadn't had a man in her home in years, had kept it as her sanctuary from the world, especially the dating world, but here and now she was more comfortable in her home than she'd ever been. In the company of another. *In the company of Tom.*

"You have," she repeated, opening her eyes to find him still staring at her. "But you can always tell me again."

Tom folded his body against hers again, his hands roving so low it made her suck back a sharp breath.

"You are amazing, Caitlin Rose, and you'd better believe it."

"I'll be back in less than an hour." Tom grinned at her as he walked backward down her driveway.

Caitlin shook her head in disbelief. Seriously? "I don't understand why you don't want to take your car?"

Tom stretched his legs out and she couldn't stop watching him. The way her eyes were following his movements, his body, was…indecent. She wished she could turn away but couldn't.

"I can't believe you run *every* morning. It's…"

Tom stood still, watched her. "Obsessive, I know," he said. "But I'm kind of like an addict, and I'll run back and get my car later."

"For fitness," she suggested, wishing she could scorn

him but admiring him instead. "A complete fitness junkie," she teased, but she was going to have to stop that sometime soon and come clean that a few years back, she'd been no different.

"Yeah, for anything that involves exercise."

"Great," she goaded. "Just great. I'm dating a fitness junkie."

Tom started walking forward then, his grin even wider, his mouth turned up in the biggest smile she'd ever seen. "Dating, huh?"

"Let's see how long you take to get back, then we'll talk about dating," she said, feigning a bravery that didn't come naturally.

Tom blew her a kiss and broke into a jog. "I'll be back with her soon."

Caitlin pursed her lips and fought the question waiting in her mind. She had no idea who he was talking about, but so long as it wasn't a secret wife then she didn't care.

She watched him pound down the footpath away from her. It was exhausting just watching him running this early in the morning, when she was still so tired from the night before. Although… She cast a quick glance at her watch. Technically it wasn't that early, but it was a Sunday and she was used to lying in bed until her stomach drove her into the kitchen for brunch.

Her belly growled at the thought of food and Caitlin turned from Tom's disappearing silhouette. She could track him with her eyes all day—he wasn't exactly hard to look at—but right now her fridge was calling to her.

Fruit, she mused. It would be healthy and wouldn't leave her feeling guilty about her lack of exercise, because it was going to be a while before she was allowed to use her ankle properly.

Caitlin limped carefully into her kitchen and paused

at the fridge, looking at the old black-and-white photo of a ballerina she had pinned to it. No one else would know it was her; they would presume it was a take-home from a show she'd seen. But it was her, and sometimes she felt like staring at it for hours.

But not today. Today she ignored the woman in the picture and hauled the fridge door open, searching for goodies instead. The woman in that photo had haunted her for long enough, and it was about time she moved on. She'd thought she had. After all these years she'd thought she'd been brave and positive and moved on from what had happened, but she hadn't.

Caitlin put her fruit on the counter and reached for the photo, pulling it out from the magnet holding it in place. She gave it one last look, pressed a kiss to the girl looking back at her with her beautiful position, and slipped her into a drawer.

She was a teacher. Her role was to coach others to fulfill their dreams, and she was okay with that. Caitlin had loved the discipline of ballet, had lost herself within the structure of the dance. It had allowed her to be in control, and no one had been able to take it away from her. Until the accident that had ended her career forever.

Ballet would always be in her heart, but it was time to move on for good. And she was finally ready to, or at least she liked to think she was.

Caitlin smiled to herself as she cut into the melon, popping a piece in her mouth. Tom wasn't exactly a bad distraction, and she couldn't wait for him to get back.

Tom wasn't ready to pull over, but he also wasn't prepared to forfeit seeing Caitlin again. He'd run home fast, punishing himself, when all he'd really been interested in doing was getting back to her.

Last night had been… He stroked his hand over the steering wheel as he parked his vehicle. If he had to choose between Caitlin and his car right now, he'd give up the car, and that was saying something. Tom almost dialed his brother but jumped out instead. Daniel would laugh all day if he knew his brother was so keen on a woman he'd give up his car. Hell, it'd be like admitting he'd give up a limb for her. And he'd *slept*. After he'd woken and she'd held him, he'd slept like a newborn baby for hours. No waking up in a hot sweat, the sheets damp and tangled from his nightmares again. He'd gone to sleep with Caitlin in his arms and he hadn't woken until morning.

"Tom?" Caitlin was calling out from the front door when he stepped out.

"Come and meet her," he called back, inviting her down.

Tom tried to keep a straight face as Caitlin walked slowly, carefully down across her porch and toward him. She looked confused and her ankle was obviously tender from the way she was hobbling.

"You got a new car?" she asked.

Tom closed the distance between them and looped an arm around her shoulders, pulling her in for a kiss before taking some of her weight from her leg. "This isn't any old car, Caitlin."

She groaned. Over-the-top-loud kind of groan. "Please don't tell me this is who you wanted me to meet?" she asked, looking at him as though she pitied him. "Here I was thinking you were Mr. Perfect, but instead you're actually a car nutter."

Tom squeezed her closer and forced her to walk by his side to the car. "I am *not* a nutter." He tried not to laugh. But he sure liked the sound of *Mr. Perfect*.

"Oh, yes, you are," she goaded, poking him in the ribs. "Absolute nutter."

Tom gave her a push sideways, nudging her with his hip to move her away without letting her put any weight on her leg. "I'll have you know that this beauty is a 1965 Ford Mustang convertible," he said, as proud as if he were introducing Caitlin to his own flesh and blood. "I restored her from the ground up myself, whenever I was home."

Caitlin's gaze flicked from him to the car and back. "Okay, I'll concede that the car looks nice, but I'm not so sure about the formal introduction."

"Sally," he said, trying not to smirk.

"Excuse me?"

"Her name's Sally."

Now Caitlin was roaring with laughter, holding her belly and looking as if she was going to hyperventilate. "You named her? Oh my God, you *are* some kind of weirdo."

Tom tried to act offended, hurt, but her amusement was contagious. "Just get in the car," he ordered.

"And here I was stressing that you were going to have a secret wife and kids or something," she muttered.

"What's that, I can't hear you? You've got my bad side," Tom joked. He'd never thought his lack of hearing was something he'd ever be making fun of, but away from work and his usual life, Caitlin seemed to make him capable of laughing at anything.

Caitlin poked him in the ribs again and tried to do a fast shuffle-limp around to the passenger side. "I'm not falling for that one again, Cartwright."

He intercepted her, moving fast to pin her to the side of the vehicle before she could open the door. "What did you call me?"

"Cartwright," she said, her voice bold as she looked back at him defiantly. He liked that she looked so confident, none of the seriousness he'd once seen remaining in her eyes.

Tom didn't know who this guy was or where he'd left his real self, but he slid both hands to Caitlin's waist, skimming down to her hips and locking her in place, shuffling his body closer so that they were pressed together.

"You can disrespect me, but not the car, okay?" he told her, his lips hovering above hers, waiting for her to invite him closer, to kiss her.

Caitlin tilted her head back, taking her mouth farther from his instead. "Where're we going?" she whispered back.

Tom thrust her forward, tighter against him. "Anywhere you want." He didn't let her ask any more questions. Instead, he kissed her, relaxing in the warmth of her mouth against his, of the warm, willing woman in his arms.

A few weeks back, he'd resented everything about his life. He'd hated his job, not wanting to teach, and he'd hated the way his life had changed. But this was helping more than therapy had so far.

He still wanted to be out on the water, working in the field and doing what he loved. That longing would probably never go away, but he was liking this, too. Caitlin was helping to heal his wounds, if that were even possible, and today he intended on thanking her. She was like a ray of the brightest sunshine, a fluffy white cloud in a patch of azure blue when the rest of the sky was black with rain-filled storm clouds. There were still things he felt he didn't know about her, things she was holding close to her chest that he didn't want to push, but she was starting to trust him.

He pulled back before pressing one last kiss to her lips. "Thank you."

She raised her eyebrows in question. "For what?"

"For making me remember who I am again."

Tom ran his hands down her sides before forcing them away from her body so she could get in the car. He'd admitted to being addicted to exercise, but he was fast seeing how easy it would be to become addicted to Caitlin, too.

CHAPTER ELEVEN

"So, where's Sally taking us today?"

Tom would have thumped her, but she looked far too little to deal with one of his lighthearted punches, and besides, she was probably right. It was stupid to name a car, even if he wasn't going to admit it to her.

"I thought we'd take a drive and stop for lunch somewhere."

"Anywhere in mind?" she asked, head tilted to the breeze, hair pulled up off her face.

He was tempted to pull her hair tie out so he could watch her dark mane whip around in the wind, but he didn't. Because even though they'd just spent the night together, he didn't want to ruin anything, to risk mucking up what was happening between them. Whatever that something was.

Tom pulled at his earlobe and tried to forget about his deafness, but times like today, when he could barely hear through that ear except for a weird ringing sound sometimes, he resented what had happened to him. No matter how hard he tried to fight it, he was close to being sucked back into the pathetic "why me" thoughts, when he knew he should be happy to be alive instead.

And fortunate to be in the company of someone like Caitlin. The kind of woman he'd never thought would be a part of his life, a life that involved being on call every single day, never knowing when he might be needed and how many days or months he could be away from home.

"Tom?"

He refocused, annoyed he'd lost concentration. "Sorry, what were you saying?"

Caitlin cast him an amused look that he caught from the corner of his eye. "I asked you what was for lunch," she repeated. "Did you have somewhere in mind?"

Tom nodded his head to the side, indicating for her to look in the backseat. "I picked up some food on my way over to your place. Sushi and sandwiches."

She laughed. "Sushi *and* sandwiches?"

He raised his shoulders. "I wanted to get something you'd like and I had no idea what that was," he admitted. "So I figured you'd like one of the options."

"I like both, for the record," she told him.

They kept driving, content in silence. He liked that. Tom had spent plenty of time talking to Caitlin, but he'd never really been one to open up, to chat for the hell of it. But she'd drawn him out of his shell without seeming even to make an effort. Without realizing what she was even doing.

"Tom, do you have to see a specialist about your ear?"

Her question took him by surprise. He hadn't expected her to bring it up. "Ah, yeah," he said, not wanting to talk about it but not wanting to be rude, either. "I have regular checkups, if that's what you mean."

She was silent for a beat before answering. "I just wondered if you're planning on teaching indefinitely, or whether you're going to be sent back offshore again."

Tom gripped the steering wheel tighter, hating what he was about to admit. "I'd do anything to give up teaching, but it's all I *can do*. The docs have been pretty clear about the realities of my injury." He fought to keep any bitterness from his tone. "I'll never be a SEAL again."

"Once a SEAL always a SEAL though, right?"

Caitlin's tone was kind, understanding, but it still grated on him. In his heart he was a SEAL all the way, but in his mind he knew that he wouldn't be ready to go back even if his ear did miraculously heal. After losing one of their team, they'd all struggled with it, but Tom had been the one closest to the explosion. He'd never stopped wondering if there was something he could have done, something he should have seen that would have saved the other man's life.

Which was why he didn't want to be having this conversation. Not now, not when the mood between them was so happy and light. *So easy.*

"Why are you asking me all this, Caitlin?"

He watched confusion and then…hurt cross her face. He hadn't recognized it straight away, but he could see it now as plain as he could see the weather in the sky.

"Because I like you—isn't that reason enough? Because I want to try to understand what you're going through," she replied, but her tone was different now. The lightness, the warmth that had rested between them had disappeared to be replaced with something cooler.

"I'm sorry, it's just…"

"What Tom? It's just what?" she asked.

Tom didn't answer her, he kept driving instead. Caitlin kept her head turned, was looking out the window, and he didn't disturb her until he found a place to pull over. He drove into the parking lot, well off the street, and looked out at the beach. He'd imagined a picnic, laughter, kisses, but not this. He should have known it would come up again, eventually, but he hadn't. Why was it that she was so desperate for him to confront his past?

Tom got out of the car and waited before going around to her side, but she'd already opened her door and was stepping out. He'd needed the burst of fresh air before talking to her again.

"Let me help you," he offered.

Caitlin's gaze stopped him. But she still didn't say anything, was clearly waiting for him to answer her question.

He walked slowly and she hobbled alongside him onto the sand, looking out to the water.

"Caitlin, I don't know what to say to you. What you want me to tell you."

Her gaze was sad, almost sorrowful, and it hurt him. He didn't like seeing her in pain and she was clearly hurting, but he didn't know what to do, either. Didn't know how to make this right when she was asking something of him he didn't want to give. He was used to being pitied by those closest to him, not confronted like this, and right now he didn't know what was worse.

"I want you to tell me how you feel," she told him, her bottom lip quivering. "I want you to open up to me instead of keeping your pain bottled away inside. Because we can keep pretending that everything's fine with you, but we'd be lying. And then we're only kidding ourselves that something real's happening between us."

Tom looked away, fought the urge to focus on her again. His temper was bursting, fighting to emerge from within him, like a fury he hadn't ever experienced before.

"Caitlin, there are some things better left unsaid and this is one of them," he told her, firm but trying not to show his emotions.

She looked angry. "Yeah? Well, there are some things that need to be said, and what happened to you, wherever the hell you were when that bomb went off, is one of those things."

He didn't trust himself to answer so he didn't. Tom clamped his jaw down tight, as if it had been wired shut, and tried to focus on his breathing, to deflect from the situation until he was capable of acting like the man he wanted to be for her. For Caitlin.

"I like you, Caitlin. I *really* like you," he admitted, reaching for her hand. She gave it, not immediately, but when he grasped her fingers with his own she didn't resist. He tugged her closer and ran his hands down her back when she faced him. "Last night was incredible, and I don't want to argue today and ruin how happy we should be feeling."

She returned his kiss when he dropped his lips to hers, but the feeling was empty. Not the electric, excited current they'd had the night before or this morning, and he knew it was because she felt let down somehow.

Caitlin pressed her palms to his cheeks. "Tom, every time I ask you about the Navy, every time I try to tell you that I understand…"

He pushed her away, couldn't fight the surge of anger any longer. "When will you get it?" he barked, his voice colder than ice. "You don't understand and you *never* will."

She didn't move and he couldn't stop.

"You want to know what I've been through?" He was yelling now but he'd lost the ability to keep himself in check. "I've been through *hell,* Caitlin. I've seen the depths of a hell that you couldn't even imagine, worse than any pathetic nightmare you've ever dreamed of."

She went to back off but he grabbed her hand. "You want me to open up, well, *listen here.*"

"Let go of me."

Tom didn't realize, was too angry, didn't see the tears in her eyes until it was too late.

"Let go!" she screamed, clawing at him, pulling away as hard as she could.

He dropped contact with her as if he'd had hold of a burning ember.

"Caitlin, I'm sorry, I'm so sorry. I never meant to…"

"Stay away from me. Don't come *any* closer."

He could see how scared she was, *of him,* but he stayed still. Did what she asked.

"Caitlin, I'd never hurt you, you know that."

"Do I?" she questioned, looking so fragile it physically pained him.

He went to move forward but the wildness in her eyes made him stop.

"You better believe that I know exactly how you feel, Tom."

Imaginary bristles spiked along his back but he stayed put.

"You're wrong," he said.

Caitlin shook her head, almost violently. "No, Tom, I'm exactly right. I'm not going to hold my tongue because I can't admit to you that I *do* know what you're going through. I know how it feels to walk away from something you love, and I sure as hell know how it feels to lose someone you care about, okay?"

"No." He wanted to shout at her but he kept hold of his frustration. Just. "No, Caitlin, you don't."

"Stop saying that, Tom. Stop and listen for once." She glared at him. "But don't you take a step closer to me."

"Damn it, Caitlin!" he fumed, darkness surging within him. "You don't understand and you won't ever understand, got it? What would make you think that you understand what I've been through? That you have any idea what it's like to lose what I've lost?"

CHAPTER TWELVE

CAITLIN was furious, her head pounding as if it was going to explode. "You're not my superior, Tom, so don't think I'm going to say *yes, sir,* and roll over just because you tell me to." Her body was shaking but she didn't move. She forced herself to stay strong.

"Caitlin, you know I didn't mean…"

"Didn't mean what?" she spat, so angry that she wanted to walk away. But she didn't, because she wasn't a coward. She never had been. She would have taken anything, even the worst of beatings, to save her mom from being hurt. "That no one in the world could know how you feel? That what you're going through is worse than what anyone else has ever felt?"

Tom stared at her, his gaze cold again. It made her stomach turn.

"Grow up, Tom. Just grow up."

Caitlin turned to leave. She didn't even care anymore, or maybe she did care too much but she sure as hell wasn't going to let him know it. She knew every single emotion he'd experienced and then some. Because no matter how much he wanted to pretend otherwise, she did know, and if he took the time to listen to her he'd know it, too. She'd held her tongue too long now, when she should have said something that very first night they'd argued about it instead of letting things go this far without confronting what stood between them. What would always keep them apart. She'd been stupid to put it to one side.

"Caitlin, stop." His fingers moved then curled into fists at his side again.

"Do you honestly think you're the only one who's ever lost someone? Who's ever had something they love more than heaven and earth stolen from them?" she asked shakily.

Tom looked down, then slowly raised his eyes. "I lost one of my guys out there, Caitlin," he said, his voice soft, low now. "And when I lost my job it was like I'd lost part of me. Like a vital organ had been taken from my body and I had to figure out how to live without it, without any warning. So yeah, I doubt you or anyone else in my life knows how that feels."

Caitlin sighed. They could argue all day; he could tell her until he was blue in the face what had happened, why he was behaving the way he was, but he'd never truly understand until she told him. And he needed to understand as much as she finally needed to get what had happened to her off her chest.

She looked out at the coast stretching for miles in front of them, wished they didn't have so far to drive back. But maybe it was a good thing. Would give her time to calm down and think, to cool off. She shouldn't have brought the subject up at all, or she should have been honest with him from the start. When he'd noticed her scars that day out hiking, she could have told him. Before they'd become close, before they'd spent the night together and she'd met his family.

"I won a scholarship to the School of American Ballet in New York when I was sixteen," Caitlin told him, staring at a tree she could barely see, trying to distance herself from what she was saying. "It was just me and my mom, and we didn't have a lot of money. We'd left my dad after he hit Mom one time too many, and it was the most amazing opportunity." She looked at Tom, saw that he was listening, hands shoved in his pockets, eyes trained on her. "It was the biggest opportunity of my life. I thought I was going to be the famous ballerina I'd always dreamed about becoming."

She swallowed the emotion away, tried to push it back and focus on what she was saying. She had a story to tell and she needed to get it out. No thinking about what she'd lost, how hard it had been losing her identity and being alone.

"What happened?"

"It was amazing there. I was doing so well, and I had the most incredible job lined up. I was going to tour the country doing what I loved."

Tom took a step closer, touched her arm. Caitlin didn't shrug him off this time.

"I was dating an army guy. Things started out so nice. I thought he was charming and kind, but it didn't take too long before…" She wasn't going to describe the ways he'd hurt her. How he'd abused her.

"Did he—" Tom paused "—hurt you?"

She nodded. "Yeah, he did. He was violent, just like my dad."

A wildness grew behind Tom's gaze, as if a fire had been lit within him and he was glowing with the rage of it. "You know I would never, *never* hurt you Caitlin. You know that, right? Please tell me you're not scared of me?"

She wanted to tell him that, but it was hard to trust him. Hard to believe, when you'd had a father and then a boyfriend think they were tougher and stronger than the women they were with, and want to prove it, that another man could be gentle. Could commit to never raising a hand in anger or wanting to fight other men. It was something she would never forget, would always be traumatized by.

"You've already hurt me by not listening, Tom," she said, her voice low, on the verge of cracking. "You need to understand that you're not alone in how you feel."

She could see him struggling, not wanting to admit that anyone could know what he'd been through, but he stepped closer again, this time wrapping his arms around her from behind, holding her.

"Tell me what happened," he asked. "I need you to tell me."

Caitlin leaned back into him and shut her eyes. "He'd been drinking, but I didn't know until it was too late. I was already in the car. He'd come to pick me up after a show in the city and I'd been planning on breaking it off. As soon as I knew he was violent, I had no intention of him ruining my life, of holding me back." She paused. "When I told him I wanted to get out, he only got more angry, and before I knew it we'd hit another car and I couldn't move my legs."

Tom held her tighter and she squeezed away tears. She'd never spoken about it, not truly, to anyone.

"It took me six months to recover fully from the accident, but at the time I wanted to die. I couldn't see what the point of living was if I couldn't dance, because it was my whole life."

Tom pushed her away slightly before turning her to face him, holding her at arm's length. "But I've seen you dance. What happened?"

Caitlin shook her head slowly from side to side. "I can dance enough to teach because I spent hours and hours trying to regain my strength and ability, but the

damage to my left leg meant I could never dance to the
same level again." She walked away, needed some distance. "So when I tell you I know what it's like to have
your body fail you, to have to give up the one thing in
the world that makes you who you are, you need to start
believing me."

She tried not to choke on her tears, because it still
hurt. It hurt because what she loved had been stolen from
her through no fault of her own. It hurt because she'd
trusted a man she should have run a mile from, and he
was responsible for what had happened to her.

And now she was hurting because she'd been so close
to letting someone else in after all these years, and he
was on the verge of hurting her badly, too. It *hurt* to remember, to talk about it, but she needed to get it out.
After so long keeping her past to herself, she was ready
to open up.

"Caitlin, I'm sorry, I wish I'd listened to you."

She smiled at him over her shoulder, trying to be brave
and failing. "Me, too."

He stopped moving, became immobile. "Please tell
me you'll give me a second chance," he said, eyebrows
creased. "I know I should have…"

Caitlin put her hand up, fingers touching the air. "I've
heard a lot of *should haves* over the years, Tom," she told
him, needing to get everything off her chest here and
now, not wanting to leave anything else unsaid between
them. "I had a dad who let me down time and time again
until he eventually gave up and left me alone, and I had
a boyfriend do the same thing to me. So when I tell you
that I don't need to be hurt again, I mean it."

"I haven't always been like this, Caitlin. This—" he
threw his hands up in the air "—everything that's happened changed me. I used to be the guy wanting a wife

and a family, and now I can't even figure myself out, let alone be there for anyone else." He paused, looking defeated. "I'm embarrassed by my behavior and I'm sorry. I want to protect you, not hurt you. I know it might be hard for you to believe, but it's true."

Tears stung her eyes. He was being honest, brutally honest, and she couldn't blame him for that. But it hurt. Damn it, it hurt! Because at one stage she'd thought that maybe, just maybe, he could be the guy for her. That he was capable of giving her what she so badly wanted in a man.

"Do you know the difference between you and me, Tom?" she asked, even though it pained her so badly it was like carving a hole through her chest.

He shook his head, waiting for her response.

"You have people around you who love you. They love you so much," she said, wiping at her eyes with the back of one hand. "You have a mom who'd do anything for you, a brother who loves you, a sister-in-law and a niece. You know who I had?"

Tom took a step toward her, but she stepped back, not letting him any closer.

"I only had *me,* Tom. *Me.*" She put one hand over her heart. "My dad was out of the picture, my mom died before she ever saw me dance again, and none of my New York friends cared enough to look out for me after the accident."

Tom looked at the ground, scuffed his feet in the dirt. "I'm sorry."

"Yeah, so am I," she said, not bothering to fight the tears now, letting them wet her cheeks. "You have no idea how lucky you are, how great your life is. What happened to you is awful, it *sucks*, I get that, but you're going to be fine."

Tom reached out, fingers skimming hers. "Why does this feel like you're about to say goodbye?"

Caitlin shut her eyes, squeezed away the tears before braving a smile. "Because it is goodbye, for now anyway." She took a shuffled step backward, and then another, before turning and walking away from him. She kept her shoulders squared, back straight, proud of herself for being so strong.

"Caitlin, I'm sorry."

She didn't stop, only held her head higher, forcing the distance between them before turning and giving him one last look, saying the words that needed to be said. "I have to go, Tom. You need to figure out what's going on in your life before I can ever consider letting you become a part of mine."

Caitlin heard him call out again, but she kept moving forward, focused on putting one foot in front of the other, even thought it hurt like hell and she probably should have been on crutches. It was one of the hardest things she'd ever done, but it was also the right thing.

Tom meant something to her; it was the only reason this hurt so bad, but it was also the reason she'd had to be honest, and why she had to walk away.

Maybe he'd never seek her out again, and she wouldn't hold it against him if he didn't, but the thought of never ever seeing him again made something within her break.

She'd get back to the road and figure out how to get home. She didn't want his help, and she didn't want to be coddled as though she was in danger of breaking. After all these years with only herself to count on, she wasn't useless and she didn't want anyone to pity her, not ever.

Especially not Tom.

* * *

Tom watched her go but he didn't move. Couldn't. Even thought it hurt him to see her limp off like that, made him want to run to her side and help her, to be there for her.

She was right. She was so damn right.

How could he have been such a jerk? Behaved as he had, when Caitlin had faced the same type of heartache, gone through so much in her life? If he'd only listened to her, given her the time and respect she deserved, she'd still have been standing beside him right now.

He was supposed to be able to read people, to understand situations and figure out how best to proceed. It had been what he'd trained for all these years, what he'd always been good at. He was meant to *protect and serve*.

But instead he'd stuffed up the one good thing he had going for him right now. Just because he hadn't wanted to meet anyone, because he didn't feel ready for the things he'd once craved, like a woman in his life and a future, being a father, didn't mean he could let Caitlin go. Couldn't let his demons get the better of him and regrets ruin his life.

Seeing Caitlin walk away was almost as hard as saying goodbye to his career.

And that told him everything he needed to know.

Tom turned away, refusing to watch her retreating figure any longer, and instead started to run. She wanted to be alone and she'd made it clear that she was used to being independent, so right now he needed to do what he was good at. Burn energy, push his body to the limit. What he needed to do was sprint until his lungs were burning so hard he could barely breathe, and his mind was so exhausted he wouldn't be able to think.

Maybe he needed to walk away. Maybe he needed to figure out what he'd done here, how he'd managed to stuff this up so bad. When had he turned into the kind of guy who'd taken center stage and refused to let anyone else show him that he wasn't alone? The kind of arrogant ass who thought that what he was going through wasn't on par with what happened to other people every single day? That he wasn't alone in his pain?

Tom ran faster, pushed himself, tried to empty his mind of thoughts and get into the zone, the head space he'd become so good at getting into when he'd been on a mission, out in the field.

He had flashbacks, visions of the morning when it had all gone so terribly wrong. Bursts of images behind his eyes, of the explosion, of what he remembered of it, of losing his buddy and not being able to hear a thing.

Tom wiped the back of one hand into his eyes, rubbed the blur away, stopped. He dropped his head, knees bent, *heaving,* hardly able to breathe. He felt as though he was going to suffocate, drop where he was standing.

He forced his body up and took off at a sprint again, knowing he couldn't keep up the pace but not caring. He needed to push himself as hard as he could go, to stop thinking and focus on his body.

That's what he *needed*. Only then would he be able to deal with what had just happened, with what he was up against. And figure out what he was going to do to make it up to Caitlin.

If that was even possible.

CHAPTER THIRTEEN

"OKAY, go for it."

Tom sat back, nursing a beer but not remotely interested in drinking it. He deserved whatever Daniel gave him.

"Idiot, loser, moron." Daniel grinned before shrugging. "You know I don't mean it, right?"

Tom sank deeper into the sofa. "Yeah? Well, I know I meant it when I said it to you."

It wasn't that long ago that he'd ripped into his brother for being an idiot and almost wrecking his marriage. Now he was the one who'd stuffed up big-time.

"Advice?"

Daniel shook his head. "All I know is that I'd hate to be without Penny. If I hadn't had you and mom to kick my butt over the whole thing, I could have lost her forever."

"So what're you trying to say?" Tom asked his brother.

Daniel leaned forward, intent. "If you think you stuffed up, then suck it up and say sorry. Do what you have to do to make things right."

Daniel was right. Everything he was saying made sense, but it didn't make the situation any easier to deal with. "I have a scary feeling that she's the one, Dan. It's in my gut, it's keeping me awake at night." But it wasn't the only thing keeping him awake. His dreams, his nightmares, were worse again—back to what each night had been like since he'd been home, nothing like the peaceful night he'd had lying in Caitlin's arms, with her tucked against him.

Daniel laughed, sipping on his beer. "If she's the one, then I pity her." He held up his beer, raised it to the ceiling. "To Caitlin, you poor, poor girl."

Tom scowled. "What makes you think making it up to her will be that easy? There's more to it than just saying sorry. I don't think she'll even want to hear me out."

That really made Daniel laugh. "That's the thing, bro. It ain't going to be easy. She'll chew you up and spit you out, then stomp all over you. But if she's the one, she's the one." He shrugged again. "Besides, saying sorry is always a good start."

Tom put down his beer and dropped to the ground. It was the only way he knew how to deal with whatever was going on in his head.

"Whatcha doing, Tommy?" Gabby's singsong voice stopped him in his tracks.

"Press-ups," he grunted, lifting his body up and down, hands planted into the carpet, muscles pulling back and forth.

"Your uncle's punishing himself."

Tom didn't bother to glare at Daniel; he kept his eyes trained on the ground, focused on the rigid up-and-down motion of his arms.

"Why?" Gabby asked.

Tom listened to Daniel snigger but ignored him. "Because I like to work out when I've got stuff on my mind."

"Like my teacher?" she asked.

Daniel burst into laughter now, slapping his hand against his thigh. Tom rose, stood up and glared down at Gabby. She was standing all cute and innocent in front of him, twisting her hair between her fingers, not scared of him in the least.

So how the hell was it he'd managed to scare Caitlin? When he should have been doing his darnedest to show her he'd protect her no matter what?

"Why? Why would it have anything to do with your teacher?" he asked.

She giggled. "Because Miss Rose's been all sad this week, just like you have been. And I saw you *kiss* her." Gabby looked proud of herself, as though she'd just divulged a major secret. "So that means I know you like her."

"Gabby, does Cait— I mean Miss Rose, teach ballet on a Saturday?"

Gabby shrugged, but he didn't care. This was his chance.

"Daniel, I didn't understand what you were going through when you gave everything up for your family," Tom admitted, hoping his brother recognized his words as an apology.

His brother smiled over at him. "Yeah, maybe not, but I decided to walk away from the Navy. You didn't have a choice."

"What if it wasn't the worst thing that could have happened to me? Maybe it was time for me to do something different."

Daniel raised his eyebrows. "Maybe, but jeez, Tom, I don't know. You can talk it to death, but at the end of the day you're out. You're not a SEAL now and you need to make the most of what you've got."

Daniel's words seemed to echo in his mind. *He wasn't a SEAL anymore.* The sooner he got over that, the sooner he had a chance at being happy and making a new life for himself.

"Your ear's damaged but you still have all your limbs and you have your mind. You're alive."

Tom looked up. Penny was leaning in the doorway, arms folded, watching him. He didn't look away, because she was right. Penny had every right to be the one to tell him that, because she'd made it home from war, had been a soldier and a brave one at that. And she'd lost people she was close to while she was away peacekeeping—he knew that, too.

"How much did you hear?" Tom asked her.

She smiled widely, making him feel that he was the most important person in the room, as she always managed to do. "Most of it," she said. "Figure it out, Tom, and do it quick."

"I gotta go." Tom grabbed his coat and raised his hand in a wave as he rushed to the door.

"Tom and teacher up a tree, *K-I-S-S-I-N-G*..."

He didn't even bother to scold Gabby for singing her little song, although her squeals of laughter told him that Daniel was probably play-scolding her on his behalf. His brother had listened to him when he'd needed an ear, his sister-in-law had put everything in perspective in one sentence, and his niece had made him realize that maybe, just maybe, Caitlin had been moping about, too. That maybe she was hurt and wishing things had turned out differently, just as he was.

It was up to him to make this right.

He'd been an idiot, a fool...everything his brother had called him. What he needed to do now was make it up to her. Because Caitlin had told him to figure out who he was and what he wanted.

Now he knew. He wanted *her,* and nothing was going

to stand in his way. That's what he wanted. But even if she wouldn't forgive him, he needed to change his attitude for *himself.*

Tom was used to getting his own way, to being the boss and working a certain way. Caitlin had changed all the rules and he still wanted to play the game.

And that told him everything he needed to know.

She was right and he was wrong, and that wasn't something he'd ever liked to admit before.

Caitlin stretched in front of the mirror, showing her class exactly what she expected of them. They were older girls on a Saturday morning, young women who were starting to remind her more and more of herself at the same age. They might not want to become professional ballerinas, but they loved what they were doing and that's what mattered to her.

She stopped to survey the room, looking over each girl to make sure they were stretching and moving correctly.

Oh, *my.*

She hadn't heard the door open, but she knew it had. She'd been so consumed with dance that she hadn't seen him, but she had now.

Tom. The man she so desperately wanted to stop thinking about, but who'd been in her thoughts every minute of every day since they'd parted so badly.

She'd missed him.

"I'll be back in a moment, girls, then we'll run through the rehearsal," Caitlin instructed in a firm, unwavering tone.

When she met Tom's gaze, she didn't feel so confident. Didn't have the core strength that she was usually so good at summoning. Because Tom rocked her off her axis and made it tough to rebalance. Even if she wasn't physically scared of him any longer.

"Caitlin," he said when she neared. "I'm sorry to interrupt."

She smoothed away imaginary creases in her snug-fitting top, touched over her skintight leggings, all the time watching him. Seeing him. Realizing how much she'd missed him, even though she'd tried so hard to fight it. To tell herself he wasn't worth the pain.

"I can't talk here," she said, wishing she could throw herself into his arms. Wishing they were more, but then knowing they couldn't be. That it was never going to happen. Caitlin looked into his rich, dark eyes, at the softness of his mouth as he smiled at her. "Why are you here?" she whispered.

"Because I was an idiot and I'm here to make sure you believe it," he said, holding her gaze. "Can I see you after class?"

Caitlin looked over her shoulder at the girls still dancing, then back at the man before her. She wanted to say *yes* so badly, but...

"Why?" she asked, her voice low, not quite able to say *no*.

"Because I'm hoping you believe that everyone deserves a second chance," he said, his voice husky and low, too. Tom reached for her hand, squeezed her palm inside his. "Just give me this afternoon. Hear me out."

Caitlin wavered, the desire to say yes stronger, then disappearing. But she couldn't say no, could she? Not when he was standing before her, honestly and truly asking for a chance to prove himself. It didn't even mean she was giving him a second chance. Maybe it just meant that she was prepared to hear him out.

"Just this afternoon?" she asked.

Tom grinned, nodding. "Just this afternoon. If you still think I'm an idiot after that, I promise I'll never bother you again."

Caitlin touched her hand to his cheek, smiling back at him. No matter what he'd done, she knew he was kind. That he was a nice man, a brave man who did nice things in his life and for his family. What she didn't know was whether he was the right kind of man for her. Or if she was even capable of letting a man in again.

"I never thought you were an idiot," she told him before stepping back.

"Yeah? Well, I sure acted like one."

Tom didn't move; she could feel him watching her, but she wasn't going to let him distract her or her class, at least not until after their lesson was up.

"No viewing in the classroom," she called out, confidence back.

Caitlin didn't have to turn around to know that Tom had disappeared.

CHAPTER FOURTEEN

Tom was starting to sweat. Not just a damp line touching his brow, but a panicked, wet kind of break-out that was making him nervous as hell.

He had less than half an hour to figure out what to do, how to show Caitlin the kind of man he could be, and he had no idea what that was going to be. Where to even start. But he'd asked her and she'd said yes, and that's what was important. What was spurring him into action. *Penny.* Penny would be able to help him. She'd tell him what to do. He should have told her the whole story earlier, confided in her, instead of running out of the house in such a hurry.

He pulled out his mobile and hit speed dial.

"Tom!" Penny answered, sounding breathless.

"Bad timing?" he asked, one hand nervously rubbing back and forth over his head.

"No, it's fine. I'm just outside kicking a ball around with Gabby."

Tom stood up straighter, pulled himself together. That's what he wanted. He'd resisted it, fought it, but he wanted to be the guy hanging out with family, kicking a ball around a yard. Not with his brother and his family, but *with his own family*. And he wanted it now. Maybe he hadn't realized it before, but now he knew, he didn't want to stuff this up. Screw his past, to hell with the demons chasing him in his sleep. He wanted Caitlin in his life and he would do whatever it took, whatever he needed to, to make that a possibility.

"Pen, I need help," he admitted, realizing how desperate he sounded but not caring. This was his sister-in-law, someone he loved and trusted, and if he couldn't turn to her, then there was no point even trying to make something happen with Caitlin. "You were right, but I don't how to tell her, what to do."

There was silence, before Penny answered. "Daniel filled me in on the whole story."

He'd presumed his brother would have spilled as soon as he'd left their house. "So what do you think I should do? How can I make it up to her? I need to show her that I care enough not to walk away. That I was a jerk."

Penny laughed. "Have you tried telling her all that?"

"Should I?"

This time her voice was serious. "I'm not going to tell you what to do, Tom, because it's what you *want* to do that matters. Just tell her how you feel, in your own words, and show her why you're serious. Only you know what's in your heart and what you need to tell her."

"But I've got less than—" he checked his watch "—twenty-five minutes to figure out what to do."

He could almost see Penny shaking her head. "I can't help you, Tom. I wish I could. All I can say is that if she means that much to you, you'll know what to do and what to say." There was silence for a beat. "I know about her, Tom. She told me a little about her past, and I'm guessing she finds it hard to trust men. You need to show her why she can trust *you,* that you're different."

"I know. I just don't know how." He sighed.

"The Tom I know will figure out what to do. Okay?" she said.

"Okay."

Tom said goodbye and hung up, walked a few paces, before stopping dead in his tracks.

That was it.

If he wanted to prove himself to Caitlin, he had to show her that he'd changed, that he'd accepted who he was. That he was ready to let someone else in, to be there for someone else, and to listen. And that he'd listened to her. That even though he'd been a jerk to start with, he had listened eventually, and most importantly, he'd understood.

He pulled out his phone again, but this time he had to look up the number before dialing. If this didn't work, then nothing would.

Because he was all out of ideas.

Caitlin usually stayed in her dance clothes after class, but she hurried to the restroom to switch back into her prelesson outfit. She wriggled into skinny jeans and pulled on a low-front T-shirt before letting her hair out and quickly running a brush through it.

Tom had her all jittery. A jangle of nerves. It was stupid, because she'd promised herself she'd stop thinking about him, stop pretending that something could ever happen between them, because they'd tried and it had failed. Badly.

Maybe she just wasn't going to have a man in her life. Maybe it was time she accepted that.

"Caitlin?"

A voice echoed out through the building. She was the last one here, didn't usually hang around on her own, but it didn't matter. It was Tom, and it was now or never.

"Hold on," she called back, stuffing her clothes into her bag and reaching for her makeup. She touched up her foundation and mascara and pressed some gloss to her lips.

Just because she didn't think anything could ever happen between them again didn't mean she didn't want to look nice. *For herself.*

Caitlin took a deep breath before walking out into the studio, forced her eyes to stay up instead of letting them drag to the ground when she saw him.

He was gorgeous, there was no reason to pretend otherwise. From the moment she'd first seen him, looking across at her in her classroom, she'd thought he was handsome. Strong. Confident-looking. But then she'd also thought he wasn't her type.

But his smile made her want to crumple to the ground, to tuck into him to calm the rapid pound of her heart, to feel small against his big frame, braced by his body and knowing that nothing could ever hurt her.

Even him. Because that was one thing she'd been wrong about in the beginning. No matter how much he could hurt her emotionally, she knew now that, without a doubt, he'd never lay a hand on her or threaten to, either. It didn't make her any less annoyed with him over what had happened, or make her want to forgive him, but she did admire him for his strength.

"Caitlin," Tom announced, standing near the door.

"Hey, Tom," she said back, feigning confidence.

"Did you have anything planned for the rest of the day?"

She moved her head from side to side, not sure what he was getting at. "Why?"

"Because I might not have you back until late tonight."

He was grinning at her, making her want to run in the other direction again.

"I'll need to feed my cat, but…"

"Come on," he said, standing back and holding open the door. "I know I said I didn't need long, but I do."

Caitlin followed his lead. She didn't have the strength to turn him down. Didn't want to push him away or argue.

Because if he thought he could change her mind, could prove himself to her, then she was prepared to give him a chance. She told her students all the time that everyone deserved a second chance, and no one liked a hypocrite. No matter how sure she'd been that she didn't want to see him again, she couldn't turn her back on him. Not yet.

She liked Tom. With every beat of her heart she liked him, so what was an afternoon? Or an evening? He deserved it. After all those years serving their country, for being kind to her and coming to her class that first time she'd met him.

She had nowhere else to be and she wanted to hear him out. Even if that was making excuses for him.

"You ready?" he asked, walking alongside her and gesturing to his car.

Caitlin nodded, holding her bag close to her side. It was now or never.

Tom resisted the urge to touch Caitlin's hand. Just because he'd figured out what he wanted didn't mean she felt the same, or that he even had a chance with her, or that he could prove to her that he'd changed.

But the fact she was with him right now made him confident enough that he had a *chance,* and a chance was all he needed.

"How's school going?" He didn't know what else to ask.

"Um, good." Caitlin twisted in the seat to face him, eyes searching his face, as if she was trying to figure him out and not having a clue. "I have a feeling you didn't turn up at my dance class to talk to me about school, though."

Tom sighed. "You're right."

"So?" she prompted.

He couldn't tell what she was thinking or feeling. Whether she was hopeful or pitying him. "I wanted to say sorry."

She nodded. "I appreciate it."

Tom cleared his throat, suddenly feeling as if there wasn't enough air in the car for the amount he needed to suck back into his lungs. As if there wasn't enough space between them even to think, for him to get his head around what he needed to say.

"Caitlin, I was an idiot. An absolute idiot, and I'm so sorry for not listening to you." Tom paused. It hadn't been so hard. He wasn't used to apologizing, to admitting his downfalls, was used to being brave and pretending that nothing fazed him, but right now he was being honest. And it felt…natural. "I grew up wanting to prove myself, to be the kind of man I used to think my father was. I grew up wanting to protect."

A frown marred the pretty expression on Caitlin's face. "You've never talked about your father before."

Tom swallowed, made himself push through what he usually kept to himself. If his brother had learned to open up, to talk frankly with his wife when they'd had the same hopeless father, then he was going to have to man up and do it, too. "My dad cheated on my mom, and when we chose her over him, when we told him that we wanted to live with mom, he cleared out. Didn't want anything to do with us anymore."

"I'm sorry." Caitlin reached for him then, did what he'd wanted to do but hadn't had enough guts to. "No one deserves that."

"I know, but you know what?"

Caitlin shook her head.

"You've had it easily as rough as I have, but instead of moping about it, you got on with your life. Even when the going got tough." He'd never spoken so honestly in his life. A choke of emotion pulled at his throat, burned behind his eyes, such as he'd never felt before. Or at least not for a really long time.

"I haven't always been this together, Tom," Caitlin told him in a quiet voice, her hands moving to fiddle with the edge of her top, as though she was nervous. "But I didn't have any other option but to pick myself up and get going. I had no one else to depend on, I had to survive, and to do that I had to look after myself."

Tom leaned back into his seat, on an angle so he could look at her. "And you've watched me be an ass when I've got more than you've ever had to live for."

Caitlin smiled, eyes soft. "Let's just say I understand, okay? If I'd been able to I would have hidden away forever. I didn't think I had anything to live for, but I did." She laughed. "I was lucky I found a good friend—she helped me through a lot, but sometimes we need someone else to show us what we've got to be thankful for."

Tom slowly reached out to her, skimmed his fingers across the side of her face, across her cheek, curling around her chin before pulling away. Letting his hand drop back to his lap.

"Thank you," he told her, wanting to kiss her so badly but holding back, not wanting to push his luck. He'd never felt like this before, as if he couldn't lie if he tried, as if he'd do anything in his power to protect this woman, to be honest with her and make things right. For once he didn't care about his past; all he cared about was his future.

"What do you have to thank me for this time?" she whispered back.

"For giving me a chance today."

Caitlin didn't say anything. She only smiled, her aqua eyes showing her kindness, that warmth within her that he'd been drawn to from the very beginning.

"For the record, I'd never hurt you, *ever,* and it kills me to think you were scared of me. Even for a second."

Her smile told him that she wasn't scared of him now.

"Come on," he said. "We don't have long."

He jumped out of the car as she unfastened her seat belt. Tom's palms clammed up again, his pulse raced.

He hoped his plan worked, because he didn't have anything else up his sleeve if it didn't.

CHAPTER FIFTEEN

CAITLIN had no idea where they were or where they were going. She followed Tom, their bodies close but not touching, that awkward feeling between an argument with a loved one and making up—neither knowing quite how to act. What to do. *What to expect.*

"This way," he said, reached for her hand. "How's your ankle?"

"Getting there," she replied. "It was only a mild sprain according to my doctor, so nothing too serious."

Caitlin let him take her hand, gave in to the warmth of his palm against hers, the strength of him guiding her. She wished she didn't like his touch so much, but the truth was she did and it was no use trying to pretend otherwise.

"We're here."

She had been so distracted she hadn't known where they were, but now it was obvious. They were on U.S. Navy property, the bold letters of the signwork telling her so.

He'd brought her to his work.

"This is where I feel most at home, and I want to show you why," Tom told her, his voice low, huskier than usual. "If you'll let me."

"Is this where you train your recruits?" she asked.

"Yeah." Tom nodded, looking at her as they walked. "This place has been like my second home for years. It's where I trained after being accepted into the program. It's where I became a SEAL, where I came back to when I wasn't overseas or on a mission. And now it's where I teach the new guys, put them through their paces."

"Why did you bring me here?" Caitlin asked, stopping, her hand in his making him come to a standstill, too.

"Because I want to show you who I am and why this means so much to me," he whispered, reaching out to touch her hair, catching strands as they blew in the breeze and tucking them gently behind her ear. His fingers stayed there, keeping her hair in place, tickling the side of her face. "I want to be real with you, and this is me showing you who I am."

Caitlin looked away, needing to break the contact, to pull away from the intensity of his stare. She breathed deeply before feeling courageous enough to look at him again. His open palm found the side of her face, warm against her skin, and she turned her cheek to him.

"I've been an idiot, Caitlin, but I want to show you why. I want you to know why the Navy means so much to me, why it'll always be a part of my life."

Her stomach fluttered. With hope. With want. With *wishes*.

Could she trust him? Could she believe that he was ready to move forward, to listen, that he wasn't still trying to hold on to the past? That he'd truly acknowledged that he wasn't alone in his pain?

"Just like your ballet will always be part of your life, this is part of mine."

His words were soft, low…gentle. And she believed

him. Believed that he wanted to try, to make an effort and prove himself to her.

"Show me," she said, leaning into him, letting him wrap an arm around her and pull her close. "Show me your world."

Tom didn't hesitate. He pulled her into him and held her tight. She was like a fairy tucked into her protector, tiny beside his height, small against his frame.

And she liked it. Liked feeling, for once in her life, that another human being genuinely wanted to protect her from harm.

Caitlin pushed aside her fears, the worries trying so desperately to take hold of her mind.

If Tom could do this for her, then she could give him a chance. Had to let him prove himself, do what he had to do. She couldn't let her past hold her back for the rest of her life, and Tom was the man to show her there was a different way.

Maybe life held a different path for her than she'd thought. Because if he could move on, then so could she.

Tom walked through the double doors with Caitlin at his side. He stilled the alpha within him wanting to get out, refusing to get all protective over her. She was beautiful and he had to deal with it. Other men were always going to look at her, and, from what she'd told him, she wasn't entirely fussed on overprotective male behavior.

"So this is where you train, huh?" she asked.

Tom stopped, gave her time to look around. "When I first walked through those doors, I knew I'd found where I belonged," he told her, speaking honestly, from the heart. "I thought that'd be my career for life. Making the SEALs was everything I'd ever wanted."

Caitlin turned sad eyes his way. "Like all your dreams

had come true and you'd found the one thing you were destined to do," she said.

Tom reached out to her, squeezed her hand. "Finding what you loved and making a career of it," he agreed. "I thought I was so lucky."

"You *are* lucky," she insisted, moving in toward him, not letting go of his hand.

Tom liked it, liked that she wanted to touch him when he'd expected her to back off.

"Come on," he said, tugging her with him. "I want to show you something."

Caitlin followed, curiosity plain on her face. "You're not going to make me do anything, are you? Have I mentioned how much I hate the water?" She was cringing and it made him laugh.

"I can arrange a swim for you if you like…" he teased.

Caitlin's eyebrows turned into a frown. "I can't swim," she confessed.

"Oh, I can definitely help you with that," he said, laughing, taking her through to the huge swimming pools. "But maybe not today. Wouldn't want all these guys to see you in a bikini."

Caitlin stopped when they entered. "How many guys are under water?" she asked.

Tom waved out to the instructors on the sidelines before beckoning Caitlin to come forward. "Can you see any air bubbles?" She watched as one of the men gave Tom a signal that she didn't understand.

Caitlin walked forward slowly past him to peer at the water. Even from where they were it was impossible to tell there was anyone in there, had they not been able to see through the clear water into the pool.

"They've only just gone down, but they have to stay under as long as they can without letting go of so much as one air bubble," he explained. "Most of them will crack soon, but the good ones, the ones who'll make it, they'll blow your mind how long they can stay like that."

"Why?" she asked. "Why is pushing yourselves to do such insane things so important?"

Tom understood how it seemed, how ridiculous it was to most people that guys like him wanted to push their bodies to the limits, to force themselves to achieve. But it was what he loved, and it made them who they were. An elite team who could achieve the unachievable. "We have to swim better than anyone else can, stay underwater longer than any other person, survive longer than anyone else, because when we're out there on a mission, it's survival of the fittest. If we can't maintain stealth, we could be dead, and we never know what the situation will be or what we'll need to do in order to stay alive. That's why so few guys make it—because you need to push yourself to the limit, over and over again."

Caitlin laughed. It echoed through the otherwise silent building and she clamped a hand over her mouth. "Sorry," she whispered.

"You think I'm crazy, right?" he asked.

"No," she shook her head. "I think that you're an adrenaline junkie, and when I was a ballerina I think I was kind of the same. Seriously."

Tom went to reach for her but she leaped forward. "Bubbles," Caitlin announced. "I see bubbles. Oh, lots of bubbles now."

A heap of guys broke the surface almost simultaneously, made their way to the edge of the pool. Tom raised his eyebrows at Caitlin as an instructor started barking at the young men, yelling at them and making them drop to do press-ups as punishment when they hauled themselves out of the water.

Slowly, all the men came up, with only two still down. One of the instructors was on his knees, bent toward the water, watching.

"That was me," Tom said, gesturing to the pool. "I was always the one under water the longest, trying the hardest, because this was the one thing I was good at. The one place I could prove myself and succeed."

Caitlin was watching still, fixed on the water. "It's just as important to be teaching them, you know," she said, not turning around. "You can be the difference between them succeeding and not."

Tom crossed the distance between them, circling his arm around her, loosely holding her and pulling her back toward him. "I know that now," he told her. "You made me realize what I hadn't been able to figure out for myself."

Caitlin turned slowly in his arms. "I didn't take you for public displays of affection," she whispered.

Tom grinned, the corner of his mouth turning up into a smile. She did something to him, this girl, something that drove him wild and made him want to run in the other direction all at the same time. "You got me," he said.

"So why the affection?" Caitlin asked, wriggling closer, her face so close it was almost pressed into the hollow of his neck.

Tom cleared his throat, fought not to shut his eyes and lose himself to the sensation of holding her in his arms. "Because I think I could be falling in love with you."

Caitlin went still. She didn't move and neither did he. He'd said it. The words he'd been thinking, the thoughts that had been circling his brain like an eagle over prey, finally out there.

"You are?" she whispered back, still not looking up at him.

Tom sucked up all his courage. "Yeah," he said, voice low. "It just so happens that I am." He tucked his fingers under her chin, softly tilted her face up to look at his before bringing his lips down slowly to brush over hers.

She murmured against his mouth, but she didn't pull away. Caitlin's slender frame tucked into his, asking for more. Tom didn't hesitate. He kissed her harder this time, dipped her back before pulling her up tight against him.

Whoops echoed out throughout the complex, but he didn't care. He held his finger up behind her back at the guys watching, telling them to get lost. They didn't stop, and neither did he. Not until Caitlin pulled back, red-faced, cheeks flushed, eyes dancing but clearly embarrassed.

"Tom!" she scolded, peeking over her shoulder then glaring at him again.

He shrugged, grabbing her and pulling her close again. "You want me to let go?" he whispered in her ear.

Caitlin tilted her head, smiled coyly up at him. "No."

He smiled at her, waving over one of the guys.

"Don't you want to know why?"

Tom bent his head lower and kissed her on the cheek. "Sure."

Caitlin buried her face against his chest, her words almost lost. "Because I think I'm falling in love with you, too."

Tom dropped a kiss to the top of her head. "Lucky you're on my good side, otherwise I'd need you to repeat that," he joked, half-serious.

Caitlin swatted at his backside with her open palm, but she was laughing and so was he.

For the first time since he'd come home, he felt there was nothing holding him back. No weight on his shoulders, no noose around his neck slowly choking him, pulling him away from the life he'd once had.

"So this is the special lady, huh?"

The deep male voice made him turn, arm still tucked protectively around Caitlin. "Mark," he said, smiling first at Caitlin and then at his friend. "I'd like you to meet Caitlin Rose."

Caitlin didn't need to be told Mark was one of his closest friends for her to be charming to him, and he loved it.

"You're another instructor here?" she asked. "For the record, I think those guys need some lunch and a rest for the afternoon."

Mark laughed, but he didn't take his eyes off Caitlin, and Tom glared at him. He'd been one of his best friends when they'd served together, would trust him with his life, but he also knew how much his buddy liked beautiful women.

"Okay, just so you know how we operate, there's no chance of them breaking for lunch yet, not until we punish them some more," Mark told her, shaking her hand and then crossing his arms over his chest. "And secondly, I can see why Tom's smiling. You really are gorgeous."

Tom saw Caitlin blush and had to force himself not to clamp her to his side. "Caitlin, Mark was with me on my last…" He swallowed, looking at her and finding strength in her gaze.

"I survived the explosion, too," Mark finished for him.

"Yeah," he said, looking between Caitlin and Mark. "That's why I wanted you to meet him."

A whistle blew and Mark took a step backward, hand extended to shake Caitlin's again. "It was nice to meet you, Caitlin, but I've got to run. Recruits to torture."

"Nice to meet you, too," she replied.

"Let's go," Tom said, happy that he'd been brave enough to bring her here.

"Yeah, let's." Caitlin leaned back to look up at him, before nipping a kiss to his jaw.

"What was that for?" he murmured. "Not that I'm complaining."

"For being brave," she told him. "I'm so proud of you."

And Tom was, too. For once he didn't mind being called brave, because this time it was true.

CHAPTER SIXTEEN

CAITLIN felt as though she'd been knocked over and had just caught her breath. She looked at Tom, *really looked at him,* and couldn't wipe the smile off her face.

"Are we really doing this?" she asked. "I mean…"

Tom's eyes crinkled gently in the corners. She loved it. The cheeky upturn of his grin, the way his entire face seemed to smile when he was happy. "I guess we are."

As if he knew exactly what she'd been trying to say.

Caitlin sighed. It was good. Better than good. She actually felt that something was finally going right in her life for a change. She'd stuck to her guns, fought to show Tom how happy he could be, what he had to be thankful for in his life, and he'd proven to her that he could embrace that.

"There's one more place I want to take you," Tom told her, forcing her from the daydream she'd been lulled into.

"Somewhere else?" she asked, curiosity piqued. "Like where?"

Tom took his eyes off the wheel for a second and grinned again. "It's not exactly the New York Ballet, but it's the best I could do at short notice."

What? "You're taking me to a ballet recital, aren't you?"

"Yup." Tom looked far too pleased with himself. "I

don't know anything about ballet, but I know you love it, and I want you to show me your world, too. Well, the one you left behind."

Caitlin leaned back in the seat and shut her eyes. Tried not to cry.

After years of struggling with what had happened to her, of wondering if what had happened was her fault, Tom had blown in on the wind and turned everything upside down.

"You're one of a kind, Tom Cartwright," she said, opening her eyes and shaking her head slightly. "I don't know where you came from or how we ended up here, but I'm glad."

Tom laughed—a deep, loud laugh that echoed throughout the car. "Tell me why you love ballet," he asked, suddenly serious.

Caitlin looked out the window and smiled. "I was a little girl with a dream, and no matter what happened at home, my mom always told me to believe in myself," she said. It was like a movie running through her mind, remembering her first tutu, her ballet shoes, the desperation to make it as a teenager, to change her life and become something. "Mom was so proud, and I felt like I'd succeeded for both of us when I won the scholarship. That we were going to have a new life, that everything was going to be better."

Tom was focused on driving, but she turned to watch him, to study the outline of his profile, to study him. She'd been wrong to judge him as the typical tough guy just because of her past. It was mean to lump all physically strong men into the same category, to have judged him as she had. He'd been stubborn, sure, and a bit too self-absorbed in his own issues, but he was also kind and thoughtful. And now he was proving himself to be a decent listener after all.

"You know, my dad leaving seemed like the worst thing in the world when it happened, but we had a great mom and we still do," Tom said.

Caitlin reached out, touched her finger along his jaw-line, watched the way his pulse started to tick, as if he was nervous. Or uncertain. Or maybe excited, as she was. Excited about the possibilities of what could happen between them.

"I'd do anything to have my mom here still," Caitlin said. "I wish every day that I could pick up the phone and call her to tell her about my day and hear about hers. To tell her that I did okay for myself."

She watched as Tom's face pulled into a frown, even as he concentrated on the road. He pulled the car over and turned to look back at her.

"I know it's no substitute, but I'd love my mom to be there for you one day. For you to feel she was family enough to become close to like that."

Tom opened his door and stepped out of the car before she could respond, opening hers and waiting for her to get out.

"That's really sweet of you," she said, always appreciative of his old-fashioned manners.

Tom cleared his throat, looking anxious.

"What kind of ballet are we going to in the afternoon?" Caitlin asked, suddenly confused.

Tom moved from foot to foot. "Ah, a dress rehearsal. It was the best I could do at late notice. I hope that's okay?"

She threw her arms around him in an impromptu hug. "Thank you, Tom. You're amazing."

He took her hands and held her back at arm's length, eyes searching her face. "Amazing enough to marry?"

Caitlin was pleased Tom was holding her. Marry her? "What?" Was he joking?

"I'm serious," he said, before dropping to one knee. "Marry me, Caitlin Rose. Do me the honor of becoming my wife."

Caitlin was in danger of stuttering. Marry her? The question was stuck in her mind as though it was on repeat. "Tom, are you serious?"

He looked up at her. "Deadly."

Oh. Wow. "I think you need to stand up," she said, smiling but terrified all at the same time.

The grin left his face, leaving him drained, pale. "Not the answer I was hoping for."

Caitlin raised her hands, placed both her palms against his cheeks. "I can't marry you, Tom."

He started to protest, to say something, but she put a finger over his lips. She couldn't say *yes* and she needed to explain why. "It's not because I don't want to, but we haven't known each other long enough. When I get married, I want it to be for life. I don't want to rush it."

Tom looked at the ground then met her gaze. "So it's more a *maybe* than a strict *no*," he asked.

"I want to be with you, Tom, but I want us to take our time."

"I understand," he said. "Penny told me it was too fast, but as usual I chose not to listen to her."

That made Caitlin laugh. "I'm guessing Penny helped you with the whole ballet idea, huh?"

Tom chuckled. "Actually, no. I tried to get her help but she told me I needed to man up and figure it out on my own."

Caitlin tugged his hand to walk toward the building, stopping only because Tom didn't move. She had a feeling she and Penny were going to become great friends.

"Aren't we going in here?" she asked.

Tom grimaced. "If you're not going to marry me I'm hardly going to sit through potentially hours of ballet." His face went blank, serious.

"Tom!" she declared, hands on hips.

He laughed, catching her around the waist. "Has anyone ever told you how cute you are when you're angry?" he whispered in her ear.

Caitlin tried to push him away but he had hold of her and he was too strong. "No," she whispered back, wriggling so she was facing him. Tom grabbed her and she wrapped her legs around his waist as he lifted her in the air. "But you can tell me all you like."

"You're cute," he repeated on command.

"Kiss me," she ordered.

"Yes, ma'am," he replied, touching his mouth to hers.

"Don't call me *ma'am*," she told him, trying not to laugh.

"Yes, *beautiful*," he said instead, cupping his hands beneath her bottom to keep her in place against him.

"Now that's more like it," she said, nose to nose with him.

Caitlin kissed him then. Arms and legs wrapped around him, lips pressed to his, in the middle of the street for everyone to see. As if they didn't have a care in the world.

And they didn't. For the first time in years, she was safe in the arms of a man she loved, and she couldn't get enough of him.

EPILOGUE

CAITLIN wriggled from foot to foot in front of the floor-length mirror. She couldn't stop staring at herself.

"Stay still," Penny ordered.

Caitlin sighed at her soon to be sister-in-law's bossy tone. It had been like this all day—being told what to do and feeling as though she was looking down somehow and watching herself rather than actually living through the experience. Kind of the way she used to feel when she was on stage performing, like a guardian angel looking down from above.

"I need to get down there," she said, suddenly panicked, heart racing. "Do you think he's here yet? Do you think he's waiting?" Her heart started skipping even faster. "You do think he's coming, right?"

Now it was Penny who was sighing, watching Caitlin in the mirror with a pained, almost humorous expression as she pushed a final pin into her hair and sat down beside her. "Yes, he's here, of course he's coming, and you don't have to wait much longer. Just *enjoy* this. You'll be spending the rest of your life with him, another fifteen minutes of being apart isn't going to kill you. Now stop stressing!"

A loud knock echoed out. Caitlin looked at Penny, confused, until she heard his voice.

"Hey, beautiful, you in there?"

"Tom!" Caitlin called out, she couldn't help it, even with Penny glaring at her. "Tom, come in."

"Go away, Thomas!" Penny barked, fierce, marching across the room toward the door. "Don't even think about opening that door." Her voice was low now, like a growl.

Caitlin took a step back. So this was how Penny had been such a formidable soldier. Her tone alone was enough to send a weaker woman whimpering in the other direction.

"I need to see her," Tom called back, sounding impatient. "Let me in, Penny."

Caitlin stood, hitched up her dress and marched after Penny, confidence returned. "Let him in," she said, trying to look as fierce as the other woman. "He's my fiancé and I want to see him."

"No!" Penny yelped. "You're the bride and he is *not*, I repeat *not*, going to see you yet."

There was silence and then a thud. Tom came crashing into the room, a sheepish expression on his face.

"Tom!" Penny yelled.

Caitlin laughed and pushed past Penny to get to him. To hell with tradition. "Hey," she said, opening her arms. "Hey, you."

"Hey to you, too," Tom said, bending for a kiss, wrapping his arms around her so she was enveloped in his hold, tucked safely into his body. "I've missed you," he whispered, pressing another gentle kiss to her lips.

"You two are…" Penny threw her hands up in the air, beyond frustrated.

"What?" Caitlin asked, trying not to laugh. "We're what?"

"Maybe neither of you have been to enough weddings, but you generally wait until *after* you become husband

and wife to kiss the bride, *Tom*," Penny insisted, hands on hips again as if she was really angry. "There's this little thing called tradition."

"Maybe we don't like tradition," he quipped.

Caitlin laughed and swatted at the air, shooing Penny away. "I think I'm as ready as I'll ever be," she told her, genuinely thankful for all her help. "I appreciate everything, Pen, but we can take it from here."

"Yeah, thanks, Pen, but we can handle it from here," said Tom, mimicking Caitlin and rolling his eyes at Penny as she continued to glare at them.

Now Caitlin swatted at him, but he caught her hand and pulled it into his.

"What do you say we walk down the aisle together?" he asked.

She slipped out of his grasp to check her hair and her makeup one last time.

"You look gorgeous, Caitlin, honestly you do," Tom said, walking up behind her and cupping his body to hers, bending his head to press a kiss to the nape of her neck. "Good enough to eat."

She giggled. Caitlin actually giggled, and it sounded so weird coming from her mouth that it turned into laughter. He made her happier than she'd ever realized she could be, and it never ceased to amaze her.

"I think you're right," she said, leaning into him as his arms encircled her from behind.

"That you're gorgeous?"

"No!" She turned in his arms, took a moment to put her cheek against his chest and relax. To listen to the steady, familiar beat of his heart. "About us walking down the aisle together." She'd had no illusions about her father ever walking her down the aisle; she didn't even know if he was alive. But what she did know was that the man she was going to spend the rest of her life with should be at her side—partnering her down the aisle before they said their vows.

Over the last year he'd proven to her that he'd do anything to make her happy, that he was the man she'd thought didn't exist, and nothing was going to stop her from exchanging vows with him today.

"You ready?" Tom asked, finding her hand and clasping it firmly in his.

"More ready than I've ever been," she said, scooping her bouquet off the bed and walking toward the door. She turned back when she noticed that he wasn't moving. "Tom?"

The expression on his face worried her, but the curve of his smile, kicking his mouth up at the corners, calmed her nerves.

"There's something I want you to have," he said, closing the distance between them and reaching into his back pocket.

Caitlin didn't move, kept her eyes trained on his as he slowly withdrew his hand and brought it toward her.

"Turn around," he ordered.

Caitlin obeyed, smiling to herself as she shut her eyes and spun away from him. She felt the cool touch of a chain against her neck, but waited before looking.

"I've been waiting to give this to you." Tom's voice was deep, sounded on the verge of cracking.

Caitlin walked to the floor-length mirror, felt Tom's presence behind her as she looked at the gift he had given her.

Wow.

"Your trident," she said, fingering the symbol that now hung around her neck on a fine chain. "You told my class about this that first day I met you."

Tom nodded behind her, dipping his head to kiss her cheek. "It's my most special possession and I want you to have it."

Caitlin fought the tears tickling at the back of her eyes, not wanting to cry. "Thank you," she whispered. "I love it."

"Not as much as I love you," Tom said simply.

Caitlin turned in his arms and kissed him, the slightest brush of her lips to his.

"Let's get married."

Tom touched the trident where it sat at the hollow of her throat, then touched his fingers along her chin, before taking her hand and pressing a kiss to her engagement ring. "Let's go."

They made their way down the stairs and through Tom's mom's house. Caitlin spied the small group of guests waiting for them and laughed to herself as the band hurriedly launched into the music as they saw them standing there.

The garden looked gorgeous, understated yet elegant, with a petal-strewn walkway leading down between the row of seats.

Caitlin looked up when Tom nudged her. "I love you, you know that, right?"

She looked into his amber-brown eyes, trying to stop the tears as they threatened to escape. "I love you, too," she whispered.

Tom took her hand and held on tight. "Let's not keep our guests waiting."

Caitlin walked by his side and couldn't help the smile that burst onto her face. She would have walked with him wherever he wanted to go, and that's why she'd finally said yes to marrying him.

Because he was her one person in the world, the one she'd thought she'd never find.

And Tom Cartwright had been well worth the wait.

* * * * *

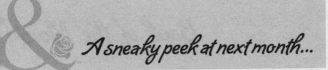

A sneaky peek at next month...

Cherish™

ROMANCE TO MELT THE HEART EVERY TIME

My wish list for next month's titles...

In stores from 20th July 2012:

☐ Once Upon a Matchmaker – Marie Ferrarella

& The Sheriff's Doorstep Baby – Teresa Carpenter

☐ The Sheikh's Jewel – Melissa James

& It Started with a Crush... – Melissa McClone

In stores from 3rd August 2012:

☐ Argentinian in the Outback – Margaret Way

& The Rebel Rancher – Donna Alward

☐ Fortune's Secret Baby – Christyne Butler

& Fortune Found – Victoria Pade

Available at WHSmith, Tesco, Asda, Eason, Amazon and Apple

Just can't wait?

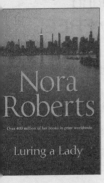

Have Your Say

You've just finished your book.
So what did you think?

We'd love to hear your thoughts on our
'Have your say' online panel
www.millsandboon.co.uk/haveyoursay

- 🌹 Easy to use
- 🌹 Short questionnaire
- 🌹 Chance to win Mills & Boon® goodies

Visit us Online

Tell us what you thought of this book now at
www.millsandboon.co.uk/haveyoursay

YOUR_SA